BURNING GLASS

ELLE KAELEE

BURNING GLASS

THE GLASS WINGS SERIES

ELLE KAELEE

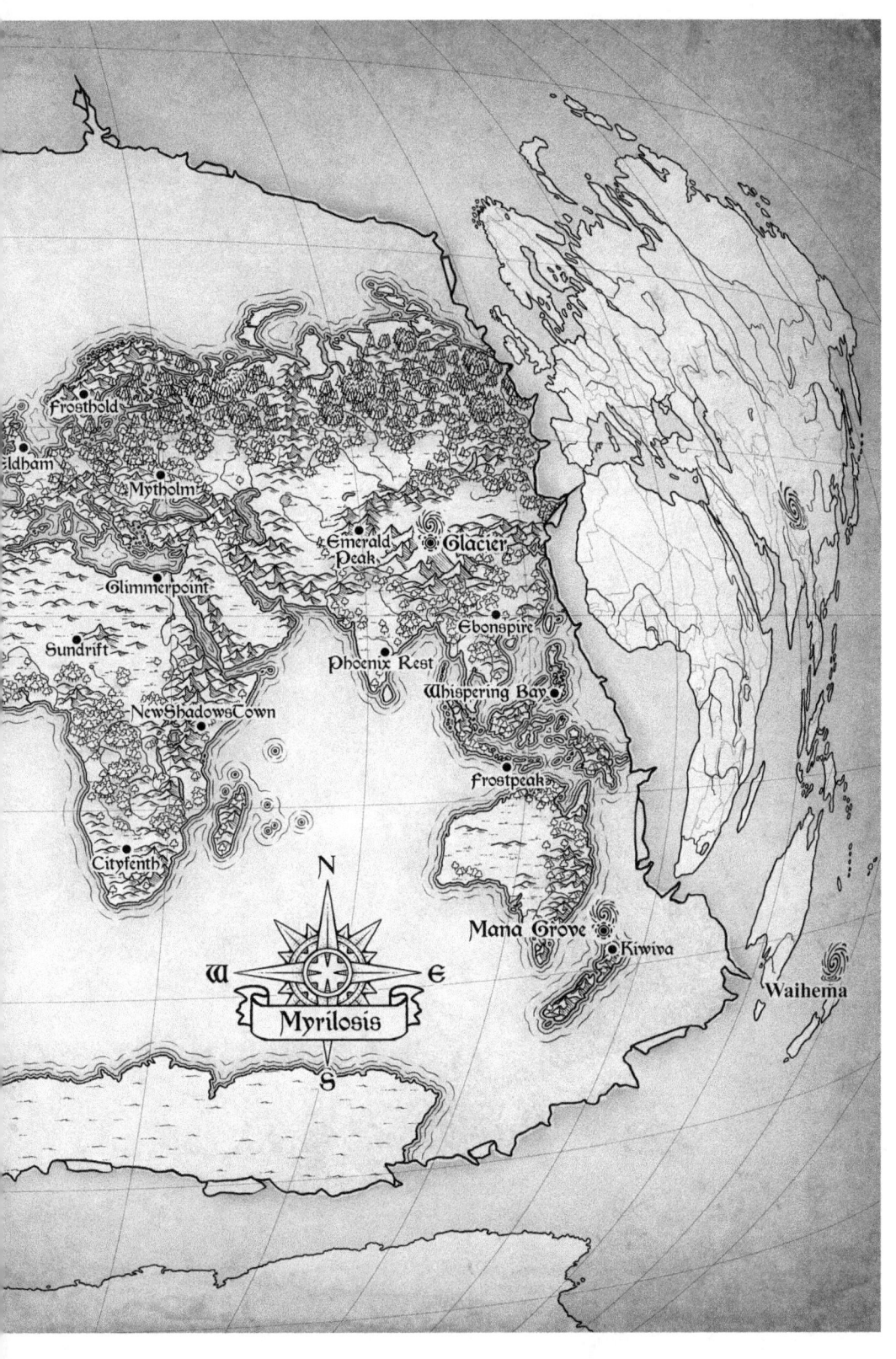

TRIGGER WARNINGS

Glass Wings is a dark fantasy trilogy intended for **mature audiences (18+)** and readers who enjoy morally complex characters, intense emotional arcs, and dark fantasy themes. Please review the following content warnings before reading. These are a continuation from the first book of the series, and these themes continue for Burning Glass and Glass Shadow:

Major Themes:

• Emotional abuse — *on-page*, throughout multiple chapters

• Power imbalance / toxic relationships — *on-page*, significant throughout

• Trauma and recovery — *on-page*, central theme, appears in most chapters

• Identity, transformation, and loss of self — *on-page*, recurring motif

Explicit Content Warnings:

• Sexual content, including consensual and dubiously consensual scenes — *on-page*

• Graphic violence — *on-page*, including deaths and battles

• Blood and gore — *on-page*, throughout

• Kidnapping and captivity — *on-page*

• Drugging (coerced bite-induced intoxication) — *on-page*

• Physical abuse — *on-page*,

• Emotional manipulation / gaslighting — *on-page*, central to antagonist dynamic

• Death of a loved one / grief — *on-page*

• Cult behavior and forced rituals — *on-page*

• Self-harm imagery (symbolic/magical) — *on-page*

• Body horror (wing growth, transformations) — *on-page*

Psychological Themes:

• PTSD and dissociation — *on-page*

• Suicidal ideation (non-graphic) — *on-page*

• Panic attacks and anxiety — *on-page*

• Shadow self / fragmented identity — *on-page*

Fantasy-Specific Elements:

• Possession by magical entities — *on-page*

• Demonic beings / monstrous transformations — *on-page*

• Forced marriage / mystical bonding — *on-page*

• Betrayal by loved ones — *on-page*

To those who are trying to heal but keep being pulled back down by the tide.

1

_____

Reifoel | The Middle Of The Sea

Reifoel loved it there, where the sky met the sea like a yin-yang symbol. He could sail for the remaining two or three centuries his body would give him without needing anything more from this life. There was such a beauty to the surface, where colors swirled to create new tones, a vibrancy that didn't exist where he was brought up. This mortal world felt like a fantasy to him.

"We are the masters of the world, Dofen!" Reifoel shouted at the top of his lungs and laughed into the breeze.

The mast's rope cut too deeply into his right hand, yet his smile brightened. His loyal dolphin friend, who liked to follow him while he sailed towards the Americas, squealed in euphoria when breaking through the ocean surface, the sound of its childlike pleasure interrupted by its splash back into the water.

The sun beat violently on Reifoel's back that day, drying out his human-skin cloak. The scales that were hidden in his arms were crackling under the heat. He could feel every ounce of moisture leaving his body, and if he went another day without submerging in water, the people of the land, the mortals, would be able to joke that he was "well done." He would smell like it, too.

Getting used to being in the air had taken a lot of effort. This would be his legacy, with no other way to communicate between land and sea. Reifoel's kind would one day see this value and then speak his name with the highest praises. He did have a kingdom to rule and protect. Even if that was a distant future, it was still a future he'd have to consider.

Reifoel's skin appeared dark, like a roll of fine leather, but it turned red if he spent too much time on the deck of his beloved ship, the *Deep Diver*. He burned fast, like a fish that had been caught and left to bake underneath the sun, and after enough time had passed, he could start to see the scales so transparent on his skin. Once he hit the water, he returned to his natural state; his milky white skin glowed in the darkest depths like a living star in the night sky.

Despite the discomfort and the scorching, Reifoel still chose to expose himself to the sun, to this world. He grabbed the rope and angled his body over the boat's edge, dangling over the open ocean with the sea breeze pushing his blue-black hair back behind his ears. His eyes, primarily gray, changed in the light, sometimes reflecting oceans and other times reflecting skies.

The dolphin, its slate and purple skin gleaming in the light, trailed him but usually stopped once they reached this point of the voyage. It wouldn't stray too far from its pod, its family, even for him. Instead, the sea animal continued to sing in the distance, the high-pitched echoing sound fading out as it dove out of sight beneath the surface.

"See you soon, my friend," Reifoel said for his own comfort. He sat on the deck for a few moments, listening to the rhythmic sounds of the waves lapping against his ship and feeling so thankful, so lucky, that his parents didn't restrict his dreams, his curiosities. He was a boy of only twenty; he could be expected to marry and live in the court. Yet, he was never pressured to.

A clangorous and urgent cawing came from behind Reifoel's

vessel. He turned his head towards the noise, his brow heavy with unease.

Birds ... this far from land?

These birds were not migrating. They were fleeing. Their calls were panicked, urgent. A storm, utterly destructive, would follow them within the hour.

Reifoel's skin prickled with goosebumps as he pivoted his human legs off the ship's side and jumped onto the lower deck. He readied the *Deep Diver* for the assumed approaching gusts of wind and sleets of rain despite the harsh sun that said otherwise.

Only quiet followed the birds as he worked, pulling on the ropes and tying them off. The sounds of water lapping against the body of the ship's hull were no longer present, leaving behind apprehension, thick and threatening.

Reifoel couldn't hear the movement of the cloth as the breeze danced with the sails.

Silent. It's too silent.

Something was wrong. Reifoel sniffed, detecting the faint smell of sulfur wafting through the air.

It took five more minutes of listening to the loud, slow beating of his own heart, anxiety filling his chest like water entering his lungs, before he noticed what was coming. The sound of a roaring fire gradually grew, only five miles from his location. It was rapidly traveling in his direction.

This was what the birds were fleeing from.

Despite growing up in a world of magic and visiting other cities and ports in Myrilosis, it was still hard to process the sight. The surface world in the mortal realm was relatively new to Reifoel, but there was no doubt in his mind that what he saw before him did not belong in this realm.

The enormous wall of fire in the middle of the ocean was menacing, dancing reds and purples leaping elegantly up to eighty feet into the sky. He squinted to study it. It rivaled the sun's brightness. There was a faint high-pitched shriek, coupled with a roar that made

Reifoel feel like he was listening to the soundtrack of cities burning and creatures dying.

That's no wall. That's a wave.

What Reifoel saw was more expansive than the horizon itself, and the heat became unbearable as it closed the distance between them. He thought he might be on fire, though he saw no flames on his skin. Hot, he felt too hot. Hysteria set in, and he vaulted off the side of his boat and into the water near boiling. He was a fish sitting in a stew pot.

His legs instantly disappeared, transforming underneath the surface while he raised his head from the water. Reifoel watched, his tail supporting him effortlessly, as the tidal wave of fire descended on him and his ship.

He gulped in the air, the oxygen hitting hard against his throat before he dove twenty feet below the surface. Reifoel's body was not efficient at using both gills and lungs simultaneously. He choked as the violent sound of the fire eating his first and only wooden ship roared above him.

My parents are not going to believe this.

He pushed back any morsel of grief for his inanimate friend and let the thick, crashing ember wave pass over him before rising to the surface again. The heat triggered his gag reflex, but he pushed past it to study what remained of his only love.

The *Deep Diver* was decimated.

Small, burnt, half-floating pieces of wood and rope struggled to keep afloat. A portion of fabric, bright blue with charred black edges, tossed itself back and forth—the final remains of the flag that once hung from the mast.

It took every effort to get the support to afford this ship. Reifoel had a hunch that King and Queen Pires would not entertain the purchase of another, especially when the story was that a tidal wave of fire destroyed the first.

I am going to be laughed out of the family.

Reifoel sighed and dove down, only changing directions once he reached the depth where sunlight could no longer go. He could navigate his way from the ocean floor's vegetation, the rocks, and sunken treasures that served as landmarks. His black tail was long and sleek, propelling him through the water faster than a sailfish diving on unsuspecting prey.

After a full day's journey, he landed about sixty miles off the coast of Haiti, where he would enter through a portal that brought him into the carbon copy realm of Myrilosis. The pressure on his body as he raised himself back up to the surface did not come without its source of agony, but his love for this realm, these mortals, made him happy to endure. Once he reached the correct coordinates, he glided towards the daylight, breaking the surface again.

It was an unremarkable section of the ocean, with no visible land in three hundred and sixty-degree views of open water. Sometimes, Reifoel saw ships passing by, but their navigation systems never had them pass directly through the portal's coordinates. He wasn't sure if this was by design or coincidental, but as far as he knew, his ship was the only vessel that had traveled between the two realms.

Reifoel swam forward, his head bobbing in the water, hoping a shark didn't mistake him for a seal today. He hurled himself through the air, ascending at least three feet above the waterline to reach the entrance.

If anyone had seen him do this, they would see something aquatic jumping out of the ocean and completely disappearing before it came down. Reifoel flopped heavily when he reached the other side, his scales making an ungraceful splash. This was where his people, the water people of Serelune, thrived through several colonies settled throughout the waters of Myrilosis.

He dove again, the last one to complete his journey, swimming deeper and deeper until he reached the black sands that waited on the ocean floor.

Agatized coral rock and bones foraged from whale shark gravesites comprised a colony of underwater domes. They were deep enough that flashes of surface light reflected off the shiny white and amber structures, but otherwise, the city was engulfed in darkness.

According to the legends of the Serelune, their kind once lived blindly and were easily killed by prey. That was before their eyes had adjusted to the murk through generations, and now they could see in the blackness quite well. Their skin provided the only luminance at the depths that they colonized.

As Reifoel swam through the domes, he passed many Serelunians tending to their kelp gardens and carrying out their day-to-day tasks. Pet fish were allowed to swim while the adolescents laughed and chased after them.

Eventually, he arrived at the last dome, slightly more amber than the rest but comparable in size. This was home.

Pushing through an unlocked door strung together of moss, kelp, and bone, Reifoel entered an open room where both his mother and father hovered over a table surrounded by other important-looking Serelunian citizens. They were all talking in hushed voices, reading and pointing to scrolls in front of them.

I just swam into a council meeting.

"It's a myth; there's no basis to this worry, King Pires," said a broad-chested Serelune with deep dark eyes and hair that matched his moon-like skin. Reifoel's lips pulled back. He had to stop himself from snarling instinctually at his cousin's presence.

"Reifoel," King Pires said, turning his large head to address him. "I did not expect to see you back so soon, my son."

The rest of the room turned, surprised that an unknown presence was in the dome with them. Presumably, any worry was simply about what was overheard. Reifoel was not a part of the council, not officially, per his own request. He would be ready someday, but until then, he had other priorities.

"What trouble have you gotten yourself into, boy?" The queen cut in, her fierce, sharp eyes wrinkled around the outside edges. Her brow furrowed knowingly.

Talk about a welcome party.

"Mother and Father, King and Queen Pires, I have turned around to come and tell you about an event I saw on the water's surface in the mortal Earth realm. It seemed an urgent matter."

"I did not notice your ship floating above us," his blond and skinny cousin snickered. "Did you manage to sink it?"

Like you could have seen it from down here anyway, you piece of plastic. Reifoel managed to keep the thought to himself.

The other four council officials floated silently around the table, shifting uncomfortably as tension filled the surrounding waters and seeped into everyone's gills.

"Isadore," Reifoel started, "just because my household took you in after your parents were eaten—while recklessly shark chasing, I might add—does not make you one of us. You are not in line to rule."

"I am if you die," said Isadore, suddenly interested in his fingernails while his long blond hair wrapped and tangled around his navel.

"Enough. You two children are always barking at each other like sea lion pups," King Pires growled. His teeth were exposed, and his muscles flexed from the tip of his fingers to a powerful, larger-than-life tail.

"Answer his question, Reifoel; what happened to your ship?" His mother asked in a tone that conveyed caring and disapproval simultaneously. All eyes in the dome darted back and forth between the four of them.

Reifoel let the water slowly pass through over his gills, only visible behind his very human-like ears, and launched into the story of the tidal wave of fire that had destroyed his precious *Deep Diver*. He did his best not to get emotional about it. Luckily, the thought of Isadore's teasing didn't leave much room for sentiment.

Isadore erupted with laughter once Reifoel had finished, clutching onto his sides. His cousin stopped only as he took in the dead serious faces of his king and queen.

"Oh, you can't be serious," Isadore nearly shouted. "You both have spent a small fortune on that ship, something that can stay intact between realm travel. All for the precious Reifoel's ridiculous dream of living on mortal land, and now, it's gone."

"Council, please leave us. This is a family matter," Reifoel's mother asked politely.

For a moment, no one moved; the water felt unsure, untested. She cleared her throat as the four other council members scooped up their scrolls and exited the dome through the bone door. Not one turned to look back. Reifoel assumed they were all relieved to be spared from the conversation.

The queen floated over to the table. It was one of the few in the community made out of wood, a difficult resource to come by when living this deep. She placed her hands over it, feeling the grainy but slightly slimed surface, and looked up while Reifoel's father moved to join her.

"Boys," she began, "I have shared many of our kind's legends with you when you were children. Do you remember the story about how the Serelune were created?"

Isadore rolled his eyes and let his body fall back into a relaxed position as the water supported him. There were no seats, no couches like Reifoel had seen in the living rooms among the land people. There was no physical need for those kinds of furnishings. Besides the table and a sparse kitchen, the dome was empty, void of material items.

"I think I remember, Mother," Reifoel said. "There was a boy, a land person. He wasn't exactly a person, however. He was . . . special . . . somehow."

"Yes, very good, Reifoel." She nodded in approval. "Now, Isadore, can I ask what you are doing?"

"If you are telling fables, I might as well get ready to propel myself around the room so I can sleep," he said, putting his hands behind his head.

Disrespectful, arrogant, piece of—

The king lunged forward at Isadore, smacking him in the nose. He cried out, to Reifoel's satisfaction.

"Just because we include you in the council meetings does not give you authority to talk down to your king and queen," his father said in a deadly calm tone.

Isadore came to attention, pinching his nose to stop blood from escaping. Reifoel's mother approached her husband's side, touching his back. His father turned his head to look at her, and Reifoel was in awe, as he always was, at the way their eyes communicated.

"This boy that Reifeol speaks of was no land person. He created all life, magic and mundane, here on Earth. This boy had large wings, like swimming in a current through the clouds, that could carry his weight. Once he grew into the body of a man, he no longer aged. He also had a family, others with similar gifts, with whom he grew into adulthood. This boy made the first water person simply by waving his hands when he was no older than nine to impress a girl he loved. That water person was known as Serene Wata.

Serene Wata eventually perished, but not before more water creatures had been created to join her. They were toys, silly things to amuse. But then they were quickly forgotten about. This boy, we know him as Kinnari."

Reifoel took in his mother's story, trying to figure out what he should learn from it.

"Does this mean that this legend is true? This boy, Kinnari, still exists, then?" Isadore asked, hiding his apparent interest in the tale by looking at the dome's ceiling.

"The legends are fact. This Kinnari created most of the species existing in Myrilosis. They do not enter our realm now, having completely abandoned their creations, but he must be found. I believe he can intervene."

Queen Pires moved through the water and reached out to her son, eyes locked on his. "We were discussing it at the table, my son, as you returned home. The Earth's rotation has slowed, and I fear we will soon stop rotating altogether. What effects that will have on the moon and our waters are unclear, but I'm assuming it will be life-ending for many species, including ours."

"The fire wave—is it related to this tale?" Reifoel asked.

"Your mother believes so," the king mumbled under a dark, stoic mustache.

They believe me.

"You want me to find this Kinnari creator, then?" Reifoel asked.

"Yes," his mother said, moving towards Isadore and touching his shoulders. He tensed up instantly. "Take him with you. An extra pair of eyes cannot hurt on this journey. Reifeol, I wouldn't ask this of you if it wasn't important. It's much more urgent than your surface life dream could ever be."

Isadore opened his mouth to interject, but Queen Pires raised a finger at him. She then held out a closed fist to Reifoel, placing a smooth stone in his palm, closing his fingers tight around a small, smooth object.

"A true moonstone for luck and protection," she whispered. "Hang onto it as if your life depends on it, as if all of our lives depend on it."

Reifoel looked at the stone in his hand, seemingly unremarkable. For all he knew, it could have been petrified bone, a very common find in their neighborhood. He felt no magic, no protection from it there in his hand. He would assume it to be just a trinket if it weren't given by such a severe woman.

"I trust that you are not sending us on a wild eel chase, My Queen, but how would we even start our search for this creator?" Isadore asked, his words long and drawn out.

"You boys will go east until you reach the Bay of Bengal. That is in the Earth realm. You are on foot from there. Ask locals about their legends and myths. You are looking for a winged man. A temple that is hidden in white amongst the clouds," the queen answered.

Reifol's mother pulled back and recoiled into his father's arms. The pair stared at the two young men with solemn faces. The queen's words were final, demanding, so Reifoel grabbed Isadore's arm and pulled him out of the dome, the bone door swaying back and forth behind them.

2

Amis | Sacramento, Ca

The dread that hit Amis made him wish for death, for a level of peace, an eternal abyss that he wasn't sure he could ever truly achieve. The Kinnari male brushed his brown hair over his shoulders, wrapping his arms around himself, looking for comfort, for hope. That silly word seemed like a luxury he didn't deserve—hope—but he had held onto it since childhood. He dreamed about creating a more peaceful world, correcting the violence. Adhering to his magic and keeping the inner workings of the living in balance made him take the long way.

Long was an understatement.

He stood in that house in East Sacramento, bursting at the seams with two ancient enemy species, watching as the Kinnari and Vrae in the entry room around him fell, one by one. There was no apparent cause, yet the shock in the eyes that fell quickly turned to emptiness, a void where positivity could never survive. The thuds of their bodies on marble tile echoed up to the enormous pentagram etched in the ceiling above.

Hoping for an alliance, Amis had supported the first Vrae, Sheng. The goal was to bring the two species, light and dark, together. This was all Amis had been working towards for more years than he could count. A significant threat loomed: an unstable goddess, a fickle sun that would fully want control of the Earth. Both mortal and Myrilosis realms would likely then be annihilated.

"She's gone," the faint trembling voice of a child reached Amis' ears, giving him something to anchor to. He pulled on that anchor, his mind breaking, every possible nightmare flashing through his eyes and ripping his will apart.

He saw the infants, every single babe devoid of magical blood, cry out as they were murdered, their mothers not even given the privilege of an hour's bond. He saw the villagers he cared for, homed, slaughtered to death by the monsters, the Vrae that stood beside him. He saw the pain, the inhumanity he had single-handedly caused, and for the first time, it broke his heart.

The fear that pooled through him, that he fought to break free from, continued to pull him back down as he cradled his knees to his chest and asked himself if this was worth it.

And, of course, he saw what had started it all most vividly. Eight immortal children, created by the Life Gifter and Goddesses themselves, playing together in their mountaintop temple before the start of life on the planet.

"If you just let go, the burning goes away," a young Allienna said to a young Arryn. She was taking the fire, the burning, that gathered under his skin away, and absorbing it within herself. That fire burned when Arryn did not let himself fulfill his purpose: to create.

"Arryn, don't be boring. Fill the sky with rainbows and provide sleds so we may slide down them. It is a command," a young Reign said, her magic binding all who hear her orders to obey.

Little Arryn flipped his blond hair out of his eyes and straightened, Reign's magic taking its hold. He focused, his eyes narrowing in on seemingly nothing in the frozen landscape before them. Arryn physically gathered atoms in the billions, energy bursting from his body that the naked eye could not see.

Shaping them as if gathering sand on the beach, an archway formed until it solidified and striped into millions of colors, though Amis could only count the traditional seven. Another slightly smaller archway followed, as did another and another, until a small amusement park was painted before the other seven Kinnari children present.

With his curly brown hair and dimples, Tristan ran up and grabbed one of the last items to appear, a sled that gleamed in solid gold.

"Bravo, Arryn, this is your best creation yet." Tristan beamed and scrambled up to the top of the first arch. Amis watched him struggle, the incline too steep, but at a glacial pace, Tristan figured out a scoot and pull technique that got him to the top. The rainbow was solid enough to carry his weight, which was essential since, at that age, none of their wings had come in yet. At that point in their lives, they were unaware that there would be additional limbs to consider one day.

They were the first—the first living, breathing beings. It would be their job and duty to foster life in the realms as their creators desired. Those days, though, were filled with happiness, with laughter as they learned to lean on one another and learn their particular skills.

"How does it feel?" Precession, twin to Roksana, asked in a dreamy, out-of-this-world tone.

Tristan set his sled down on the rainbow and let his hand caress the colors underneath him. Initial surprise was followed by a full-toothed grin as he picked up his hand and held it out, examining it.

"It feels like warmth, love, clouds, and fields of lavender. It is smooth, solid, but there's a pulse underneath, a rhythm like a river, a stream."

"Just go down the slide," yelled a young Djoser, his hands cupped over his mouth, his head shaved even back then. "I call next."

The eight Kinnari children spent the next few hours giggling and screaming with joy, gliding up and down the arches. The cold and snow that filled their landscape left them unaffected, while their fast, energetic movements kept them warm.

Amis remembered looking down from the top of the largest arch. The temple's roof seemed just a short jump down. He pushed off, sliding on his stomach, with the wind hitting his face and a howl of both joy and fright following him.

That might have been the first time he had known what it was like to fly. The exhilaration, the feeling that no one could touch him. They were all invincible.

"Should we head inside to eat?" Amis suggested, his stomach rumbling after the excitement calmed down. The others began to walk towards the temple door, the heavy latch taking two of their bodies to lift fully, while a third pulled the door wide with all their body weight.

The children walked through the hall, heading towards the great open room where they all dined, slept, and lived together.

"Something hot today, please," Djoser begged Arryn, whose eyes reached a large communal table. Arryn used his magic to fill it with bowls of hot purple rice, plates of steaming seasoned vegetables, and roasted duck.

"My hero," Allienna said, reaching up slightly to nuzzle her nose against Arryn's cheek. He blushed a deep red as the others sat down, grabbing chipped clay plates that were left from their prior meals together.

"I think your stomach needs to calm down," Tristan jabbed at Djoser. "It's growling so loud it sounds like it's an animal."

"That's not my stomach," Djoser became very still, sucking the energy out of the room. He cocked his head to the other side of the temple, where another hallway and another door existed. That door was not one that they were supposed to open. That door went into

Myrilosis, a realm to separate magic from the ordain, to hide the creations that Arryn got too carried away with.

That hallway was consumed with shadows and darkness. No torches lined the walls since no one ever bothered to walk down it, other than Arryn, occasionally wrestling with something out of the ordinary. Sirens, dragons, and all the like were thrown in there to be forgotten and never thought of again.

A movement rushed through the shadows, followed by the appearance of blood-red eyes just twenty feet from their table.

"That's not something I made," Arryn mumbled, his fists clenched by his side, words through gritted teeth.

Four creatures jumped out into the light of the great room, exposing themselves. Their skin was slick and reflective, like oil on rubber. They bared long, thick, pointed teeth that filled their mouths so entirely that they needed extra space. Their heads were able to open horizontally a full ninety degrees. They were bald, with ears pushed too far back on their oval-shaped skulls.

Allienna cried. Roksana, standing near her, was unintentionally heightening her panic as a result of her magic. The closest creature formed what Amis assumed was a smile. It let a lengthy tongue slither through the air as if tasting their fear before diving towards the group, claws extended.

Reign jumped back, pulling on Precession's arm and toppling over the opposite side of the table as it flipped on them, plates crashing and full cups splashing. The creature let out a howl, its tongue still out but now it's leg pinned under that flipped table.

More screams erupted from the group as Arryn jumped to attention. A sword appeared in his hand, and he clumsily thrust it towards the monster pinned by the table.

It shrieked as the blade pierced it, cold red blood flowing freely. Arryn looked utterly surprised, stunned. He didn't know what to do next. He had never killed anything before with his own hands. He had never even held a weapon. He had seen some early humans make clubs, but this, this was sharp and nearly effortless to use.

Amis saw the struggle painted over his face and ran towards him, shouting.

I can do it. I can kill.

"Weapon, give me a weapon."

Arryn threw the sword into Amis' hands, the blade slicing through Amis' palms as he gasped. The other monsters seemed triggered, more focused as his dark blue Kinnari blood dripped onto the sword, which rattled as it hit the stone floor.

They attacked.

Chaos erupted as two of the monsters tackled Amis, their hot breath and saliva shooting straight to his open wound, bears at a beehive looking for honey. Teeth punctured his hand, and Amis froze. Anxiety like he had never experienced before pulsed through his veins.

"Roksana, sleep," Reign shouted, her voice filled with the same edge that flowed through Amis. The monsters drank, two more now on his arm. The panic died down with each gulp, and he began to feel relaxed, seduced even. He would let them do that forever, perhaps. Maybe they all should get bitten.

The red-headed twin collapsed asleep in Reign's arms from her command. Precession and Allienna stood frozen, holding each other tight behind them.

"Get back to Myrilosis," Tristan shouted as he ran ferociously towards the sword on the ground, picking it up and struggling under the weight before throwing his entire body towards one of the monsters that was lapping up blood oozing under Amis.

The pinned monster under the table was growling and chanting while still stuck, sitting in a small puddle of its own blood. Each growl became more audible, as if it were its power source.

Vrae. Vrae. Vrae.

It broke free as Arryn shouted in warning, but the new weapon he made appear in his hand was too far away to be effective. The single monster jumped onto Tristan's back, opening its mouth entirely before pulling out a piece of Tristan's neck with its teeth.

The girls screamed, and Tristan fell to the floor. The blood, spurting freely like a fountain, attracted the others. Their focus turned away from Amis as they joined and tore the Kinnari child into pieces.

Amis sat up, horrified, panting yet still in a daze. He saw Arryn, his hands shaking and his eyes darting around the room, helpless and lost in the fear. He saw the girls crying behind the flipped table, and then Amis noticed Djoser. Djoser, who showed no evidence of power, of magic, was now his focus. Amis' body seized, as if it no longer belonged to him, as his magic seeped out, invisible and quick. The power of balance surrounded Djoser as the olive-skinned Kinnari breathed it in, unaware of its presence.

But he wasn't unaware for long.

Djoser stood to the far side of the great room, his back facing the hall that exited into the mortal realm. He stared at his hands, rage hot and growing in his eyes. Black wisps rose from his fingertips, something Amis had never seen before. They needed help, and Amis' magic of balance had found its way to give it.

What can you do?

Djoser looked at the monsters, the Vrae, and the sounds of tearing flesh and squeals from traumatized youth filling the room. He was not scared. He was not crying. Instead, Djoser reached out his hands, flexing his fingertips, and then crushed them into tight fists as if controlling the air. The monsters froze and then, bit by bit, began to disappear as if they were sand being blown by the sea breeze. There was no struggle, no indication of pain. They were just gone.

"What the hell was that?" Arryn turned to Djoser, who looked devastated, to Amis' surprise. The malice in his eyes had turned into despair and disgust. He hated it. He hated this new magic.

The sobs from the girls heightened as they trembled over the wreckage of what was left of Tristan's body. Though the tears formed in her eyes, Precession remained a beacon of serenity. She stood as if made of stone while the others mourned.

Never, never can this happen again. I won't let it.

Amis stood up, his mind clearing now, and looked for a broom to begin clearing the wreckage. The temple balance had been altered, and he felt out of control.

This isn't happening. Your fear is from a memory.

AMIS MANAGED to pull himself out of a paralysis, seeing that whatever had a hold on him, pushing his fear, still had everyone in the foyer on the ground. The Vrae and other Kinnari were cradling themselves underneath the large pentagram carved above them. Hadley, the girl, she was not there. She was missing.

The memory that held him down, that rooted his fears, was something that made him. It was not a looming threat. It was not his worst nightmare. He didn't have one of those because he had already lived it. Whatever magic used here was still in effect and had a hold on him, but his magic was off balance, and his internal rhythm would always correct itself.

"Get up," he shuffled over to Reign, whose eyes were closed, with tears dripping down her chin. The fierce general, the powerful woman who had fallen to pieces before him, looked no different now than in that memory. She seemed no older than eight after the Vrae had torn her to shreds those few weeks ago, her body regenerating as an immortal child.

Reign's eyes fluttered open, and the panic in her face was evident as she skirted away from Amis as if he were a monster. She wouldn't have been entirely wrong. Keeping the balance required a fair amount of sacrifices.

"Snap out of it," Amis said, scooping her up into his arms. Amis wondered if the horrors in her mind, the fear placed inside her, was made of the same memories as his. "She's gone, Hadley is gone, and we are all clutching our bodies on the floor."

Reign looked up at him, her body starting to relax.

"Can we go after her? Was she taken?" Reign jumped out of his arms, the forty-eight inches of her body landing in a fighting position, ready to strike a target that didn't exist.

"They did this," Reign pointed to the Vrae and at Sheng, who were all still under the influence of this fear, this spell, this magic.

Whatever it was, Amis knew it originated from the girl. Whether she knew what she did was still an unanswered question, but it affected them all at once. An untrained power like that could have some interesting results if they chased after her.

"No." Amis did his best to keep his voice calm. He had sacrificed his entire life for Sheng's cause. He would now be seen as a traitor, as a murderer, and he wouldn't endure what that brought with it for nothing. Amis would ensure this bond, this alliance that Sheng sought, was accepted and honored.

"If we were looking for the one true villain, the one that needs to be eliminated, dear Amis"—Djoser, the physical embodiment of destruction, stood up without any lingering effects of the fear paralysis—"then I think we found it with you."

Shit.

Amis let out a quick breath before jolting towards the door. He had no battle skills. His magic couldn't have been more obscure and less helpful in most conflicts, so all he could do as the wisps of black poured from Djoser's fingertips was flee.

"Djoser, you will not kill Amis," Reign commanded. "At least not right now." Her arms were folded across her chest, and she tapped her foot impatiently. "Honestly, you are all children."

"You're one to talk," Djoser said, strained as he fought Reign's command with all he had. Out of the Kinnari, only Arryn seemed to be able to resist her commands, and he had practiced a lot to only have a far-from-perfect success rate.

"Normally I wouldn't volunteer, but can I kill them, then?" Djoser asked, his head cocking towards the Vrae, their red eyes beginning to appear under their cloaks as the magic that held them to the floor seemed to be lifting.

"No," Amis said, his body out of the front large double doors but his head remaining inside.

Djoser chuffed, still very much on edge.

"Losing Hadley is a minor inconvenience," Sheng, the original

Vrae, said as he stood to attention. The demon leader's smooth skin, kissed by gold, and almond eyes were endearing, the perfect facade to trap victims.

"Minor?" A woman's voice fluttered from one of the cloaked Vrae behind him. "She's the entire reason we are here."

"Jenny, we will have a word later about your . . . insubordination."

The Vrae woman shrunk back, her red eyes and face no longer visible as she cowered inside the hood of her cloak.

"As I was about to release her to you, for goodwill, I feel it's only fair that your kind retrieve her. Make her feel like she can trust you. Then, you will return my wife to me once your family is bonded so we can use her in our fight against the sun. Ayurveda will burn this realm down. Make no mistake about it."

"Just one word, Arryn, and I pull them apart, atom by atom," Djoser said through his teeth, talking about the Vrae but very much staring at Amis' head poking around the door frame.

"Find the girl. I must find out what happened to Allienna," Arryn stiffened. "From there, give these bastards their damn alliance. Who cares? Who cares about any of it."

Amis saw a real sadness behind Arryn's eyes, saw his heart breaking in front of them, new cracks forming with every added piece of this conversation. The Kinnari leader, who created the world before them, was forced to grieve again.

Arryn wouldn't have cared about the fate of this realm. He didn't care about the Vrae before him. He didn't consider that he even had a living child in Hadley. No, Arryn cared only for his lost love and was left with no more of an explanation than he came here with.

"On that cheerful note," Amis said, stepping again fully into the foyer, "I will fly back to Waihema. I've got a village to free."

3

Djoser | Zion National Park

D *amn, it's hot.*

THE SUN PEERED in and out of the clouds overhead, and when it was exposed, the one-hundred-degree temperatures intensified. This place was beautiful, otherworldly, with its bright red cliffs stacked up so high that Djoser was sure he could exit the atmosphere if he flew to the top.

Dinosaurs once roamed these lands, drinking and cooling in the river running through the national park. He remembered the day where most of them were killed, when both realms, the entire planet, had to start over, leaving only sharks and bacteria. That was the first and only time a Kinnari did not follow the Life Gifter's order. Djoser had been the one to disobey, the first order he refused, still a child, still grappling with the monstrous power he suddenly possessed.

Ayurveda had been the one to carry out the punishment that time, a meteor six hundred miles in radius being pulled into the planet's atmosphere. The punishment worked; he corrected his behavior and became obedient right after the wipeout. How much more death the Gods could create for him was now apparent.

Djoser hadn't left America since standing before an entry room filled with Vrae. They stared at him, thirsting for his blood, their hunger plain in their blood-red eyes. He imagined their jaws unhinging, their dagger-shaped teeth that seemed larger than their heads coming down on his own head and dislodging it, but instead, they had stood there before him with the appearance of mortals. That was the first time he had seen that the oily, smooth, black-as-night monsters could disguise themselves as humans and even live among them.

Djoser's mouth went dry at the thought. How many deaths had been happening without him knowing? How often did someone defenseless become a meal for his natural enemy? They didn't need Kinnari blood to survive, if they were still out there all these years later. He struggled with his feelings of being more like a fine wine, a delicacy, his blue blood delectable to the demon monster palates.

"You are fucking killin' it, man!" shouted a man standing on the cliff's edge, his dark, greasy hair wrapped up in a bun. "I seriously worship you!"

Djoser rolled his eyes and continued to focus. His bare toes were wrapped around the one-inch piece of slack line supporting his weight as he stood suspended three hundred meters between two cliff points within Zion.

"He's not strapped in, everyone. My man Djoser here is a straight-up God," man bun shouted again.

"Thanks for the support, Greg," Djoser shouted, his leg muscles slightly trembling to keep balance.

You can shut up now.

Vivid red mountains surrounded him, their distance making him feel parallel to their peaks. The stone he had walked off of went straight down, nearly perfectly straight and smooth. The side he was heading towards hosted green, tall trees that grew on an incline. The life in front of him was encouraging. He strived to be around life.

It had been six months since they were all in that house to save Arryn's daughter. The Vrae stood behind her like she was their queen, yet horror lived in her beautiful dark blue eyes. That horror turned to anger when she saw her father, the very Kinnari who was driving the rescue mission.

Djoser's ankle wobbled as he pushed himself forward. Only eighty-six steps to go; he was about halfway across now. A group of climbers, two females, and three males, stood at the start watching, their ropes hanging off their hips and helmets unclipped. Greg was a salesman to draw in such a crowd during the off-season.

Even suspended over the valley, Djoser couldn't stop thinking about her, the new Kinnari who left them all there, staring at each other with no accurate recollection of what had happened. Her mother, Allienna, had hidden this child from them, from Arryn. She was the first biologically conceived Kinnari ever to be born, and what a wonder she was. His mind couldn't leave those horror-filled eyes of hers. He wanted to protect her and, for the first time, he wanted to kill. He wanted to destroy anything that kept that horror there.

Djoser's stomach dropped as he pushed his hips forward violently, his balance entirely off. The threat of fall loomed underneath him while he could physically hear the stress from his growing fan club.

"You got this, you got this, you got this," Greg chanted softly.

Slack-line with a guy for two days, and he thinks you're best friends.

Djoser's dark olive Egyptian skin was soaked in the sunshine after a cloud passed, bringing back the heat while the male regained his balance. Not breathing, he was able to tuck his hips back underneath him. The triangular marks on his shoulder blades remained intact, as he had not had to save himself from the pain of such a fall. He wouldn't have died, of course, but it would still hurt like hell.

Djoser had done all he could to distract himself from the girl,

Arryn's daughter. Snowboarding out of helicopters, ice plunging, and cave diving hadn't succeeded, so here he was. It was all too dull. There was no risk. Even now, with the fall that eagerly awaited him below, he couldn't get the girl's wings out of his mind.

They had rounded edges, magnificent and translucent. Kinnari's wings were meant to match the patterns in one's eyes, but she held a different kind of power from theirs. One he was eager to learn about.

Incredible. That girl was incredible.

"My name is Hadley," she had said before Djoser remembered falling to the floor, feeling nothing but paralyzing terror. Flashes of memories that he kept down in the darkest, deepest parts of his heart played out in his in mind. When it was over, she was gone, leaving her rescue group staring into red eyes, feeding them silly stories about an alliance.

There was a darkness about her that drew him in. One that he couldn't let go of, like an arrow that pierced an organ. He could bleed out if he pulled it free, facing eternal darkness. Instead, he would leave it, obsess over it. His own sadistic lips grimacing with every movement as he was painfully reminded that now, the arrow existed. Hadley existed. Her face, her wings, her hips, with him now always.

The sun had disappeared as quickly as it had come, and flashes of lightning illuminated a now eerie sky above him. Djoser looked up as his fan club vanished from the threat of the desert's monsoon season, descending the trail to safety.

Djoser knew this storm well. He dreaded it, wishing it was only what the mortal hikers thought it was. Thunder erupted through the clouds, a black and purple haze overwhelming all other colors above him. It had the same texture as a cloud, though nothing was whimsical about it. That cloud held the promise of looming death—a death by Djoser's own hands.

What existed over his head was his creator, his god, The Life Gifter. A power so unassuming that it took no form, no comfortable creature to connect to, relate to.

"I can't remember the last time I've gotten a special visit from you," Djoser said casually, continuing to hold his arms out and finish his route.

This, his purpose, and his powers made him flee the temple even as a young child. The day of the attack, of Tristan's death, was the first time he had discovered them. He had always assumed before that he had no gifts, that he was straightforward and lucky. No one else seemed happy with their magic, except maybe Reign.

Djoser ran out into the snow after that, his childhood self in mourning after discovering what he was. Shortly after, the Life Gifter visited him and gave him one of these special assignments for the first time. He'd never returned to the temple to live with his family after that. He'd started his own and fostered a history, an economy, and a country throughout his millennia of existence. He had a lot to make up for.

As far as he knew, the Life Gifter had created Djoser for a purpose, and that was one of destruction. Though mostly left alone, he was expected to obey and participate in the bigger picture. If he looked at the bright side, if he had hope, who he needed to eliminate would be someone who had once hurt *her*. At least then, he could feel better about it.

A monster. I was made to be a monster.

No audible voice filled the valley, though internally, Djoser felt the command, felt the words in his dark blue magic-filled blood.

"A girl, a Kinnari, must be eliminated."

Djoser's heart sank, his mind assuming that the death order was for Reign. She had violated the laws of time hopping multiple times to save her friends and her family, and she had been warned that the penalty would be death.

Djoser thought she had gotten away with it since the Vrae had mutilated her, sending her to be reborn as a young child.

She did technically die, didn't she?

If he pulled her apart, would she still be reborn as a child, or would she be gone permanently? He suspected the latter.

How could he do it? How could he pool the blackness in his fingertips and stretch to find her atoms? How could he pull her apart, looking like a child? He hated this. He hated who he was. There was no retribution, no pleasure in this.

"Glass wings," the Life Gifter continued, snapping Djoser out of his worry. The description no longer fit Reign. The God was demanding someone else's life. His command was to destroy the girl who now consumed him—the girl who had disappeared six months ago. The girl who had made him face unbearable horrors in his mind, left him in paralyzing fear on the floor. He was expected to kill Arryn's daughter. He was expected to kill Hadley.

Djoser was never given a reason or explanation. Leaders of war-torn countries, pop stars, and a magical creature or two had all been sent into darkness at his own hands. He followed his commands, fulfilling the reason his creator had made him.

He jumped off the slack line, no longer visible to any humans as they navigated the rocky trail down to the valley. His body flipped through the air as bones cracked, pushing out the triangular marks on his shoulder blades. Djoser's wings, at full length, supported his body in the air with ease. The fifteen feet of leathery muscle and skin matched his light green eyes, with gold etchings peppered throughout.

The sky began to clear as Djoser touched his feet to the dirt below him, stinging with the rope burn from the slack line, before pulling his wings back into his skin. His body was already healed as the climbers who had abandoned him reached the start of the trail. Their surprise was evident as they took him in.

"How did you get down here faster than us?" Greg asked, astounded and holding his arms towards the Kinnari, ready for an embrace. "Never mind all that, I'm glad you're okay, I am. I don't think we have any cell service to call for help, so that's a load of stress off my plate."

"I wouldn't have expected you, of all people, to leave me to die suspended between two cliffs, Greg." Djoser's rough voice echoed through the valley.

Greg chuckled awkwardly and played with his bun until his hair was let down loose.

"That was a wild storm. I've never been in something that came and went so quickly like that. It had us all pretty scared there for a minute."

Djoser grabbed the hiking pack strapped to the front of Greg's chest.

"I thought I'd bring that down for you," Greg said awkwardly, his pack strapped to his back. The other hikers left him behind to face the large, grumpy person in front of him.

Asshole hippie.

Djoser turned and headed through the valley trail, leaving Greg behind him. Surrounded by lush greenery, he headed in a direction different from the group slightly ahead of him, his nose filled with the faint scent of vanilla from the surrounding trees and mountain rain until he reached the Virgin River.

Calm, cool water welcomed his feet as the smooth rocks underneath had him stumbling and slipping. He fell forward, his hands and knees splashing down, and laughed before the goosebumps forming on his arms and legs reflected not the chill from the river but what he was now expected to do.

He didn't know the girl. He couldn't be attached to her in any way, but he saw how connected the Vrae were to her. She was beautiful and powerful, but she caused drama and contention. He contemplated if her death would ensure a full-out war between Kinnari and Vrae. This supposed alliance couldn't have any truth in it.

Djoser thought back to the infants at Amis' village, Waihema. He thought of the mothers screaming out from the torment of their children being murdered for what they were told was the common good. He thought of the villagers being raised there only to be slaughtered, a farm, a food supply for the Vrae that had found a portal between realms in the New Zealand forest. Djoser stood upright, wings out wide, his head towards the sky.

Good, let those bastards come.

4

Hadley | Coachella Valley

She didn't know what she was doing there. Hadley tucked her blonde hair behind her ears, utterly self-conscious of how ordinary she looked, never having been to something like this before.

Desert Music Festival: May 12-16th, the sign she passed read.

She was in a golf cart, wearing filthy black running shorts and an oversized t-shirt with the lineup of a 90s rock series. She had fished it out of the dumpster—along with a pink linen baseball hat—which was littered with so many discarded pieces of clothing that she wondered if she could open a thrift store with it.

Ahead of her were a row of white tents with larger yurts on the other side. The two girls in the golf cart's back seat snickered and teased each other, their long braids whipping the back of Hadley's neck.

"He spent almost thirty thousand dollars for one of those yurts," the brunette, who looked younger than her, snickered. "Why else would I be with him? You are either a loser or a winner, and I've never seen anyone work their way up to being a winner."

"You're so wise," the platinum-blonde friend said, her voice utterly stoic.

The golf cart slowed and stopped in front of one of the larger yurts. The middle-aged male driver turned his head to Hadley, pulled his sunglasses down over his nose, and pointed to the one on their right side.

"That one is all yours, miss," he said, clicking his tongue.

"Wait, you are staying in one of these?" The brunette, covered in thick gold bangles and little more than a bejeweled pink bra, turned to notice Hadley for the first time. Hadley stood up and jumped onto the grass, the only piece of lush, watered vegetation she had seen other than the thriving Joshua trees.

"Who are you? Like, what do you do? Are you a performer here? Do I know your name?" The brunette kept berating her with questions. "Let's get a drink together tonight. I'm staying with my boyfriend just down the row."

"Do you need help with your bags?" the golf cart driver asked.

"No bags on me." Hadley smiled, shaking her head, and raised her eyebrows at the girls before turning away without a word, listening to the golf cart's electric hum as it drove away.

Hadley stood before the white, circular, tent-like structure, reading the number twelve etched in gold on the elegant wood door. Two palm trees lined the walkway up to it, and she sighed at the extravagance before her. She had spent months in the mountains, sleeping on the rocks, only surviving the threat of hypothermia thanks to the Goddess with fire in her hair. And, of course, that dragon Ayurveda kept around helped, too.

Hadley didn't know what that Goddess had planned for her there. There was little conversation, little understanding, only the fostering of her own broken heart.

"Greetings, Miss Kin," an upbeat voice said behind her.

Hadley turned around, her heart thumping. Being around people again was going to be complicated.

"I'm your attendant, Ursula, assigned to this yurt. Your companion is already here, though she left a short while ago. Would you like me to come in and show you around?"

"No, no, thank you," Hadley sputtered, her cheeks red from the heat and the forced conversation. She missed the solitude, staring at the skies, the coldness from the altitude, and the rough dragon scales against her bare feet whenever it came to visit her.

"I understand. You have full access to the performer's lounge, with a buffet for all three meals of the day. And of course, access to the best stage views in the festival. Just shout, I'll come running and help you navigate it all."

Ursula curtsied for Hadley. She was dressed like a hotel employee, wearing long khaki shorts and a deep purple polo shirt. Hadley gave her a weary smile, pulled open the door to her yurt, and stepped inside.

She remembered camping and sleeping in a small two-person tent, snuggled up in a scratchy sleeping bag on the ground, her mother's breath expanding her rib cage against Hadley's back. She remembered not sleeping, not feeling safe with nothing but trees surrounding them. Nothing but cloth had protected them from the outside world.

This, what she stepped into, was nothing like that.

Plush, blue-carpeted flooring covered the ground. Hadley immediately needed to sink her toes into it. Once she kicked off her shoes and let the threads tickle her feet, she studied the vaulted ceiling of white fabric, supported by wooden beams. There was a large painting of a resort pool against a desert landscape on the far side of the yurt, supported by a gold metal frame. A white couch against a white bar, martini glasses, and a silver tumbler were displayed on a silver plate that faced the art.

There was a California King-sized bed to her left, white bedding and white pillowcases, and two casual plush chairs to her right, surrounded by palm-leafed plants in decorative planters. It was beautiful. It was also clean, and she was suddenly very conscious of the dirt and grime that had built up on her over time.

Hadley walked over to the bed. A small yellow duffel bag sat at the end of it, with her name written on the paper lying atop it. She opened the zipper and began pulling out clothing that made her roll her eyes. There was barely any fabric in these tops to cover her. She ultimately pulled out a halter-top sundress made of loosely knitted material that would still show plenty of her skin, but at least she would fit in with the other girls here.

Her shoulders were bare, the triangle birthmarks on each blade prepped, ready for her mental command. Letting her wings grow and unfold had gotten smoother since the first time they'd surprised her, locked in Sheng's closet with a lock around her ankle, but it still hurt like hell.

Hadley closed her eyes and let her head roll forward, chin to her chest, while her arms relaxed by her sides. The sound of bones cracking and skin ripping danced around her ears as she held her breath, unable to breathe from the pain.

Bone exited through those birthmarks and folded together until wings formed behind her. This new part of her existed casually, as if her wings were no more extraordinary than her arm or leg. The first time she'd sprouted her wings, they were heavy and made it difficult for her to move or balance. Now, she was stronger, having them pulled out during most of her time in the California mountain tops.

Hadley walked over to the private bathroom and looked at herself in the mirror. She was much thinner, her cheeks hollow and gaunt. Her eyes appeared much too large for her face, like a damsel, like someone with much more innocence than she herself possessed.

Her wings took up the entire length of the bathroom, six feet long on either side of her when fully spread out. They were perfectly balanced for her height to support her during flight. She tucked them into her, curving around her like a draping towel. The layers of translucent skin were too easy not to see until light reflected specks of color through them.

She fit in now; it all looked like a costume. Hadley looked just like every girl at this musical festival: pretentious, young, and filled with the trendy allure of a bohemian lifestyle.

Okay, Ayurveda, what's the plan now?

As Hadley exited the bathroom, the front door opened, and a beautiful woman with fire in her hair stepped inside.

"You're looking a little more human today." Hadley smiled as the Goddess, whose normal form was that of a blue, see-through woman's body, inflamed. Now she wore clothes. She had skin that was both golden and dark. It was smooth, like precious metals forged in fire.

Ayurveda smiled, her mixed platinum and cinnamon-colored hair unable to hide the blue flamed tips entirely. She was the sun, and she needed to be worshiped, should be worshiped. This Goddess had watched after Hadley after escaping a kidnapping, a supposed family who tried to rescue her but didn't want her. This Goddess had been there for her; she deserved Hadley's backing and devotion. That was the kind of family she wanted to have.

"We are here to start building your fan club," Ayurveda said, holding a hand out to Hadley. "Are you ready for it?"

The moment reminded Hadley of the first time Ayurveda had held out her hand to her.

"Would you like to destroy the world with me?" she had asked. Hadley could only say yes, her rage boiling inside her, her fear of this new being, this living flame, intertwined.

The two of them stepped out of the yurt, and instantly, a golden electric golf cart appeared with her attendant, Ursula, smiling too widely at the wheel. Hadley pushed her sunglasses up her nose and sat down next to Ayurveda. It was a bit shocking still to see her as a human woman.

"Those wings are amazing. I love that they are see-through; no one will be yelling at you for blocking their views of the stage," Ursula, was still quite chatty.

The heat had picked up, and more than a gentle breeze was winding through the festival grounds as they passed through security. Dust was collecting in Hadley's eyes despite the sunglasses.

Why do people willingly go to this?

"I'll be here to pick you up whenever you are ready to go," Ursula squeaked. "I would fully recommend having dinner with the performers tonight. The buffet is usually at its hottest point around midnight, when they are all winding down."

Ayurveda gave the human a friendly nod and wrapped her arms through Hadley's, pulling her out of the golf cart and into the festival —wide dirt paths filled with people splayed out before them.

Human. The attendant is human, and you are not.

The crowd before them stood in lines to stand in more lines. They pretended to be interested in art and shrieked delightfully atop a gigantic Ferris wheel decorated in pastel colors. They were downing shots in small, jam-packed designated areas like sardines in a tin before bursting free and running to one of the various stages around them.

These people were dressed like they were in a futuristic catalog, their bikini tops with gold reflective covers, their makeup overdone, ethereal yet melting off from the sun's heat. A group of shirtless men in their twenties poured water bottles over their heads, creating small, muddy puddles, since the ground below their feet was not porous.

Hadley stared at these people, all of them incredibly beautiful. They were all who she'd hoped to be at one point—swept away into the creative celebrity world with her writing, the plays she once wrote. Now she looked down on them all, feeling surly, dust sticking to her skin. Her mouth curved down.

This Goddess beside her wanted to burn the world down, and Hadley was getting over her fear of the gigantic scaled creature that Ayurveda sat upon when she'd first approached her in those mountains.

Hadley remembered falling into the snow, not knowing how to land, as her back muscles screamed from exhaustion from her first flight. Ayurveda held out her translucent blue hand towards Hadley, who didn't blink twice and took it. She had never seen a Goddess before, but nothing could surprise her anymore, especially with everything she had just gone through.

Hadley had climbed on top of the dragon and sat directly behind the Goddess, separated by a thick black spike as it walked them through the terrain, trees bending as they hit its belly, the ground trembling with its steps.

"I helped create you," Ayurveda had told Hadley as they found a cave, making a base. "You are a powerful being. Your mom gave up her immortality to ensure yours."

Immortal. She said I was immortal.

The cave was surrounded by snow, with gray rock lying underneath. Beyond, an azul lake lay, surrounded by bright green trees under a crystal clear sky.

"Your magic manifested in a way I didn't expect," the Goddess' voice had echoed through the cave as the dragon spit embers at small gamey animals for its dinner. "But I suppose you are what you need, and you, my dear, will never be alone again. You will practice working with that shadow, calling it, learning what it can do."

Hadley nodded, agreeing. At the time, she'd known nothing about it, why it appeared, or what it acted on. When it saved her from the Vrae, from being nothing more than a breeder held captive, she'd felt like it acted entirely on its own.

Now, after all this time, she knew that wasn't true.

Ayurveda had split her time, leaving Hadley alone, often with the dragon's company. She hadn't trusted the creature then. Judging by the side-eye it usually gave her whenever she wandered from the cave, it didn't trust her either.

"Your wings will be my convex lens, my burning glass," Ayurveda had told her weeks later. "We will eliminate everyone and everything on this Earth together."

"And do what then?" Hadley had asked.

"Then this galaxy will revolve around me once more. There are millions more galaxies, and I am their star and anchor. Though none are quite like this, none have a planet with two realms that host the living."

Hadley had frowned at this. She certainly would have loved to hear that Sheng had died and paid for his crimes against her. She had nightmares regularly of the group of hooded, cloaked figures around her while teeth sank into her neck. She had been so helpless then, no more powerful than an ant under a magnifying glass.

"If you want to be worshiped, we can do it without mass destruction," Hadley had gathered the courage to say after more weeks had gone by. Her shadow self was seated right next to her and quite comfortable. The figure would disappear often, but was always there when something was happening. Hadley was never alone for the big moments.

Ayurveda had shown her a new way, mothered her, but gave her enough distance to learn who she was and what she could do in those mountains. Hadley was fully committed in return. There was no other life to return to, even if she hadn't been. It was a new path marked by ember, rage, hurt, and desperation.

The Kinnari and the Goddess stepped through the crowds, people parting for them as they approached.

"Yes, queen," an onlooker yelled at them from the side as more wind and dust floated around the two of them. Hadley's hair blew around her face, framing her heart-shaped face and emphasizing her now exposed collarbone. She was thin, having eaten much too little in those mountains, but here, thin was something to be proud of. This was not weak. It was not malnourished. Here, it was revered.

Ayurveda rolled her womanly hips from side to side like a lioness on the hunt for her pack. "It's time, young one, for you to get mad."

Hadley raised her eyebrows, letting Ayurveda continue.

"If victim was a people, you'd be their queen. Get mad, girl."

She was right. She had no one to lose anymore, nothing to hold her back. This was what they were doing in the mountains, trying to heal, trying to figure out her magic. It was all still so new, so underdeveloped, she could tell. Untested bombs, however, can often be the most deadly.

A hand reached out and grabbed Hadley's, and she gasped, pulling away. That courage she was building, that defiance and raw power, vanished. She was a scared cub again, looking for safety. All confidence, all power, now gone at the mere contact of skin.

She hadn't been touched, not really, since Sheng had woken up beside her in bed as her husband. She had been drugged. The venom in his jaws forced her to love him, to honor him. She once had sold her body to survive in the real world, this very same world, and it had cost her so much more than she ever could have predicted.

No, she didn't want anyone ever to touch her again.

"Woah, woah, Hadley, it's me," a familiar accent floated to her ears. Her suspicions did not waver; she did not let her guard down, but she turned to face the stranger who brushed her skin to find that it was no stranger at all.

"Hello, Hector," she said, staring at the Portuguese man smiling widely. This man was once her best friend. There was no love in her eyes, no warmth as the memories came flooding back of how he had convinced her to take one last job. Sure, he had returned to get her, but just that one time. He accepted the situation and never checked on her again, at least not while she was still captive in the East Sacramento mansion.

"You look so different," Hector said, his smile faltering slightly at Hadley's expression. "Absolutely gorgeous, but I honestly wouldn't have recognized you if I wasn't staring at your amazing costume like I was your stalker."

Hadley looked Hector up and down. His festival attire consisted of silver pleather shorts that were cut off and hugged in all the wrong places, as well as a matching tie. He had a gold hoop earring in one ear, and three males dressed identically cautiously hung out behind him.

"Thanks," Hadley said. "Who are your friends?"

"Oh, them?" Hector turned to wink at the group. "I did it, Hadley. I thought you'd be so proud of me. I made the move. I live out in West Hollywood now. I have six roommates in a two-bedroom apartment, but I'm actually here as a backup dancer for the artist on the main stage in a few hours. I wish you had come with me, but who am I to break up love? How's Sheng? Who is this?"

Hector nodded to Ayurveda, and as he did, the star turned on the charm.

"Call me Sunny," Ayurveda held her hand out for Hector to kiss. He immediately did so.

Hadley's chest was tightening, her breaths short and quick. She wasn't ready for this, to see someone from her past—especially someone she had loved.

A dark figure, Hadley's double, appeared. Her shadow danced around Hector, doing a few pirouettes while sticking her tongue out at him. She gestured to him, asking Hadley for her permission to strike.

Hadley smiled, her shoulders relaxed slightly as she shook her head no.

"Let her strike, Hadley. This is the reason we came." Ayurveda's voice, now motherly and encouraging, dug its way into Hadley's heart. "We want undivided loyalty. Love."

Hadley nodded as she allowed it, letting her shadow figure plunge into Hector. She watched as he fell to his knees.

5

Djoser | Coachella Valley

The pulses rang through his chest, rising and falling with every inhale and exhale. Djoser took a breath from his nose and held it.

One. Two. Three.

He let his breath out, the hushed release, the vibrations as it passed through his lips, carried his voice by air as it escaped into the valley below.

One. Two. Three.

He continued his meditation, sitting cross-legged in the dirt, the sun beating down his exposed back and wings. He wasn't ready to open his eyes, to face why he had come here. He wasn't ready to be a monster, a killer once more. He had to prepare, to get himself there, into the mental state of someone ready to rip life away from the living. There was no romance in it, no fantasized grim reaper tale. He had a contract, a job to do.

The Life Gifter demanded devotion, and he would always serve his creator. Djoser had faith and knew that things were so much bigger than him, more significant than those he was ordered to kill. He took some comfort in the fact that pulling atoms apart did not seem like a violent death, but still, his next target was down below in that valley somewhere, and now that he was there, he didn't know how to push through this.

It took Djoser three days to get to Joshua Tree from Zion, catching a ride with that backstabbing mortal Greg. Listening to the pretentious stories of having too many craft beers and growing out handlebar mustaches was torturous. Nothing was wrong with either of those two things, but hearing about it for miles and miles with club music seemingly on repeat was enough to make Djoser regret not flying, taking that risk in broad daylight.

Despite Greg being insufferable, Djoser had intentionally been taking his time. Now that he had arrived, there was no other way to avoid it.

Djoser opened his eyes, looking down at the too-large plot of land holding what seemed to be hundreds of cars packed in so tightly that he wondered how anyone was able to back out. The faint echo of heavy stereo systems used for live music made its way to him, even all the way up in the San Jacinto mountains.

A yellow hot air balloon hovered slightly over the scene, making the festival seem more hopeful, more fun than he anticipated it to be.

Djoser sighed, throwing his head forward.

Suck it up. You don't even know her.

His thoughts returned to simpler times, times of beautiful Egyptian women sitting in steaming hot baths, their legs and minds open to his council. He missed the never-empty wine mugs and the hieroglyphs carved into sacred temples in his honor. He even missed the awful priests who always hated him, the proof that their religion was not entirely accurate.

Still, Djoser let them have those stories. He let his people shape their own culture. They were only human, and he loved them.

Djoser stood up, stretching his wings wide, creating a mythical shadow in his wake. He wore jeans, cuffed at the hem, with flip flops, which was fitting. He supposed he'd fit right in with the crowd below.

There was a good amount of wind, so Djoser stepped into the air. The mountain was descending underneath his step, and he was immediately carried. The air groaned beneath his wings, though it was not quite powerful enough to truly hold his weight, so he pushed his wings back, giving him more lift as he floated effortlessly down to the valley.

He was visible. Anyone paying attention would have noticed him. Luckily, most everyone was on drugs or working. No one was looking towards the mountains.

He landed, his feet on flat dirt, and walked to the fence surrounding the festival grounds, hopping over it as if it was no taller than a highway divider. He pulled his wings in after he landed and walked forward, passing stalls serving fried chicken sandwiches.

Do your job, and you can get one covered in buffalo sauce.

"How the fuck am I supposed to find her in this mess?" Djoser growled, chin tucked low, and hands balled into fists.

He was surrounded by humans, all showing as much skin as possible. This was a terrible climate to do that in. They would all get skin cancer unless they inhaled too much dust and got lung cancer instead. Humans were much too fragile for this.

"Can you see it?" a woman, slurring her words, shouted while still too close to her companion's ear. "Something is happening over there. There's a huge crowd, and there's no stage there."

Djoser watched as the young couple rushed over to an area three hundred yards away, noticing a gathering with the most peculiar body language. There was no dancing or enjoyment. There was no panicked excitement about getting the chance to take a photograph with a performer.

No, the group he watched looked like they were praying. Their shoulders were slightly hunched over, yet their necks and chins pulled upwards, giving their full attention as if waiting for a command.

Djoser had never been to this music festival before, but he

assumed religion was pretty far removed from it. Maybe he would find the girl in the crowd, much easier to spot if she wasn't moving freely. He would pool his magic, the blackness reaching for her atoms, and pull them apart in one swift movement. Then, it would be time to go home, back to Egypt. Letting Arryn drag him out here to North America to save the very person that was now his mark made him realize that he needed to return to his roots. He needed to be as far away from Kinnari, from magic and grief, as possible.

Djoser moved through the group's onlookers, curious people like himself who did not entirely understand what was going on. He was looking for a vantage point since he couldn't see what the crowd surrounded while on their same level.

He found more food stands and a portable bathroom ahead and climbed up to the roof. He scanned the crowd, hoping to see that same blonde hair that had plagued his thoughts since those many months ago.

He began searching from the perimeter of the crowd and stopped quickly, something odd catching his eye. The onlookers, the people who were not quite part of the group, were one by one, jolting upright. Their eyes suddenly emptied before flashing to expressions of destiny and love.

The gathering was growing larger, and more and more festival-goers were becoming a part of it, bowing down, ready for what was in the center. Djoser shifted his eyes, now understanding that this group was dealing with something much different than fame.

His heart skipped, and his jaw tightened as he laid eyes on his mark. There, in the middle of the ever-growing crowd of worshipers, stood two women. One looked so familiar, but he couldn't quite place her, with platinum blonde and cinnamon-colored hair. The other, with translucent wings that shimmered in the sun, was Hadley. He had come for her.

Djoser stared at Arryn's daughter, the creature created from Alli-enna's unknown sacrifice. This being caused so much hate and grief, even though none of it seemed to be directly her fault.

Black wisps of magic pooled at Djoser's fingertips. He could just do it now. She would disappear in front of everyone's eyes, and they would applaud, thinking it was part of a show. It was the perfect setting, so visible, and yet, nothing here was real. It was all a spectacle.

Djoser halted as he took notice, blinking twice to make sure what he was seeing was real. The woman beside Hadley was floating, her feet just inches off the ground. No one reacted to it. Hadley turned her head slightly and smiled at the floating woman, reaching out her hand towards her. Their fingers intertwined.

"This is your moment. Make them worship you," the woman said, letting go of Hadley's hand as she ascended higher into the sky, her skin turning blue and her hair catching fire.

Ayurveda. Shit.

"Look at the fucking hologram. Coachella has gotten epically wild," Djoser heard some people passing by, pointing up to the Sun Goddess that hung in the sky. The wind grew stronger as canvased topped awnings began to creak under and moan, their metal stakes holding them into the ground disturbed.

Kill her. Kill her now.

More and more of the crowd fell to their feet like something was hitting them, a spell or magic that looked physical. They all reacted the same way: stunned. They got up to their feet, and their expressions turned into awe.

"It's her!" a few in the crowd called out. Although the sun floated above them, manifested as a woman, the crowd was talking about Hadley.

She was so dainty, looking at the faces that stared back at her. There was no lust for power on her face, no indication that she was drinking this attention in, but Djoser had little doubt that she was causing the crowd's reaction.

He watched as she held her head high, eyes darting to the goddess above.

She doesn't know what to do next.

Djoser tilted his head, letting his neck crack as he grasped for those wisps of black magic once more. It was time to get this over with, and whatever was going on with these humans should probably stop before things got really weird.

He reached out into the air, feeling and weaving his way through the atoms that existed between them. Humans, statues, food, it was all getting in his way.

Once this is done, you get to go home.

He was inches from her now, excited to feel the translucent glass-looking wings that sprouted from her back. Djoser snapped his head up to Ayurveda, his heart stopping as a shriek flooded through the valley, ringing his ears.

Ayurveda was expressionless, a portrait of what she was expected to look like. She hung in the air, hair of fire blowing in the wind with increasing violence. The crowd below her did not look around; they did not seem to notice the same ear-piercing sound, and Djoser began to wonder if he had made it up. He hadn't heard a sound like that since Arryn was a child, making magic-wielding creatures that he threw into Myrilosis.

The light from the sky had disappeared, and Djoser realized that he was within a large shadow. He looked up, mouth gapping in surprise, unsure of what to do with the twenty feet of dragon that flew above him.

"Are you fucking serious?" he muttered under his breath.

Stay focused. Stay focused on the girl.

Gasps and screams came from further away, pointing to the massive creature in the sky. It had smooth, deep burgundy scales that blended into solid brown on its wings and legs. The dragon hovered momentarily and then pushed its powerful wings down to make a shallow circle around Ayurveda, a pet showing loyalty.

Djoser eyed Hadley, staring up at the scene above her before she was airborne, fluttering her wings quickly. He'd never seen a Kinnari move their wings like that before. It was almost like a bee, a hummingbird, moving so quickly that it appeared her wings didn't exist. When he flew, he used powerful, slow pulses. If it were a bike, his gear would be set at ten, hers at one.

He pushed his dark wisps through the air towards her, the crowd of festival goers underneath her now all raising their arms up as if they were trying to follow her. The humans gathered, bringing themselves in tighter until they began climbing on top of one another. There was a desperation, an emptiness in their movements, as if Hadley leaving them would mean their deaths.

Djoser forced himself to ignore them, the tower of humans steadily growing higher and higher as his magic got closer. He was inches from her now, his dark wisps traveling through the sky as he tried to avoid the hecticness of the human tower. All he had to do was reach out for her long yellow hair that was getting violently blown around her face by the wind. All he had to do was commit, but he didn't. He hesitated, and that fucked him over.

As soon as he moved forward, ready to make Hadley disappear into a forever darkness, the dragon swooped down into a descending corkscrew. Its heavy tail thrashed behind it as it let out a sound of mourning, surprise, and lethal anger. Djoesr's magic had hit it, and though he immediately pulled back his touch, it was too late. There was damage done.

Ayurveda's gaze scanned the area momentarily before settling on Djoser. He froze. It was possible that she didn't know what his true intentions were, but either way, he was there hurting one of her pets.

The dragon rolled in the sky, shrieking its disapproval over its now missing limbs. It landed with only two remaining legs over the humans' climbing tower. Sounds of crushed skulls, like that of children stomping on sticks in the wilderness, filled the valley.

"No, no," Ayurveda clicked her tongue at the creature as it looked around the group, contemplating if it should crush more skulls.

Djoser watched Hadley, his eyes rarely leaving her. She was still in the air, her eyes locked with his and her wings fluttering furiously. She lowered herself to the ground, her hand landing on the dragon's tail, giving it soothing pets.

"Followers," she started, looking around at the festival goers who were not reacting to the carnage but instead staring at Hadley as if she were their God, the only one that mattered. This was cult-like behavior. His mind flashed to the terror that hit him in the East

Sacramento mansion, wondering what she did, how the two were related.

"Come, we have work to do. We have a word to spread."

Hadley began walking towards the festival exit as the dragon, now technically a wyvern—gods, how long had it been since he'd seen one of those—took flight and soared over her. Ayurveda nodded her approval at the scene below and ascended higher into the sky until she was no longer visible.

Thousands of mortals began stomping after Hadley, their faces giving nothing away but undoubted loyalty to the Kinnari women they followed.

She has an army.

Djoser stood there, letting the breath in his chest return as he considered the possible consequences. The festival grounds were now eerie, and thudding music on loudspeakers emphasized the area's complete emptiness. Everyone was gone: the attendees, artists, and employees; they had all followed her.

It doesn't matter. None of this matters. You have been given a task that you must complete.

Djoser jumped down from the stall, his knees cracking slightly under the impact, and began walking after them.

6

Reign | Sacramento, Ca

Reign sprawled out on the floor, her knees swaying while on her back. She watched the ceiling fan overhead spinning with a rhythmic thump as it completed its circle repeatedly. If she focused on one of the fan's arms, it slowed slightly enough to where she could follow it, and when she let her focus zoom out, chaos ensued, and the five white plastic arms blended back into a perfect circle.

"What are you doing?" Arryn came down the stairs and stared at the immortal woman stuck inside an eight-year-old child's body.

"I need to pay my mortgage," she sighed, regretting not buying the house in cash when she easily could have. Business was good back then, and figuring out how to launder the money was not even worth the stress. "I'm trying to think of jobs I can do now, considering that I am not a legal adult in polite society's eyes."

"Child actor? Can children still perform in the circus? Can you even do a backflip?" Arryn chuckled. It was the first time she had heard him laugh in months. Between the two of them, an almost visible cloud of despair hovered over her modest Sacramento townhome.

"What I don't get is why you need a job at all," Arryn walked over and laid down on the floor next to her, the sides of their heads touching, blending blond hair and black. "You could go into any bank and command the teller to give you the entire contents of their vault. It seems you, out of anyone, would have the easiest time surviving in a mortal life. Even in this youthful body."

Reign sat up, supporting her weight with her arms bent behind her. She looked down at Arryn, her face showing pure disgust.

"I have worked hard to build a life without cheating. I use my magic sparingly in the mortal world."

"Okay, okay, calm down," Arryn said, holding his hand up to her. "Here, I'll use mine then for your cause."

What once was Arryn's empty palm suddenly lay a purple paper bill adorned with stars and the number five hundred in the bottom left corner.

"That's European money; it won't hold any value here." She sighed in defeat and flopped back down to the floor. "Also, you need to learn how to speak to women. Telling one to calm down is usually not the recommended move."

The two had gone back and forth multiple times a day, trying to make one another feel better. They'd once considered themselves best friends and had bonded over their love for Allienna, and now were working on getting back to that point. Neither of them knew what to do with their time, so they just slumped around Reign's townhouse, being completely unproductive and useless.

Enough time had passed, and Reign was ready to start figuring out how to live again.

"Sorry, I went to visit the twins before I came here to find her," Arryn said. "That's the only reference I have of modern money."

"You mean your daughter. You have a daughter, Arryn, who probably needs you." Reign sneered back. She was choosing violence today. "Allienna's gone, but you still have a chance to savor this other relationship. Allienna gave up her existence for this girl. You should show more interest."

"I'm just not," he said bluntly. "I'm heartbroken. She left me. I can't get through it. This daughter I have, someone I never even knew existed, might have been the cause of all of that."

"What if she's like me now? What if Allienna is walking around as a child? Alone?" Reign stood up, hearing the doorbell ring.

"No, it's not possible. She would have come home. She would have known the kind of pain I'd be in."

Arryn, you're an idiot.

"I've got to go get that," Reign said, leaving Arryn on the floor as she walked down the steps to the first story of her townhouse. She passed the small but modern kitchen and a loveseat couch surrounded by her bookshelves to reach the front door.

Thud. Thud. Thud.

"I'm fucking coming," Reign yelled out, walking up to the door before turning the deadbolt and throwing open the door.

"Don't you see this place from the outside? There are four fucking stories. Show some patience." Reign stopped her angry spiral once she looked up and took in her familiar, unexpected visitor.

Grant. Shit.

The middle-aged male with skin that indicated he no longer went outside stared at her in surprise. They used to be so close, speaking every day. Sure, it was usually about work, but the man had a big, misguided heart. Although he was gross in more ways than one, he did take good care of her as her pimp. Grant would prefer the word manager, but sex work was sex work.

Grant's greasy hair was pulled back into his familiar ponytail while he leaned on the side of the door, stroking his goatee.

"You seem a bit young to be speaking with a mouth like that," Grant said to her.

"What do you want?" Reign exhaled and crossed her arms over her chest.

"I'm looking for the woman that lives here. She looks a lot like you; maybe you're related?"

Grant put his hands in the pockets of his jeans and shrugged his shoulders. Regin stood there for a moment, staring right back at him in silence with a judgmental brow.

"That's my mom," Reign said, deciding this was the better lie to move forward with.

"Your mom? I didn't know she had kids," Grant scuffed, his eyes wide from surprise. "I thought we'd had a relationship where she would tell me something like that."

Reign tossed her hair back over her shoulders. "She's my new stepmom. She got hitched and traded in those tall boots of hers for an apron. Pretty anti-feminist if you ask me, but whatever." Reign rolled her eyes, taking on the new role of a spoiled, angsty stepdaughter. It didn't feel too off base.

"Anyways, if you're some heart-sick past boyfriend or something, it's best to probably forget her. My dad's pretty loaded, works in tech and drives into San Francisco three times a week. Judging by the quality of that haircut, I'd say you couldn't compete."

Grant gaped at her before darting his eyes behind her, looking for another sign of life.

"You're a brat, ain't ya'?"

"Are we done here? Should I call my dad down?" she asked before turning over her shoulder, "Oye, Dad, someone's here to see that gold digger you married."

Grant laughed. "Don't worry, I'll skedaddle. It seems like she will have her hands full with you. I mean, she could have called or sent a simple text, but you can let her know Grant's on standby."

"I won't."

"Great." Grant threw his arms out wide and turned around. Reign watched him stomp down the cement path leading to the sidewalk before closing the door and turning around.

"What did you do that for?" Arryn said, walking down the stairs and leaning against the kitchen counter.

"I was a dominatrix, Arryn. Can't really do that these days," she said, pointing at her adolescent body. "Regardless, I've got a few ideas on what I can do for money."

Arryn widened his eyes at her and tapped his nails on the counter. "You've been extra grumpy lately, have you noticed?"

Reign ignored him. "I'm going to build a website, sell some shit that people don't need." She shrugged her shoulders, looking down at her feet. "It's practically anonymous. No one needs to see my face. Maybe I can design skin care products for people who want the skin of an eight-year-old."

Arryn raised his eyebrows at her and cocked his head.

"What's a website?"

Reign groaned and pinched between her eyes.

"I think it's about time to kick you out, old timer." She threw her hands up in the air and started stomping up the stairs. "I won't be able to get anything done if we are both just supporting each other's misery."

"I agree," Arryn said.

"You do?" Reign's head popped out from the side of the stairs, lips pursed.

"Yes. I have plans to leave, and I think that you should come with me. You mentioned Europe earlier, and I think we should connect with the twins. I don't think anyone has told them what's happened."

"We can just call them," Reign said. "Unlike you, we all have phones. Besides, Precession probably has a good grasp on the situation. She's always had a bit of a precognition."

Arryn shifted, leaning back to rest his elbows on the white countertop.

"I'm leaving, hoping they might have more clues for me. I can go figure out what happened to her."

Reign scoffed, and her head disappeared from the top of the staircase.

"Oh, of course, this would be about Allienna. You need to let it go," a faint, high-pitched shout barely reached Arryn. He shook his head and looked down at his feet before heading upstairs.

"I can just fly from the roof, right?" he asked. Reign knew that the fire under his skin had to be burning. He needed to release magic, create a storm, create anything. That money had been the first thing she had seen him do in months as he kept himself in a state of torture and self-loathing.

"You're leaving right this second? You aren't going to bother to pack?" Reign stood in the second-floor living room with her hip sticking out.

"I make whatever I need—besides, flying at distances with luggage? I'll pass," he said with a perfect, pearly white smile.

Great, so I get to clean up all your shit after you leave.

"Fine, I'll travel with you. Let's go to France, and then I'll come back here alone." She didn't actually know how to start a website and would rather leave it to future her to figure out.

Reign marched up the stairs, passing her third-floor primary bedroom, and continued up to the rooftop. Arryn followed, twenty seconds behind her.

"You know, you really are a bratty child," Arryn said as they looked out at the city view.

The twilight sky overlooking the Sacramento Bridge was positively breathtaking at this hour. Unlike the Golden Gate Bridge in the Bay Area, this bridge was actually a warm gold, illuminated under the dark blue skies that were fading out to black before their eyes. The calm river flowing underneath reflected the scene above like a mirror, including the stars that glimmered as they appeared in the darkening horizon before them.

Reign looked up at Arryn and let her wings, dark brown with specks of gray, flow out through the black, too-loose tank top that she wore. It had been hers when she was an adult; she'd used it when she pretended to exercise.

Arryn ripped off his shirt in response, and his own wings, cyan blue with streaks of gold, cracked and grew out of the triangular Kinnari marks in his shoulder blades. Reign was facing 5,500 miles in the sky. Her wings were smaller now. She frowned.

We should have just booked a flight.

Reign's bare feet lifted off the ground, and she debated whether her toes were likely to freeze off during the airtime. She always hated that about being in the sky, the bursts of cold, the numbness. Modern society might have ruined her with its comforts.

She caught up to Arryn, who patiently waited for her. He slowly moved east on his back, his hands supporting his head as if he were floating on top of water.

"I can be patient," he said as he flipped his body around and held out his hand. Reign took it, her body's underdeveloped back muscles grateful for the support, as they began their long trek.

Sixteen hours later, the two touched down in the charming town of Chartres. The sun had already set due to the nine-hour time difference, making the large cathedral sitting amongst a large cobblestoned open area seem threatening, menacing.

Looking away from the building, Reign was delighted to see the many gelato shops that lined the pathways and local tourists out walking arm in arm, love plaguing the scene. Many small cafes were still open, as waiters pouring wine into clinking glasses hurried through service.

The air was warm, with the occasional slight breeze. Summer was approaching, and the blooming flowers and trees filled with leaves left a natural fragrance as the two began walking over a small footbridge, gentle water running underneath.

"Where are we going?" Reign asked, noting the looks she was getting for being a barefoot child walking with a grown man at a late hour.

"I don't remember how to get to their chateaux; the last time I was here, I was just able to find Roksana in a bar. I was hoping that we'd have the same outcome here."

Reign stopped walking and scoffed, shaking her head no.

"Fuck's sake, Arryn, you cannot be serious."

Reign pulled her phone out of the back pocket of her jeans. She pressed *call* on Roksana's contact number and put the phone to her ear. The phone rang a few times, the tone deeper than what she had become used to while in the United States, before the familiar voice of a fiery redhead answered the phone.

"I can't think of any reason why you might be calling me," Roksana said on the phone.

"Always a pleasure. I miss you, too. I can't wait to visit and braid one another's hair. Do any of those sound realistic?"

There was a short pause before Roksana breathed into the phone. "You're here then. Where are you? I'll send you our address, and you will show it to the cab driver. They likely will not speak English."

"Got it," Reign said.

"Your voice sounds different," Roksana pointed out.

"You'll see why when I get there."

The phone beeped, indicating that Roksana ended the call. A few seconds later, it chimed when a text message came through with the promised address.

"Let me hail the cab," Arryn said like an enthused child. "I learned how to do this the last time I was here. Plus, you know, you're so short that no one would be able to see you, anyway."

Reign looked at Arryn with daggers in her eyes and pulled her wings back in. Couples walking in the background looked away quickly, not understanding what they were seeing.

Arryn followed suit as they walked towards the nearest street, finding the cabs that waited for tipsy couples leaving their dinners. The two of them were quickly inside a cab, the driver putting on his glasses to see the address that Reign showed him on her phone. He entered it on his GPS, and they drove off, arriving only fifteen minutes later.

The cab drove through a gated entrance as Reign tried not to balk at the gorgeous estate before her.

"Moo-ne-ey," the cab driver tried to over-enunciate to Arryn, and Reign's attention snapped back to the inside of the cab.

"How much? Combien devons-nous?" she asked, grateful that she remembered a bit of French from her romps around Europe in the late eighteen hundreds.

The cab driver held up his fingers, indicating nine euros, and Arryn held out his palm as an orange, tan, red paper bill appeared.

The cab driver nearly smiled from the tip he received before aggressively pushing them out because "time is moo-ne-ey."

Arryn and Reign stepped out of the cab as it drove away, staring at the countryside chateaux surrounded by deep green trees. The gravel under Reign's feet stung, so she wasted no time making her way up to the large, arched front door.

Reign raised her hand to knock, but the door groaned before she could, opening to reveal a foyer abundant in moonlight as it bounced off of tile flooring. There, standing before a grand spiral staircase, stood two petite women. Their hair looked like flowing lava in the unlit room, with the window light highlighting it from behind.

"Precession, Roksana," Arryn greeted them.

Precession, so frail, hanging off of her much stronger sister, her protector, looked at Reign, curiosity in her eyes as she bit her lip. She began to open her mouth but was cut off, sinking her head back into her sister's shoulder.

"This is the second time you've shown up here uninvited, with no notice." Roksana smirked. "I forbid this from becoming a trend."

Footsteps sounded behind the twins, followed by cloth dragging on the flooring. Multiple bodies with hooded cloaks emerged. Their blood-red eyes, like daggers, stared at the new guests as if they were pieces of meat during a famine.

7

Arryn | France

"Do you care to explain why ten Vrae are standing behind you, inside your home, like they are guests?" Reign asked, her big child-like eyes wide, her fingers clenching. The tile flooring gleamed in the moonlight as the twins in elegant, long silk robes intertwined their hands, looking out at their unexpected visitors.

Arryn couldn't bother to look at them, the pitiful demon-like creatures, leering from underneath their hooded cloaks. He recognized some of them who had once stood from a distance, under the shadows below the Sacramento pentagram ceiling. There was a blonde man with shoulder-length hair that bared his teeth before showing a crooked smile.

Saul.

There was a brunette woman, tall, with long legs and eyes that bulged even from the darkness surrounding her face.

Jenny.

These were the two that their leader called by name that day. The others had also been there, though they were never introduced as individuals. They were a group, a cult, there to worship a leader plunging them further into darkness. Kidnapping Kinnari daughters and feasting on Waihema villagers were just a recent list of their vices. He hated them all.

Arryn wondered if they had anything to do with Allienna's disappearance, with her supposed death. None of the others had died, Tristan or Reign. Were they keeping Allienna prisoner as well? He opened his mouth, searching for answers in Roksana's or Precession's faces. He found none, as the twins remained stoic.

The hairs on his arms started to rise, and goosebumps appeared. Arryn's heart rate sped up, and a cold sweat settled on the back of his neck. Panic was setting in, and his anxiety was so deep that his mind became empty to help him cope.

Stay calm. You'll kill them all later when they think you're asleep.

"Roksana," Arryn said softly, "please stop."

The right side of Roksana's mouth twitched up, her magic being chaos, even to herself. Emotions would heighten around the Kinnari twin, regardless of her intent, and Arryn was feeling that, his edge, his burning intensifying. It was a slow trickle, but even small drops can eventually cause a flood.

"Unfortunately for you, Arryn," Roksana said, sneering. "I'm not pushing at all. What you're feeling isn't intentional and is likely a sign that you must build a better tolerance for me. To answer your question, Reign, someone who can explain better is coming now."

Arryn looked toward the hallway directly behind the group of Vrae and did indeed hear someone, or something, making its way down to them. The smooth clicking sound of dress shoes eventually hit the tile as a male with long midnight black hair and dark golden skin entered the foyer. His eyes were the color of charcoal, and he brought a feeling of calm. as if any pending danger was inevitable, and it was best to let it happen. Arryn's breathing began to return to normal, embracing the balance that had come forth.

Arryn made a mental note to kill him first, but he might need

Djoser for that particular task. It was an easy feeling; there was no anger or hate, just the zen knowledge of *that piece of shit should be dead*. It was hard not to appreciate someone who could cancel out Roksana, though, Arryn could admit that much.

"Are these Kinnari bothering you, my sweet?" Amis asked, walking up to Roksana, putting his hands around her waist and nuzzling his nose into her neck. Arryn remembered that when they brought a battle to the Life Gifter, to plead and fight for the lives of their small species, that these two were freely flirting. He wasn't prepared then to think of it with any significance.

"Amis, what are you doing here?" Arryn asked, stepping forward, malice filling his eyes for the Kinnari who left them, deserted them when barely older than children, all to aid their enemies.

"I suppose," Amis said, beaming, "there's only one thing to do to keep us bonded through this little alliance."

If I try to kill Amis, will Roksana go after me? We can try to blame the Vrae.

"Pfft," Arryn spit. "This alliance isn't real. You all will attack me the moment I turn my back. My blood runs deep blue, which is their drink of choice, Amis. Not that I should have to remind you."

"It's settled, then, a drinking game." Amis clapped his hands in excitement as the room shifted uncomfortably. Arryn watched Roksana as she, too, inched a bit further away from him. Amis looked around the room, seeing Reign's shocked gaze as she moved into a threatening pose, despite being unarmed.

Arryn pulled together a group of atoms, leaving a small dagger in her clenched fists. She loosened her grip immediately as the emerald gems in the silver handle cut into her hand. The toughest of them, the Kinnari always ready to fight for everyone but herself, stood beside him, feeling small and defenseless. He didn't approve.

"Keep that blood inside your body for the night, will you? Roksana, please bring out a few liquor bottles, and we will meet you in the dining room," Amis said, clapping his hands together.

Arryn looked down, meeting Reign's gaze. She was pouting, and she bounced on her toes, dagger held tightly against her chest so that it gleamed across the room.

"I think the little one wants to go to bed," Arryn said, wanting to pull her away from any danger.

"Speak for yourself," Reign's meek voice managed to boom. "I can drink you all under the table."

Saul chuckled. "Careful, little one, if you get any angrier, your eyes could turn red like mine." He flashed a glare, blood coloring his irises.

"What's that supposed to mean?" Arryn asked gruffly.

Reign ignored it as her small body stomped towards the left side of the foyer, going through an opulent framed doorway surrounded by glass windows that led into the dining room. Still visible from where Arryn stood, Reign pulled out a chair noisily and plopped down, throwing her feet on the table and leaning back in her seat.

"After you," Amis said to Arryn with a grin, his hand motioning to follow Reign. "If you have questions, playing along will be the best way for you to get your answers."

The level headedness that Amis' magic brought to the room was everything Arryn didn't want. He wanted to be angry. He wanted to fight for the people he loved. He wanted their blood smeared on the shiny tile beneath their Vrae feet.

Arryn shook his head as if to wipe out the hate, the murder, and the incredible feeling of those thoughts bringing him peace. He realized the effect of Amis and Roksana being together would ensure a tortuous night.

"If anything happens here tonight, Amis, I promise you won't wake up in the morning," Arryn said as he walked into the dining room. Amis and the group of Vrae walked behind him in dead silence.

"If I remember correctly, Arryn, you're no killer. In fact, that only seems to get accomplished if someone else does it for you."

Arryn looked at Amis, the burning under his skin somewhat more noticeable, the magic inside him clawing to get out. The things he could make to ensure torture, to ensure suffering for everyone in the room playing out in his mind.

The dining room table only sat ten bodies and filled up quickly, leaving two cerulean linen chairs open for the chateaux's owners. Precession, eyes hazy, daintily collapsed into one of them, lashes fluttering wildly. She gripped the table with her hands as if she were about to float away.

A chandelier was suspended over the center of the table, featuring draping crystals on top of bronze curving arms. Twelve electric candles sat atop, sending bursts of light to the wide metal-framed mirror on the back wall and illuminating the room as if it were day.

Four of the Vrae were left without a spot at the table and stood behind Precession, looking down at the back of her neck. Their lips frowned under the shadows of their hooded cloaks.

"I was on my way back from Waihema," Amis said, locking eyes with Arryn as he took the seat across from him. "And decided it would be good to remove these Vrae from Sacramento for their safety. There were Kinnari with a vendetta living in the area. I'm just dropping them off here."

Reign scoffed since Amis could only be alluding to her, shifting as the dagger pushed against her wrist hard enough to break skin. A smooth one-inch cut revealed a red hue underneath before it quickly scabbed over and began healing.

Arryn noticed a few seated Vrae gulping audibly, their nostrils flaring. All of the Vrae bodies in the room stiffened, and their gazes narrowed due to the copper scent of blood wafting through the air.

"Red?" Arryn whispered to her.

"Since I've become this, my blood is no longer blue." She shrugged, keeping their conversation private and her cut out of sight. "What about Roksana and Precession? What about their safety? Why would you let them stay here?" Reign asked, ignoring the attention on her now scabbed wrist. She turned to Precession, confusion settling in her eyes. She was given no answer other than an unassuming smile, though little more than that was ever expected from Precession.

Three clear frosted bottles filled with bright yellow liquid thudded down onto the table. Roksana then slid a tray of two-inch-tall smooth glasses with round bottoms meant for liquor onto the tray.

"Limoncello," she announced with a tinge of pride, "for whatever this occasion is."

Amis wasted no time, pouring the liquor from the frosted bottles into the tray of glasses and handing them to the Vrae that sat next to him with auburn hair and gray-green eyes,

"Killian, my rugged little viper, take this and pass it down, so it goes around the table."

The Vrae took the glass, his eyes not moving off of Reign, and handed it to his companion. He reached out to take another, then another.

"They may stay," Precession said with an airiness to her voice, "because I am losing my grip on the moon. It's happened more than once these past few months. It feels like I am hanging over a cliff with a rope. The rope starts getting pulled right out of my hands . . ." Precession trailed off, her gaze focused out the window, chin up towards the sky.

Reign pulled her feet off the table and sat up, staring with her mouth open.

"Are you going to elaborate on that?" Arryn prodded.

"Uh-uh," Amis tsked. "The game has started. The rules are simple. Empty your glass to ask a question. We might as well get the formalities out of the way and introduce everyone in the room. How silly of me."

No one laughed, no one shifted. Arryn just stared at the traitorous Kinnari with pure malice. Amis stared back, refilling Arryn with a mellowness, a willingness just to be present with no expectations. He did his best to fight that, push away that balance. He did his best to pull in the energy around Roksana, but she was a few steps further away. He couldn't get through Amis' fog.

"Now, everyone here knows the Kinnari, my childhood mates, but I have been living with this group for quite a long time, and they have yet to eat me, at least against my will. Those are definitely stories for another time," Amis laughed out loud, his belly pulsing before he slapped Killian on the back and pulled himself together.

The corners of Arryn's mouth tried to move in an upward motion. He shook his head; he refused to have his spirits lifted.

"Seated here," Amis continued, "we have Saul, then Jenny, Killian, Leonardo, Priscilla, Francis, Dravus, Bruce, Marcus, and Ramsey."

The Vrae collectively began to take their hoods off, as if the introduction had given them permission to do so. They all looked so normal, like groomed and polished mortals from proper political families, American royalty.

Leonardo sat next to Killian, who had high, elegant cheekbones. It seemed like he had modeled his human skin from a drawing, thin and gaunt in the most captivating way. Arryn did not doubt that he would lure someone in only to rip out their throat. Priscilla and Francis, the other two Vrae sitting down, could have been siblings with their matching eyes and silver hair. Unlike Francis, Priscilla had five piercings on her earlobes. Each piece of jewelry inserted was a small, elegant gray pearl.

Just play their game.

Arryn raised his glass to the table, nodded, and then gulped it back easily before gently setting it down. He licked the sugar off his lips and nodded his head towards Roksana in approval.

"Now," he said, clearing his throat from the slight burn of the liquor, "Precession, please explain what you meant about the moon."

Roksana took a deep breath and walked over to her twin sister's chair, pushing the four huddling Vrae out of her way as if they were nothing of note. She had no fear of the murderous creatures right next to her throat. Dravus, Bruce, Marcus, and Ramsey seemed to be the mightier of the Vrae as they all towered over Roksana, nearly twice her height.

"My magic, my purpose, as you know, tethers me to the moon. I alone keep the earth spinning through its rotation. There have been two instances where something has hit the moon with incredible force, stopping me for seconds at a time. The earth stops spinning, and I feel like I'm personally being attacked. If we are using analogies, someone is on the other side of that cliff, pulling that rope out of my hand. The planet is on its way to standing still before I snap to and recover."

Precession also seemed at ease and carefree, though this was always her normal demeanor. Even as children, Precession held that air of mystery, that unbelievable burden that Arryn could only imagine to be a curse, though she never showed it. They had all been cursed by their creators in some way.

Precession looked up to Roksana and smiled, a slight twinkle in her eye. "My guess is that it's solar flares hitting the moon. That would make sense if what the Vrae are saying is true. They may not be the real enemy; the Earth may actually be under attack by Ayurveda. It all lines up with what I had been experiencing, so I told my sister to let the Vrae come in when they showed up at our gate yesterday."

They had only been here for a day. The Vrae could still have every intention of feasting upon them, and it would probably be fine if they did.

"How do we stop it?" Reign asked.

"Tsk tsk, buttercup." Amis smiled. "Bottoms up."

No, no, not fine. Snap out of it.

"Oh fuck you," Reign yelled before gulping her glass down, letting it thud against the mahogany table. "Are you happy now?"

"That counts as a question."

Reign stood up and threw her empty glass at Amis. It sailed past his head and hit the opposite wall, shattering.

"That's okay. That's fine," she said, surprised at the overwhelming conflicting emotions that hung in the room.

"Those are expensive, handmade," Roksana hissed.

"Then I'd advise you to stop intensifying my anger," Reign snapped.

"I can't control it. You know that."

"Oh, it's probably Roksana's fault, little cousin." Leonardo winked.

Reign's nostrils flared at the insult.

"What? Would you consider your blood trickling down my throat not enough for us to be considered family? I would say it's as close to biological as it gets." Leonardo smiled.

"Leo didn't take biology in school, I suspect," Priscilla mused.

There was an uncomfortable shift around the table before Amis cleared his throat. It was then Precession who picked up the glass before her and drank.

"One drink, one question." Her eyes danced like ice during a sunrise. "Arryn, what made you come here to our home?"

Amis stood to refill the two empty glasses on the table and then filled an extra glass still on the tray, pushing it toward Reign.

"We wanted to warn you, to tell you about the confrontation over my daughter."

Precession stiffened a little at that and smiled.

"Yes, I see great, terrifying things for your little daughter, Arryn. You should consider making an effort before the world burns."

"Will everyone stop talking in riddles?" Reign crossed her arms over her chest.

"But you are lying, that's not why you came." Precession's voice played like a soft melody.

He couldn't say her name here, where there was so much vulnerability. Arryn bit his tongue and looked down at his hands.

"A drink for an answer." Amis laughed, putting his hands behind his head and nodding to the silent Vrae. "You guys too. Let's all get involved."

Two more Vrae entered the room, surprising Arryn since he hadn't even noticed they were not together.

What are they hiding?

Saul, the blond man who hunched over Amis, twitched his hand and grunted, his eyes gleaming red before returning to a neutral brown as he picked up the glass from the tray and chugged the liquid back. He flopped heavily into the last empty seat, leaving his companion, Jenny, to stand.

"That's quite nice," Saul said in a raspy voice. "Was that homemade?"

Roksana beamed and nodded. "I've been working on the recipe for a good decade. It's the little habits that keep life entertaining. I'll get another few bottles. I have an entire freezer full."

"She's been waiting far too long for an excuse to entertain. Though she'd never admit it, of course." Precession's smile was bright, infectious.

Amis bit his lip as he watched Roksana dance around, and the room's mood lifted considerably. She disappeared behind the northern door frame, where Arryn could see classic white French kitchen cabinets from afar.

"You're a genius," Arryn heard Amis mutter to Saul while Roksana pushed small amounts of joy into the room. "You're invited to all the parties from now on if you know how to get the energy up like that."

It was true. Suddenly, Arryn needed music. He needed to shake his shoulders and grab his best friend's hand so he could spin her around the room. He wanted to hear her laugh and see a true smile on the childish, innocent-looking face. She deserved it; maybe they all did.

"What's it like to fly?" Killian asked, pouring the contents of his glass smoothly down his throat. Precession stood up, moved over to a deep brown credenza near the end of the dining table, and pulled out a record, the sound of vinyl rubbing against its cardboard enclosure audible before being gently placed on the player.

"What's it like to die?" Priscilla yelled out as club music filled the room, refilling her glass immediately after she drank it.

Roksana reappeared, her hips swaying to the beat while setting down three more bottles of the sugary homemade liquor. The drinks continued to pour as the crowd around the table got looser, grins appearing behind tough facades, and Vrae and Kinnari raised their glasses to one another as question after question got less serious.

"Who thinks orange is a terrible color?" Dravus asked, his voice deep and rough.

"Who thinks we should find a better record to play?" Laughed Reign, her small body somehow holding onto the night.

The air filled with lust as Roksana swayed back and forth, grinding against Amis to the melody playing while Vrae failed to look away, pining for the two Kinnaris in their inebriated state.

"What kind of pet would you have if you were just living a normal, typical life?" Leonardo huffed, his lips barely off of the rim of his glass.

Arryn sobered for a moment at that question, remembering for the first time in many moons that he did have a pet.

I have to get back to the temple.

The baby dragon he created had been left there. It had to be full grown, boxed in those four walls. It had to be starving. It had to be pissed.

Assuming it's still alive.

The brunette Vrae woman, Jenny, stood up and slunk over to the opposite side of the table. She nuzzled up to Arryn before flopping on his lap. Curious eyes flickered across the room as she pushed her ruby-red lips up to his ear and whispered.

"Would you be open to letting me have a little bite?"

The blood rushed to Arryn's cheeks and forehead as her hot breath tickled his neck. He put his hands around her waist and gently tugged her closer.

It took a few moments before he let the words sink in before her teeth braised his skin.

"Who the fuck do you think you are?" Arryn bellowed, standing straight up and letting her fall to the floor, hitting her head on the table as more glasses shattered and littered the area around her. Roksana let out an audible sigh and turned to walk out of the dining room, angrily yelling at the ceiling in French.

"Way to ruin the mood there," Amis said, his shoulders sunken and eyes puffy.

Jenny stood up, dusting glass off of herself as her skin darkened, turning black and smooth before Arryn's eyes. Her eyes gleamed red, and her mouth widened as her teeth elongated and thickened, resembling daggers.

"I think you're right, Arryn." Reign's trembling voice made him jump. "It is my bedtime."

Jenny, in her full Vrae state, jumped and slammed into Arryn as he fell to the ground, teeth gnashing, piercing his ear and the side of his cheek as blue blood freely spilled. His head throbbed and his ears rang.

Reign acted immediately, running up to the attacking Vrae and stabbing Jenny in the back with the dagger Arryn had made her. Jenny screamed. The sound piercing the dining room was that of a wounded animal, a predator whose howl turned into a roar.

Arryn staggered to his feet, head still heavy. He shook his head, trying to push the concussion away, but Jenny jumped, her Vrae body covered with red-brown tinted blood and her mouth open almost a full one hundred and eighty degrees while her teeth grew into the open space.

"Everyone stop." Amis' voice pulsated through the room as a mellow wave fell over the bodies. It was quiet that moment, except for the faint sound of Roksana cursing about her broken liquor glasses in the kitchen. The edge she created was faint, but still present.

Arryn was grateful for the stillness and the confusion. It allowed him to collect himself, to understand what just had happened. The two Kinnaris manipulating the mood around them, along with the ample liquor that he had consumed, had fully pulled him away from himself. He was little more than a shell, there to enjoy the company and create a false sense of bonding.

He couldn't see how Amis could know that they were coming. None of this could have been planned. Even though he was detestable, Amis was far from brilliant.

I will come back and kill them all.

"We will be on our way," Arryn said, his mind returning to the dragon stuck inside the temple. He pushed the scene of it breaking out and ravaging the nearest human village out of his mind, burying the panic. He would be responsible for all of those deaths.

The fire under Arryn's skin began to return, the relief from creating the dagger already subsiding. This is why he let that fire burn him from the inside out. Most of what he created here on earth created suffering.

Reign tugged on his arm, eyeing Jenny, whose huffs and growls rumbled from inside her chest. The expression in her red eyes, no whites or pupils to be seen, was unmistakable. She wanted to rip them apart slowly, painfully.

"I think that they may be best." Precession floated up to her feet. "I will be going to bed as well. I expect our guests to clean up after themselves." Roksana appeared at his sister's words, giving everyone a disapproving stare, before taking Precession's arm and leading her out of the room.

Arryn let Reign pull him out of the dining room, but she stopped to turn, looking at Amis, standing with his hands casually in his pockets. He shrugged his shoulders as he made eye contact with them.

"How could you do this to us?" Arryn heard Reign ask, her voice filled with youthful innocence. She didn't wait for a reply as she turned away and continued pulling Arryn out.

"How's your head?"

"It's about healed."

The two left the foyer, the grand double doors groaning as Arryn pulled back on the handle. He looked at his friend and frowned. A deep purple streaked under her puffy eyes, and her round cheeks hung low.

"You're exhausted. We can go back inside and rest."

"No," she turned to him, shocked. "Where to? My place? I can make it."

Arryn looked up at the starry night, the warm country air burning itself into his stiff neck and relaxing his shoulders. He let out his wings and watched as Reign followed.

"We need to go somewhere a little colder," he said and heard her groan as he took off into the sky.

8

Reifoel | The middle of the sea

So much delight was garnered from the surface, smells being one of them. Reifoel had never known that the ocean had a smell, one that clung to him and everything that lived inside it. He was surprised to learn how unpleasant the scent of fish out of water was as it wafted through the air. He was even more surprised that humans still ate it despite that aroma.

Being raised in an eternal darkness so far beneath the waves had its perks. Reifoel, in fact, had a delightful childhood with endless freedom. Fear was absent, leaving only trust to foster and grow within his community, for everything living around him simply wanted to be left alone. Sure, there were accidents, Isadore's parents being a prime example, but a jellyfish would only sting you if you swam into it. Even being a prince was no more than a title. It meant so little to his classmates in primary school. He was not glorified or treated any differently for it, except he suspected that he got teased a bit more than anyone else.

No, the title was almost more of a burden, a sad understanding that he would one day have to grow up and have a real responsibility. None of those memories, tender moments, compared to the life, the colors, the customs, to the world he discovered in the open air. That first time he was on his own, wandering into the magical villages ashore in Myrilosis, had been the first time he felt that burden of the crown. He couldn't leave, he couldn't forever live where the grass wasn't greener.

Where there was actually grass.

At twelve years old, Reifoel started exploring even further than the shores and beachfront towns of Myrilosis. Eventually, he discovered the open ocean portal entirely from luck while amusing himself one afternoon to see if he could jump out of the water to reach the height that the birds flew in the sky. He had spent much of his youth hunting, learning the myths and the legends about a mortal world, so it made sense that it was real. At first, he thought it was fiction, something to learn obscure life lessons from. But when he went through the portal for the first time, he didn't know it had happened until he dove deep, finding that his home was not there, only trash and debris piling up in the black sands. It took days after that, of searching, of eventually finding land until he figured out what happened. That was when he saw his first human, and that was when he discovered that they thought he was human, too. Reifoel was enthralled by the mundane, obsessed with mediocrity. He had found a place where you didn't have to be special to thrive, not even physically strong, and that idea traveled with him on all his journeys.

"Do you really expect us to swim the whole way there?" Isadore's green eyes squinted with his arm over his head, blocking out the light. The milky white skin on his forearm quickly turned into a cracked, brown texture.

"What is this?" he asked, frowning at the sight of his arm.

"Your face and neck look like that, too." Reifeol smirked at his cousin's irritation. "The sun above us, that big bright thing in the sky, does that. Our scales don't like it too much, so we will have to make sure to refresh them at intervals throughout the trip."

"I know what the sun is, cousin." Isadore's blond hair fell flat on the surface. It was pin straight, pulling tightly over his facial structure. He looked like a drowned rat. Reifoel beamed at the thought of using the human expression, knowing Isadore had no reference.

"That Goddess in the sky is precisely what our lineage and species is meant to avoid at all costs."

Reifeol rolled his eyes.

He is going to be like this the entire way.

"We are right underneath the portal. We must get a few tails' lengths into the air and we will catch it, falling into the water in the other realm on the way back down."

"Is it really exactly the same? There are no differences?" Isadore asked, raising his hand in the air as if he was trying to catch something solid in his palm.

"Only in the creatures; geologically it's the same. Ready then?"

Isadore nodded. Reifoel noted his nervous gulp, and tried not to show his satisfaction. This journey would have been a lot more enjoyable on his own, so he would not miss the chance to take joy inIsadore's misery. Sure, he knew it was petty, but if pettiness was the secret to happiness, Reifoel might be on the right track.

Reifoel pulled the moonstone his mother, Queen Pires, had given him. It was now set in a band and hanging around his neck on a chain. Each time he felt the smooth, cool texture, he expected to feel power or luck, but he was suspicious of it being nothing more than ordinary, smoothed over the many hundreds of years. His mother must have given it to him for a purpose. If only she had told him what it was.

He held up three fingers, signaling to Isadore, whose eyes narrowed, focusing on the jump. One finger went down as he sped up the kicks of his fins. Another finger went down while he used his opposite arm to brace himself against the surface as if it were a wall or a desk. The last finger went down as the two Serelune flung themselves vertically into the air, a gleam pulsing through the sky as they caught the right spot of air. Gravity pulled them down into the water as they dove gracefully, their skin momentarily fading back into their familiar milk white with matching scales.

"That was it?" Isadore asked, their heads breaking the surfacing again. He pushed his hair out of his eyes and shook the water off of his face.

"There's really nothing too special about a portal. They're pretty casual." Reifeol shrugged. "Now, we find a ship heading east."

TWO DAYS HAD PASSED of endless swimming, endless motion through the water. Their bodies traveled twenty feet underneath the surface to avoid being spotted, not that there was a soul in sight that would cause them to worry.

"This feels wrong," Isadore moaned, kicking his tail lazily while lounging on his back in an attempt to sleep. "We haven't run into anything, not even a whale."

"I don't know what you mean, my dolphin friend followed us for the first few kilometers."

"Yes, yes, you are best of friends with all of the adorable sea animals. It's a bit embarrassing, really. I just wanted to make sure that we are in the right realm. Are there more portals that go elsewhere? Is that something we could have mixed up?" Isadore asked, his face frozen in his permanent scowl.

Reifoel let his mind drift momentarily after shaking his head in reply, imagining the possibility of more than two realms—a *wrong realm*. What could be hidden there? It sounded delicious, an entirely new world worth exploring.

"I know that look," Isadore said through a yawn. "You're daydreaming again. Do you even know what we are supposed to be doing? Are you leading me on?"

He certainly asks a lot of questions.

"We are looking for that." Reifoel looked ahead, smiling. He did nothing to hold back the cockiness in his single raised eyebrow as ahead of them, something large was blocking out the beams of sunlight that shone through the water. It was a ship, a giant one at that.

Reifoel and Isadore increased their speed, no longer plagued by sleep and isolation. They had a new, small mission: They had to get on that boat. That boat had a direction; it was going somewhere. Right now, the two of them were lost at sea, and they had no way of knowing where the Bay of Bengal might be. All they knew was east.

After they had broken through the water's surface, Reifoel took in the full scale of the vessel in front of them. It had to be hundreds of feet in length, with the deck elevated into the air. There was a bright orange strip of paint a bit higher than the sea level, with a deep blue color taking up the majority of the hull. There were large white letters painted on the side: "S.B.V." Several birds flew above the ship, touching down on the hundreds upon hundreds of storage containers piled on top of one another, sitting on the deck.

"How are we supposed to get up there?" Isadore asked, his eyes wide as he took in the vessel's size.

Reifoel scanned the vessel, swimming feverishly fast to be able to get a full-circle view of it. He frowned slightly, seeing only one option.

It might be easier to swim the thousands of miles.

"Come," Reifoel instructed, pulling Isadore closer to the back of the ship where large thick ropes hung down, making an upside-down arch while being tied from both sides of the deck. The ropes were still easily thirty feet in the air. Reifeol knew they could not propel themselves out of the water that high, but a metal chain was ten feet up from the surface, pushed out of an opening likely for a bilge pump with a ledge wide enough for him to stand on his toes.

That'll have to do.

"Are you crazy?" Isadore splashed his hands down into the ocean and huffed. "Couldn't we just wait for another boat?"

"Any ship traveling this route will likely be a similar size. Here, help me up."

"No, I'll go first to make sure it's safe." Isadore swam off, splashing Reifoel in the face and approaching the ship. He held his hands up, gauging the distance he needed to go to get to that first point.

He can make that jump. He can do it.

Reifoel watched as his cousin propelled himself up and out of the water, his thick tail dividing into two legs once oxygen combined with his scales. His cousin easily caught the chain. He took a moment to balance himself on the ledge, his movements robotic and stiff.

"Legs are wild," Isadore yelled back over his shoulder. Reifoel shook his head, not bothering to hide his grin.

Isadore bent his knees into a deep squat and bounced himself up, flying past feet of that deep blue paint. Reifoel's confidence lowered as Isadore's speed was pulled back by gravity, his hand only centimeters from the wide, braided rope. Reifoel's stomach lurched to see him fight, his shoulder hyper-extended and fingers touching, skirting up and then grabbing the rope firmly. With a swiftness that made Reifoel a bit jealous, Isadore scurried along the rope before throwing himself up and over the ledge. His blond head reappeared to watch his cousin attempt the same.

If I fall, I will never hear the end of this.

Reifoel pushed his tail muscles against the smooth water underneath the surface, activating any underlying strength. He was never a fighter or a sportsman; he was always just curious. He'd follow whatever compelled him to a near-obsessive degree. The presence of his cousin tainted his usual inquisitiveness, leaving an air of insecurity around him. He did not want to fail his mother and father ever, but doing so in front of Isadore would make him wish he'd never jumped off the *Deep Diver* as it got eaten by the flaming wave.

Here goes nothing.

With a thrust, he was in the air, his legs awkwardly flailing as the oxygen exposure made him forget that he had to use his inner thighs to keep his human limbs together. With his hand outstretched, he grasped the smooth metal chain, knees bent deeply as his feet landed too close to his hands, somehow not slipping off the ship since his feet were much higher than the ledge.

Reifoel pulled down on the chain and pushed through with his thighs, grabbing the rope with ease.

Maybe you can be the action hero after all.

He gloated, swinging his body while putting one hand in front of the other like a monkey traveling through trees. The rope burned his palms and he fought the urge to let go, simply because he would never hear the end of it if he did. With a final few swings of his body, letting his legs go back and forth to gather momentum, Reifoel successfully joined Isadore on the stern of the oversized ship.

"Took you long enough," Isadore said, leaning against the edge of the ship with his forearms, wind violently pushing and pulling his wet, sloppy hair around his face. They were nude, a problem that neither of them planned for.

"Well, this thing is neat. Seems easier to use than what we are equipped with. You can just stick it into something," Isadore said, looking down, flopping his pelvis back and forth.

"You should go around and test it. Stick it into any hole you can find." Reifoel smirked, goosebumps sharply appearing on his ashy skin. Reifoel turned around to take in the massive size of the vessel they were on. The two were at the very end of a row of shipping containers, tan and burgundy and yellow. They needed to find some clothes at the risk of freezing to death, their human skin much more sensitive to cold than the gills and scales that lived so effortlessly in their environment below the surface.

"Can't say that I run into stowaways often on deck," a rough male voice with a Mandarin accent said. Reifoel whipped his head towards the yellow and tan containers ahead as a human emerged, dressed in a hard hat and a neon reflective vest. He wore thick gloves on his hands and carried a clipboard.

"You're not the usual stowaways though, are you?" He looked the two boys up and down. "Normally, that kind sneaks into the containers, and we pretend we don't hear them. You two, though, seemed to crawl up on the ship from the middle of the ocean."

Isadore turned his body back towards the water, hand on the ledge, ready to jump. Reifoel put a hand on his shoulder, grabbing him to see how this could play out. They were tired, they were nowhere near their destination, and they could use help.

"You two really are lucky, you know. Most of the crew would have simply thrown you back overboard. I have a private corridor with an extra bunk that you both can sleep in. We will land in Morocco in about nine days." Reifoel noticed the gruffness in the man's voice disappear, his accent also changing as if he were putting on a show for everyone else around him.

The man turned away from them and began to walk down the row. Reifoel glanced over at Isadore, who met his eyes with a raised brow.

"We can still jump off the ship, cousin," Isadore whispered, every bit of the alpha male he worked so hard to be.

Reifoel watched the man's steps, rhythmic and lazy. The human worked so hard to drag his feet, to keep his knees from coming up too high. Reifoel could see that there was so much perfection in this man's fallibility.

"We stay."

The promise of exploration, of unanswered questions, gripped Reifoel as he let his left foot step forward. He had to remind himself to let the opposite one catch up. Swimming was much more efficient. Isadore followed Reifoel, his face in a too-obvious scowl as he walked further and further from the ledge, from the ocean, from his home.

The three of them continued down the row of shipping containers, occasionally encountering another crew member wearing the exact same combination as their escort. Most didn't notice when they walked by, too consumed in their work, but the third person they passed once they had climbed up a short set of stairs stared ferociously.

"What's going on here, boss?"

"Go along with your business," was the only reply, the man's voice gruff again, his words thick with an accent. They then went down a longer set of stairs, moving below the deck. The interior corridors were tight and made of metal, leaving Reifoel with a sterile taste in his mouth. Heavy clangs sounded from the waterproof boots their escort wore, and after several minutes of making their way through the metal maze, he stopped and opened a tightly sealed door on their left.

"After you," their escort said.

Reifoel, followed by an untrusting Isadore, walked into a moderately comfortable windowless room. On one side, there was a bed big enough for two smaller bodies and a bunk bed on the other. An overcrowded, messy metal desk sat against the north wall, and its matching chair lay several feet away, toppled over.

"Don't worry about the mess," their escort said, his accent faltering enough to where Reifoel cocked his head. "We hit some waves earlier in the day." The man moved towards the larger bed and squatted down, flipping the beige cotton blanket up so that he could access the underside. With a clunk, he pulled out a drawer and began digging through fabric.

"Here." He tossed several clothing items towards them, landing at the floor near their feet. Reifoel slowly bent down to grab a pair of cotton pants and stretched his legs into them.

"Fit might be a bit snug. You both are on the taller side, at least compared to me."

"Are you the captain?" Reifoel asked, next pulling a black, thermal, long-sleeved shirt over his head. He noticed Isadore standing there, in all his glory, with his arms tightly knitted over his chest. Reifoel smirked at his cousin's distrust and threw a shirt his way. It hit him and clung to his head.

"No, nothing like that. Best to keep me out of the control room, honestly." The man held out another pair of pants, a different waterproof material than Reifoel's, and inched his offering to a still unmoving Isadore.

"Why are you helping us?" Isadore snapped his eyes to Reifoel, annoyance evident.

"My name is Sheng," the man said. "My family owns this ship, or should I say, I own this ship. My family doesn't actually exist. That part is made up." He chuckled.

Reifoel's mind flashed back to the letters painted on the side of the ship.

S.B.V

"Answer my question," Isadore hissed, still not accepting the clothing.

Sheng laughed, taking off his hard hat and glasses and setting them on his desk.

"I needed this, the anger, the challenge. It's been months since I've been around anyone like me."

"Like you?"

"Anyone that could be a threat."

Reifoel couldn't tell if what he saw was real, but when Sheng's smile reached his eyes, they glinted red. He gulped and took a step back, grateful that Isadore was more than ready for a fight.

"What is the owner of a shipping company doing aboard a long passage?" Reifoel mustered out, pleased with his recollection of how this modern human world worked. He had studied them hard. "Don't you have board meetings to attend? Stockholders to appease?"

Sheng smiled with his pearly white teeth, his dark brown eyes softening.

"I'm impressed. You seem to know a lot about businessmen, then."

"I can read in human English and Spanish. Ouch."

Isadore slapped Reifoel on the back of the neck and gave him a look that clearly communicated that he was oversharing.

"You should put some clothes on," Reifoel said, rubbing his now reddened skin.

"I might need to jump into the water, the clothes seem restrictive," Isadore hissed, teeth clenched together.

"Well, as fun as this game is . . . it's not. It's not actually fun at all." Sheng laughed. "We all come from Myrilosis. You are both Serelune, I assume? You can relax. I am aboard this ship because of some crew rumors I've been hearing that have a special interest to me. You have safe passage here with me. At worst, I'll have some company that won't bend over backward to serve me. What's life without a little bite?"

Reifoel and Isadore stared at Sheng in silence.

I wish Isadore would put on the pants so we can move on.

"I'm heading to the food hall. A hot cup of coffee seems like a good excuse not to sit here and deal with him," Sheng said, raising his chin to Isadore.

Reifoel's stomach ached from the involuntary fast they had gone through on their journey there. He wondered if there was fresh fish, maybe even algae, that he could fill up on. Then he remembered smells. He did not like the smell of fish coming out of the water.

Maybe they have burritos.

They were the most perfect creation. Burritos should be celebrated and appreciated more. Mortals didn't know what they had.

"You can join," Sheng said, commenting on Reifoel's stomach's loud rumbling. But there is a dress code. Not officially. I doubt we've ever had this problem before."

Sheng walked the few steps before reaching the door and opened it, leaving the two alone.

"He's one of us, magic-wielding. You can calm your flipper."

Isadore's cold eyes stood focused on the door, watching it shut tightly.

"I think we should leave."

Isadore kicked the clothes a little further away from him and turned to face Reifoel.

This guy is going to make this trip so hard.

"Ask him what the *V* stands for on the letters of the boat, Reifoel. I know you saw his eyes. Only darkness and shadows live in that being. There is no kindness there, only something ulterior that we cannot see."

Reifoel did know the stories, though they had never met one of the demon-like creatures with red eyes. He did not often set foot on the lands beyond the shores, exploring and meeting the creatures in the thick trees in their realm.

Vrae. Isadore thinks Sheng is Vrae.

Reifoel wondered if his skin changed in this realm as his own did outside of the water. Were all creatures of Myrilosis able to seamlessly blend in between worlds? The separation wouldn't have made sense to him then, and he felt his mind wandering to places of unity between all living in both realms. There were no stories of a fight, of hate, or a reason for their separateness. Maybe a mortal would be accepting or even open their arms wide.

"I'm going to the food hall," Reifoel said, his excitement having him balance on his toes, heels suspended a few inches in the air. "I have so many questions for him."

Isadore balked, an expression that Reifoel loved to see from him.

Who's the tough guy now, you coward?

"Fine, wait. I'll go with you," Isadore huffed, grabbing the pants off the floor in a fit and shoving his feet through them. They rose up high on his ankles, and the button didn't come anywhere close to closing, though there were thick stretching straps attached that he could put his arms through to keep them from falling too far down. Once the shirt was on as well, Reifoel suppressed a fit of laughter. The shirt barely went down to his navel.

Isadore ignored him and marched out the door, leaving Reifoel to run after him. He turned left and marched down the textured metal floor, his bare feet stomping too hard to not be painless.

"Do you know where you're going?" Reifoel yelled up at him.

"It's a long hallway; there's only two ways to go."

Fair.

Isadore turned sharply as the hallway split off into a new direction. They jumped down another set of stairs, their pace too quick to feel wild and loose. Reifoel had to steady his breathing, his lungs burning slightly for more oxygen.

The hallway widened and opened up into a larger common area with a cafeteria line towards the back. Long metal tables and benches were welded to the floor, able to sit fifty bodies at once.

Sheng sat at the middle table, a plastic tray with a plated slop of baked beans in front of him and a mug of hot steaming coffee in his hands. He looked up, noticing the two, and waved them over.

"You two can go up to the line over there and fill yourself up with a plate. Please, make yourselves at home."

Reifoel looked warily at the beans on Sheng's plate.

"Quick question," Reifoel said as he turned to head to the food line. "You said that you were on this ship searching for something. A sailor's rumor. Tell us what it is."

Sheng set his mug of coffee down and folded his fingers together before bringing them down to his lap.

"Did I ask you why you climbed onto my ship? What fun is life with too much transparency?"

The fluorescent lights overhead flashed on and off, leaving them all in seconds of pure darkness before a loud pop sounded, and the room slowly illuminated with a red-hued light.

"Generators. The power is out," Sheng said, standing with urgency.

Reifoel tensed, and his cousin moved into a defensive position, hovering over him. Reifoel looked at him in surprise, the gesture completely unsuspected.

"You are the heir of Serelune, my next king," Isadore said, the words looking physically painful to say. "Maybe you will die, and I will rule instead, but it will not be at my hand."

"What's going on?" Reifoel turned to Sheng, whose eyes were sparkling. The Vrae seemed giddy as he stood, eyes wide. An alarm sounded, the red lights now flashing rhythmically along with the emergency siren.

The few bodies that were sitting in the cafeteria began shouting orders at one another, running off in various directions to perform their duties.

"I think we found what I've been looking for," Sheng said with a grin. "Let's go. Best to be on deck if the rumors were true."

9

Reifoel | The S.B.V.

Crew members were running down the long, narrow hallways, the deafening sirens blaring through the loudspeakers, covering the frantic thumps of work boots on metal floors. The workers all seemed to understand what kind of threat they faced. The red lights of the alarms placed throughout the ship filled Reifoel with a new sort of dread that he wasn't feeling particularly fond of, one that reminded him of how little he knew.

Isadore, militant and untrusting, focused his eyes forward while he followed the Vrae up towards the ship's deck. Sheng moved up the longer set of stairs, leading the three of them. His right hand stayed in his pocket, though his feet were quick. Unlike Reifoel, the two creatures that he followed did not seem out of breath. They did not smell like fear. How perfectly out of place he was for an emergency.

You're a prince, a leader. You do not let fear rule you.

The light began to change, a red hue slowly washed out with the mixture of natural sunlight from the stair entrance ahead. It would be okay if this ship went under. Reifoel and Isadore would be fine, navigating underneath the water. The sunlight, however, pulled Reifoel back to the moment he lost his beloved ship. It was a moment that he was alone in, a moment that would push the anxiety into his chest, his heart. No one would ever share that moment with him, and no one would ever truly believe it. His moment of loss was Isadore's moment of ridicule.

Sheng disappeared at the top of the steps, the light near blinding as Isadore followed. There was something about the air, the sound of birds squawking and screaming, that made his stomach pulse. He sniffed, searching for the scent of sulfur but finding none. It was eerily familiar, and his suspicions hit the pit of his stomach. This ship was filled with men, filled with mortals. If this was happening again, there would be so many deaths.

Reifoel stepped out onto the deck, watching the chaos that played out around him. Hard yellow hats zipped past him, nearly running into each other, frantic. Their breaths were shallow and filled with panicked slurs if he got in their way.

"We are readying a helicopter now." A crew member ran up to Sheng, bowing. "We must go, the size of this wave . . . the radar. . . we must go now."

"No, wait," Sheng said, "I have to see it."

"With all due respect, sir, anyone aboard this ship will surely lose their life."

Isadore was perched against the railing, looking down at the commotion on the lower-level deck. He turned his head to the crew member speaking, jerking his right shoulder down as if he were getting ready to pounce.

"What exactly is happening here?"

Hell. We are in hell.

"What is that noise?" Isadore continued, no one bothering to answer his question. The buzzing grew louder until it was evident that it wasn't buzzing. It was roaring, it was scorching, it was the sound of flame. Then came the pungent aroma, the one he had only smelled once before.

Sulfur.

The sky darkened, the sun somehow leaving the horizon, as a dance of violent colors rushed towards them. Even from miles away, the tinge of orange and red hundreds of feet above the waterline emitted enough heat to dry out Reifoel's skin. He was being cooked alive and had to suppress every survival instinct he had to keep from jumping into the water and leaving everyone behind.

"I told you so. I didn't make it up." Telling Isadore was enough reason to keep his feet grounded. It was a very odd but still satisfying victory. Isadore looked up, his eyes unimpressed with the fiery wave that came at them with a ferocious speed.

Screams and prayers could be heard from the crew now that the wave of fire was in sight. A tear stained the cheek of the man who was urgently trying to get Sheng on the helicopter. Reifoel's head snapped to Sheng, realizing that he had just passed on this ship's only salvation. Vrae could not survive in water like Serelune could; at least, that was Reifoel's limited understanding. The Serelune were one of a kind, even amongst the other magic-made species.

"There are three chairs inside that helicopter," Sheng said, a smile on his face as he rocked back and forth on his heels, staring at the wave. "If you run now, you can grab another man and jump in it. Go."

The crew member nodded and bowed before hastily running off, Reifoel not bothering to hide his surprise as Sheng's eyes shifted toward him.

"You don't seem to be acting like them," Sheng commented, nodding at the crew members. "You seem calm."

"We should jump into the water," Isadore interjected. "Reifoel and I will be just fine. Are Vrae able to withstand fire? Why do you seem so gleeful?"

"I lost someone, my wife. She disappeared months ago. The company that I own had a ship destroyed, crew members reporting a wave of fire, and I knew that if it were true, it would lead me back to her."

The Vrae is a lovesick romantic. Of course.

"None of that"—Isadore pushed away from the handrail, towering over Sheng—"makes a sliver of sense."

"No, I suppose it wouldn't," Sheng mused.

The fire approached closer as the helicopter lifted into the air behind them, shaking from side to side as a nervous pilot worked to turn them in the opposite direction.

"I hope they have enough fuel to reach land. We are very far from any shore," Sheng said, shrugging.

The ocean seemed to part, bowing in submission to the ferocity of flame that savagely engulfed all the oxygen in the air. It came closer. Then closer. The flames were a mile away, and Reifoel felt like his hands might as well be fully in the flames, his skin on fire.

Isadore pumped his arms and ran, hooking Reifoel under one armpit and Sheng under the other. Their feet were swept fully off the ground. Gravity pulled Reifoel down despite the tight hold on him, causing him to choke. He grabbed Isadore's forearm, trying to free his throat by protesting against the pain.

Without warning, they were in the air. There was a moment of quiet stillness, as Isadore let go, his arms hovering high above him after jumping off the side of the ship. Reifoel's stomach dropped. The empty pit feeling was something that he was learning to despise as he fell the full height of the vessel.

The fire was behind them, and they hadn't yet hit the water. Reifoel could feel the flames licking his back, the screams from crew members rushing to emergency escape boats down the sides of the ships. They were too late. The booming sound of the flames hitting the metal and fiberglass hull echoed through the vast ocean, freezing Reifoel's heart, the grief hitting him at bodies splashed into the water faster than his.

Overwhelming relief flooded Reifoel as his body plunged underneath the ocean's surface, his skin drinking deeply, his gills refreshed and renewed. He had to remind himself not to savor it or revel in the first comfort he had felt since boarding the ship and rushed to pull his head above the surface as hundreds of shipping containers hurled into the water around him.

Reifoel swam and dove, avoiding the one thousand pound structures. His legs ripped open the pants as they thickened and fused into a tail from the instant water contact.

He had lost sight of Isadore, who he assumed was waiting it out in safety twenty or thirty feet below as pieces of the ship cascaded off, the angry, heavy groan of metal bending against its will.

The fire had passed them now, the flames seemingly satisfied with their ship as its target. Reifoel studied the carnage, studied the nearly silent scene, knowing too well that the loss of life existed underneath him.

"Look," Reifoel heard a voice shout as he whipped his head away from where the powerful ship once stood whole. Reifoel's eyes widened, realizing Sheng was floating in the water just a few meters from him now, pointing into the sky in the same direction that the tidal wave would have continued to progress.

A shriek that, for a moment, gave Reifoel a sense of hopelessness filled him with awe. The first time he had seen this wave, this hellscape of fire and ocean, he had not seen what followed behind it.

How could I have missed that?

The wave of fire had a source: a creature with burgundy red scales and wings, a long, thick tail, and powerful fangs that soared through the sky, huffing small mushroom clouds of flame on its exhale.

"What am I seeing?" Reifoel asked himself.

A dragon. No, a wyvern.

Both of those creatures had once existed in Myrilosis, in the legends of the villagers who settled on the land, but as far he knew, that's all they were. Stories. As far as he had been taught, they had existed alongside sharks, older than even trees. There had never been any proof, though, that they were anything more than a deadly fairy tale.

The wave didn't originate from the ocean, from natural elements. The one-hundred-foot tall wall of flame that traveled so fast had come from the throat of a single wyvern. Reifoel's blood chilled watching the creature pump its wings, and then it did something horrendous, something that made his own empty stomach flip. The wyvern flew in a half circle, turning around to come back towards the wreckage, the bodies in the water.

"You should see your face right now." A chuckle followed by a splash came from Sheng, who had floated closer to him. "You look very freaked out."

The wyvern's shriek pierced the air, surprisingly high-pitched. If Reifoel could take a moment to appreciate the ancient piece of history heading straight toward him, he would note its magnificence, its beauty and strength. But instead, the realization hit. The wyvern wasn't simply flying in their general direction, no, it was looking directly at him.

"You know, I almost threw you two right back into the water," Sheng said. "If it weren't for that necklace you have there, I would've. I couldn't believe my luck, sitting on a ship, hoping that I wasn't following false rumors, and then you just show up with a moonstone, of all things, gleaming spectacularly."

Ocean water had shifted as Isadore pulled up from underneath the surface, looking unharmed but particularly pissed.

"I think we are past the point where we turn around here, Reifoel. That thing in the sky is about to boil us alive."

"Oh, don't leave yet," Sheng cooed, "you'll miss all the fun."

Miss all the fun, he said.

Miss the smell of burning toxins, miss the death that surrounded them. How many bodies were floating nearby? How many were stuck under a ship sinking below? They'd also miss the giant black smoke cloud billowing from what was left standing. Isadore was right. Sheng was Vrae and had already proven he was not to be trusted.

The wyvern dove as it approached them, coming down toward the water, its wings bringing a violent gust down over them before it tucked its legs. It hit the water so gently, like a bird skimming the surface, before fully landing. The creature was only ten meters from Reifoel and floated lazily like a seagull or a goose despite weighing thousands of pounds.

Reifoel laughed, his hand quickly covering his mouth. He was so damn nervous, and he could feel Isadore's eyes rolling without having to look at him. The creature eyed him, eyed the moonstone around his neck.

"It gives them comfort, in some way. No one ever fully understood it even when these beasts ran amuck through Myrilosis, but a true moonstone, its rareness, and purity gave a sort of serenity to their temperament."

"It . . . floats," was all that Isadore said in response.

Sheng began swimming towards the wyvern, his hands and arms ungracefully moving just below the water's surface as his head bobbed.

"Hollow bones, I suspect."

Sheng reached the wyvern and, to Reifoel's shock, grabbed its backside and started pulling himself towards the creature's tail as if he were bouldering. The wyvern huffed, heat forming from its two large nostrils, but otherwise, did not react.

A small current created petite waves in the water, breaking on the wyvern's gradient hide. Sheng flashed Reifoel and Isadore a big grin as he triumphantly shimmied up to the creature's backside and carefully moved over thick black spikes until he was settled near the creature's neck.

"Are you coming?"

Reifoel blinked, Sheng's fingers outstretched and coming back into a fist. Reifoel looked at Isadore, his brow heavy. He had just experienced more destruction than he had seen in his entire life. He gulped, his mouth dry and his lips pulling down into a frown. It didn't feel right.

"Where will you fly?" Isadore asked. "We cannot be out of the water for too long. Our skin, it dries and withers."

Reifoel was surprised by the willingness in his cousin's voice. The Serelune, who had made his every move painful, had been nothing but protective since the start of this journey. He had been skeptical and had not wanted to do anything involving someone he didn't know, yet Reifoel could see the contemplation in his eyes. There was a genuine chance that his fellow water creature would willingly fly through the sky.

"We fly wherever the beast takes us, but I hope my wife will be there." Sheng's teeth gleamed.

The wyvern released a hearty breath, a tiny ember extinguishing into the ocean.

"Sorry." Sheng patted the back of the wyvern's head. "You are not a beast. You are a beautiful, sophisticated creature."

The wyvern grunted and wiggled in the water. Sheng momentarily lost his balance, hugging both arms around the wyvern's neck, and laughing.

"Hadley," Sheng said slowly, directed to the wyvern, over-enunciating. "You will bring us to Hadley."

It didn't react. It didn't show any sign of understanding. Sheng shrugged.

"I think we should go," Isadore muttered out of the side of his mouth, his arms crossed in front of his chest and his eyes entirely focused on the sixteen feet worth of beast floating on top of the ocean.

Reifoel did his best to keep his face neutral and hide his shock and discomfort.

You are an explorer. You love adventure.

"What if we fall off?" Reifoel blurted out, his milky white skin turning a shade of pink.

Isadore gave Reifoel that look that he hated, the look that brought him back to the cousin he knew. With his eyebrows raised and amusement dancing in his eyes, Isadore could make Reifoel feel like such a child—but he wasn't a child. He was Isadore's future king.

The competitiveness that Reifoel usually felt flickered within him as he moved towards the wyvern, scowling at his cousin. He would not seem scared, meek. No, not compared to Isadore.

"It was a joke," Reifoel did his best to recover. "Besides, I can't quite figure out why you would want to go now when I could barely get you to stay on that ship."

Without looking back, Reifoel floated forward, very aware of the ocean he was leaving again. He thought back fondly on the last time he was on land, of those burritos. He gulped but carried on, reminding himself that amazing smells and colors would fill his mind, his world, once again.

Reifoel hesitated, the webbing on his hand disappearing as he raised it out of the water and inches over wyvern scales.

Here goes nothing.

With a breath of sea air, he found the courage that he needed, thinking of his beloved ship and the type of Serelunian he yearned to be. He pushed his body out of the water and onto the thick tail, half-submerged in the ocean and began to climb up, sitting behind Sheng.

"It's a good thing you chose to come," Sheng said as Isadore began his ascent. "Or I would have had to kill you to leave with that stone."

After a few seconds of Reifoel's uncomfortable silence, Sheng chuckled and kicked the heels of his wet boots into the wyvern. The creature huffed and shimmied its body. Reifoel's stomach lurched, and the movement made him able to imagine what sweating might feel like. He held on tighter as Isadore put his arms around his waist, not having a spike to hold on to.

Mighty wings on both sides of him lifted. The wyvern's back muscles rippled underneath them as it fluttered its wings forward, its body quickly hovering off the ocean. With a forceful push-down, the wyvern shot forward as Reifoel held on for his life, terror shooting through him.

10

Hadley | Joshua Tree

The desert wind had been unrelenting, pushing Hadley back hard. She felt like her wings could have snapped off. The tendons that connected them to her shoulders and back were screaming from the pull. She let them settle back into her body as she approached their new temporary home.

Home.

The word made her tingle, feeling uncomfortable, out of place.

Ayurveda had made her promises of a home, a place they wouldn't have to leave, where they could carry out their goals together, growing stronger every day. That promise was so heartbreakingly beautiful to Hadley, something she wanted with every fiber of her soul, but now that it was here, she didn't know what to do with it, what it meant now. This wasn't the same, didn't feel the same. Her heart felt empty rather than swelling, that feeling of comfort, of home, void.

Miles.

They had traveled miles and miles on foot with the wrath of the desert sun beating down upon them. All the people behind Hadley had done this for her but also for the Goddess that wouldn't give them a break.

You'd think you'd be able to pull back on the heat, Hadley thought, eyeing the flaming sun in the middle of the sky.

At first, two local news helicopters attempted to follow Hadley and her closest two thousand new friends. Her shadow self walked along her side, head held up high and unmistakably cocky after her performance. She was impressive; Hadley had to give the figure credit. To manipulate and to put intense feelings of loyalty into this many humans was unthinkable. And yet, as she turned her head to look behind her, she saw that they all were there.

The group, their glitter and shine dulled but still there, all stared at her. Hadley knew, without a doubt, that they would all jump off a cliff if she asked it of them. What to do with this kind of power was the newest question. It was easier just to ignore it and take another step forward, easier to follow the Goddess' wishes, instead.

Now that their large group approached private property, the media faded, though Hadley could only imagine the scene that the world got to take in. America's wealthy youth, dressed in their most revealing festival outfits, marching away from the stages, away from the drugs, away from the picture-worthy backdrops.

"What do I do now?" she whispered, her shadow self trying to hold her hand, warm air pooling into her skin.

Hadley looked up at the sun, waiting for a direction. The ranch that she was to take this group to was in front of her, and it was another level of opulence that she didn't want, didn't care for. It didn't look like a home. It didn't feel like one either.

Ayurveda didn't descend. The Goddess left her on her own as she often did when they were together in the mountains, occasionally descending in a ball of flame to stare into her eyes and teach her to focus, teach her to communicate with the shadow that had seemed to wrap itself around Hadley's soul. The power that Ayurveda seemed to believe was inside her, untapped, reminded her of her own mom.

That endless belief and confidence in her was both invigorating and a shit ton of pressure.

Hadley stomped her foot and pouted, her head falling back as she exhaled and closed her eyes. She wasn't ready to be a leader. She was still just learning to exist, learn to survive, and learn to live despite the betrayal and the trauma.

Hadley tried to shake off the feeling. She wouldn't let Ayurveda down.

But who might I have been if my mom hadn't died? If my dad was around?

A hand touched her back, and Hadley nearly screamed, jumping away, her feet skidding on the dry, cracked rocks and dust that made up the landscape. She turned and fell, her hands pushed back to catch herself as she looked up at Hector's face.

"Please, forgive me," Hector said, his brown eyes concerned as he immediately came down to his knees, holding his hand out toward her. "It's just me, your best friend. It's okay."

Hadley's gaze shifted back and forth between her shadow self and Hector, trying to figure out if he had somehow broken her spell. She supposed she had never tried to talk to someone controlled by her shadow emotions, but he seemed too lucid for comfort.

"Slap yourself." The words fell out of her mouth like scalding porridge. Without missing a beat, Hector raised his right hand and then gathered momentum as he brought his hand to his face, hard. The sound echoed through the vast desert area, canyons and mountains surrounding them.

Hadley's magic was still pulsing through him; now she was sure. They would do anything for her, lick the ground she walked on. She was their messiah, their chosen one. The loyalty, the worship, and the passion that her shadow shelf forced into their bodies would stay in effect until distance broke her connection to them all.

"Do not ever touch me," she said, picking herself up from the ground. "No one is to touch me," she yelled out to the sea of faces that stared at her, worship and awe filling them.

This is going to take a lot of getting used to.

The private ranch in Joshua Tree that Ayurveda had sent them to was an oasis of green, blooming cacti. A pebbled path led up to a tall, half-dome building that looked big enough to house half the group. Thirty or forty miniature versions of the half-dome were scattered among the grounds, highlighting the acres upon acres that were now only for them.

Hadley stepped over the property line and began walking again, this time to a bed, where she might settle for a long while. Even if it was not what she wanted or envisioned, it was still a promise of safety. She was missing the dragon then, wondering where it flew off to once the group had left the festival grounds. Knowing the beast was there was so much comfort, even if their bond was still forming. There was a sort of connection there, though, she couldn't deny it.

It will be fine.

The main building's exterior was made of concrete, and thick wood sheets crossed over each other to form a mid-century modern facade near the tall, thick, maple-colored door. The dome was connected to a slightly smaller one through a concrete patio, with hundreds of solar-powered fairy lights strung tightly over the top. It was a modern, magazine-worthy escape.

Hadley looked back at her following and frowned. Fitting all these people here was going to be extremely tight. However, she knew that they likely still did not have enough bodies to accomplish Ayurveda's goal. They would still have to find more people and cram them in this compound.

"Make yourselves at home," Hadley whispered, though it seemed loud enough for them all to hear. They were all connected to her; the loyalty and magic that was forced within them were all pieces of her. Individuals walked in all directions on the property, some sitting in the dirt, content to camp without shelter. Others walked into the tiny geodomes, keeping the doors open as they stared at her, leaning against the frames.

Hadley walked into the large half-dome, Hector right on her heels. She remembered how endearing that used to be, how she loved his attention. He was, at one point, the only person she had.

Now, she looked back and saw a desperate, sad version of herself, a version of herself that would do anything to hold onto that friendship.

The inside of the structure was beautiful. Thick, wicker chairs lined a living area complete with a desert-sand-colored rug and green cacti plants in coral pots. It was bright, overflowing with natural light reflected by white interior paint. A record player sat on a coffee table, and two thick redwood square slabs sat purposely misaligned for aesthetics.

Hadley let her wings free, lazily falling behind her as her shadow self appeared in a full-length mirror, shiny chrome-decorated pots on countertops, and other reflective surfaces. She felt more at peace when she saw this new part of herself, like she could conquer the world. She liked that feeling and reveled in it. That was Ayurveda's doing, showing Hadley her own strength.

Dozens of people withered around her, exhausted from the heat and the distance, as she continued to explore the space. She smelled food cooking in the communal kitchen, saw furniture being pushed around, and saw others instantly fill the space with their bodies, making circles and holding hands.

Seems like some of the festival still made it here with us.

With the dust still covering her body, her thighs chafing together from endless walking in a barely there dress, Hadley headed towards the bathroom and delighted in the wide floor-to-ceiling green tiled shower, multiple shower heads gleaming chrome and welcoming her at different angles. She undressed and let her wings out wide, wanting to clean every inch of herself. It was her first shower with them, having only bathed in frigid streams since she was in Sheng's home.

Her throat tightened just thinking about him, thinking about that house.

Steam filled the room, and she marveled at the solitude while still being able to hear the chatting and movement of thousands of people around her. The hot water trailed down her hair, wings, and breasts as she stood soaking it in, letting the dirt pool at her feet before it whirlpooled down the drain. After turning the water off, she jumped, seeing a young woman her age staring at her through the glass pane. The brown-haired beauty with pink rhinestones decorating the sides of her cheeks offered her a fluffy towel and stared down at the floor.

Hadley stepped out, wrapping the towel around her as more people entered, pulling brushes through her hair after an unsure nod of approval, and offering a beautiful white, flowing skirt decorated with daffodils.

Once dressed in a matching white halter top, her wings free and unbound, she walked back out into the living area. Hadley planned to find a bed and let herself dream while sunken beneath pillows and blankets. She wanted to escape the attention of her new cult following, knowing little of what was in store for them, but knowing enough to where she didn't want to get to know any of them.

Hadley pushed down the guilt that tried to gather in her stomach as they all aided her, spoiled her. It was hard to avoid them and disappear as she walked out of the bathroom barefoot. That's when she saw Ayurveda, in her flawless human form, lying on a velvet blue sofa surrounded by more followers, their devotion limitless despite the slight edge of nervousness that bloomed from those who stood closest to the Goddess.

"So soon?" Hadley asked as she watched the goddess nod in response, the tips of her hair a flaming blue.

"What would be the point of waiting, child?"

Hadley looked around the room at the followers, who stared at her with wide eyes. They were all so beautiful, yet so dusty and worn.

"Hector," Hadley called out as his sun-kissed face jumped through the crowd, making his way up to her. If they were all to have the same fate, the same journey, she might as well start with the person who would remind her of her shame. It could be done, and she would never have to see, hear, or think about him again. Just like he had done to her as he left her in that East Sacramento mansion and jolted off to chase dreams instead. Hadley took a clipped breath, looking for her shadow self for the nod of approval to help get her through this.

"Hector, today you will happily die for me," Hadley explained, seeing no falter in his smile. Hector nodded at her enthusiastically while there was a slight protest from the crowd. The sounds of distress surprised her, and made her heartbeat skip until she took in what the crowd was saying.

"Choose me instead," a female voice yelled.

"No, no, I will make a better sacrifice," a deeper voice bellowed.

You can do this. They want this. They are begging for it.

Hadley lifted her hands, instantly settling the bodies around her.

"You will all get the chance to express your loyalty, to prove yourselves here," she said to the group. "My dear old friend Hector simply gets the honor of going first."

She watched Hector as he leaned in to kiss her cheek but stopped once he noticed her pull away. Hadley was still learning her magic and was surprised that he had disobeyed and not listened to her. Though she had said not to touch her, he had still tried. If Hector was filled with the most unwavering loyalty that he as a person could offer, then she didn't know how to interpret that.

"He is ready." Hadley turned, an offering to Ayurveda.

The goddess, filled with a heartbreaking radiance that pulled everyone towards her, smiled. It was a dangerous smile, one filled with unmatched power and hunger. If she had not grown accustomed to it, Hadley might have flinched.

Ayurveda's feet floated over the floor, placing her body right before Hector. His eyes never left Hadley, his smile showing her love, admiration, and pride. Hadley looked to the floor before more guilt caught in her throat.

You've prepared for this. You knew him once, in another life. That life is gone.

Hadley understood that with every person, it would get easier. The guilt would wither away, taking with it the compassion that began to stir in her heart. A tear slid down her cheek, their friendship flashing through her mind. He had done it; he was out in the world accomplishing his dreams. She wondered if that was what she was truly hurt by, bending her fingers by her sides as if she was reminding herself what it felt like to type, to write.

They all abandoned me. They all abandoned me and would have let me die, just like my mother.

Hadley forced herself to look up, meeting Hector's gaze, her eyes hard and unwavering. Ayurveda opened her mouth, an opera singer performing a ballad, but a hot, ashy breath pulsed out from her diaphragm instead of a song.

A minute passed, then another.

Hadley didn't break Hector's gaze but did notice that he had stopped blinking. There was a tremor underneath his skin, his sudden stillness broken by what seemed like a cascading cooling within him. Moments later, he was violently shivering, his face still an expression of contentment. Hadley's magic still held him, as his life, his essence, the stardust that made him, was drawn out torturously, slowly.

Hadley watched as Hector's vibrant, luminous skin began to drain of color. His eyes were widening but flickered down, his only indication so far if there was any pain.

White, he had turned a ghostly white, as if someone had thrown a bucket of paint on him. The opacity lessened, the white becoming see through before finally turning a translucent cerulean blue.

Hector looked like a solid piece of arctic ice, beautiful, but broken, fragile, defenseless. There was no scream, no plea. His eyes, still frozen from the floor, were now empty, like there was no life, no soul there any longer.

Burn the world down together.

Hadley took comfort in the thought, seeing the replay of Ayurveda's arm reaching out for her as she was alone, lost and helpless in the mountains. Together, they would create a home here, where they both belonged. The Goddess, the sun, would be worshiped as she yearned for, and then Hadley could do whatever the hell she wanted.

Disappear. Then, I can disappear.

Ayurveda had not changed her posture, her mouth still open, welcoming what were now speckles of ice, melted drops of what was once Hadley's best friend, floating while changing from blue to black to clear before drifting inside the Goddess' mouth. She was eating them, that was what it came down to.

All the other humans, the festival goers in their rhinestones and cowgirl boots, all stood around, hovering, waiting their turn with an eagerness that reminded Hadley of the few minutes before going trick or treating as a child, walking up to that first house. The anticipation, the slight horror of knocking on a stranger's door was there, in their faces and yet, they wouldn't save themselves. Not as long as her shadow self remained, keeping that loyalty, that magic intact.

You were once bound by magic, by Sheng's fangs, not able to make the right decision, either.

Hadley blinked away the water pooling in her eyes and turned to face her followers.

"Who's next?"

Hands clamored over one another, bodies pushed and slammed with urgency as the group of followers overflowing from the front door were begging to be chosen. She couldn't sit here for this, for the thousands of people that had followed her from the festival.

"You will all wait your turn calmly, orderly. Do not leave here," Hadley announced as she walked away from the scene. Ayurveda pulled a girl her age towards her from the crowd as Hadley moved towards the door, bodies shifting to let her pass. Every person that surrounded her would soon be gone. Then they'd find more.

Once outside, she let her wings flutter, fanning out more of the crowd around her that was clamoring to get inside, to be next. She lifted herself into the air, her wings fluttering hard, humming so softly that only she could hear. It was not effortless yet, flying, though she suspected that one day, it might be. Hadley landed on top of the half-dome's roof. The metal underneath her bare feet was too hot for her comfort, but the burning of her flesh did not matter. What mattered was the male, sitting unbothered on the other side, his feet hanging over the opposite edge.

He had a clean-shaven head and dark olive skin pulled tight over his muscles. What made her realize exactly how out of place he was were the full-length wings that sprung from his back. They were not exactly like hers, dainty and translucent. No, his hung mightily off of his shoulder blades and were dark like leather, even tucked back, she could see how massive they were. She thought of the dragon and how similar their wings were in shape.

The Kinnari turned his head toward Hadley, taking her in as his lips tugged up into a gentle smile. His green eyes looked too familiar.

"You," Hadley whispered, surprise evident on her face. "You were at the house. You were with my—"

She couldn't finish her sentence, her throat dry as more wind whipped around her.

You were with my dad.

"Yes, it's me," he said, his stare pouring into her, his gaze so intense. They stared at each other, the silence between them other than their slight pants from the desert heat. He was the first to break the moment, his voice gentle, as if trying not to scare off a stray cat.

"My name is Djoser. Would you like to join me? It's a beautiful view." He patted the spot next to him.

She stood there, unmoving, unsure.

"What are you doing here?"

A chuckle came from deep in his chest. Hadley closed her eyes, savoring the sound. There was something about him, something about his presence that made her relish his grin, drawing her closer to him. It was like she knew him, from a distant life, a faraway memory that whispered the word that mattered most to her, tickling her ear.

Safe.

But his presence was wrong. It was not a part of Ayurveda's plan, otherwise she would have been warned.

Wouldn't she?

"I could ask you the same thing," he responded. "I know death when I smell it. You host the Goddess Ayurveda right under this very roof. I don't believe you'll meet anything that is quite as terrifying as the sun."

Hadley's fingers curled into fists, letting seconds pass in silence.

"She saved me." Her words were filled with pain. "She saved me from being used as a puppet, as a body. They wanted to breed me, they held me captive and told me I would love it one day."

Djoser looked at her and she saw something that she hadn't seen in a long time. There was kindness and empathy in those green eyes. There were flecks of gold there, highlighted by the light bouncing off the metal roof. Hadley shifted, her body reminding her again that she was touching something seething hot.

She kept watching though, studying the way he looked at her. His gaze did not tell her that she was a prize to be won or a charity case. He looked at her like she was ordinary, like she was wrong, but they could fix it, fix it together.

Djoser moved to his feet, swift and silent despite his size. His body, his wings, were casting a shadow over her from the opposite side of the roof. For the first time, she noticed his hands, a fine black smoke emulating from his fingers.

"Forgive me for saying so; I can only comment on what I've observed, following you," he began. "But it seems like you are still in the same situation, just obeying, held captive, by someone else. Someone who has tricked you into thinking you are here by choice."

Following me . . .

Hadley didn't know what to do with that, but she shook her head. No,

She disagreed. This powerful Goddess had helped liberate her, taught her how to use her magic and protect herself. She gave her—a nobody, a nothing, someone who was constantly thrown aside, left to the wills of others—an autonomy she never could have dreamed of. Yet, she knew, without a doubt, that she was still so broken.

"Your hands," she whispered, her eyes still on the darkness steaming from his fingertips. "You have magic too?"

Sensing a shift of energy that even she did not feel, Hadley's shadow self emerged from behind her, moving in and out of the shadow cast by Djoser's wings until she hovered right next to his body.

Djoser froze at her question, assessing her gaze as he noticed that her eyes were not looking at him, but something next to him that he could not see. She couldn't tell if he could see her shadow.

Hadley shook her head no at her shadow self, the mischievous part of herself ready to jump into the Kinnari body that towered over her. There was no threat here.

Was there?

She could sit there with him forever, staring at the sunset in silence. The thought almost made her smile, almost made her trust.

Never again. You won't trust ever again.

She was numb, less than a person. Pieces of her soul, her heart,were missing, with only moments that reminded her who she was, who she was supposed to be.

"I have orders to kill you," Djoser said to her, unblinking.

Hadley's shadow self bared her teeth at him, ready. She got no permission from Hadley and stomped around impatiently, puffing and throwing an absolute fit like a toddler who was being denied an extra cookie.

"Will it hurt?" Hadley asked Djoser, her voice soft but held no hint of fear.

"You will not feel a thing. You would just disappear, then there would be nothing."

Hadley nodded and closed her eyes, tears rolling down her now nearly sunburnt cheeks. He stood there, patiently, waiting for an answer, a movement, anything.

"That sounds nice," was all that she said.

11

Djoser | Joshua Tree

Djoser heard the breeze hitting buildings and pushing against dying greenery. He heard the faint clamoring of mortals underneath him volunteering to be next, though he didn't really know what exactly that meant. The group was getting smaller. Despite the huge mass of bodies flooding the property, he could tell that slightly less land was covered.

What is her magic?

He looked at the Kinnari woman standing before him. She was completely heartbroken, not afraid of the death that he had promised her. She wasn't afraid of him. That was new. There was no underlying scent of fear from whoever stood near him. Peace, together, there was a promise of peace. His heart sunk—how incredible it felt, like ice-cold water after being left out in the heat.

The heat.

The hot metal under his bare feet burned, and Djoser wondered how it was not phasing the young Kinnari in front of him.

Ayurveda was under them, under the roof that refused to cool. Whatever the Goddess was doing, it had pushed the Vrae to connect with its enemy, the very species that they hunted. It was a team of convenience, with little trust and little belief, but now that he was there, watching the crowd lessen by one person at a time, Djoser realized how essential that team might be. This was it. This was why he was commanded to kill the girl. She was the sun's aid, a key point to her plan. However the girl's magic worked, she could manipulate the masses, the people there, were certainly not of the sun's doing.

Djoser stared at Hadley's face, her eyes closed and her tear-streaked cheeks flushed from the desert heat. He wasn't a monster to her; he was a savior. That alone gave her a power, one that was worthy of his. He was a match, and she was the flame. There was no fear, no intimidation, only a hunger for understanding that her flame would bring to him. He thought of what they could be together, the life between two powers like that. He could hold her, help her heal, and tell her she was protected. She could help him feel human.

The Kinnari male lifted his hands, turning them over as he gathered his magic, feeling the billions of atoms that made up the ten-foot distance between them. His breath hitched when he was centimeters away from her skin, his black wisps tickling her chest as it rose and fell, savoring the last few moments of life. She moaned at the contact, a sob breaking out and up into the sky.

"I'm sorry," she said, whipping her face with the bottom of her long, billowing skirt.

Djoser pulled back, letting go of the atoms that surrounded her. She was apologizing for crying as she prepared for death. He looked at her lips, the bottom much fuller than the top, dry and cracked. He was supposed to now be okay with never seeing them again. He couldn't imagine the perfectly human, mortal-esque body with imperfections in front of him gone. The slightest gap existed between her front teeth, and he loved that the more he studied her, the more he was convinced that she was no mortal, no Kinnari. She was a goddess herself, kissed and loved by the ferocious sun goddess under them.

Hadley deserved to be worshiped. She deserved to have every inch of her kissed, every curve of her held, loved.

I won't do it.

Djoser let his hands fall by his side. His wisps faded and disappeared. When that meteor had hit the planet in his childhood, it had been dark for months, the debris from the impact creating enormous clouds. But she was worth it, she was worth that consequence, more world destruction. The suffering would be on another scale, with humans now populating the planet.

But still . . .

Hadley shifted and pulled her chin down, opening her eyes to take him in. "I gave you your opening."

Djoser hid the smile playing on his lips, and he knew, in that moment, without a doubt, what his feelings meant. This was new. No other lover had brought him such comfort with just a glance. He wasn't being protective because of who she was to Arryn. He wasn't in awe of the power or beauty she possessed. There was no envy. His feelings were simple, and that cut deepest of all because he knew what it meant. This woman, who he didn't know, would be the love of his life. His tragedy. His downfall.

"You should head back inside," he said to her.

"She's killing them, every single person. I can't sit through it all."

"It unfortunately seems, Hadley, that death is enamored with you." Djoser folded his arms across his chest, knowing that the words wouldn't sit well with her.

She stood there staring at him, unmoving, frozen as if he had shot an arrow into her heart. Djoser regretted the words, but they were true.

"I knew your mother. She wanted you more than anything. She would give up her life again and again to know that you were happy." It was the only thing he could think of to say to comfort her. Comfort wasn't his specialty. It was something he was willing to practice for her.

Hadley didn't hold her tears back any longer. She turned her head away from him, her shoulders shaking and her wings blinding him as the sunlight bounced through them and reflected back into his eyes. He watched her, loving her, giving her the distance that he knew she wanted and needed, despite wanting to hold her and kiss her.

"Please." Djoser's throat was dry, coarse. The Kinnari mourned alongside her but refused to let her see. "Please, go inside."

Hadley nodded, looking away from him, and stepped off the roof, gently gliding down as the mortals beneath her welcomed her like a beloved queen. Djoser sighed in relief. She didn't have to watch what would come next. He couldn't bear it, having her see.

I disobeyed.

Dark smoke and clouds began to roll in as Djoser watched calmly, staring overhead. There was no point in running; he would never be able to hide in any realm. He, himself, was not a god; he was a tool—a tool that, after centuries of use, was now broken, unusable. This wasn't his first offense, so it made sense that the punishment be more severe.

The desert wind disappeared, and now an eerie quiet and subdued storm hovered, awaiting him. Djoser thought of Hadley, thought of her willingness to die, her hope for eternal peace, and wished the same for himself. If she could accept it, so could he. This world would be better off without him, and he found so much solace in that alone.

I accept, Life Gifter.

Dark matter pulled down from the sky, surrounding him as if he were the eye of a storm. Djoser watched his hands and feet turn into flakes, breaking apart. His own magic was eating him, tearing him from the inside out. There was no pain, just like he had promised Hadley. At least he wasn't a liar.

It was a peaceful death, almost whimsical. His disappearing body transformed into those familiar wisps, smoke that was redispersed into the sky. He lifted his chin, thinking of her until the last of him faded.

There was only peace, darkness, and then nothing. His magic went out into the air, a whisper in the wind, with no body to attach itself to.

12

Amis | Waihema

The tide moved in and out before him and cool sand stuck to his legs, gritty and itchy when mixed with the salt water. Amis stared at the moon, feeling the pull and tug of the elements on the Earth. It was alienating, the constant internal war of needing to self-correct, to fulfill the balance of power.

It was the only thing that had driven him since he could even remember; it wasn't something he had control of most days, though he could turn it up and defuse a situation, giving the facade that he was level-headed and collected.

How he wished that were true.

Amis was certain that, instead, he was deranged. Or at the very least, lonely.

His magic was a chore, utterly unremarkable. He couldn't explain it other than an urgent need to act, fix, and heal. More often than not, his physical actions brought things back into balance, his choices and the beating of his heart guiding him like an eternal compass of equilibrium.

Serious magical fixes, on the other hand, were usually out of his control. His free will became nonexistent.

Amis' heart was pounding, his breaths short as if he had just sprinted across the country. Instead, he was sitting still with his chest held high and elbows resting against his knees.

The dark-haired male had been cultivating this village, this home to half-Kinnari-blooded mortals, for too many years to count.

Now that there was an alliance between Kinnari and Vrae, however fickle it felt, Amis supposed there was nothing to do except set them free. He wasn't a terror himself, no, but he certainly was no do-gooder. If the relief of the decision weren't overshadowed by the most incredible, tremendous magical imbalance that he had ever felt, he would be singing, skipping, and dancing with the villagers who prayed to him, worshiped him as their God.

Something happened after he left the Vrae in France, after he had landed on the volcanic ash shores of New Zealand. An energy had disappeared from the realms, from the Earth. It left Amis with a crippling anxiety, one he hadn't felt since he was a child.

There was a lack of peace, and the promise of eternal rest was gone. It was big, so big that he feared it could mean one thing.

One of them was gone.

Amis looked up into the night sky, the stars shining brightly overhead as the pupils of his eyes disappeared. His body started shaking, sand flying off his skin and hair. It hurt, the violence of the seizure. The muscles in his body tensed and jerked until the light in the sky changed, and the sand turned into snow beneath him. It was always a relief to realize it wasn't real.

"I think we all know now that you can be present in the physical world, Tristan," Amis said, grunting, getting to his feet while cracking his neck. "I am over a million years old. I'd say it's best to let this old man stay out of your induced hallucinations."

The distinct smell of flowers, as if he were in a botanical garden, overwhelmed Amis, though all he saw around him was a frozen landscape where nothing could thrive. Nothing was notable around, just miles and miles of snow and rock over flat earth. It made him think of the temple, their childhood home.

A wet, plopping sound of shoes marching through slushy melting ice made Amis turn his head as the boy he had been expecting appeared.

"You know, I do keep expecting you to age eventually," Amis said with a smile as Tristan stood before him with curly brown hair, large eyes, and the stature of a nine or ten-year-old child.

"'I've stopped hoping that it would ever happen." Tristan shrugged, his hands in the pockets of his cargo pants.

"Where are we?"

"A man's dream. I found him snoozing in a hut near you."

Amis' eyes blinked, not understanding how one of his villagers could dream of a landscape like this.

"Is this a nightmare?" Amis asked, his eyebrows raised, the floral smell slightly sickening.

"Most of the action in this one is over on the other side of that boulder. It's a recurring dream, I've seen a few different renditions." Tristan pointed, his disinterest evident. "I would think it obvious why I pulled you into this dream."

"Yes, the obviousness is a bit tiring," Amis teased, having no idea why he was there until he remembered what he had just been feeling. That pent-up anxiety, that feeling that brought him back to powerlessness, was the same as if he was still that child who watched the boy in front of him get ripped apart.

"The balance is off," Amis said more seriously.

A loud bang sounded from behind the boulder, even from the distance, making Amis jump and jerk his chin in that direction.

"Hey, focus, stay with me here." Tristan snapped his fingers until Amis' gaze met his again.

"That's not real, whatever is happening over there. What is real, though, is Djoser's death. Someone needed to know about it. No one else was there to witness it."

No.

Hearing his suspicion confirmed by someone else made his senses temporarily disappear. He couldn't accept it.

"What do you mean, death?" Amis demanded. "He would not be a child then, like you? The balance wouldn't shift this drastically."

Tristan slowly shook his head, his eyes hitting his feet momentarily before he exhaled and met Amis' stare again.

He didn't have to say it. Amis knew.

He had felt the moment it happened, when Djoser was erased. Amis had never felt something like that before. He'd had no idea what it was then, but unfortunately, the pieces fell perfectly into place thanks to Tristan.

The Life Gifter had come, had claimed Djoser. All of that death was erased from the Earth in one swift motion.

"I know neither of us were exactly close to the brute," Tristan said, "but he had refused an order. Refused to eliminate upon Life Gifter command. I saw it walking through a dream, a memory of a mortal as their life flashed before their eyes, before they were killed, too."

Screams erupted from behind the boulder, and Amis looked toward it, his eyes narrowed.

"Will you shut up over there? I'm trying to be sad," he shouted as Tristan erupted with laughter. The melodic, youthful sound made it impossible for Amis' lips not to curl upward.

"Sometimes you are my favorite, Amis."

"That's a relief," Amis said, "to be your favorite all of the time sounds exhausting."

The bright white sky began to fall apart, the darkness of the night with blinking stars, and the sounds and smells of the ocean started to wrap themselves around the reality of Amis' mind. He was back, his head snapping forward, his neck sore.

Fuck.

"Tristan," Amis yelled into the sky, feeling ridiculous. "You can't drop a bomb on someone like that and disappear."

What he could do, what he could focus on, was putting one foot in front of the other and walking into his beloved, but always tragic, Waihema.

Amis wanted to get the villagers away from the portal that lived within the forest he had to walk by to reach their village path. He wanted them not to be regularly on the menu now that the monsters from their legends were not supposed to be hunting or feeding off of Kinnari.

Vrae didn't need Kinnari blood to survive. It was merely a craving, an addiction, and without the regular rush from the Waihema feeding frenzy every couple of decades, Amis imagined that the Vrae might be more challenging to control.

He planned on letting them continue to feed off him, whatever had to happen to spare more lives from then on.

Amis moved, stepping over a large stump, moving to the visible path that hosted small huts on either side. It was late. Not a soul was in sight, and the faint, soft sound of snores came from the doorless huts as he passed by them. This was the village that had made him a murderer, turned him into something that could live devoid of empathy. It was somehow for the greater good. It brought the magic into harmony.

The path opened into a modest communal area. A wooden stage sat by a fire pit. The site was witness to death, to carnage. More often than not, even Amis had not been there to witness it.

Past the ceremonial area and up a small cleared hill was a protected building sacred to their village. It was where the village mother lived, tending to pregnant women, growing and birthing future Kinnari blood. He would start here.

That fear, that memory that flashed through Amis' eyes. It had felt so real in the Sacramento house with the Vrae. Whatever Hadley had done hadn't left him, wouldn't leave him.

It is time.

It was time to correct what he had done here. It was time to be moral. He could feel it in the air, in his magic, pressing against the swelling of his heart and conscience.

It took Amis' eyes a minute to adjust to the dark. Hand-woven mattresses were strung out all across the floor and occupied. Someone stirred near the back of the room.

"Who is there?" the village mother's voice croaked.

She was protective and unpleasant. She had lived a hard mortal life. Amis held more appreciation for this single person than anyone else.

The elder lit a candle, standing at her strangely short height, her gray hair neatly tucked into a braid. She squinted her eyes, disapproving of the intrusion. Mother Waihema quickly realized who stood before her and shook her head.

"No," she said, "It's too early. You're not due for a visit yet."

Amis loved her firmness, the unrelenting protection of the women here. She had been taught well by the generations before her, each one stronger than the next, each accepting their responsibility to the village unquestionably.

This elder had nine children, and only one had Kinnari blood. The despair and sorrow had aged her significantly with every infant she birthed that had to die. By the last one, she hadn't even looked at the child. He could remember it well.

"Mother," Amis hissed, keeping his voice low so as not to awaken and alert the sleeping women, "I have no ill intent."

"Of course," she sighed, "I will go into town and pull anyone available for breeding should you desire. The infants born since your last visit have had time to bond with their mothers, and that separation will be quite difficult should any be fully mortal. I'd like to have some time to prepare them."

The woman shuffled her feet in the dark, finding slippers covering her long, thin toes. Despite the thick nightgown draped over herself, she covered herself and kept her eyes low, not ever quite meeting Amis' eyes. He didn't like that. Showing up unannounced and unplanned seemed to change so much between them.

"Please, Mother Waihema." Amis bent his knees into a low bow as the elder blinked at him, turning her chin towards the exit. "This visit will not follow the same events our history has held. This visit brings a new chapter to Waihema."

"What is your command?" was all that she said.

Amis smiled, his heart uplifted, knowing that there was good news to be shared. His visits typically forced him to remain stoic, unattached, and empty of emotion. Normally, only death and rape would follow.

"We are leaving Waihema," Amis said, not bothering to keep his voice low. The elder did not return his enthusiasm, and her face was even more skeptical than before.

"I do not understand."

"I have secured a building in the northern part of the country. It has sixty homes with electricity and modern furniture. Some have more than one bedroom. Some even have three."

The elderly woman kicked off her slippers and blew out her candle.

"Most of us prefer to sleep in one space. We are fine here."

Confusion struck him. The mother had implied she would not wake up her most vulnerable. She would not have them moved.

"Besides," she added, "I cannot have my entire village moving by foot in the middle of the night through brush and trees."

"I will fly them all, one by one."

Mother Waihema laughed.

"You must rest, my humble God. At first light, I will be more willing to debate the future of our small village."

The mother's mattress skidded on the floor as she lowered herself into it, pulling a thin blanket up over the rest of her body.

"This hut is reserved for women. Unless, of course, the ceremony is being performed." She yawned. "I'm just following your rules."

Amis rolled his eyes and turned to leave through the door, the village before him. Despite the old woman's stubbornness, he would get everyone out. His heart could take no less. It was time to fix the imbalance that bored into his conscience.

He slumped down, his wings and back scraping against the exterior wall of the ceremony hut. As he stepped outside, he flopped down, looking up at the blinking stars. This time, he had the whole night before him to remind him that he had no answers. If Djoser was gone, then that meant only one thing: defeating a goddess without death seemed a fool's dream.

DAWN BROKE out over the horizon, towards the sea, bringing a dance of reds and oranges against a thinning dark sky. Amis let his eyes close, his mind wander, before jumping to his feet in a panic, startled by the sound of footsteps.

"Now that I am awake," the elderly voice crooned, "you can make your case more convincing than it was before."

Amis held back his laugh. He had lived her lifetime too many times over. She knew this as well. Still, there was a charm to her aged face that he would never himself have. It alone commanded respect. She was mortal, yet still survived. That was not an experience that they could ever share.

The two walked down the path toward the ceremony site. A handful of villagers had been working on starting a fire and preparing breakfast but quickly scattered at the sight of the Kinnari male.

"I am ending our legacy today. Waihema will be vacant."

"What if the villagers disagree? This had always been our home. We have all been raised with stories of magic, of us being here to protect the outside world, of some of us being destined to bear children with wings. I do not think that all will agree to it, even with a promise of a more contemporary life."

Amis stopped walking, his hand over the fire pit, which was smoking, though not properly lit.

"Everyone here in this village is meant to feed the monsters from our stories," he confessed, his eyes not meeting the mother's. "The visits, the slaughters, are not random events. Mothers can stay with their children and promise them a life that can actually be lived. I will financially support it all. I take all responsibility."

A small hand touched the bottom of his left wing, and Amis

swung his upper half around to see a female child staring up at him, her eyes brown and filled with horror.

"Are you going to take me away?" she asked, tears spilling down her cheeks. "I heard you say it. You said that our village is no more."

Amis knelt down, his hands slapping the sides of his thighs.

"Only in the best of ways. It is a treat, a gift. I want you and your family protected. What is your name, child?"

"This is Salome," the elder mother cut in. "She is one of three children in the village that possess a mark."

Amis' heart sank; that mark on these bodies was a curse. They would have the blood that was to be hunted. They were the successful outcome of what this village had been trying to achieve.

"Then you, Salome, will be the first that gets to settle in their new home."

13

Arryn | The Kinnari Temple

Reign flew behind him, struggling to keep up as Arryn sprinted through the sky. His heart felt like it wasn't going to pump blood any longer. Pressure built up inside his chest while the burning under his skin heightened. This was just another thing he had failed at, someone else that he couldn't care for, that he had let down. He could leave Allienna for months and months. He forgot that a baby dragon likely could not take care of itself in captivity.

Mist clung to the air, soaking through his clothes and drenching his body while shivers ran up and down his forearms and chest. He felt everything all at once, making him forget who he was and what he wanted. He was running on instinct, out of fear that a dragon either lay dead, emaciated in their temple, or even worse, out in the world, free.

"Slow down," Reign yelled, her voice lost in the sky behind him.

His wings cut through the air like a knife, pushing down and pulling back with strength and speed.

The air grew colder as they narrowed in on their temple, which was too high and out of reach for anything living. Arryn gasped out a breath, his lungs about to burst. He continued to plummet through the air, a bullet shot from its gun.

Ice, snow, and soul-shattering pain ripped through him as he plunged into the side of the mountain peak. Everything was gray, the sunless snow blending with the dreary sky. He had been going too fast; he likely would have collided even if he had noticed it.

Arryn couldn't move, he was surrounded by frozen earth, his blood mingling with the brown and the white that surrounded him. He suspected that his nose, shoulder, and spine had been broken.

He let out the frustrated yell of a wounded animal, teeth gnashing and grinding until the sounds coming out of his lips turned into sobs, thick tears angrily caressing his lower lashes.

Pathetic. You are fucking pathetic.

"I don't know if I've ever seen you fly that fast. It was pretty cool," Reign said, landing on the rim of indented snow. "I've got to say that if I fly even half that fast, I wind up lost in another time. I'm a bit jealous."

Her smile was wide and infectious, and Arryn winced as he tried to sniffle, imagining the child version of himself getting into trouble with the girl who stood before him.

"Please, I know you to—" He groaned, trying to turn to face her properly.

His spine was definitely broken. Even the slightest movement shot a pain that was impossible to move through down his back. He would have to be still and let it heal.

"Reign, get to the temple. Tell me what you see."

Reign's smile vanished, and she crossed her arms over her chest.

"How about we start with my questions instead? What is it that you are hoping that I see?"

Arryn growled, his nose already snapping back into place.

"Reign . . ."

"Arryn." She smirked.

"A dragon. You are looking for a godsdamn dragon."

Reign threw her hands back behind her, hitting her own wings with an open mouth, moving in an array of expressions.

"You would send me into a building with a dragon unprepared? Do you see me? I look like a mouse, an appetizer, to something that gets that big. I can't believe you."

"You would have been fine." Arryn rolled his eyes, groaning from the shooting pain that came from barely moving his neck.

"Hmph." Reign's footsteps mushed through the snow, ascending the peak before her wings carried her out of Arryn's immediate view.

He could feel the pull of the tendons in his wrist and his arms as they healed and tightened. Sharp staccato pops rang through his body as the bones in his vertebrae and shoulder were repaired. He looked at his hand, closing and opening his fist, satisfied with the movement.

Arryn wiped the blood from his hands onto his pants and pushed himself up out of the indent he'd made, letting his wings spread wide behind him.

She hasn't come back yet.

How long it had been since Reign left, Arryn wasn't sure. However long it was, it felt like too long. His brow lowered, his adrenaline pumping, the anxiety returning to his chest like a welcome friend.

Lifting off the ground, Arryn moved with a lethal quiet, his wings delicate and the air around him seemed filled with thorns. If that dragon was still up there, then Reign was likely right in her worry about being a snack.

There was no fire in the air, no smell of charred flesh. He was hopeful that a battle for life had not broken out, yet as the temple came into view, Arryn's world came crashing down again and again and again.

Reign sat at the foot of the temple, where snow, ice, and sleet normally covered and hid their childhood home. Her legs were pulled into her chest as she rocked back and forth, the snow underneath her soaking into her clothes. She was looking forward at the crumbled walls that lay scattered in a thirty-foot radius of the once-existing building.

Packed snow had fallen throughout the rubble, with small hills hinting at architecture and stone underneath. Arryn stepped forward, his shoes crunching as Reign snapped her head towards him, eyes hard.

She blames me.

He moved to sit beside her, and she scooted a few inches further from him.

"What would Allienna tell me to do?" he asked.

Silence, with the occasional sound of wind hitting the sides of their faces, was all that passed between them. Arryn let it continue, his grief heavy, recognizing all that he had lost, all whom he had lost. It was a chapter of his life that he would have to close, but his mind couldn't find the right door.

"Rebuild it," Reign said. Her words were so soft, so solemn, but it was a command, nevertheless. Arryn's instinct was to fight it, the straightening of his back, the bend of his will. The fire burned under Arryn's skin, his breath choppy as he inhaled through his nose, as if his magic was eager to be let out.

"She would tell you to rebuild it."

Arryn nodded and stood, letting the flood of emotions pour out of him. His fingers twitched when he let out the burning under his flesh, searching and collecting the atoms around him. It was so luscious, like wrapping himself in silk sheets while euphoria from his body's chemicals hit his brain.

Allienna wanted you to create. To create life with her.

Arryn blinked, and his heart sank even further. Atoms mashed together, the stone began to rebuild. The rubble pulled together as snow shifted and sparkled in the daylight.

Reign stood beside him, never faltering, while she grieved, too.

The beauty of ancient stone gleamed in gold tones as light bounced from its wet glow back to the snow. There was life and beauty in the air. Arryn didn't shudder but let a chill run through him as he continued to work.

I forgot that this is how life can feel.

Arryn's eyes opened wider as the blood that pulsed through him turned, filling him with energy and relief. He had never tackled a project this big, at least not all at once.

When he finished, the temple measured thirty feet in the air, and the stone was meticulously carved with their stories, the Kinnari story.

Reign gasped as she approached, letting her fingers run over the indents from top to bottom. Her hands passed over Tristan, Precession, Roksana, Allienna, Arryn, and herself, their wingless child bodies standing in a row, holding hands.

Reign's fingers followed the carvings up to explore a forgotten history. There were depictions of a young Arryn creating trees and the fruit that hung from them, and then a story of sorrow as his creations took off, causing the first plagues and famines that wiped out masses of people. There were more stories showing war, greed, and environmental disasters that Arryn all took direct responsibility for.

Reign walked her fingers along more stories, more depictions on stone. One of herself, standing tall and proud as the Kinnari children stood around her in worship.

Arryn could see her heartache; he knew she was likely thinking back to when she discovered her power of commands, the things she ordered others to do all for her youthful pleasure and games.

Reign had found herself alone too quickly, with no real friends. Everyone around her had been just a body, too quickly willing to bend to her needs. She'd been isolated and begged for years for forgiveness. During those dark years, Arryn had been the only one who stood by her side in understanding.

They had all been awful at one point. Everyone except for Djoser, who was always depicted as strong yet alone, always slightly on the outside of the group, grappling with who he was.

Arryn continued to watch Reign explore the stories and memories that were etched into the stone, his heart feeling bright and his body full of testosterone from the creation. He didn't want to stop. He had held back for so long, so scared of what other misery he would create. He couldn't live like that anymore.

Allienna would want you to create.

Holding back tears of grief and acceptance, Arryn placed his hands over the snow, letting the ground heat and the soil pull in minerals and richness that it had never before possessed. Green sprouts began to emerge, growing thick before displaying leaves and small, white flowers. Soon, the radius around the temple was technicolor, with flora in dark reds, yellows, whites, and blues. The scent of sweet pollen in the air reflected spring and brought a sense of immediate joy.

Reign continued her journey around the temple, hovering near the top as her hand moved over more memories, memories that made up who they were. She turned her head and gasped, taking in the scene.

"It's so beautiful, all of it, Arryn."

Arryn wasn't done; he was in a state of euphoria. A high rang through his body as he continued to pump, mold, and bring more life together. Pure white rabbits began to hop among the flowers and a handful of foxes watched them with interest nearby.

Wobbly kneed horses, black and tan with shining coats, playfully romped at the edge of the grass, kicking up snow and earth. An animal so pure it almost shined blue emerged with four legs and a spiraled horn upon its head. It swished its white long tail back and forth as it stood on its hind legs, kicking before coming back down.

"Oh, Arryn," Reign said, letting her feet meet the ground.

"Your magical creations, they can't exist in this realm. They couldn't survive here; they would be hunted; it would be cruel."

It had been so long since he had thrown something through that portal.

He chose to ignore her, continuing to create with a savagery in his eyes as the power pulsed through his body. He felt like could create an entirely new mountain and wouldn't feel tired or slowed down. The pleasure that circled through him as he released more and more was euphoric. A hunger awakened.

Numerous unicorns appeared, bringing more grass and life to a larger area further from the temple. A pair of massive goats that seemed to have the capability of speech were now there, half huffing and half enunciating sounds as they began to self-teach themselves language.

"Arryn, it's enough," Reign said, though Arryn continued to ignore her. He continued as hawks the size of pterodactyls began screeching through the air, swooping down with yellow talons and picking up horses. The unicorns began shrieking as more animals ran in a panic, stomping the flowers, eradicating the beauty.

"Stop," Reign commanded.

Arryn felt the pull, the tug of her magic, but it was nothing he couldn't shove off, especially in his current state. It did make him pause, however, and he could see the manic state that was beginning to unfold. He took a step back, shaking his head and kneeling down on the ground.

I can't do anything right.

He felt a hand on his shoulder, a touch of comfort. "Let's bring the magic beings into Myrilosis," Reign whispered. "Other than that, you are doing great. You just brought so much life and so much wonder to this world in a matter of minutes. I nearly forgot what you could do, Arryn. It's breathtaking. It truly is a gift if you let it be."

Arryn nodded and rose slowly to his feet as the large hawks circled around him. He had a strange suspicion that he was their next target and wished that Djoser were there to aid him, to make them disappear, so that he wouldn't have to figure out how to get them into the temple portal.

"What were you thinking when you made those monsters?" Reign asked, pointing up.

"I wasn't thinking at all. I just did what felt good."

Arryn jumped into the air, his wings moving tantalizingly to attract the hawks. He was their perfect prey, and he counted on the chase. The unicorns and goats would be easy enough to track and gather. He would leave them for later.

"Reign," Arryn yelled, dropping to the ground. "Open the latch to the temple and to the portal. Make sure no one else comes through."

The hawks screeched to each other, now circling Arryn. Reign sprinted to do her part. The hawk on his immediate right was the larger of the two and snapped its beak, jolting towards him. Arryn pushed back to get out of its reach just in time, not wanting to lose any organs. He'd save that for a different time.

The smaller hawk sang out before it dove towards Arryn. This time, he was ready. He flipped his body up and horizontally, wrapping his arms over the animal's neck, catching it by surprise. It thrashed violently while Arryn squeezed tighter, making it harder for the hawk to breathe.

The larger hawk dove towards them, whether to help or to selfishly claim Arryn for its own, he didn't know. Whatever the reason, Arryn didn't care as he steadied himself enough to lift his upper body while wrapping his legs around the hawk's neck.

More thrashing came from underneath him as Arryn beat his wing on the larger hawk's face, startling the creature. He grabbed its wing. Several giant feathers fell to the ground as Arryn turned himself in the opposite direction, kicking one of his legs over and pulling in.

Arryn was now on top of both hawks, his feet dangling over both sides so that they could each only use their outside wing. They started to plummet to the ground as the animals fought and shrieked. Arryn pulled his wings up, slowing their fall and giving them enough direction so that they glided through the temple door, still with too much speed.

"Holy fu—-"

They shot past Reign as she dove flat against the floor, coming through the opposite temple door and the portal into Myrilosis. Arryn jumped off of their backs as the hawks fought and snapped their beaks at each other, struggling to get their inside wings free. Once they did, the two soared off into the distance.

Arryn looked around, seeing the mountain peak, ice, and snow. Below the summits were villages and towns of intelligent creations that were stowed away, that he had never planned on visiting. Everything he had made growing up into the man he was today lived in this realm, discarded and left to their own devices.

Arryn was not to come here, his own rule. Some of the creatures he had dreamed up and brought into existence were terrifying, made of his nightmares. They could be vengeful.

This realm could only be a danger, a mistake, and yet the thrill of using his magic made him feel so free. He hadn't felt this good in hundreds of thousands of years. For the first time, he wanted to explore it, to see what a life around his own gifts could look like.

It's time for new dreams.

The sound of galloping hooves behind him made Arryn turn his head, his blond hair falling over his blue eyes. The rush of three and then four unicorns running past him brought a smile to his face. He began to walk up the mountain, coming closer to the portal door that would bring him back into the temple.

"You stubborn piece of shit." Reign was panting, using her entire body to push up against a mountain goat, trying to urge him through to the other side.

"Piece of shit," it repeated, breathless and all, as it mimicked her.

"Reign, they're like toddlers. You can't have them running around the realm yelling obscenities at anything approaching them."

Arryn grabbed the goat's horn and pulled it into the snow as it huffed in protest. The second goat followed, casually following its leader.

"There, all magic back in Myrilosis," Reign said, clapping her hands together.

Not quite, he thought.

Arryn didn't want to think about the dragon running rampant in the mortal realm. He felt too good at that moment to be dragged back down with grief, which surely would hit him again if he went back for it.

"Have you ever been to the village at the base of the mountain?" He turned to Reign. She shook her head no, her eyes wide with a hint of fear.

"This realm is where Vrae live, Arryn. Where they and creatures you have created, want you dead."

"Maybe," he said. "I think enough time has passed for us to go check."

Reign sighed and pulled the temple door shut, the deafening sound of stone hitting stone echoing through the area.

"Let's go," she said, her nose in the air, stomping through the snow as they began their descent.

14

Hadley | Joshua Tree

Like a whisper in between trees, a breeze that wasn't not really there, Hadley's shadow self jumped between all of the festival goers on her sideline. Hadley watched the crowd clamor with desperation for their voluntary demise. It prompted her to keep her distance. She sat outside of the larger half dome where it all took place, clinging to the last bit of shade before the sunlight moved further overhead and made it disappear altogether.

Hadley closed her eyes, feeling everything and nothing all at once, wondering why that Kinnari, with green and gold specks in his eyes, had left her there alone.

Another soul she had felt safe with, and yet, another soul to vanish.

She went back to look for him after spending twenty minutes clinging to the wall inside, watching Ayurveda steal the life from three more bodies. She shouldn't have listened to him; she should have clung to him as her sweat clung to her, like a desperation to cool off, to find comfort. But he was gone, and despite the declaration of his intent to kill her, she felt a kinship with him, a promise that she had found her place.

Maybe her place was with another, but his absence proved her wrong again. Still, she couldn't get him out of her head, and that emptiness, that tender gift of death, was an option she hadn't realized would be a comfort.

The crowd of festival goers had thinned out immensely. Ayurveda had been at it for hours. Hadley had guessed that five hundred, maybe six hundred bodies had since evaporated in donation to the sun's cause.

She stared ahead at the end of the group, realizing that the backs she stared at were those two girls she had shared a golf cart with. She smiled and rolled her eyes. Maybe the world would be better off without those two. The brunette stood out, kissing the tall, slender man who hovered over her. His hands lingered around the back of her thighs, sliding up little by little as their passion grew. They were celebrating, joyous, as they waited. Their free will still allowed them to be them. There were no empty zombie stares from her loyal fan group.

She continued to study the effects her magic, her shadow self, pushed into people. Even with all her practice in the mountains, the effect on humans was entirely different than she expected.

Hadley sighed, knowing that it wouldn't be long until she had to go and wrangle more people for Ayurveda to accomplish her goal, to grow so powerful here on this planet in a human form that could be worshiped. She could go to Palm Springs and gather everyone on Spring Break next week. Still, ideally, she would need the entire states of California, Oregon, Arizona, and Texas to get close to giving Ayurveda the power she craved.

Maybe it was too much, maybe what they had was enough, though Hadley certainly wasn't brave enough to challenge the one being that hadn't completely left her alone, that hadn't forsaken her.

Hadley tried to distract herself by guessing where the Djoser went. There was a thunderous roar, and a storm was approaching despite there not being a cloud in the sky. She noticed the sky darkening, a dangerously dark and violent purple. Perhaps that scared him away. Perhaps that sky was him, a result of his magic, of his pacifying kiss of demise.

Another roar, a shriek, deep and brooding, erupted from behind her. This was not thunder, not the sudden rush of a desert storm. No, she knew that sound and found both dread and comfort from it. Hadley searched the sky for Ayurveda's dragon, hearing the heavy thrusts of wings against the air as it came into view behind her, dipping down to only fifty feet in the air.

"Here, here." She clicked her tongue, letting her familiar voice catch the creature's interest. The dragon noticed her immediately, its massive underbelly more visible with its two front legs now gone. It made wide circles over her head before settling down, the earth shaking as its body touched down in a cramped space between the tiny cabins.

The creature shook its wings, eyes wide, staring right at Hadley.

"Woah, hang on," a male voice yelled as the dragon huffed angrily, opening its mouth in a snarl.

Poor, blasted thing. I don't want him around me, either.

Hadley's own nostrils flared, anger filling her up like boiling water being poured into a teacup, as she placed the male voice. She stared right at the monster who had been her captor. He was sitting on the dragon's back and he was not alone.

The man, the demon, the devil who arrived had impeccable skin, the color of warm sand. He wore work boots and an orange vest and displayed a large grin across his face while he dismounted the dragon like a prince dismounting a white stallion. His boots hit the ground, and he stood back up quickly, as if he hadn't just fallen ten feet. He shook out his ear-length black hair as he strutted right towards her.

"I have been looking for you, my dear wife," Sheng said, his white teeth gleaming in the desert sun. He looked dirty and gritty, but underneath that was the unmistakable, utterly attractive monster that she had gotten to know while being held prisoner all those months ago.

His wife.

"Did you start a cult? I could get into something like that. Did I mention just how stunning you look with those sun-kissed cheeks of yours?" Sheng motioned towards the group of festival goers waiting to enter the house and chuckled.

"Seriously, what's going on there?"

"Help us," a weak dry voice demanded, and Hadley gazed upon the other two bodies clinging onto the dragon. Both looked minutes away from death.

"More hostages, I suppose?" she asked, raising an eyebrow. Sheng took a step closer.

"Ah, but we are so alike, are we not?" He winked at her, and her blood chilled.

"Don't come any closer," Hadley warned, her shadow self dancing out of the cast made from a rooftop.

"I should probably get those two into some water. I saw a pool on the property when we flew over," Sheng said as if he didn't have a care in the world, never breaking eye contact with Hadley.

She blinked, unsure, nervous.

"It's behind the main building. The pool, I mean," she said. "This way."

Sheng moved slow, cat-like, walking backward and not breaking his view of her, as if she might just evaporate. He eventually turned around and walked back to the dragon, apparently satisfied that she would not run.

Hadley watched as the two bodies dropped down. Sheng caught them both and propped them on either side of him, bending slightly at the waist as he willed the three of them towards her.

"What are they?" Hadley asked, making eye contact with the smaller one. Though they both had human forms, their skin looked like cracked, dry desert terrain, severely red and leather-like. It seemed painful when Sheng's moving legs and hips brushed against them, neither of them able to hide their grimaces.

"Let's save the small talk when I'm not carrying two full-grown adults," Sheng said.

Hadley kept a ten-foot distance between herself and Sheng while leading them to the pool. It was a simple, modest-sized rectangular lap pool of light gray cement. A few vinyl beach chairs sat at one end along with an oversized, inflatable pink flamingo.

The sound of bodies heavily hitting the pool's surface sent adrenaline pulsing through Hadley's skin. She lifted her chin, arms tightly bound to her chest, and took a few steps closer to the pool's edge, trying to peek. The two mystery creatures did not immediately push off the bottom of the pool, not even to take in breaths of oxygen. Instead, they stayed at the bottom of the pool. No bubbles floated to the top.

"Are they dead?" she asked, eyebrows raised. Her shadow self hovered beside Sheng, sticking her tongue out at the monster in front of her.

He probably did this to them.

Sheng laughed. "They are right where they want to be. In all seriousness, though, what's going on inside that building? No one batted an eye when the wyvern landed, which seems like an unusual reaction for humans."

"The what?"

"The wyvern. The two-legged dragon. That big fire creature of death that we casually just walked away from."

Hadley rolled her eyes. She had never even heard that term before.

"It used to be a dragon," she mumbled under her breath, irritated.

"What did you say?" Sheng asked before the bodies in the water emerged from the surface.

Hadley stepped back as two heads powerfully emerged from the water. The creatures had completely transformed, their skin now so milky white that she wouldn't have been surprised if they glowed in the moonlight. A splash of a tail, thick and wide, showered the cement sidewalk. One was blond, with long, beautiful hair; the other's hair was dark, a shade of black rivaling the closet she was once locked into.

"So thankful there's no chlorine in here. Saltwater should be the standard," the dark-haired creature announced, his voice filled with relief and his gray eyes that reflected the blue in the sky flashing in curiosity.

Hadley's gaze followed their bodies down into the water, peaking at the swishing body parts that had her feeling like she knew nothing of the world. An inch below the males' pectoral muscles, their skin gradually darkened, turning a dark, murky green color on the blond and a black that shined a blue that reminded Hadley of her own blood on the other. Where their hips would connect to legs, a powerful, thick black tail was instead, their thighs merging into one muscle.

"Are you just going to sit there and gape at us?" the blond one asked while the other stared at him disapprovingly.

"What are you? Who are you?" Hadley asked.

They came with Sheng. It doesn't matter. Do not trust them.

"Are you a . . . mermaid?" she hated herself for saying it; she felt like a two-year-old. Hadley's shadow self pouted and gave her pleading eyes as it hovered behind Sheng, ready to leap.

"An offensive term; mermaids are from human children's stories. Do you know how young humans are as a species? They are barely a blip in comparison. I am Reifoel, and this is Isadore," Reifoel said. "We are called Serelune. What is it that your wings say about you?"

Hadley's mind went blank as Sheng stepped in for her.

"This is Hadley, my wife. She is Kinnari."

The two bodies in the water nearly gaped in surprise but pulled back their expressions to reveal nothing more.

"We are familiar with that word. I thought it was someone's name," Reifoel said sternly.

"There are a handful of her kind that float around this mortal world." Sheng chuckled. "They really are all a bit too dramatic if you ask me."

"No one asked you," Hadley snapped.

"Pure marital bliss."

Hadley took a few dramatic steps back. "We are not married. That is false."

"Should we take it to the gods?" Sheng smiled.

Hadley looked between the three of them, all staring at her with expressions that made her feel like a little girl. She was not going to be the insecure one in front of Sheng. She had made that promise to herself while getting strong and surviving in those mountains.

You have already survived him. There is nothing left to fear.

"Yes, let's ask one," she smirked, turning her head towards the building that Ayurveda occupied as they spoke. She felt her presence, her fire, even from here, as if they were linked.

Sheng tilted his head, a look of panic hiding behind his dark eyes.

"What is happening inside that building, Hadley?" the Vrae leader asked.

It was Hadley's turn to smile, just one side of her lip curling upward with a single eyebrow following. It felt good to hold on to the horror that was taking place. It felt like a personal threat to the monster that stood before her. The same monster that begged the family that had abandoned Hadley her whole life to unite and fight against precisely what she was helping with.

"Ayurveda is inside there," she whispered, her words sharp with malice. "She is pulling energy, life, from mortals. I am helping her gather them, to keep panic and edge out of the process."

"To what end?" Sheng asked, ruffling the top of his hair with his left hand.

"If she consumes enough energy, she can become a dark star, the true and only god that would matter in any galaxy."

"Ah, yes, our jealous little Goddess." Sheng shook his head.

"Excuse me, ma'am who is helping destroy the entire planet." Reifoel raised his hand like a child in school, water splashing from the movement. "Are you aware that any natural disasters that happen in this realm also happen in Myrilosis?"

Hadley pinched her nose with two fingers and lowered her head at all these new words that were so casually used in conversation.

"I don't know what most of that means," she muttered, "but no one is trying to destroy Earth. She wants to rule over it."

"That is certainly false, princess." Isadore shook his head. "A dark star will emit little to no heat or light. It would plunge this planet into darkness. This would wipe out most natural food almost immediately. The planet will be freezing and uninhabitable. Life will die out for most within the first few weeks. It is an odd thing for you to support."

Run. You need to get away from them. They want to stop you.

"I—I don't believe any of that," she stuttered, taking steps back towards the house. "Let's go ask her. She will explain it better."

Isadore and Reifoel came closer, resting their elbows on the edge of the pool, looking at each other with uncertainty in their eyes.

Turn around. Run.

Hadley looked around for her shadow, suddenly unable to see her when she needed her comfort most. She whipped her head around and turned her back towards the pool, walking towards the building, toward the Sun Goddess who would surely protect her. She nearly fell over the wyvern's flopped wing as it slept deeply, bathing in the desert heat and shaking the nearby rocks and debris with its snoring.

She laughed at herself, at the panic that stirred in her subconscious as she straightened back up from her stumble. Relief flooded her when she saw her familiar mischievous shadow lounging on the creature's back, kicking her feet and making patterns in the sky.

Her shadow looked over at her, and her eyes widened. Her mouth gaped open, and she pumped her arms as she jumped down from the wyvern.

"I missed you, too," Hadley said, smiling.

That smile faded quickly as she realized her shadow was rushing, alarmed.

What's wrong?

Hadley's knees buckled, her weight completely falling to the ground while something, someone, held her up. Blue blood dripped down her arms from the thick, piercing teeth that had sunken into her, and a familiar, cozy feeling swept through her as the Vrae venom mixed into her veins, her heart.

She felt like she was swooning, drunk, and in love. Hadley was temporarily transported back into Sheng's silky bed, drenched in her blood, while she obsessed over his body, his attention, his kisses.

Fight. Wake up and fight.

Her brain yelled as her body disobeyed.

"You know," Sheng grunted. "I prefer these wings not to be here. They so do get in the way."

She looked up at him, her eyes glazed from her fog, seeing only perfection despite the carnage that dripped down his chin.

"There's my wife," he chuckled, noticing the change in her expression.

"Let your shadow jump. Let her help," Hadley said out loud, not noticing Sheng raising his brow.

Hadley's shadow self frantically ran around the two in a circle, screaming as if she were behind a glass pane and no one could hear her. She was trapped, looking for the weakness in Sheng's spell so she could jump through. She needed the complete freedom of Hadley's mind, even if it was only for a second. That could be enough, all that the shadow needed.

"That crowd of mortals is getting smaller. There are barely any outside anymore." Sheng smiled down at her, still supporting Hadley in a backbend as if they were ballroom dancing. "I think it's best if we leave here, regroup, and confront that Goddess with a bit more power. I am very interested in learning who you are talking to when you are standing here by yourself. What is this power you have that I cannot see?"

Sheng leaned in and nuzzled his nose against hers. It was so tender, so affectionate, and Hadley felt herself melting even more in his arms, staring into his impossibly deep eyes. Her chest rose and fell with her shallow breaths, her stomach jumping as every inhale brought her body closer to his.

"What is going on here?"

Hadley didn't bother to break Sheng's eye contact as Reifoel and Isadore walked up to the two of them, now displaying tan-skinned legs. She couldn't pull herself away from her intoxication with the monster whose breath gently caressed her cheeks.

"You two certainly look cozy. I could have sworn she hated you just a few minutes ago," Isadore said, his legs shoulder-distance apart and arms held strongly by his side.

"You guys are naked again. We've got to find a way to get you through that," Sheng said, not taking his eyes off Hadley.

"Is this not the human form? Do you not look like this?"

Sheng sighed and gently supported Hadley to stand, only taking his hands off her once she was steady on her feet. There was a gleam in her vision. Everything seemed dangerous, a red flag—everything except for clinging onto Sheng.

Hadley watched her shadow self silently scream, still stuck behind that invisible panel on the other side of the sleeping wyvern. She wondered why her shadow was so upset. She frowned at the poor thing as Sheng gave her a side-eye. He smiled at her before turning his attention back to the two males.

"My wife here has turned a corner and decided to support my cause, the same cause as her own species, in fact. This means, boys, that I need to get her away from here. She is a match to a very explosive flame, it seems."

Hadley stood there, silent but in complete admiration for the man now talking for her, taking her voice.

You have a voice. Don't forget.

She shook her head as the thought crept into the back of her mind, making Sheng look down at her and frown.

"We need to get to the Bay of Bengal. Is that on your way?" Reifoel asked while dodging Isadore's dagger stare. "What? It would be convenient. They have a giant flying—"

"Deathtrap," Isadore interrupted. "We almost died on that thing. We dried out so fast. I have never felt anything like that before."

"What on Earth are you going to the Bay of Bengal for?" Sheng asked.

Isadore looked at Reifoel, shook his head no, and then pouted like a toddler when Reifoel opened his mouth to answer regardless.

"We are looking for a being named Kinnari. In our stories, there is just one, and he created our people. He created natural life."

Sheng's face lit up, looking back and forth between the Serelune and Hadley.

"Interesting," he said slowly, flicking his teeth. "Your stories know of his location? They can lead you to the Kinnari temple? It has been searched for, but it seems you have to have wings to find its Earthside entrance."

"We have hints, that is all," Isadore said before pressing his lips together.

"I was going to take you to France for a lovely honeymoon and, of course, to see the friends that are waiting for us," Sheng said to Hadley. "You two can always drop off at some point in the ocean. You have a long journey, especially if your search is led by *hints*."

Hadley noticed her shadow self was reaching a new level of hysterics, running back and forth and jumping into the air, trying to get her attention. Hadley cocked her head, her brow furrowed, and then she noticed the wyvern.

The creature was fully awake, staring towards the larger building, its breaths rapidly increasing in pace. She knew that look. Sheng's eyes danced around the scene, trying to figure out what was happening.

"I think it's time to get on the dragon, guys," he said.

"It's called a wyvern," Hadley said, her voice floating while still in her harmonious state.

"Up you go," Sheng said, ignoring her as he picked her up, her knees and legs hanging over his left arm. "You too, let's go, guys."

Sheng hoisted Hadley up on the back of the wyvern, and she watched as the two Serelune males climbed up behind her.

"I don't need to be on here. I have my own wings," she chuckled to herself.

You don't need to be on here.

"Is she okay?" Reifoel muttered to Isadore.

"Can you not leave some space between you and my wife?" Sheng spat out as Reifoel instinctually held onto her from behind for dear life. She could feel his skin, a slight sliminess rubbing onto her wings. His pelvis pulled back from her, pulling her weight further back.

The wyvern let out a welcoming screech as the large domed top building exploded, exposing a small section. There stood a Goddess dressed in flames and drunk off power as black clung to the edges of her fire. Her face had no expression. With feet that didn't bother to touch the ground, Ayurveda moved through the air towards them.

"Oh, Mother, how lovely to see you," Sheng yelled, holding his arms out towards the traveling fire. Sheng's grin was large, but despite the rose veil, even Hadley could see the tick in his brow. She had never seen him terrified before. Her hands squeezed tightly on the wyvern's spike in front of her as she tried to decide if she could pull herself together long enough to help him.

Admit it, you like it when he's scared.

Sheng slapped the side of the wyvern even though his feet were firmly planted on the ground. "Time to go, old girl."

"Just where do you think you are taking her?" Ayurveda demanded.

"I just wanted to let the wyvern spread its wings. She's getting a bit fat, don't you think?" Sheng laughed as he shoved too obviously against the creature's hide. The wyvern blew out a bit of fire in protest and rose. Hadley felt Reifoel's grip tighten on her.

"The girl," Ayurveda whispered, though it seemed to echo through the area. "The girl is mine."

"The mortal church recognizes her as my property now, so I'd have to disagree," Sheng said as the wyvern spread its wings, casting shade over him. "Would you fly away already, you damn beast?"

Ayurveda, still showing no emotion on her face, erupted, hot blue flames pulsing through her body, signaling that she was less than pleased.

"You have to come too," Hadley pleaded to Sheng, her body realizing his intention for the first time. "You can't send me away."

Run so far away that none of them can ever find you.

Hadley began to sob. The emotions building in her chest were overwhelming, an unthinkable grief. The logic that worked so hard to sneak into her brain cast doubt over all of it, over who wanted the best of her.

None of them. You are a tool, nothing more.

"Stop," yelled Ayurveda, her voice powerful but too late. The wyvern was already in flight, airborne. The mighty wings on either side of Hadley created a gust that nearly propelled her into the sky.

Fly away, jump off, and disappear.

Hadley watched from the skies as the wyvern began to shoot off toward the east, her eyes wide in horror as Ayurveda pulsed fire, exploding like a bomb onto Sheng. She didn't hear him scream, couldn't see him writhe in pain under the flames before they flew out of view. He was protecting them, making sure they had enough time to get away.

He is amazing.

He is psychotic.

Sheng's venom, still in her blood, screamed out in protest, and she slumped over, not bothering to hold on. Her eyes were closed, she couldn't think, couldn't breathe, the separation nearly causing a heart attack with the bite still so fresh.

"Woah, woah, I've got you," Reifoel shouted as she grabbed her shoulder and her head, and pulled her back onto his chest, his arm wrapped around her tight as his skin began to dry out, redden and crack.

15

Precession | France

Bright red hair collected in the bristles of her two-hundred-year-old silver hair brush. Precession looked at the strands, and her shoulders lowered before she placed it back on the vanity. She pushed her arms up on the stained wooden surface and stumbled still, always light-headed, as if she had a mild flu or fever.

The constant strain, the never-ending pull she felt on her body from both the earth's spinning and the moon's rotation around their planet, relied entirely on her power. She had never known anything else.

When she had been in the snow, the mountains, surrounded by her fellow Kinnari, she was youthful and filled with promise, dreams, and goals. For the briefest second, she had felt normal. But the next moment was accompanied by the feeling of being hit by a rock after indulging in a gallon of the finest wine, or at least that was what she remembered.

Suddenly, magic had pulsed through her, one that tied her to nature, to cycles. Her young eyes had dulled for the first time.

Without her, Earth was uninhabitable. Without Precession, the Earth could not rotate the sun, could not hold on to the moon, could not spin on its axis.

No one else knew when it had first happened except the twin sister, who sat back to back with her loyally. Precession suspected that Roksana was the first to understand what mixed with her blood, what magic beat in her heart. She was often the first to know things, always so in tune with the energy that moved and danced around her, a hidden waltz only for her.

"Sister," Precession said, the airiness in her voice suggesting that she had been running for the last fifteen hours. "I'm afraid there will be a problem today, announced on the public news channel."

Roksana appeared instantly by her sister's side, her hair wild and tangled as if allergic to the very brush Precession had just used. That hair was a testament to Roksana's wild heart beating under her breast. She grabbed Precession's arm gently as if she were handling a newborn.

"That is an interesting inclination," Roksana said, her tone strong, unwavering and deep. "Come now, let us have breakfast before those hooligans eat everything in the icebox."

Precession could sense her sister's fondness for the Vrae, for having real company staying in their estate. It had been a few weeks since Amis left without them, and the air in the room that her sister manipulated had been slowly changing from utter disdain to tolerance. Precession was thankful that the constant feeling of looming anger and hate had drifted away.

Both women strolled out of their shared bedroom. The large, silver four-post bed gleamed in the morning sunlight that flooded in from their high, square windows.

They walked down the corridor, passing the feminine French portraits while their black and pink ankle-length skirts swished and bounced with each bare-footed step. Roksana led Precession to the dining room and sat her at the otherwise empty table, both savoring the peace and quiet that she knew would be short-lasting.

"Blackberry jam or peach?" Roksana asked, turning towards the kitchen. The room warmed and then cooled with Roksana's words. It was so faint that no one else would have noticed it, but for Precession, finding the key to her sister's heart was no more difficult than breathing.

"Blackberry," Precession answered, the area around her emanating love and respect.

Roksana began banging around in the kitchen just on the other side of the dining room while Precession sat, staring at the curved patterns on the table. In her moments alone, she let the full effect of the world's weight crush her as she sat, forced to let it happen.

Roksana brought out three trays, one by one, setting them on the surface before them. One was adorned with toast, scones, and a saucer-shaped like a rooster holding blackberry jam and butter. The others held eggs, both devilled and poached. Small bowls of salads and fruits were on the last.

"Always a show." Roksana smirked as she got ready to sit. Her head turned to the left, and she heard the slams of bodies billowing down the stairs.

"Do you think they try to sound like elephants?" Precession asked, a wry smile hinting as ten Vrae in human form entered the dining room, bringing the chaos of a large family home.

"Hey, there's my sunshine," Killian said, rubbing his scruffy dark facial hair against Precession's cheek and kissing her there before sitting beside her. The seats filled with bodies as the table overflowed with a larger breakfast spread; Dravus was the first to reach for a plate and began loading it.

Precession noticed how the silver-haired Priscilla and Francis did not try to eat human food today.

"Not hungry?" Roksana asked, eying them as her disapproval spiked goosebumps into Precession's skin.

Saul laughed a little too loudly, his hands slapping the top of his thighs before reaching for the elegant pitcher of coffee. "You could not feed me enough, that's for sure."

The male winked toward Priscilla and Francis, and it could have been her premonition or Roksana's paranoia, but something was different that morning.

"Sister," Precession said, "fetch the milk and morning paper. They should be there by now."

Leonardo jumped from the table, nearly skipping out of the dining room.

"I've got it," he yelled behind him.

"Jenny." Precession turned to the brunette, her voice a soft song, "is there a plan? Have you heard from Amis yet?"

Jenny sighed and shrugged, returning her attention to the untouched blackberries on the plate before her. Like the other female in their clan, she didn't hide her boredom and displeasure at being there. The males, however, generally acted like the American frat boys she saw in the shows Roksana watched late at night.

Leonard came back in, holding four glass bottles of milk. He walked by the dining room shenanigans to set them on the kitchen counter.

"Can I have the paper, please?" Precession asked, yelling in comparison to her average volume. Leonardo lifted his head into the dining room and smiled at her.

"Ah, no paper today,"

"Then what's that under the back of your tee shirt?" Roksana asked, pointing out the too-obvious rolled-up newspaper outlined.

"Ah, this?" He pulled the newspaper out of his pocket. "This is an old one. I kept it from last week."

Roksana closed the distance between them and grabbed the newspaper as he turned to her aggressively, his eyes gleaming red.

"Why are you being so weird?" she scoffed without a tinge of fear pulsing through the air. The twins had learned so much about their houseguests, more than even the demon creatures would have suspected. They would keep it to themselves for now, but the fear of attack for their own personal safety did not hang over their heads any longer.

Roksana dropped the paper on the table in front of Precession, and the smacking sound drew the attention of all Vrae in the room.

"Here is your old newspaper, sister." Roksana turned her head to Leonardo and smirked.

Precession nodded her thanks and rolled the paper out, boldly displaying the current date in black ink. The headline story made her hold her breath; it was exactly what she expected. She slowly raised her head and looked around the table, most of the Vrae avoiding eye contact with her.

"Does anyone want to explain this?" she asked, her voice soft and gentle, like a loving mother. She stood up, a little too wobbly, and tossed the paper on the other side of the trays for all to see. A few of the Vrae males looked at it curiously before turning their faces into expressions of shock and disbelief. Jenny rolled her eyes and went back to pretending to eat her berries.

"Seven bodies found off a country background near Chartres," Roksana read aloud. The room immediately tensed, Roksana's temper bringing unnecessary tension into the air. "We've fed and housed you pieces of shit this entire time, and you go sneaking off in the night to murder mortals?" Roksana huffed.

"You seem to have forgotten that we are predators. We live off of blood, not the bird food that you princesses eat." Priscilla sniffed and turned her nose away from her plate.

"I guess we are not denying it then, Priscilla? Who were you to decide that?" Saul drawled lazily, tipping his head back and pinching the bridge of his nose with two fingers.

"This is all ludicrous, and we all know it. The Vrae and Kinnari of this house sit and wonder what the point of us being here is." Priscilla slammed her hands on the table and rose from her seat before storming off.

"If it makes you feel better," Jenny added, "some of us shared a body to, you know, stay incognito. It wasn't exactly a feast."

Roksana laughed and picked up the paper, reading the article closer out loud to the room.

"The victims, all seemingly unrelated, range in age and occupation, their lives brutally cut short by an unseen assailant. All these victims were found within fifteen meters of each other, and though it is unclear if this was a single assailant, residents are warned to look out for cults or unknown group gatherings and newcomers.

Each victim bears deep puncture wounds on their neck. The wounds are jagged and irregular, suggesting a frenzied attack. In a disturbing display of brutality, some victims' limbs are found twisted at unnatural angles, suggesting a savage manipulation of their bodies post-mortem. These macabre details add a layer of horror to the already grisly scene."

Roksana slammed the paper down on the floor and walked back into the kitchen while muttering curse words in French.

"I think it would be better to focus on the positives here," Killian chimed in.

Precession smiled at him, amused.

"Go on then, list them loud enough for my sister to hear back there."

Killian stood, leaning against the table. He looked around, making eye contact with all the Vrae, some who seemed just as curious as Precession to hear this list of positives.

"Well, let's start with the fact that none of these mortals were fully drained of their blood. We showed proper restraint."

"Go on." Precession raised an eyebrow.

"Then, you have to consider that we all just abstained for . . . how long has it been . . . three weeks? I can't tell you a time in all my very long years that I have gone that long without proper nutrition."

"I'd like to add a positive," Jenny chimed in. "We have spent all this time living with our natural prey and haven't eaten you entirely in the middle of the night." She flashed Precession a large white-toothed smile, the sweetness of it not hiding the sinister intent.

"Yes, yes," Killian agreed. "That one does seem important. Overall, I think we are doing a bang-up job here at your estate. None of us have managed to go crazy from boredom; the farmhouse chores you've assigned us are always completed, and I think we deserve to indulge ourselves and let loose once in a while. It's not like back at home, where we can jump through the pentagram and come out to our own private Kinnari breeding farm."

Precession stared back, not breaking Killian's intense stare, and tilted her head. She didn't have the energy to decipher what his comment implied, though she tucked it away to ponder later. She closed her eyes as she pushed, pulled, and let herself get crushed before bringing herself back to the room.

"As I understand it, some of you work in politics," Precession said. "How do you propose we clean this up? I feel like anybody left behind is a job that is not finished. Do you disagree?"

Roksana stormed back into the room, her hands balled into fists.

"No, absolutely not. You do not get to turn my sweet, loving sister, the better one of us, into an accomplice."

"There is little innocence about me, Roksana, as you know. There is no need for facades at this point." Precession let the sweetness and frailness of her voice act as Jenny's smile had moments before. She, too, could bite back.

All she had to do was destroy the Earth by simply no longer continuing the spin or the rotation. She had wondered precisely how her powers would manifest while untethered.

"We have to work together, be more in sync. We have no idea when Amis will be back to collect you." Precession took a breath. The murders were not the real issue, not what her body had been feeling.

"I did have one question, though: how did you kill a Kinnari? There has been a hole, a missing power from this planet, for the past few days. It took a moment for me to recognize it; I do not possess the same kind of magic Amis does. Wherever he is, he likely knew right away."

She trailed off, her mind wandering to worlds of unbalances.

Roksana cleared her throat, snapping her sister out of it.

"How did you do it? The killed Kinnari has not come back as Reign or Tristan did."

Everyone blinked at her, confusion on their faces. Roksana stopped moving towards the table with another tray in her hands—this one adorned by a blue tea kettle—and stared at her sister.

"No one here knows what you are talking about. You are the only two Kinnari we've seen, smelled, or even fantasized about since Amis left here," Dravus said, breaking the silence.

"Fantasized?" Jenny mused.

"Yes, of drinking their blood, eating their flesh. Don't worry, I'll make sure you are filled with my cock later. There will be no other kind of fantasy there."

"I don't know, sex while draining someone of their blood? No one can tell me that they haven't thought about it, or hell, even tried it." Saul winked.

"I'm afraid your . . . cock . . . would just about shrivel up once I was ready to attack it, Dravus," Jenny said, studying her nails while a few Vrae laughed. "You just don't seem like the type that could handle me."

"Oh, but Sheng is?" Dravus spat back while the smiles disappeared quickly.

The sound of Jenny's chair pushing back on the tile floor filled the otherwise silent room as she stood. She kept her head bowed as she laughed, drawing out the sound as her nails turned into claws.

"Sheng could kill you all without even bothering to look at you. We follow him for a reason, and I will not stand to hear your insubordination."

She raised her head, eyes red, lethal.

"Woah there, tiger. We just fed; why are you so uptight, baby doll?" Dravus lifted his hands, palms towards her to offer peace.

She snapped, turning to grab her chair and lifting it over her head before she slammed it down on the floor. It snapped, as did Roksana's heart as she saw the mistreatment of her possessions.

"Because I'm surrounded by fucking Kinnari blood, you assholes," she said, now collected, with a deadly calm.

Without another word, Precession stood, and Roksana rushed over to take her arm and assist her. They walked out of the dining room, through the foyer and out the front door, letting it slam behind them.

Precession let the sun bathe her skin, the warmth sending shivers up her back and across her chest. She took in a deep breath of the air, mildew on long-leaf grass mixing with her sister's woody, sultry perfume.

Roksana placed her arm on her back. The two walked side by side around the estate's circumference, listening to the birds singing and bees humming, their bare feet squishing over the damp earth.

Eventually, the clamoring of chickens rushing to their morning feed came into view, along with a pen of three large pigs, a horse, and three goats that roamed free but still chose to hover close to the feeding troughs.

"Morning, mademoiselles." a Frenchman in his fifties tipped his blue hat to them while keeping a thin cigar secure in the corner of his mouth.

The twins both smiled at their groundskeeper, the only permanent staff member allowed on the property. They were not princesses; they would not shy away from working with their hands, milking goats, and plucking chickens, but when the Vrae were not there to boss around, the land was too big for just the two of them to care for.

"Did you hear about Miriam? She lives at the end of ze street," he asked, pulling feed from his apron pockets and throwing it down for the chickens. "Her daughter was among the recent murders. How horrible."

"It is sad indeed," Precession responded, using her most empathetic face. "I will send over a casserole this evening."

"Where is that group, those lively Americans you are hosting? Interesting that these murders happen shortly after they arrive, no?" He avoided their eye contact as he moved over towards the chicken coop, grabbing a push lawn mower and getting ready to move through the estate.

"I do not appreciate the comment, Michel," Roksana said, trying to sound innocent as he slunk off.

"I suppose you brought me out here to talk about the Kinnari death," Precession said, watching her sister's suspicious eyes following their groundskeeper.

"He is obnoxiously observant. It could be a problem for us." Roksana sneered. "Yes, I needed time away from the Vrae and some fresh air to deal with something so serious. The bigger blow to my heart, though, is that you omitted this from me. How can I continue to trust you when you do not trust me?"

"I had never felt something like this before, sister," Precession said, her head hanging down low. "I couldn't bring it to you until I understood what it was that I was feeling."

"Who do you think it is? Do you think it's Arryn?"

"My first thought was Amis, since the balance feels so jolted, but I do not know."

Roksana bit her lip and tapped her fingers against her shoulder. "What do we do?"

Precession sighed and looked apologetically into her sister's eyes. "Unfortunately, I think we ignore it. We have a life here to focus on. We have nine murders to cover up in a town filled with suspicion and gossip."

Precession snapped her head up towards the back doors on the west side of the house as they burst open. The full group of Vrae bounced out, wearing working gloves and smiles, as they pushed each other around and laughed.

"They are like a toothpaste ad," Precession giggled. "So cheesy, no?"

Jenny strayed from the pack and ran up to the twins, her demeanor positively sunny, as if she were a different person.

"Hey, girls," Jenny panted. "I wanted to apologize about your chair. It was a beautiful piece of furniture, and I plan to find a replacement of equal quality."

"That is fine," Roksana said, crossing her arms over her chest.

"We, as a group, also only have a few more weeks in us here before we lose control and murder your entire town. I just wanted to let you know. I'll go get my chores started; lots of eggs to be sold at the market this weekend."

16

Reifoel | The middle of the sea

There was so much blue, so much incredible ocean underneath them. Reifoel wanted nothing more than to fall hundreds of feet from the sky and plummet into his life force, his home. They had been on the wyvern for over three days. The animal flew and landed as it pleased, usually in an empty field where it could slurp up a few wild horses, the sounds of their neighs, their smothered screams lingering in his ear for hours after.

The girl, the woman who sat in front of Reifoel, was something that he didn't know how to deal with. He couldn't see her face from where he sat, her blonde tangled hair constantly whipping his own face through their journey, but he could feel her body breaking down.

With each hour that passed, he felt her posture lower, her chest cave in, her wings wilting at her sides. Both of the Serelunes' skin cracked and tightened, and the two males felt desiccated as if even blinking could shatter their entire bodies.

"I can't keep going," Isadore meekly yelled in Reifoel's ear.

Reiofel could feel Isadore's arms, which clung around his waist, loosen a bit more, and Reifoel knew that he was right. None of them could keep going.

They would have to pick a place to get off sooner or later. It seemed like no one knew what they were doing, just clinging on, closing their eyes, and hoping they'd end up where they were supposed to be.

This wasn't his world, though. His experience in the mortal realm was limited to a small area that he had sailed to from the portal. He didn't know where they were or how far away from his goal destination they were. If they got off in a bad spot, who knew what they would be expected to face?

They didn't have a choice, though. Death was upon them. Water creatures were not meant for the skies.

"We have to land," Reifoel said into Hadley's ear. Her shoulders pulled back slightly at his words, but then, only stillness came from her.

Maybe she didn't hear you.

Reifoel raised his hand to tap on her shoulder to get her attention, but instead, she turned her head and upper body to face him. She was entirely comfortable on the wyvern as it soared in and out of clouds, the moisture giving Reifoel a slight life boost.

He looked at her and was met with painstakingly deep blue eyes, like the color of the middle of the sea. For a moment, he forgot that he was dying. He forgot everything. He saw home, the ocean, in those eyes, and there was a second where he was stunned.

It wasn't the first time he had looked upon her face, but it was the first time he saw her wounds, her suffering in the crinkle of her nose and worry lines around those sapphire eyes, with specks of green and gray like the light coming in from underneath the water.

She didn't speak. She just nodded before turning to face forward.

Hadley thrashed her heels into the sides of the wyvern and patted the patch of skin in front of her five or six times. The wyvern, flying rhythmically, bobbed up and down, disrupting its transit route before diving at a sharp degree that made Reifoel feel like his stomach had dislocated and had flown out of his mouth.

Reifoel used his left hand to grab the tattered, rough skin on Isadore's leg, holding him down, suspicious that he could fly off behind them at any moment. He used his right arm to squeeze them both against the winged beauty before him, trying not to get distracted by her softness, the way his arm sat amongst her. This was for survival, and this was holding on for their lives.

That was all.

Hadley shifted uncomfortably. Reifoel could tell that he was hurting her, but he had nothing else to hold on to. She kept him on the wyvern and did not complain or comment about the feel of his rough, crumbling skin against hers.

A sound like a cannon boomed, and they moved so fast that the world around them was a blur. Relief flooded Reifoel an instant later as he realized they were in the water. That sound was the wyvern diving into the ocean below them.

Energy and the soothing feeling of seaweed over burned Serelune skin made Isadore's grip on Reifoel's waist tighten, his fingers able to bend again. Reifoel's legs morphed into a tail. They were moving fast, the creature propelling them underneath the shadows of ships above.

They had been under the water for a minute now, and despite how great he felt, he could feel that Hadley had tensed up, her whole body rigid.

She can't breathe underwater, can she?

Reifoel watched, feeling helpless as her blonde hair floated towards him like a ghost, her chin rising up towards the direction of the surface, her eyes closed with her face in agony.

He started counting the seconds after that.

Twenty-four, twenty-five.

She turned, and her eyes met his. Panic seeped from her, and her face looked scarlet even underneath the water.

Forty-nine, fifty.

She opened her mouth and choked as water entered her lungs, her arms going rigid as she began floating off of the wyvern that was still propelling them under the surface of the ocean. Reifoel grabbed her, pulling her into him, her wings slimy, wrapped around her like a wet piece of paper as the speed at which they shot through the water pushed them harder and harder together.

One hundred and eight, one hundred and nine.

She felt lifeless, her skin radiating like a siren on the hunt, like a ghost lost in the sea.

Reifoel ducked his head. The wyvern's motion changed abruptly. It moved upward and broke the surface with such force that they all hovered in the air as if gravity did not exist. After a breath, the creature floated back down to the water like a feather, a sway in its back and a turning in Reifoel's gut.

Hadley was gagging, choking on air as it filled her lungs, her shoulders falling to the side as she hung slightly upside down with her legs still straddling the wyvern.

Reifoel blinked at her, listening to the agony that was her burning throat, her writhing lungs echoing throughout their surroundings.

She is alive.

"Are we going to help her?" Isadore asked.

"I don't know how," he said, realizing the wyvern was still floating on water. They were surrounded by darkness as if they were at the bottom of the sea. The air was cold, slimy even.

The two Serelune just sat there, not taking action, watching the outline of Hadley's body recover from the underwater journey. Once she stopped gagging and got her breath under control, she lay in silence, listening to drops hitting the surface of the water, the only clue to where they were.

What do we do now?

Hadley sat up in front of him, her body rising like there was never any trauma, no fatigue, and leaned over, hugging the wyvern, whispering what sounded like coos. The creature let out a raspy breath in response.

"You two seem close," Reifoel cleared his throat as the words echoed, bouncing back to him.

"We've spent some time together," she said.

Reifoel could feel her looking at him through the darkness. She made a noise, a clicking of her tongue against her teeth, and in response, the wyvern let out an elegant blast of fire, giving visibility to their surroundings.

He looked around and got to his feet, water flinging off the tail that was once there, balancing against the wyvern's spikes. They were in a cave. Delicate stalactites formed over hundreds of years clung to the ceiling, formed by the ceaseless dripping of water. Rocky walls lay barren, but an opening, a path forged by the stream of fire and light, urged Reifoel's curiosity forward. There was a world there to explore.

"The king and queen will be expecting us back soon," Isadore said. "We should get back to our search. The water is just below us."

Reifoel looked down, seeing the mineral-infused water that filled the cave, so clean and clear, likely from the help of the many coral reefs that lived just outside it. The wyvern's tail began to push them forward, following its fire's path.

"This ride isn't over." Reifoel shrugged, already settled, comfortable in the moisture surrounding them.

The darkness was interrupted by a faint glow, an etherealness that clung to the water before them. Bioluminescent algae clung to the walls as they narrowed, creating a shallow tunnel where the pocket of air was getting tighter and tighter.

Reifoel looked at the back of Hadley's head, a nervousness pulsing through him at the thought of her drowning but not dying again and again and again. He shook his head at the thought and wondered where his protective instinct for her came from.

The cavern stretched deep into the heart of the ocean floor. Small fish darted in and out of crevices, seeking refuge from larger predators. They continued through into an open chamber bathed in an azure light. On the far side of the chamber, a rocky floor fanned out from the water, and crystals reflecting purple and white hues peaked out from small cracks in the surface.

The wyvern crawled onto the rocks and curled up, with every intention of falling into a deep slumber, ignoring the passengers it carried. Once its breaths became deep and rhythmic, its belly rumbling, Hadley quickly jumped off while her wings, nearly invisible except for the reflection from the crystals, floated her down. Her feet daintily hit the rocks, and she moved towards the wall in front of her.

Reifoel realized what she saw: pictures and carvings on the cave walls. He tapped Isadore and pointed, not waiting for a response. He clumsily slid off the wyvern and winced at the rocks hitting his naked feet. Isadore jumped down with no issues beside him, reminding him of how truly unathletic he could be as they moved to join the girl at the wall.

She followed the carvings with her fingers. "This one is a mountain. This one is me."

Reifoel saw the mountain and saw the stick figure body with rounded wings drawn behind it, standing on the top.

"Who are you?" Isadore asked her, "Why would you be depicted here?"

She shook her head and furrowed her brow.

"Maybe it's not me after all," she said, "and if it's not, then it's one of several bodies with wings I want nothing to do with."

"Do you know where this mountain is?" Reifoel asked her. She turned to look at him, her face disappointed.

"Anyone I've ever met with wings has only abandoned or lied to me. My kind are not to be sought out. My kind might be better off eliminated."

Reifoel blinked at her. A simmering rage settled under the sweetness of her voice. The casual tone of her words made it seem like her opinion was a common fact, nothing to be baffled by. He inched away.

"We will be leaving now," Isadore said, breaking the silence as they stared at the carving. Reifoel wondered who was here, who had the ability to come to such a place and make such a marking. He wondered if they belonged to the mortal world or to his.

"Where are you going?" Hadley asked.

"We are looking for the creature in this carving. It's as if the wyvern has brought us here just to show us what we needed."

Hadley rolled her eyes. "The wyvern brought us here because it is completely isolated from masses of humans that will likely attempt to kill it. She really is a misunderstood beast, isn't she?"

"Did we know that it's a she?" Isadore asked. "Does she have a name?"

"She doesn't. She belongs to a goddess who is above something like that, the commonness of names."

"Then I shall leave her with a gift, a name as we leave. I have never imagined that a creature of fire and air could swim with such grace, so I deem you, Aqurya," Isadore said, bowing down to the sleeping beast.

"You're going to leave me." Hadley turned to Isadore and Reifoel. "You're going to swim out of this cave and leave me here."

Isadore crossed his arms over his chest, clearly offended, the corners of his mouth almost bending into a slight frown.

"You have indicated that you want nothing to do with us or your kind. How can we include you in a quest that exclusively concerns the very beings you'd like to see destroyed?"

Hadley's face fell, and she nodded, turning her back to them and looking back at the carvings.

Reifoel thought of Sheng and how important Hadley seemed to him. She was essential to a Goddess, too. She was valuable in a way that he didn't know how to describe quite yet, but leaving her there seemed to be the wrong decision.

"I think you should travel with us," Reifoel announced and was met with a murderous look from Isadore.

"If she travels with us, that Goddess could light us on fire. Doesn't that seem risky?"

"He's not wrong." Hadley sighed at Isadore's words. "Ayurveda needs me to fulfill her current plan."

"I'm honestly not one hundred percent sure that you are not, in fact, the one I am supposed to find." Reifoel shrugged. "You have wings and are connected to the wave of fire that destroyed my sailboat. Can you create life?"

Hadley smiled sadly. "I only seem to create heartache, unfortunately."

Reifoel looked at his cousin, his eyes wide and brows high as he took in Isadore's unwavering disapproval. He chose to shake it off before walking back over to the wyvern.

"Let's rest, and the three of us will swim out of here when we wake."

"Only if we are looking for that mountain," Isadore grumbled, following him and laying down on the rocks, a tail forming again as his toes dipped into the water.

Reifoel looked over to Hadley, unmoving from the cavern's wall, moving her hand back and forth as if looking for a shadow. There wasn't enough light on her to cast one, making the motion seem purposeless.

"You need to sleep, too," Isadore yelled at her before his snores quickly joined the dripping sounds to create a sleepy white noise. She didn't react or acknowledge either of them before bending down to sit, still staring up at the carving.

Reifoel struggled to keep his eyes open, each blink heavier and heavier as he sank next to Isadore, letting his legs dip into the water as well. The cooling temperature lulled him to sleep instantly as he gave way to his natural form, no longer able to worry about the girl, the wyvern, or the mountain.

17

Hadley | Underwater Sea Cave

"Wake up," a voice said as someone prodded her arm. Hadley began to come back into consciousness and realized immediately that she wanted nothing to do with that as the soreness of her muscles peaked and screamed within her body. She wiped the crust off of her eyelashes and groaned.

Something jabbed into her calf, and she whimpered.

"Don't kick me," she strung the words together, the memory of where she was, creeping back.

"Aqurya left while we were sleeping," Isadore's stern voice sounded over her. She pried her eyes open to see the man standing before her. His stance was wide, displaying his nudity while his face remained expressionless and cold. It would be funny in any other context; Hadley could tell that he was being dragged along even more than she was.

"The water level is rising, too. I have a feeling that you cannot breathe underwater, so it's better to leave before panic sets in."

Hadley forced herself to get up, brushing small rocks and soot off her damp dress. Her body shivered, reminding her how unremarkable she still was. She had no strength, no inherent way to survive. Just getting into the cave, she had drowned over and over again, the water stinging her lungs like poison and knives.

Yet, she still hadn't died.

Her mind flashed back to the Kinnari man she met on the roof, the one who had promised her death. He had disappeared when she had fully expected to see him again, to let him finish the task he had been given. The pure relief of the promise flooded through her as she grappled with this strange level of immortality that she was painfully discovering.

She wanted nothing to do with it.

Hadley gazed around the cavern, the moonlight flowing in from the small opening overhead, making the gems and crystals in the rocks sparkle. A large imprint from where the wyvern slept was underneath the stream of light, the heavy trail of its tail lazily pulled from behind, leading to the water. She wondered if it went back to seek Ayurveda or if it just simply got hungry.

Her own stomach growled, though maybe a growl would be much too quiet to describe the actual sound.

She let her wings stretch and flutter in rapid succession, gracefully floating into the air. Hadley flew up to the opening, following the moonlight, and managed to get her head and arms out of the small hole as she stared up at the stars. Her arms struggled to hold herself in place as she kicked her feet back and forth, unable to get her shoulders fully through. She didn't fit; the rock was too strong to claw open with her hands.

Hadley stayed there for another moment, letting the ocean breeze kiss her hair and caress her face before she sighed and let herself fall. Twenty feet rushed past before her wings caught her, and her bare feet lightly pointed and touched down right at the water's edge.

"Let's go, then," she said, looking up at Reifoel, who was already waist deep in the water. She pulled her wings in, wincing from the sensation of not quite perfecting the move and let the surprisingly warm water hug her calves, her knees and then her navel. Something brushed against her.

"You're quite jumpy." Reifoel grinned at her. "It was just my tail. No need to be worried."

Hadley tried her best to push her sense of dread into the back of her mind and looked around the cavern one last time, hoping to see a glimpse of her shadow self but finding no success. The feeling of helplessness, of being alone, crept back into her.

Isadore moved into the water, collapsing down as his body transformed. He reemerged moments later, fully upright, right next to Reifoel, the two holding out their arms for her.

"We will help you propel through the water as fast as we can," Reifeol said, his eyes full of assurance and kindness. He seemed so innocent, like the golden retriever she used to take care of for her neighbors when they traveled during the summer.

Hadley swooped an arm around Reifoel and Isadore, sandwiched between them as they pressed tightly against the sides of her hips.

"Take a breath," Reifoel said.

Before Hadley could fill her chest with air, the two males dove and brought her with them, water filling her mouth and nose, burning as her lungs tensed.

There is still space to breathe above the surface.

Hadley opened her eyes and then closed them immediately; the water pummeled her face, stinging as they jetted through the sea. Her legs and hips ached from two tails constantly hitting and brushing against her, the scales rougher than she'd imagined.

Even with her eyes closed, she could tell when they exited the cave. The water was immediately lighter than the previous pitch black. She fell limp, giving into the seething pain as her lungs screamed, as more and more saltwater filled her chest, squeezing her heart.

The water began to calm around them and Hadley felt an intentional poke against her left thigh as Isadore tried to get her attention. She opened her eyes, fully submerged in her misery to see the surface above her. There was air up there, and life. Maybe she did want to keep going. Maybe she wasn't truly ready to die.

She reached up toward the surface; they were at least twenty meters down. Her ability to communicate under the water was nonexistent as she tried to kick her legs to raise herself up despite Isadore and Reifoel keeping her in place.

Hadley looked into Reifoel's eyes, hers shooting back up to the surface, pleading to be brought up. Reifoel shook his head no, and panic shot through her body. They wanted to keep her down; they didn't want her to breathe.

Isadore's grip loosened, and he gripped her head with his hands. Hadley wished she could scream, wished that she could do anything as her head was jerked down. She pushed Isadore away, or tried to.

Reifoel grabbed her shoulders and shook her gently, moving in front of her to connect their eyes. He pointed down but then stilled, acting as if he needed her to sense the danger nearby.

With every inch of her brain fighting against it, wanting to flee without knowing what she needed to see, Hadley tilted her head down. For the briefest moment, she saw only a coral reef. The colors were magnificent: purples, reds, and golds, while bright orange and yellow fish swam in and out of their hiding spots.

A shadow flickered in the corner of her eye, and despite swallowing more and more water, she felt calm, knowing that her shadow self had returned to her. She would be okay; she wouldn't be alone.

But she was wrong.

The shadow caster came into view, and a sense of dread replaced Hadley's calm. She immediately started kicking towards the surface. Fins brushed over her leg as Isadore and Reifoel dove down and pushed a large shark off of the three of them. Hadley didn't look back, she didn't look down, she just swam and choked and hoped for air. She was missing her Goddess, the warmth and protection she felt through her relationship with Ayurveda.

Sheng had pulled her away from Ayurveda, and she cursed him in her mind while continuing to kick, continuing to reach. She was desperate to vomit and purge her body of the water, and likely the blood that now contaminated the ocean underneath her. She could get a breath in, one last breath before she got pulled under again by the jaws hunting underneath her.

Hadley broke through the water's surface, spitting out and coughing, her gag reflex active as her stomach flipped over and over again.

"Are you okay?" Isadore's voice, protective and firm, boomed over her, his body effortlessly floating in the water, watching her with no expression on his face.

"Where is . . ." she choked as Reifoel broke through the surface, seemingly unharmed, his eyes filled with concern and worry.

"We didn't get eaten by a shark; thanks for the concern." Isadore rolled his eyes at Reifoel, who shrugged his shoulders innocently.

Hadley looked around, seeing an endless ocean. Her breathing slowed and steadied as she used her arms and legs to keep herself afloat despite the lap of waves splashing her in the face. Her arms were retaken, the males keeping her over the surface as they began the long trek, bobbing through the water in the moonlight.

She had no way of knowing how much time had passed, but she watched as the moon dipped behind dark clouds, reemerging to grow fainter in the sky while the sun began to make its appearance. It was beautiful, the most supernatural thing she had experienced, watching the golden glow explode over the dark water surrounding them. She stared at that sunrise, not averting her gaze until black dots danced along her vision.

Hadley blinked, feeling the sunlight bathe her face. Nothing in her life had felt as good or as nurturing. She would fulfill her promise to Ayurveda. She didn't know how, but she would find her way back to her.

Then we will burn the world down.

Hadley's feet dragged across rough pebbles and sand, the contact unexpected, making her gasp. Looking ahead, pulling her gaze away from the light, she realized they were washing up on a beach. Her eyes widened, and she couldn't help but smile.

There was land. They made it back to land.

The grip on both of her arms loosened once Reifoel and Isadore realized that she could stand and carry herself the rest of the way onto the shore. Hadley panted and flailed like a fish out of water while working on becoming just that.

"You're not the most graceful swimmer," she heard Isadore grunt through her hurried splashes. Moments later, her hands touched the sand, and she was able to crawl until she was fully on the shore. She turned around before collapsing, sand covering her legs and arms while she debated falling asleep right then and there.

"Hey," someone shouted from further up on the beach. Hadley turned her head up to see who it was with her eyes half open. An angry small teen boy was stomping heavily, carrying a pile of towels. Hadley sat up and angled towards him, seeing the row of orange and yellow beach chairs with matching umbrellas that he was working on setting up.

Isadore and Reifoel had also managed to drag themselves out of the water, their tails replaced by legs. They kept their bodies down, lying on their stomachs.

"Unbelievable, you fucking tourists," the teenager shouted at them. "You keep your freaky wild nights to yourselves. That's what you pay for a hotel room for."

Hadley cocked her head, wondering if she heard him right, and then realized that Reifoel and Isadore were fully nude. She burst out laughing.

"You, American witch," the boy spat at her while dropping a few towels, "cover them up. You're going to get me in trouble here."

Hadley clunkily got to her feet, her body so heavy, needing rest, and picked up the towels while the teenager turned his back on them to continue setting up the chairs for the day. Hadley threw the striped pinked towels onto Reifoel and Isadore's bare backs. The two males stood awkwardly and wrapped their lower halves up.

"What now?" Reifoel asked them, shaking the water out of his hair.

Now I leave you. I find my way back.

"We find a mountain," Isadore said as he walked up the beach, not looking back.

Reifoel shrugged and gave her a soft smile, moving to follow him.

Hadley stayed planted. She didn't belong in their quest. She had been dragged along, begrudgingly saved from the very Goddess that she never wanted to leave.

You can fly. Let's see how far.

Before she could let her wings rip out from her skin, Reifoel turned around, his gaze catching hers with his eyebrows raised. He held his hand towards her, bowing slightly like a prince offering her his kingdom.

She didn't think much of it; her mind had already been made up. But then her heart fluttered, relief shooting through her fingertips and teeth, as a dark familiar hand appeared to accept Reifoel's offering. Her shadow self stood in front of him, giggling and flipping her hair around like an endless flirt. She turned and waved for Hadley to join them.

"I'm waiting for you," Reifoel said to Hadley, his voice faint against the crashing waves, hand still held out to her.

Hadley stepped forward, not wanting to lose her shadow self again, her safety net.

He could lead us to Ayurveda. It's not like I know where I'm going. She could have left the compound, searching for me.

With a sigh and conflicted heart, Hadley placed her hand in Reifoel's as the two walked behind Isadore up to the buildings and city beyond the paved streets with metal signs indicating they were at Cox's Bazar.

Wherever that is.

Hadley's shadow self danced around the three of them as if she had never left, hadn't disappeared. Hadley didn't take her eyes off of her as she continued to walk hand in hand with Reifoel.

"That seems overly familiar," Isadore said, his eyes on their intertwined hands before awkwardly pulling apart.

"I thought she was going to run," Reifoel grumbled.

"So what if she did?"

18

Amis | Northern New Zealand

Amis stared at the plastic grocery bag on the clean and otherwise bare countertop, gleaming from the sunlight pouring through the windows. For the first time in his existence, he had felt the urgent need to make spaghetti.

He would create a home for all seventy-eight villagers he had individually carried to Mt. Maunganui. He loved this area, the vibrance, and the small-town beach charm it possessed when tourists didn't flood it. The culture shock might come on a little strong, but otherwise, he could house them all in a single apartment building.

Waihema still had its closeness. Their tribe had not broken apart. Most importantly, they were much further away from that damn portal, less accessible to those who might wish them harm.

A small hand slid into his, and he looked down at Salome, one of his many children. She had come to investigate what he had been looking at.

"I am going to make you some dinner," he said, shifting to pull dried pasta and canned sauce out.

"It doesn't seem like that will feed us all," she said before running off towards the spacious entertainment area, where a television played cartoon children's shows. The rounded sectional couch that backed up against the floor-to-ceiling windows fit sixteen children while a few others lay out lazily on the floor. The youth were adapting quickly to convenience.

The apartment door opened, and the elder shuffled in, followed by several mothers carrying boxes and baskets of more food.

"We've got this, godly one," Mother Waihema said, her usual attire replaced by a more modern-day fitting purple dress that hung down to her ankles.

"I can cook," he said, unmoving and his brow lowering. "I once made someone a grilled cheese, and I enjoyed the process."

They had been in these apartments for a few days now. Most of the flats had three to four bedrooms, each housing a mother and her children, even the adult males still living within their small family pods.

Amis glanced over at the couch, the three children who would one day bear wings at the forefront of his mind. There was, of course, Salome, around seven years old, but there was also fourteen-year-old Luca, who was so close to manhood. Without the promised death sentence hanging over his head, Amis was curious to watch how this child flourished.

There was also a two-year-old boy, Noah, who often pouted and stumbled around, reminding Amis of himself when he drank too much ale.

This was his family, one that he had abused over too many generations to count, but now, things were different. Now, he had a separation, a freedom from his fear and indentured servitude from Sheng, from the Vrae. Working with them had been the right thing for this world, the right thing for the Kinnari, who had only a tiny idea about the sacrifices he made for them.

Before him was a beauty he had never been able to appreciate before.

It was the beauty of life, of giggles and children running around while mothers nurtured. Though there was still a wariness in their eyes, no one flinched at his presence; no mother stood protectively in front of their child. He was grateful they didn't know about his deal with the Vrae, and thankful his only known infraction was the culling of non-Kinnari blood.

Thick metal knives hit cutting boards as the mothers chopped onions, broccoli, mushrooms, and beef. A large pot sat on top of a gas stove, and plops of broth sounded as ingredients were continuously added while Amis' dried pasta noodles sat pushed aside.

"What do we do now?" Mother Waihema's dry voice asked, shaking Amis out of his thoughts. "Once we've settled, that is. This is a completely different life; we cannot freely grow all our food or garden in the same way. How will we fill our days?"

Amis smiled and raised a single eyebrow. This woman before him had worked her body to skin and bone daily. The gift of nothing, though possibly unfulfilling, seemed like the most incredible gift she knew how to provide.

What a uniquely immortal problem to have.

"This is now an era of learning who you are. This is now your era of doing what your heart desires."

"I know who I am," she said flatly. "Do you?"

Amis rolled his eyes and stuffed his hands into his gray pants pockets while three children tip-toed to him, holding the television remote. All of them were wearing mismatched combinations of T-shirts, skirts, and colorful socks as they learned how to dress themselves in this new world.

The tallest girl held it up to him and tilted her head towards the 60-inch screen. Amis nodded, grabbed it from her, and walked over to the couch. They all jumped and danced behind his footsteps. Their program had ended, and a dull news channel had begun playing. Finding another channel playing something bright and musical was an easy task that he could focus on.

"The death toll through the Centre-Val de Loire region in France has officials stumped as it leads international headlines today. Local officers beg for any insight or tips as the twenty-fourth body has been found just yesterday. We have a clip from a resident in the area that we will play now."

Amis' finger hit the remote too fast before he processed the new headline story. His stomach lurched, not knowing how many times he had pressed the buttons to help him get back to the news. Once he had found it, the screen showed a stout older Frenchman, the name Michel at the bottom on the screen as he spoke to the camera in heavily accented English.

"The attacks are frightening. No one knows if this is an animal or if it is a lazy killer. If it is a killer, we are all doomed. They attacked the bodies with no fear of being caught. There is no cover-up, just broken bones, graying skin, and wound marks that are made from teeth or a blade; no one can quite tell."

Fuck me.

"Some of the children are a little young for such stories, no?" Noah's tall, thin mother voiced from the kitchen, holding a raw handful of seasoned meat. She popped her hip out. Though it did add an element of sass, the insecurity still showed in the creases around her eyes.

"Yes, of course," he replied, changing the channel quickly until stopping at an animated dog that immediately made the children giggle in waves. He bowed his head and excused himself, leaving the apartment and entering a hallway with dark burgundy carpets that led to an elevator.

Amis paced back and forth, following the gold patterns that appeared along the beige wallpaper every few feet before turning back around, his hands on the back of his neck. He had been so preoccupied with doing the right thing that he forgot the consequences, the reason behind what had started it all. He had been a fool to think that Precession and Roksana could control the group of Vrae.

Even still, Roksana was all things considered, his equal. She should have been capable of watching them for just a handful of weeks. Sheng had to return to them all some time. Amis couldn't be solely responsible for demon babysitting.

He would need to get back there. His balance was so greatly unhinged that he felt like he was walking through the world with an atrophied third leg, causing him to trip and struggle under the unneeded weight.

Djoser was gone, mortals were being murdered by Vrae in France, and Sheng was still gone, with no communication and no assurances.

This is going great.

Amis didn't panic. He barely reacted in real time due to his magic, but worry and regret sat within him for the entirety of his life. He tightened the bun on top of his head, keeping his medium-length dark hair out of his face, pulled in a breath, and decided to walk back into the apartment to face his family with the intent of letting them know that he would be leaving for just a couple of days.

He worried for them, finding themselves in this new world, their safety, their happiness.

Once back inside, Amis strolled past the spacious kitchen island, now taken over by wooden bowls filled with rice and stew. The apartment smelled like onions, garlic, and bay leaves, and hungry children began to creep towards the kitchen, peering their heads over countertops taller than they were.

Amis walked over to the window, studying the ocean view and the waves that whispered against the shores of Pilot Bay. He watched several groups of people pointing up at the sky, covering their eyes with their other hands, and after a moment, realized that the sun appeared much larger in the sky than he might have ever seen it before.

A flash in the window made Amis jump back, nearly tripping over his feet.

For a split second, gold and silver hair with flashes of starlight appeared, and an impossibly regal face was there to remind Amis of the goddess he had once met. Ayurveda was in the mortal realm, even if just for a moment. A chill ran through the muscles of the backs of his arms and traveled down his back. He tensed, immediately on high alert.

"Are you scared of the fire?" Salome's sweet voice asked, pulling his attention down to her as she stood up against the window, pressing her forehead against the glass.

"There are large caravans. The men with hoses will save us. You don't need to be afraid," she continued, her voice hushed, as if she were only talking to herself.

Amis bent down, putting his hands on his knees to reach Salome's level while peering into the scene before them. It wasn't easy to see with the bright daylight, but wisps of smoke were floating through the air closer to the shore.

As more children gathered around Amis and Salome, Noah pushed right through and took Amis' hand. Gemma, Noah's mother, had joined the group and stood directly behind Amis. He could feel her breath on his neck before her hand timidly touched his shoulder. Amis did everything he could to ease into her touch, not flinch away, to encourage a closeness that had never existed between him and the Waihema villagers.

"The dock," Gemma's words were gentle but urgent, "it's burning."

Amis moved his eyes up towards the water, the sand surrounded by lush glaucous foliage and Pōhutukawa trees that, when in bloom, would sprout bright red flowers with thin, sharp leaves. Just beyond lay a small dock, where Amis regularly spotted people with fishing poles over the past few days. Now, only onlookers were watching from a safe distance as flames consumed the wooden platform.

A red fire truck parked on the beach while seven or eight firefighters walked closer to the dock with thick, heavy hoses. Water poured from their metal spouts, and the fire hissed as puffy white smoke tangled with the dark wisps, rising high into the air.

"Let's get back to our meal, children," Gemma said as she pushed on a few children's backs, guiding them towards the counter where the food was served.

There was a disaster, nothing horrific, but Amis couldn't turn away as his magic, his need to bring balance, froze him. He was missing something but couldn't see or understand what it was. Noah tugged on his hand, and his muscles relaxed as he looked down at the smiley young face with teeth spread out from one another, reminding Amis of a cartoon whale.

Amis let Noah lead him away from the window, but after a few steps, he turned his head over his shoulder to look back and check on the fire, and he was glad that he did.

"Let go," Amis commanded as he walked right back to the window, his clammy palms squeaking against the glass as his jaw dropped and his eyes widened.

Despite the thirty or forty meters between the dock and street, the fire had swept up the sand and rocks, enveloping bushes and trees as the breeze carried the embers up to a campsite. They were faint behind the closed glass, but shrill screams haunted the scene as people ran out of their tents and camper trailers carrying children and bags.

Three more firetrucks frantically rushed in as fire enveloped a fifty-foot-tall tree and collapsed its branch, which fell on top of the common facilities building. Within minutes, the entire facility was a larger-than-life bonfire, a sacrifice of materials to whichever deity humans prayed to.

"You're scaring the children," Mother Waihema's voice grunted from the other side of the room.

Maybe they should be scared.

As more and more firefighters showed up, multiple buildings were caught aflame.

Three black helicopters dove over the flames, releasing water and powders as citizens ran and dove for cover. Amis didn't understand how the fire was spreading. He searched through every new flame and scared face as the fire came closer and closer to their building, but he stepped back, his heart no longer beating as he finally figured out what he was seeing.

"Everyone out," he bellowed to the apartment. "Everyone in this building needs to be evacuated. There's no time, take nothing."

No one moved at first. Many pairs of eyes, young and old, looked at Amis with a range of emotions, from horror to suspicion. Mother Waihema grunted before she walked out from behind the kitchen island and set down the wooden bowl from which she was eating.

"Do we disobey our Kinnari God now? You heard him, children, women, we go."

Everyone followed their safety net, their person, their familiar out the apartment door, filling the hallway as they proceeded to the stairs. Amis waited for the last to clear out while monitoring the window as building after building caught fire.

He watched a blue ember of a person walking freely. She was nearly indistinguishable from the fire as she hid behind the flames, and Amis might have missed her entirely if he had not been watching so closely.

Ayurveda was there, in this town, burning it to the ground.

Amis followed the group. The rumbling sound of the Waihema tribe stomping down the metal staircase echoed through the sterile, white space, which eventually opened up into a primary lobby where the screams outside could be heard more easily.

Mother Waihema stared out the glass doors, her withered fingers pressed against the door handle and the skin on her cheeks hanging down. The building right across from them had caught fire.

It had moved too fast. They might have been too late.

Amis pushed himself toward the front and turned around so the weight of his back pressed against the hot glass. His body opened the doors with force. The air was filled with ash, and the children began coughing immediately when it hit their lungs. A warmth that felt dirty and vile spread up and down Amis' skin, his brow dripping sweat as the fire only ten feet across the street grew and grew.

"Run away from the flames," Amis coughed, "and hold up your shirts over your noses."

Amis grabbed Mother Waihema's arm and guided her out of the building while the others followed without hesitation. Teen and young adult males picked up crying toddlers, while the mothers and older girls carried the young.

With his back to the flames, Amis felt the heat scorch his skin through his dress shirt, but continued guiding his family and children away. He had to make this stop. They moved too slowly. They would never make it if Ayurveda—

"Finally, I've found one of you," a woman's deep, monotone voice said behind him. Amis could feel it through his bones, the words of a Goddess filled with calm malice, and it hurt. It hurt in a new way that he was not used to, in a way of failure or regret. Amis slowly turned around to face Ayurveda, her body translucent and every moving part of the fire about to engulf the remaining tribespeople who were too far behind the group.

"No," Amis pleaded with her, tears pooling in his eyes. "Please, let them go."

"I have no interest in killing your half-breeds," she said, no movement in her stone-cold facial expressions. "The girl was taken from me, and I need her back. I will hunt all Kinnari down for her, starting here with you."

She's talking about Hadley.

"What do you want with her?" Amis's magic felt like it was about to split him apart down the middle, like a zipper on a jacket. There was too much power here. There was too much imbalance.

"My baby," a woman screamed in the background. Amis tried not to look, afraid it was one of his. He could hold her attention just long enough for the group to keep going, to get to a safer distance away from the flames, or at least not be trapped inside the lobby building trying to get out as it collapsed from the fire.

"There is no point in ruling this earth if no one is left on it alive," she said. "Hadley is the key to my patience. Without her, I might as well wipe it all clean. Let only pure things grow from the ash and cinders, things that will look up at me with appreciation, devotion."

"I don't know where she is." Amis looked down and gulped. "I only speak the truth."

Ayurveda's eyes flashed gold as she momentarily considered him before raising her hands and smiling.

It was like a bomb; pure power and energy pulsed out of her in the form of an inferno. The conflagration threw Amis back, hitting solid mass and glass while a scorching pain wrapped around his body until he could feel no more. His skin was gone, his eyelids were gone, and he was forced to stare in horror at the sun while her smile brought hell down and incinerated all its path.

Amis was completely immobile, but the raging pain that absorbed him as his nerves and scorched muscles began to heal made him wish that his body would stop regenerating. He tried to push the burning and snapping away, he tried to see how far the explosion had traveled, to calculate if there was a chance of his villagers getting away and finding safety.

There was nothing. Nothing but ash and rubble from where he stood to the beach, to the lazily lapping tide brushing against the shore. He heard no cries, no screams, no sobs. He heard only the breeze and the wheezing from his lungs as they healed, as they took in the white ash that rained heavily down on him. That he wasn't dead, that he wasn't awakening as his childhood self, was unbelievable to him.

"I believe you have a realm to balance," Ayurveda's words were clipped as she nodded to him once before she disappeared in the breeze, letting herself rise in the form of smoke up transforming into her celestial form, toward the orange sun that beat down violently from above.

Amis rejoiced as the ability to close his eyes came back to him. Newly grown skin blocked out the light, the destruction, and the heartache. He sat there, waiting to heal and move, and unleashed the tension, the discord that pulsed in his head and chest to make it right and bring magic into balance.

In another world, in another realm, a fire started. Amis prayed that there was no city where he stood on this land so that no one else burned to the ground, for he knew that what happened to the land in the Earth realm also happened in Myrilosis.

19

Reign | Myrilosis

Reign was gliding; the cool air, holding promises of snow and ice, slapped her face like a tough massage as she let her wings carry her through the sky.

Her body tired so easily now from long distances, so Arryn followed behind her. She could feel his version of road rage building from their increase in speed and it made her smile. His annoyance at trying to care for her was exactly who he had always been.

They were surrounded by endless snow, the height of the white mountains staggering. The visual evidence of avalanches was brought to her attention by clean cliffs where snow was soft and vegetation became nonexistent in areas otherwise surrounded by hearty trees and shrubs that had the will to live.

There was still a romantic side, flying without the limitations the Kinnari placed on themselves in the Earth realm. She wasn't compelled to fly above the clouds, as there was no worry about being spotted. Arryn and the Life Gifter had created this realm for magical creatures that would have been in great danger from the masses of developing mortals.

Despite that, those creatures of magic hated Arryn, and many wished for his demise. That, at least, was what Arryn had always told her, and she had no reason not to believe him.

Reign knew that the rest of the Kinnari must also have been included in that hate. She had been raised to believe that setting foot in this world would bring only pain, only violence. Now that they were there, flying freely in sight, she felt like thousands of eyes hidden from her were staring, watching, waiting for her feet to touch ground.

Reign's eyes flagged a glimmer sixty kilometers ahead.

There was something there nestled in the valley before them. It wasn't eyes, and her paranoia faded. She increased her speed, actually pumping her wings as her muscles protested, comfortable in the stillness. Arryn caught up, flying by her side and looking less irritated, thanks to this new pace. His eyes were determined, and he seemed to understand where she was going. He saw it, too.

With so much beauty cascading out in front of her, growing larger with every foot flown, it was hard not to be reminded of how small and defenseless she was. She could not fight an army. She could command groups here and there with enough direct eye contact, but to truly fight while in the body of a child was something she had a hard time accepting, being useless, being weak.

If they were met with malice, she would be of little use.

Her mind drifted to the dagger Arryn had made her, clinging to her, strapped to most of her left calf. Reign was grateful that there was something for her to hold on to, something for her to throw into someone's chest.

The two Kinnari gazed at what lay before them as they continued to fly toward it, the beauty and light existing where Reign was promised violence and death.

She replayed her death over and over again in her mind. The day that she was torn limb from limb, Vrae teeth pulling her muscles apart, had begun to haunt her, to follow her, and cast something foreign to her.

Doubt.

Buildings of ice and snow caught the daylight in a mesmerizing dance of prismatic hues. Each edifice bore intricate frost patterns that seemed to whisper ancient tales, ones of history that they were never invited or allowed to be a part of.

We are intruding.

Arryn must have noticed the shift in her, the forced gulp of air that she took only to keep up the illusion that she wasn't completely losing her shit as she continued to move right toward it, structures and buildings becoming more and more visible.

Reign landed, her feet sinking through powdered snow as she cursed the moisture seeping into her pants. She would never get used to it, the undeniable misery and unforgiving nature of the environment that raised her, that had raised them all. She had settled quite easily into hating it, into finding an environment that was more even-tempered, not minding hot summer days one bit.

"You're so small that you're going to get eaten up by this snow," Arryn teased as she fought her way forward with snow rising as high as her hips.

"We should tuck in," she said, referring to their wings. "For all we know, there is a wanted poster with your photograph hung in the town square. The wings could be a giveaway."

Arryn nodded, his cheeks purple from the cold as his wings disappeared underneath his skin. Reign followed her own suggestion and continued to push against the snow, trekking for another thirty minutes while trying her best to ignore Arryn's effortless stroll while walking intentionally a step or two behind her.

I'm not a child.

But she was.

The town now stood before them, the snow thinning out and cleared to create a path filled with slush, water and ice. Reign looked up, a flickering catching her eye. Smiling, she took in the life fluttering above them, a type of ladybug that was the size of a puppy, glowing while the colors on its wings switched from red to orange to yellow.

The path eventually shifted to cobblestones, giving Reign's toes relief from plunging into more moisture. More glowing creatures appeared as if lighting their way, their wings humming from the speed against the cold air.

"I remember these," Reign said, pointing up at them. "You made a few of them when we were children when you thought you needed to illuminate the mountains and hills during the dark winters. I thought Djoser had ripped them apart, but you sent them here and they got very busy breeding. What was it that you called them?"

"Lumes." Arryn cracked a smile. "We were kids; of course, it has to sound awful."

"They're way better than those weird-shelled spiders you created. Those things were pure evil. I can't believe you let them roam the Earth realm."

"I think the humans named them Horseshoe Crabs. Awful name for my first spider. I had to retaliate somehow."

Reign let out a hearty laugh, so youthful and high pitched that four or five lumes took to her, flying in an intricate weaving pattern around her, through her legs and circling them both.

"This is what I miss," she said faintly to Arryn. "This creativity, this kind of unbound energy that showed how possible anything and everything was. We had so much fun. We were all so close, a real family, perhaps."

"I miss those days, too," Arryn said as they approached more life, more evolutions of all of their childhood imaginations. This was a place created to hoard wonder and hope, a place that they had been forbidden to travel and explore.

The path walked them into a town square. Cottages and shops made a circle around them adorned with tan and red bricks, the only warm colors that Reign could see. Icicles as large as she was hung from dramatically sloped roofs, and small piles of snow were neatly arranged through the open square while citizens moved about their daily lives.

Standing at fifteen feet tall were dainty giants, women with Victorian hairstyles piled high on top of their heads, wearing dress shirts and large skirts with intricate floral patterns that made it seem as if they floated across the snow in a bed of purple and dark red roses.

Their skin colors varied, just as the Kinnaris' did. However, much like giraffes in the mortal realm, rectangular-like shapes of different pigments decorated their hands, faces, and any other visible skin.

Reign couldn't take her eyes off them. They were regal and ethereal, with a feminine energy that she hadn't seen before. She took a few steps, turned her head away for just a moment, and let out a faint scream as she unexpectedly made eye contact with lifeless, frozen eyes behind a wall of ice.

She took a few hurried steps back as her brain caught up to her eyes, and her heart dropped faster than the temperature outside.

Large blocks of ice lined the far west side of the square, and each one held a body.

Some were men, some were women, some were children, but all were utterly and completely frozen, as if they had sat in a large ice cube tray.

"Are they . . . what is . . . why?" she gasped, looking closer to the first pair of open eyes she stumbled upon. At first glance, he looked like just a teenage boy with long wisps of dark hair and a scrawny build, but there was something about his expression. His eyes were so alive, as if he were processing everything that he could see. Not all of the frozen bodies had their eyes open, but the ones that did gave Reign the stark impression that she should be wary of them, afraid, even.

"We don't see out-of-towners too often here," a peppy voice came from behind. Reign turned to see one taller being staring at her from ten feet away. She bent down in a graceful swoop as her skirt of roses billowed around her. The creature put a lovely manicured hand against her own chin, her eyes so blue that they blended in with the snow kissed by dusk.

"These harmless things are called Glaciels," the gentle giant said. "The big city south of here, Ebonspire, didn't know what to do with them so they moved into the mountains and started this town. That's why it's named after their kind. Welcome to Glacier."

"So they are alive?" Reign asked, turning back to look into those frozen, open eyes.

"Oh yes, quite." She giggled in response. "The daytime is too warm for them to survive, so they sleep, a short hibernation until the temperature drops."

"An ice coffin?" Arryn said, his brow furrowed.

"What was that?" the giant woman asked.

"Nothing, never mind. How do they get out?" Arryn's face got so close to an ice block that his nose nearly touched it.

"Oh, you'll see in a few minutes." The woman said. "You are in for a treat; it's spectacular."

She wasn't wrong. Moments later, Reign held her breath as the eyes that once stared at her immobilized blinked back, still entirely frozen in ice. With no shifting, melting, or cracking, the glaciel's shoulders wiggled, and its fingers flexed.

"They're waking up. I've heard rumors of some of them getting caught in the Earth realm, can you believe that? Stuck in an eternal loop, never able to find their way home," the giantess said, daintily clapping her fingertips in excitement.

Reign jumped back into Arryn's arms while they watched the glaciel emerge from the ice, leaving the blocks seemingly untouched. They floated up out of the tops of the blocks as the sun began to set and the temperature dropped so low it seemed impossible to survive in.

She followed them rising, her chin raising as they did like balloons filled with helium, their bodies fluid as if they were only made from air. They kept the same color, the frozen blue sheen they'd had while encapsulated in the ice block, as hundreds of them rose into the sky like lanterns.

"Are they ghosts?" Reign asked, slightly in awe as the sky

blackened and stars came out too, the figures now barely visible in the sky.

"Spirits of some sort, yes." The woman nodded. "They don't communicate, or are at least nonverbal. Not much is known about them. Our town's treasure, but our mystery as well."

The woman stood, towering over Reign and Arryn, her smile beautiful, radiating with a glamoring sort of magic. Reign shivered, hypothermia setting into her body. But nevertheless, she felt at ease looking at the woman's face, the beautiful tan patterns against even darker skin.

"There is a pub and inn just over there. The creatures that need warmth to survive will gather there as they tend a fire for anyone with a coin." The woman pointed to the building beyond her, one of the few with lights and life visible from the windows. The rest of the town seemed to be strolling outside, casting curious looks in their direction.

"Thank you. What is your name?" Arryn asked, rubbing his hands over Reign's arms and gently pushing her toward the inn.

"I am Cera." She smiled, "I am what is known as an Articiren. We are peaceful creatures. May I ask your name, little ones? What magic are you made of?"

"We are Kinnari," Arryn said, his voice already defensive.

Cera stiffened, the joyous expression on her face lessening just a bit.

Why the hell would you just say that? We could be anything!

"Well, it's an honor to know that there are gods among us." She bowed her head, the amber hair stacked high on her head bobbing.

"We are no gods," Reign stammered, unsure if she should feel awkward or ready for backlash. There were unspoken words that hung around Cera, her eyes razor-sharp as she began to back away. Reign looked for her feet and could not see them. Her skirt seemed full of air, pushing her where she wanted to go.

"Let's get you inside. Your skin is turning every decaying color that I can think of," Arryn said, hand on her back as he turned her to the inn. They walked through the center of the town square, lumes creating a symphony of buzzing overhead as they brought a glowing soft light to a town otherwise encompassed in night.

Reign didn't quite understand all the stares from passersby that they collected. Other than their clothing, she didn't feel that they completely stood out, as plenty of citizens had entirely mortal features. Reign assumed that it was just an appearance that they were far from ordinary. So far, nothing in this town was like anything she could have imagined; only remnants reminded her of the life that Arryn had created in adolescence.

Reign stepped onto the patio that had barely been cleared of snow, but was covered in a sheet of ice. Her boots slipped immediately, and her feet were parallel with her head. Arryn's arms wrapped around her back and chest, setting her upright with her feet back on the ice. She reached her hand out to grab the side of the pillar holding up the balcony above them as the two inched along and made it successfully to the carved wooden door.

Reign pulled the door open and was immediately greeted with live music and laughter and chatter. The primary furniture throughout the open room were small square tables tall enough for adults to stand at. In a corner stood a three-piece band with fiddles and flutes, their human-like lips and hands using their instruments like they were part of their bodies, their goatlike hooves dancing on dull wooden floors while a fire raged in the opposite corner.

Cold drifted in from the open door, and though Arryn walked in behind her and pulled it shut quickly, it still caused the customers at the tables to look over their shoulders toward whoever was letting the heat out.

The heat. Reign reveled in it. Even being in the room, still so far from the fire, made the joints in her hands ache as she defrosted. It was a pain that she needed, yearned for. Her body had acclimated to the hotter climates that she spent the later years of her life in.

"You're going to have a hard time getting me out of here," she muttered to Arryn as she studied her fingernails, purple and blackening.

"It's tolerable in the middle of the day," a loud barmaid wearing a long fleece dress and fur-lined boots said as she bounced towards them, her large bosom bouncing and her cheeks rosy.

"It's sit yourself, but you caught us on a full day, it looks like," she indicated to the room. "If you head through that hallway over there, it'll lead you to the inn's check-in desk. There are some comfy couches with end tables to enjoy a pint and a meal."

She tossed her braided-back black hair over her shoulders and headed over to a table to pick up some empty mugs before crossing back over to the room.

"Go on and head back. I'll bring you both a plate of the special," she yelled at them as she rounded the opposite corner into the kitchen.

The two walked past the tables, and Reign stared at the fire longingly, sad she was leaving the room, leaving the warmth behind. They moved through the short hallway, dark green fabric wallpaper lining the sides as it opened into a cozy room with a door on the opposite side. A creature sat behind a desk, pale and white as if kissed by snow. He was reading something on his desk and lowered the glasses down his nose to stare at them as they approached.

"You're here for a room?" he grunted. His rough voice betrayed his age, unlike his face, which was void of lines or expression.

"Leave 'em alone, Balizar," the barmaid said, stomping in balance with two plates in one hand and two mugs in the other. She sat them down on a simple, grainy coffee table between a vintage-looking pink couch and its matching loveseat.

"Don't spill on the furnitcha, tha ol' man ova there will kill ya." She winked. "We've got a plate of whomlymamoth stew ova some mashed roots. A pint of ale for the grown man and a hot cuppa tea for the little lady." She winked at Reign.

"I'm not a child," Reign said, moving towards the food, her stomach growling as her body did all it could to combat the cold.

"Yeah, yeah. I know in some parts of the world the drinkin' age is lower, but here ya got at least be ten, and you look a bit younger than that, love."

With that, the barmaid turned away and left the room.

"If ya want to eat here, that be four silvers for a room," Balizar's disdain filled the now quiet room.

"What's your currency look like?" Arryn sighed and moved towards the desk. "I've got a pocket filled with different money from traveling through the cities," he lied.

Reign ignored the tea and grabbed the mug of ale, gulping the sour, bitter liquid before anyone noticed. Her body warmed and buzzed instantly. It was strong stuff.

"Aye, you don't 'ave any money. I can't take any of these fake coins in ya hand. Our coin is made outta scandium metals, kind of a dirty lookin' color once it's worn. It'll have a number on the front, and none of these coins with pictures are nonsense."

Reign watched as Balizar pulled a few coins out of his pockets and showed them to Arryn as he ranted on about trying to get past him with his "fake money".

"Hang on, hang on, I've got some of those in my back pocket," Reign heard Arryn say and watched as he put his right hand behind his back and closed a fist over multiple coins that seemed to appear out of thin air.

"Fine," Balizar grunted and took the coins from Arryn as he held them out to him. "Here is your key. We have strict rules about not covering your room in ice or snow. I don't know what the hell ya are, but I could see you 'causin trouble for me."

Reign turned her face away to hide her laugh and decided that grumpy old Balizar must be her kindred spirit. She liked him a lot.

Arryn walked over to sit with her, flashing two skeleton keys at her before throwing them down on the coffee table. He grabbed his plate of food and handed Reign hers as the barmaid returned.

"Oye there, you got that pint down fast. I'll fetch ya anotha," she said, turning right back around.

"One for me, too," Reign yelled, the barmaid already out of sight. "I'm old enough to be your great great great great great great, many more greats, grandmother!"

"I think it's pretty obvious what's happened to my ale after that comment," Arryn chuckled, taking a bite of whomlymamoth stew while pushing the contents of the bowl around, frowning.

"Everything in this stew has been pickled."

"Arryn," Reign said, not touching her briney plate of food. "What now? What are we doing here, really?"

Arryn looked at his empty pint glass and sighed, letting his head and shoulders fall forward.

"I want to find out how Allienna got pregnant."

"There it is." Reign rolled her eyes.

"There had to be magic involved. Someone in this realm should know something."

Reign let the silence fall between them as they both picked at their meal, ignoring the occasional too-loud grunts from Balizar. She knew, of course, how it all had happened. That visit from Allienna where she showed Reign her suddenly red, mortal blood.

Red, like Reign's blood was now.

To Reign's dismay, the barmaid returned with only a single ale and made sure it went directly into Arryn's hand. He made a show of gulping it down, directing a loud, satisfied smack of his lips toward her. She wanted to slap him across the face, feeling again trapped in this body. Being youthful and innocent wasn't something she knew how to do.

Reign's eyes darted over to Balizar, who was loudly crinkling a newspaper and muttering to himself.

"Well, I am curious to explore this realm. It's always been off limits,"

"And it still is," Arryn said firmly. "We will find trouble here."

"Oh, good. Our lives have been so devoid of it," she chuckled, standing up and reaching for a key labeled with the number four etched into the metal. "I'm ready for a hot bath and a bed. I'll see you in the morning."

Reign walked past the desk, seeing rather rickety stairs on the far side of the room. She dragged her feet up the first two steps, the wood creaking under her light frame. Her hand slid up the rail, which felt like she could push over with a decent effort. She watched Arryn grimace as he forced another bite of the stew into his mouth.

"Fuckin' gods," Balizar yelled, slamming his newspaper down on his desk, making Arryn choke on his food. Reign nearly fell over the rail as she jumped at the sudden noise.

"Someone burned down tha entire fuckin' island down south," Balizar spat. "Not a lot of intelligent magic in those parts, but still, it's all in ashes. Who could be so irresponsible?"

"What island?" Reign asked, her heartbeat recovering.

"Ah, it's the smaller piece of land west of the bigger one, technically two islands I think. Kiwiva, they call it now."

Reign stood there awkwardly. She didn't know how to respond.

"Don't ya worry your lit' brains about it," Balizar said, picking the paper back up and burying his head back in it. A photo of an area that vaguely reminded Reign of Waihema, lush trees on ocean shores, was printed on the front page. It was side by side with another image, an after photo, of the same space devoid of life, only cinders behind.

"You could actually do our world some good, for once," Balizar added as Reign began to turn and continue up the stairs.

"What do you mean?" she asked as she found Arryn's eyes, his fist tight, tense against the fork he held.

"Ah, I tol' ya not to worry now didn't, I?" he said, pulling the glasses down, presenting his purple irises. "I know who ya both are. Another one of your lot comes here when he's not hiding in my dreams as I sleep. He looks like a child like this one." Balizar pointed to Reign.

Tristan.

"And you don't hate us? This shouldn't threaten us?" Arryn's voice commanded the room. Balizar blinked at him and smiled.

"You should be threatened, all right, but not by the likes of me. I know what you can do. If you can take care of this realm, even for just an instant, you could go to these islands and help repair the damage that has been done. Aye, you created me before tossing me through that stone door; I'm sure you can make a few gardens fertile for crops."

Arryn stood, looking down with a bit of food smeared on his chin.

"We can help, can't we, Arryn? We can leave in the morning," Reign interjected.

Balizar only glanced at her for a moment before returning to his paper as if there was no more that needed to be said. Reign glanced at Arryn, who seemed furious, his eyes shooting daggers back at her. She liked the thought of an island, warmth, and sunshine.

"Anything to get out of this snow, am I right?" She laughed and stomped up the stairs, looking for her room.

20

Amis | Northern New Zealand

Groans erupted from Amis's mouth; the sounds followed the flow of air that tried to escape his collapsed lungs.

I need to move.

But moving seemed impossible.

His skin was still healing after the devastation that played out before him. He had to push through the pain, reminding himself how temporary the searing was, reminding himself that if he were not Kinnari, he would certainly be dead.

Dead.

So many around him were dead, burned alive, their screams muffled as their bodies were incinerated.

Amis tried to take a step, his muscles hanging off the bone with skin still smoking, still singed, not yet rebuilt. He fell, his body giving out, landing on his hands and knees, and a silent moan escaped his lips, floating to the Gods where he was left ignored. There was still no skin on the palms of his hands or his shins. The contact with the ground below was a brutal reminder of how severe his injuries were.

He didn't know where to go or look, but that didn't stop Amis from fighting every survival instinct he had to find them. All those children, the mothers, and the few males accompanying them had to have survived. They had some magic. He prayed, he wished so hard that they'd had enough time to run, to get away from the flames of a furious goddess.

If they hadn't escaped the flames, if they all had joined the mortals in the buildings surrounding the bay, then Amis knew that the blame was entirely on him again. He had moved them, all of Waihema, from an area with such little population to a place filled with other families.

But Amis hadn't known that he had a target on his back. He would have isolated himself in the Kinnari temple for eternity had it meant protecting the people who had already gone through so much. It seemed not possible for him to love and care for others. There was something about him that ensured that misery would follow, surrounding the very target he wished happiness for.

His heart dropped in his chest, the mental turmoil outweighing the physical as he looked around, taking in the nightmare laid out before him.

This is what Sheng was trying to stop, trying to protect us from.

He'd expect to see this if hell was a real place, like the mortals' depictions in art during the Renaissance period. Maybe he did die, and this was his purgatory. To live forever on an island, now devoid of life, covered in black to replay the murder and assault that he had put that entire village through for generations. No, he knew he hadn't. That would have been lucky. Facing himself, who he was and what he had done, was a far worse punishment than a fictional fiery hellscape.

He couldn't take back the events he had personally set in motion, but there was a piece of him that whispered to him late at night, caressed him, and played with his hair, telling him it was still right and asking him how much worse it would have been if he hadn't made those decisions.

Amis pictured Sheng again in his mind, his own skin thickening enough to make him a little less useless while searching. Sheng came from a creator who told him he was only suitable for death, for pain and revenge, but then, when confronted with a young girl, a child, he'd learned to skip rocks on top of the water. He'd learned to laugh and make silly facial expressions. Amis had watched Sheng love that child, Emere, possibly the first person he had ever loved. That girl's death brought humanity to the demon and solidified Sheng as an ally. He couldn't bear to dwell on the deaths of these villagers.

They have to be out there.

"Salome," Amis yelled out to the wasteland before him, listening for anything, any sound different from his wheezing, his panting, and his desperation. His head was still woozy, the thumping pounding in his eardrums. A brain injury from the blast, no doubt. His brain seemed slow to heal. He sped up his pace, imagining life holding onto them slipping away. He could be running out of time.

There was a build-up inside him; something was off balance, but he couldn't remember what it was or why it was there. He brushed it off at first, choosing to ignore it and blame it on his protesting body as he limped with haste, with a panic that would not lift. He couldn't remember what would happen if he released it and fixed that energy. He shouldn't let it out until he knew what it would cause and the cost. It lingered; it haunted him, but there was no time to focus on himself.

"Luca," Amis shouted again, returning to his feet, feeling stronger by the minute. He walked by buildings, cement foundations blackened and toppled, scattered, broken bricks that were now gray with ash. If it were not for the ocean behind him, Amis would have sworn that he had lost his sense of color altogether.

"Mother . . . Waihema," he shouted, his hands resting on his upper thighs as he hunched over, smoke still heavy over the area being recycled through his own lungs.

There was still nothing, no one.

Amis swallowed hard, his eyes down at his feet while keeping his chin high, doing his best not to fall apart. He had failed them. He had failed them all miserably.

Self-loathing is only for Arryn. Save it.

He tried to push the emotions back down his throat, pushing his feet forward, walking further into the northern island, his steps shuffling, defeated.

"Noah, Gemma," he yelled meekly, his syllables broken as a sob erupted from his lips. He clasped his hands over his mouth, his eyes wide with surprise. He had never cried quite like this before. He let out another and then another.

Amis came down to his knees, his howls of suffering carried off into the breeze, along with more ashes still raining down from the sky. He felt like he could fall asleep, clinging and welcoming the darkness between every breath and between sobs.

There was no logic to the immense sadness that swept over him. There was no balance, no pulling himself together. He let loose entirely, feeling every morsel of doubt and dread that had haunted him since childhood. There were so many fears and so much remorse; it was a hole he feared he might never dig his way out of. It was a hole that might not want to escape. Someone needed to deal with the consequences.

His body lurched as if he'd been tackled from the front, flying back a few inches as the dirt and debris flew up around him. Something invisible, something he couldn't see, slammed into his backside. Amis was thrown face down onto the ground. He didn't move despite the loose nails and metal rods licked clean by the fire underneath him. He couldn't feel them. He couldn't tell that his blood fertilized the starved earth beneath him.

What he could feel was that the crippling panic was gone. His body thrashed around as the balance within him, his magic could no longer be contained; he was consumed by sorrow.

"No, no, no," he cried out. "Where did it go," he yelled, though hardly any sound escaped his rough, cracked throat.

Where did it go? Who was now suffering? Who was now dead?

He couldn't remember. He couldn't remember what the imbalance was. His head throbbed, and he choked on a half sob.

Something big, something bigger than this destruction, had escaped from him. If it had to flee, had to fight his very will, Amis couldn't even begin to imagine what he unwillingly had done. His balance was out there, untethered, likely doing its worst. There were a lot of firsts on this day.

"Here," a faint voice reached Amis' ears. He didn't react at first, no longer processing what was around him, his senses shutting down. He needed rest, gods, he was so damn tired.

"Help, I'm here," the voice sounded again. Amis's chin turned this time, and his breathing stopped, not making any noise, trying to figure out where that voice had come from. He wasn't a hunter, and he had no skills or instincts for tracking. He needed Djoser for that. That voice was just so far away. Yet it called him, again and again, and Amis moved, forcing his feet to go anywhere, turning in a new direction, stepping on melded metal car roofs overturned and dislodged on what he suspected was a road when the voice sounded weaker, further.

"Where are you?" he called back, lost in endless rubble. "I can help. I'm here to help." His throat bobbed.

You are no hero.

Instead of more cries for help, Amis only heard screams. Young screams, children's screams. They were muffled, buried deep underneath something.

Trapped. There are children who are trapped.

Amis moved quicker, the continuous screaming guiding him better than the occasional cry out for help. Once he was sure he was standing on top of them, moving back and forth over the same spot a few times, he began to dig.

He grabbed something big, something heavy, his fingernails slowly peeling off as he pulled back with all his body weight, hands clinging and gripping into what seemed like a metal beam. It budged just an inch, but the screaming instantly grew louder.

They were under there, buried beneath hot, scalding metal that had crumbled in the blast, the explosion of fire.

His stomach dropped, not knowing how anyone could have survived. If he moved the beam more, would wounds be opened, forcing them to bleed out? Would it peel burned skin off with its movement?

"It hurts, it hurts, help, it hurts."

He knew that voice. He knew that child.

"Salome." Amis could barely get the name out; his eyes flooded with tears.

She was alive, oh gods, she had survived.

He choked out another cry, grabbing the beam, uncovering more ash, revealing hot shiny metal as he pulled back. His muscles nearly gave out, his spine cracking as he refused to stop despite the burning in his legs, shoulders, and arms.

"Amis," Salome's voice cried. She heard him. She recognized him.

Amis yelled out from the force, refusing to let her stay down there.

"Amis, it hurts," Salome's voice continued to cry.

The beam gave way. Amis watched as it toppled and flipped over itself, revealing the four meters of horror that awaited him underneath. Surrounded by a blown-out room, collapsed walls supported pipes that actively gushed water and sewage into the opening below him—a hole that held bodies, so many bodies.

Huddled in a circle, as if protecting each other, were the villagers of Waihema. The bodies on the outside were completely burned, bones exposed where flesh once had covered, and skulls crushed into the bodies in front of them from where the beam had fallen. They had made a cocoon of sorts, sacrificing themselves to protect those in the middle, who were buried under them, to give them a chance of survival. It had worked, barely.

Within that pile of bodies was Salome. Amis could hear her screams, but now he could hear others, too. He inhaled, gasping from the hope, pleading that the Life Gifter was watching, helping, giving strength. He had never prayed before, never worshiped his creator.

Another first, but he would beg over and over if it meant that those children were okay.

He cared. He cared so much that the ache tore through his chest, salty tears flowing down his cheeks, making paths through the ash that blanketed Amis's skin.

"I'm here," Amis managed to get out, holding back the vomit that climbed up his throat from the smell that erupted as he pushed the burnt flesh away from the pile. He knew those faces. He couldn't bear to look at them. These mothers and men had believed in their cause in their village, dedicating and sacrificing their children to more brutality. Make more wings to fight the monsters, and discard anyone with the blood of true red. Magicless blood, worthless blood.

Amis stopped, and the screams and the cries grew louder. He was nearly there, but there was one face he couldn't avoid looking at. One face stared at him through lifeless, wide-open eyes; her face twisted as her body held onto a child who hadn't been buried deep enough in a pile.

Mother Waihema.

Generations of elders who had served this village, and here was how the last of them had ended. Protecting, watching, as she had always done.

"I'm sorry," Amis whispered to her. "I'm so sorry."

Amis raised his hand and put it on the elder's face, closing her eyes. He placed his hands underneath her shoulders and gently moved her to the side. The child still clung tightly in her arms. He knew that child, too. That little boy had been running around the living room, playing with Noah just hours before this chaos. He would play, he would run, no more.

"It hurts," Salome cried again, squinting as the light hit her face. A handful of others gasped, the ash-filled air hitting their lungs, but still, it was air. They all choked, and Amis smiled as he watched them breathe. They were breathing. Among the hopelessness that surrounded him, Amis smiled as he saw life. He saw survival. He saw helplessness outlive a brutal attack, an attack by a goddess that could not be outrun.

"Help Noah," Salome cried as she squirmed her body, heedless of the bruises and burns on her skin, to push the two-year-old forward. Others cried out too, yelling as they were elbowed, their faces stepped on as the toddler whimpered. His eyes were wide, helpless as Amis reached out to grab him, his hands touching wetness as they closed around Noah's middle and pulled him free of the pile.

Amis smiled; he couldn't believe who he was holding. He thanked every star in the universe, every power that might be, for giving these children a destiny, a fate not covered in blood.

Noah started coughing and wailing, his body shaking in Amis's arms as he sobbed, thrashing and reaching his arms over his back. Amis's smile disappeared as he saw for the first time what that wetness was. It was blood, blue blood. Noah continued to thrash, continued to cry, and just seconds later, something sharp poked Amis's forearm as he held the toddler.

Wings. The toddler has Kinnari wings.

Small, delicate, brown, layered wings that matched the light in Noah's eyes hung limp and heavy from the body that carried them. Amis had never seen wings on a child before, the average age for them being right around nineteen or twenty. He was stunned.

"Help us," Salome's voice registered, unfreezing his movement as he awkwardly set the wailing, winged Noah down. The toddler immediately collapsed, leaning against the bodies and continued to cry as Amis reached back towards the trapped children and grabbed an arm to pull.

Amis got two more children out, who did not bear the Kinnari mark on their shoulders, and they collapsed as Noah had, cuddling him as they blocked out the horrors of their surroundings. Next was Luca, who got stuck getting through the hole, not knowing how to move with the wings that were now hanging from his back, too.

Luca was shaking but stood tall, staring at Amis, his fingers switching from flexing to clenching.

"It's only Salome that's left," he whispered. "No one else is moving."

Amis nodded, turning back to the pile and reaching his arms through, grabbing the young girl.

"I've got you," he said to her, and he meant it. He pulled, watching the seven-year-old emerge, her face heated and wincing as her own deep brown wings followed. Amis, at first, could only assume that this was the energy, this was what that explosion of magic had jetted out of him to fix. But as he looked upon Salome's face he was consumed in doubt.

"It . . . it started to hurt. I could barely walk." Salome's eyes looked away. "I couldn't keep running, I couldn't keep walking. I slowed the group down, and no one understood what I was saying; they just picked me up and kept going."

"Salome, no, no, no. Do not feel guilty." Amis fell to his knees to get on her level. "You cannot ever feel guilty for this."

"I slowed us down." The girl let out a sob. "It wasn't all day like in the village stories, they came in so fast. My blood was everywhere, it was thick and blue. The grown-ups stopped running; they looked at me like I was, wrong, broken. And then they all ran toward me, scooped up the others, and jumped on top of us. I listened to the explosion, felt the heat, felt the bodies on top of us get heavier. Then the others, their wings came, too."

Her wings came in before the explosion, before Ayurveda had even left them. It wasn't his magic; that was still loose somewhere, correcting a different imbalance.

Amis looked around, feeling slightly lost, before hugging Salome.

"It's not your fault," he assured her again.

"Then whose?" she demanded, choking through a sob.

He didn't know who to blame. Ayurveda was obviously the enemy, the one to fear, but a pull in his heart told him that he himself was still the problem. He had created these lives and put them at constant risk, raising them as cattle.

He thought back to Sheng, too, who maybe shouldn't have saved him during their first encounter. If Amis had endured that death, things could have been different. There would be a full war against the Vrae; maybe then, no goddess would need to attack.

"There are too many variables, but I can promise you again that you are not one of them, Salome. We have a long journey on foot," Amis said, standing up. "We will go back to Waihema, back to that forest."

Amis picked up Noah, his eyes fighting sleep, and cradled him in his arms as the others trudged beside him, holding hands, their chins down. He was going to take them through the portal, into Myrilosis, and hope that he could find them all some help.

21

Hadley | Bangladesh

It had been nearly a month since Hadley learned that she could not drown. She could only suffocate and endure the harshness in her lungs, praying for her vision to blacken. With each step, with each meek smile thrown towards Reifoel, Hadley focused on her shadow self, who was slithering around while trying to avoid physical contact in the crowded city where they had washed up on the beach.

I will not lose you again.

There were so many people around her, walking and talking on cell phones, yelling at cabs on the street as they drank their iced coffees. It felt surreal to be among normal people again. She expected to love it, to find a path of her own and separate from Reifoel and Isadore, but instead, she stayed close to her shadow self, keeping her anxiety in check.

They were in front of a bus station in Bangladesh, watching from a safe distance as Isadore argued with the ticketing clerk until they closed their window in frustration.

"I guess the conversation didn't go well," she said, Reifoel sitting by her side, his skin cracking in the heat. They had just been in the water earlier this morning, but she noticed that his longevity was weakening over time, especially if they were not rinsing off in salt water.

The two were leaning against a stone bench, both wearing tattered clothing that they would find thrown by dumpsters or unattended lost and founds as they slithered through hotel lobbies. Hadley did not doubt that even if Isadore wasn't argumentative, the ticketing clerk likely didn't want to help them simply from how dirty and tired he looked.

Dirtbag tourists.

The past few weeks had been filled with achy feet, and she sat on sandy beaches in the dark as she waited for Reifoel and Isadore to rinse off on the shore. Now, they were further inland, having come up with some semblance of a plan, one that was better than looking for money dropped on the beach by travelers.

Hadley wasn't quite sure what she was doing there with them, but she liked their dynamic, and so, despite the constant small voice that filled her head and her body urging her to find her own path, she stayed.

Isadore was so stern and protective, with some oddly suave moments that were hilarious yet out of place. For the most part, Isadore almost completely ignored Hadley, but there were small moments of kindness, like a cheesy grin, as he proudly held out food he had sourced for them all, giving her a share.

Her relationship with Reifoel was quite different. He joked with her and grinned at her constantly. It felt at times that he looked for her approval, her friendship. He was so easy, so casually charming that if she were not trying to figure out how to get back to her goddess, the sun, Hadley might consider letting herself get lost in it all, the normalcy of having friends.

Are we friends?

It was hard, so hard, to give them such a label.

Hadley preferred to continue thinking that they were all stuck together. They were making the best of it despite that small voice endlessly urging her away, telling herself she was getting distracted.

"Are you hungry? I'm hungry." Reifoel looked at her, their faces two feet apart when she turned her head toward him. Her eyes fell, and she gazed at his hand resting on the bench, her cheeks slightly flushed.

She liked looking at his teeth; they were a dazzling white, perfectly square, and safe without any hints of daggers or fangs. She knew he'd caught her staring at them, and since then, he seemed to smile with them fully displayed a bit more than necessary.

"You're always hungry." She shrugged, flipping her hair over her shoulder.

"Food on land is just surprisingly better. You have heat. Even seaweed, all dried up, tastes better. However, whenever I was sad, my mother would make dumplings filled with seaweed. She would sift the sand until it was smooth and colorful, like polished coral. It always cheered me up. I wish I had some now if I'm being honest."

"Your mother? You have a family?"

"I do. Isadore is my cousin. My mother and father are the king and queen of our little kingdom."

"I'm not sure the words little and kingdom go together," she said. "I knew you were sent here by your king and queen, but I didn't know that I was traveling with royalty."

Now it was his turn to blush. His face didn't turn pink as hers did, but she could see his weight shift back, his shoulders sink forward, and his dimples rise to the surface as he pursed his lips.

"I never cared for a title," he admitted.

"I think that's probably seen as a cliche in our world."

Hadley watched his fingers spread out, inching closer towards her on the bench. The sound of a throat clearing came from Hadley's right side. She turned over her shoulder to see Isadore standing with his chest puffed out and eyebrows raised. Reifoel jumped to his feet.

"So?" she asked, ignoring whatever accusations were being made in his gaze.

"We need money, and we need something called a visa to leave here. The guy at the ticket counter made it seem like it was a miracle that we were not being arrested on the spot for not having . . . that."

Hadley blinked.

Of course.

She had known this. Although she had never had a passport before, riding wyvern back through various countries had never been flagged in her mind as a legal issue until then.

"Did he tell you how to get those things?" Reifoel asked Isadore.

"He mentioned the word embassy. Does that mean anything to you?" He looked at Hadley.

"It doesn't." She sighed, looking around the area and spotting a higher-end hotel at the end of the street. It was a smaller boutique hotel, but it had a bar.

"I've never tried it this way before," she muttered, "but I know how to get us money."

She had seen countless movies in her high school years of working women finding clients in these places.

I can't believe I'm considering this.

She gulped and stood, Isadore and Reifoel watching her with curiosity.

"I used to be able to get paid to spend time with men." She didn't look at them when she said the words. "I can do it again. How much do we need to get visas?"

Reifoel put his rough, dry hand on her shoulder but pulled back as she stiffened. "I can't let you do that."

"Let's only discuss real options here," Isadore's voice suddenly boomed. "You're skinny and in need of a bath. That is an unreliable plan at best."

"You sure must be fun at parties." Hadley's eyes rolled, but she tucked her hands around her neck and waist, closing herself off.

"Thank you, I am."

All the people around her, their voices and happiness, made her feel so small. It brought her back to when she was a grief-stricken, penniless girl going into Grant's garage. Being told that she wasn't good enough even to stoop that low made her want to slam her shadow self into Isadore. To have him come down on his knees, worshiping her.

She thought of Ayurveda and her goals, and she got it; she understood why. Living beings, humans, they were all awful. She thought she just hated Sheng's mansion, but it turned out the entire world just . . . just . . . sucked.

"Little do either of you two know," Reifoel jumped in, his voice excited, easing the tension. "I've been teaching myself to juggle. If I put a little hat down, we will have enough money in no time."

"What do you juggle?" Isadore scoffed.

"Mostly rocks, but I haven't dropped one on my head in almost a week. I'm getting pretty good." Reifoel flashed a dashing smile, his face proud, staring only at Hadley. "I'm sure if we did your plan, we'd reach our goal much faster."

"How can you say that? Her hair is too oily." Isadore shook his head and marched to a street cart vendor selling panipuri on the other side of the street. Reifoel shrugged his shoulders and looked at her apologetically.

"Go," she said, reaching into her pocket and pulling out a few crumpled orange paper bills before handing them to him. "You said you were hungry. Get some food. This is the rest of what I have right now."

The smells of onion and fried snacks wafted over to her as the line at the stand gathered. Her stomach growled loudly.

"Don't worry, I'll get you something," Reifoel threw Hadley another one of his dazzling smiles as he grabbed the bills from her hand and walked to the other side of the street. She didn't take her eyes off him until he got in the line and turned his head to meet her gaze, giving her a thumbs up.

Hadley took in a deep breath and popped herself up off the bench, looking around at the vendors and booths on the wide cement sidewalk that she occupied. She turned back to look at that hotel again. Another life, one where she'd been naïve, one where she'd been too trusting, flashed in her mind.

That's what she was doing now, being too trusting, getting lost in a boy's smile and his attention because she was starved for it. She was starved for being treated like a human, like she was more than just a pawn in someone's game. Never again would she let herself be taken advantage of.

She could walk away, right there, and go to that hotel to get money for herself—money to travel, maybe find a boat that she could stowaway in and find her way back to the warmth of the sun, toward Ayurveda, who understood her rage and understood her need never to hold on to fear again.

There went that little voice again.

Hadley started walking toward the hotel. Reifoel's voice yelled across the street, "Hey, where are you going?"

She gave him a reassuring grin and a nod before turning her back to them. Isadore waited next to Reiofel, his order already in his hand.

Hadley took another step and stopped, her eyebrows raised as her foot did not come down to meet the ground. She was hovering just a few inches off the cement, not enough for any of the busy tourists nearly walking into her to notice.

The air was hot, and the smells of all the bodies and oils around her hit her, turning her stomach as she hung there, unsure how to move. Her limbs felt stiff; bending them would break her like she was made entirely of delicate glass.

Hadley's shadow self appeared in front of her, cocking its head and tapping its foot as if she were playing a silly game.

"What's going on?" Isadore's stern voice came from her left side as she stared at her. She was starting to draw a crowd like a magician performing a trick.

"This is weird," he continued, crossing his arms.

"I can't move—" she started to say until something slammed into her, knocking the wind out of her. Hadley was thrown back and tossed like a doll. She couldn't speak, think, or feel, except for the breathlessness, a thirst for air like she was back under the water.

Her body jolted forward and was slammed by an invisible source from behind. She was flung, this time hitting the ground, the skin on her forearms and chin sliding against the cement, leaving blue blood spackled on her upper body.

She didn't move as she heard gasps and panicked chatter from people around her.

"Hadley, Hadley?" Reifoel's voice was right over her, frantic and panting. "Are you okay? What happened? Were you flying without your wings?"

His hands touched her shoulders, and she inhaled for the first time.

Her body shook.

She raised her head to see that a circle of people were hovering around her, all their eyes staring, concerned, even scared.

"She's conscious," a random male voice rang out. "Is there a doctor here?"

"No," she gasped, "no doctor."

Hadley moved to lift herself, her body sore though no longer delicate. She felt different, heavy, as if she'd multiplied her body weight by ten.

"Get them to leave," she muttered to Reifoel, who nodded and jumped to his feet. Hadley let her head fall back down for a moment as she listened to him and Isadore shuffle people back to their day.

Hadley slowly returned to standing. Reifoel turned and rushed to her side to help her once he saw, guiding her up by holding her arm.

"Is it because you haven't let your wings out in almost a month? Does your body retaliate like mine when I've left the water too long?"

Hadley shook her head. "I don't think so. I don't know. It felt like I was hit by a car, and then that same car slammed in reverse to then hit me again."

Isadore just stared at her, silent, unnerving.

Her shadow self stood before her but had failed at first to get her attention. Instead of a dark figure, it was now shrouded in mist, translucent like a ghost, like her wings.

"What?" she said out loud, her eyes hard and mouth open.

That's new.

Reifoel looked around frantically, trying to see what she was talking about. His eyebrows were raised, and his posture was still.

"What's going on?" He put his hands in his pockets and let his weight move back and forth between his heels and toes.

"Nothing," she brushed it off, staring at her now ghost self. The figure flickered, its color turning back into darkness, but only briefly. "I think I just had a headache." She raised her hand to her head.

Or possibly a concussion. What the hell happened?

"Hey, American slut, get out of the way. You're blocking the walking path," a loudmouth man with a beer belly and heavy accent yelled at her behind his rack of postcards as he sweated through his unbuttoned short-sleeved shirt.

"You don't talk to a woman like that," Isadore shouted back, his chest puffed out and strong jawline tight. Reifoel also turned, looking disgusted, glaring at the vendor.

He just called me a slut.

Hadley didn't know if she was going mad, but she giggled, child-like and filled with disbelief.

Oh, how ironically right he is.

She hated that man for those words, despite the absurdity of it all.

How dare he unknowingly peg her for who she was? She made those choices that led her here. She had to remind herself to own it. Faking some pride was better than showing shame and admitting it all.

She couldn't imagine a person so cruel, a person so unforgivable, making her confront herself as she was stuck again, this time not in a closet, but in a foreign country. It built steadily, slowly, but she could feel the rage under her skin, even pulsing out from her fingertips.

Her shadow self, still barely visible even to her, nodded assuredly and walked across the street to join Reifoel and Isadore. The two were now yelling at the street vendor, causing a slight commotion.

Hadley's nostrils flared, and she realized how long it had been since she had fully controlled someone, had let her shadow self do what it often asked to do. She gave it permission, not thinking much of what this new appearance meant, and watched it jump into the man whose eyes went wide, his body still.

22

Hadley | Bangladesh

The body was stiff as it hit the cement of the sidewalk, eyes wide open but devoid of life.

The vendor's mouth was left hanging loose, tongue stiff and pointed, his reaction to when Hadley's shadow self, newly translucent, had jumped through him.

Djoser had promised her peace, nothingness. Hadley's fingers twitched, her stomach knotted. She wished for that, angry that he had dangled something so beautiful in front of her and then disappeared without a word. Now, it was this that she had to deal with instead, this that she had to face.

"He's dead," Isadore said, standing after crouching over the body, his fingers on the side of the vendor's neck as he looked for a pulse but failed to find one.

Hadley frowned, blocking out the hushed panic that began to spread out beyond her as other vendors and bystanders started to repeat Isadore's words.

"Did you see what happened?" Reifoel asked her point-blank.

Hadley forced herself to blink. She had been holding her breath, frozen, but the voice of her friend reminded her that she had quite the audience. It grounded her, reminding her that she was just Hadley, riddled with anxiety.

Hadley located her muscles, finding the operating manual to her body in her brain. Shen then nodded, still transfixed by those open, lifeless eyes. Reifoel grabbed her arm and pulled her out of the circling group, the harshness of his grip not registering.

She was just a body. She wasn't there, not really. The death that had befallen that man had come from her. It was such a power, new yet harsh. How to deal with it, how she herself could now be death, was something that she didn't have the mental space to contemplate.

"Something did happen, then. What was it?" Reifoel whispered to her, his chin down and throat bobbing.

"I don't know. I don't know how to describe it." A tear slipped down her cheek. She turned her head away, hiding the tear and brushing it off on her shoulder.

No, that was a silly thought. It couldn't have been her. He couldn't just suddenly die with no warning. Her shadow self played on emotions. If one could pull feelings, physical pain, and devotion out of someone, then her shadow self was the opposite. Death had never been a part of that before.

She wasn't a cold-blooded killer..

But there was that force. What was it that hit you?

Hadley looked around, her eyes searching for that mist, for the ghost that was now so hard to see.

"Where are you?" she whispered. They were not words meant for anyone other than her, for her shadow self.

"Who? Who are you looking for?" Reifoel asked, taking her chin and gently turning her to face him. They were close again, and she could feel his exhalation on her forehead.

"It had to be them," someone shouted, then repeated.

Reifoel let his hand fall, and they both turned to see the voice's owner, a man Hadley didn't recognize. He pointed at Isadore and then went back to her.

"That girl was just on the ground, and now that man is dead. They do not have visas or money. They must be thieves."

Isadore moved quickly to join the two of them.

"Who is that?" Reifoel asked him through his teeth, doing his best to dazzle with an insincere smile. It seemed the entire street was looking at them with malice, the makings of an angry mob, trying to pinpoint exactly what to do with their rage.

"Murderers," the voice's owner sounded again.

"Shit," Isadore mumbled, "that's the guy who worked in the ticket stand at the bus counter."

"I am not a murderer," Hadley yelled back as Reifoel pulled her into his arms, trying to calm her. The injustice in her body, in her heart, was ever-building. She was on the verge of collapsing, of letting the weight of the world hang heavy on her chest, of watching Hector die, of getting forcibly dragged away from the person she once was.

If it was her fault, if she was now death in some way, then this was her first direct kill.

"Police, call the police," a bystander yelled from the ground. "Illegal tourists. Terrorists!"

"Help," another person echoed, high-pitched, a woman's panicked voice. "Somebody's dead."

Tears flowed freely down her face, and Hadley did not bother to wipe them away.

"Please," she begged as the crowd surrounded them, trapping them. Then she saw the mist, the ghost, her shadow self. She watched it, her only friend there, the only one who could help.

Hadley closed her eyes and, again, whispered.

"Please."

Her prayer was answered with a sudden uproar, the gasps of the crowd that surrounded her.

"Again, they did it again."

"How can you say that? We haven't touched anyone," she heard Reifoel yell, squeezing Hadley tight. She opened her eyes to see another body on the ground, wearing the same lifeless expression. It was the ticketing clerk.

"No," she said half heartedly.

She didn't hate seeing them dead. Her anger still simmered beneath her skin, and she was glad for it. What she did hate, however, was the thought of her mother watching her, seeing what she had become. First a whore, then a killer.

Her stomach turned, not processing the conflicting thoughts, but also failing to bury them.

"We are not murderers," she said to her ghost as it lingered around the group, and though Hadley couldn't see the smile, she could feel how her shimmering shadow bared its teeth, ready—eager—to take more lives.

"Right, did you hear that? We've done nothing wrong," Isadore yelled back to the growing mob. Half of the crowd shouted at them, still barricading them in a circle, while the other half desperately tried to revive the ticket clerk. Women were sobbing, their hands wrapping around themselves, not knowing how to be strong.

Hadley could relate to that.

We are not murderers. Not in this way.

Hearing her thought, Hadley watched her shadow change again. It suddenly had so many forms.

Still translucent, the figure was her now, shiny and reflecting light as if made from crystal or glass. Not knowing yet what this change could mean or what part of herself it brought out of her, she still felt relief. The beauty and the reflective colors were such a reassurance against the frantic backdrop. She could focus on that and keep her eyes open for it.

"Please," she whispered.

Her shadow self, gracefully stepping and weaving between bodies, took one last look at Hadley before it disappeared back into the ticket booth clerk. The woman hovering over his body gasped as his chest began to move again, his eyes blinking.

"He's alive. He's okay," a woman's voice said, rejoicing.

"Maybe he just had a heart attack or something casual," Reifoel said to her.

"You don't know much about humans, do you?" Hadley replied as his arms left her, freeing her from his warmth. She didn't realize that she missed it and felt much emptier without it.

What is it that you do?

Hadley watched her shadow self step out of the body as if it were simply getting out of bed in the morning, back to its normal dark hues. It spun a small victory dance for her before weaving and bobbing until it was out of her sight.

"He's still not right; we still need a hospital," someone from the crowd commented.

The ticket clerk sat up, his head lolling as if there was no control of his upper body muscles. The body found her with its eyes, blank, unintentional, and through a struggle, began to stand.

The man didn't take his eyes off her.

Hadley felt cold and hard, like solid ice, as if moving meant she would turn to liquid, a puddle of undeveloped magic on the ground left in Bangladesh, forgotten. The body was on its feet now and stepped towards Hadley, closing the gap.

Reifoel's hand raised in front of her, protective, but she waved him off and let the body approach. That body was the human who was unmistakably dead just moments ago, the human who she thought she somehow killed. Her throat bobbed as she looked into his eyes, brown, dirty, skin that seemed tinted slightly gray and continued to pale. The man had no expression, no anger that radiated from him.

Lifeless, yet walking.

"I'm sorry," she whispered, though no one seemed to hear her but Reifoel, whose eyes widened as he stepped back. His position changed from defensive to offensive.

She looked at him, hoping he could read the plea in her heart, the reparations she was more than ready to offer. He didn't seem to pick up on it and Isadore began to match his posture as well, realizing what the minor exchange of glances was communicating.

She thought back to her little apartment, dancing and feeling free with her best friend. Sitting down at a computer and writing. Even those eviction notices on the door were a stress she missed and longed for. It was a time that had set all this in motion.

Her body was heavy with regret, with bad decisions. That best friend no longer existed. She had watched him die and made him happy to volunteer to do so. She hadn't even flinched.

She deserved all this. Deserved all this sadness and pain.

The man, the body that stood before her, raised his hand, his eyes vacant.

Empty.

Lifeless.

"The police, they are here," yelled someone from the crowd. "It's her, it's that blonde woman. That man was dead."

Hadley stared at her alive-again victim, his hand robotically resting in the air, and blinked. Her shadow self was now right beside her, inches away from Reifoel.

Don't, she thought. *Don't touch him.*

She turned her head to look at her shadow, the figure that hovered in darkness with a tight-lipped smile that invited her trust, pulled her into a source of magic and power that she somehow could not feel in herself. It was all this troublesome figure that was always there for her. It would always protect her when she didn't know how to defend herself.

Show me what to do.

Her shadow raised her hand to match the posture of the unmoving man before her, but paused as if waiting for her to join. Hadley took in a breath and let her trust fall within herself, within her shadow.

Chaos ensued around her as a group of police officers in dark blue vests broke into the scene, armed with tear gas guns.

"Get down," one of the officers yelled into the crowd.

The onlookers ran and screamed.

Some fell to their knees, purses and bags over their heads and mouths. Other braver souls stood unmoving, pointing toward their group, yelling at the officers before they were thrown down by the police themselves with their hands behind their backs.

"Let's go." Isadore grabbed Reifoel's arm and tugged hard. He resisted and gently reached for Hadley but stopped, letting his hand fall as his mouth gaped open and he stepped back.

Hadley placed her palm against the man's, and tears erupted down her cheeks. The man's fingers, followed by his wrists and arms, began to harden and lose color at her touch. A soft crackle danced around them as every inch of the man turned into crystal. No, not crystal . . .

"Glass," Hadley sobbed.

An instant later, an officer tackled the man, shattering him into hundreds of pieces. The officer rolled, shards piercing his skin, anguished curses filling the air.

Isadore knelt and picked up a finger, watching the sun's colors reflect and gleam on the cement underneath.

"No," he said, his eyebrows raised in disbelief. "A sand burned by ancient fire, glass formed by the burn of a dragon."

"You are under arrest," an officer raised a gun at Hadley, his face unforgiving, unfaltering.

"She didn't do anything," Reifoel defended her. Hadley didn't fail to notice how much further away from her he was at that point. His upper body leaned toward her, but his feet backed away.

"Don't touch her," another officer yelled, "she's a witch. Didn't you see?"

"Run, Hadley," Reifoel urged her. "We will find each other."

Don't run.

"Let's go," Isadore yelled.

"Freeze, don't move," the officers yelled as one moved forward with zip ties in his hands.

He's coming for you.

"Who is coming for me?"

As if synchronized with her heart, with her will, with the words her shadow self whispered within her, a vibration pulsed in the air.

Leaves on trees and weeds sticking out of concrete rippled as though alive with a heartbeat.

The chaos quieted. People stilled, most eyes fell to their feet, their breathing shallow. A brave, curious few raised their chins to the sky, their posture sinking as they laid eyes on the creature of myth that soared through the skies.

Steadily increasing in speed, darkness fell over the city as the creature passed under the sun. Each flap now sounded thunderous, sharp cracks of air slapping against its hard leather-like wings.

"Ayurveda's wyvern, Aqurya," Hadley whispered, closing her eyes as relief flooded her. She was going back, back to where she was safe.

The wyvern belongs to you.

She opened her eyes, her brow heavy as she considered the thought. The creature let out a shriek that ripped through her. She smiled and let out her wings, the back of her shirt ripping, the only sound among the stunned silence of those who witnessed the creature above.

"It's a dragon," a police officer yelled and shot his gun at it.

No.

All of the officers pulled out their weapons as the harrowing sound of gunshots filled the air. A distinct metallic pop caught Hadley's attention before she looked around to locate her shadow self. She would not allow it. She would not allow her wyvern to be taken down.

A hiss erupted. White smoke filled the air.

"You idiot," an officer yelled to one of his teammates as they began to scatter. Clouds of steam unfurled, followed by an acrid smell of gas. Hadley heard Reifoel and Isadore cough and gag, but despite the stinging, despite the blindness that swept over her pupils, she kept her head upright.

The massive wing flaps brought relief as the wyvern descended, circling as the clouds dispersed under its sturdy, clawed feet. A thud signaled that it had landed, and citizens crawled away, whimpering in fear as the wyvern let out a shriek. Camera crews gathered in the distance as onlookers shouted, telling them to run.

We are no longer hidden.

Reifoel crept up to Hadley, his eyes red, and his skin suddenly more cracked and dried than it had been just minutes ago. She could see that he was in pain, that every motion hurt. He needed to get into water.

"Hadley," Reifoel was hesitant, but did reach out to her. He was interrupted, though, by a smooth, seductive voice, a voice from the top of the wyvern.

"Whatever this thing is, best to accept that we are in it together, wife," Sheng said, his white teeth dazzling against his dirt-covered face and hands, those teeth that could turn into fangs, that could pierce into her skin.

She had never seen him look worn before; the ruggedness surprised her. Her stomach dropped, from her hatred of him or his beauty, she didn't truthfully know.

"Get on," he instructed. Reifoel and Isadore did not hesitate as the wyvern lowered its head and upper body so they could climb. Sheng held out a hand, helping each of them up.

"Stop, you are under arrest," a lone police officer shouted as Hadley began to move. The wyvern opened its mouth and let out flames, engulfing the human as the world watched.

"Waiting on you, beautiful," Sheng said with a single wink and a smile. She could have imagined it, but it looked like relief flashed across his face.

She waited for it, waited for that voice inside her to tell her to run, to get away from him, but it didn't.

"We have no time for games," Isadore's rough voice boomed.

"What he said." Sheng winked.

With a heavy sigh, Hadley stretched her wings and flew ten feet up to reach the wyvern's back. Sheng caught her wrist, pulled her down to him, sat her on his lap, and gave her a wide, wicked grin before they were all in the sky, leaving Bangladesh behind.

23

Precession | France

She lived in a dream most days; the sun warming her cheeks as the winter chill swirled around her while she fed her chickens and hummed. Her twin sister, with a severe kindness that only she seemed to see, was beside her, elevating Precession's happiness.

If her life were a musical, Precession would happily sing all her words and skip all of her steps, acting as if the world's weight didn't hold her down. Her optimism could be sickening.

It was sickening, as far as Roksana was concerned.

Yet, the two women loved one another just the same. It was a true partnership that most people looked for their entire lives. They needed nothing and no one else.

At least, Precession felt that way. She knew better, though, to speak for her sister. She knew that loneliness had found its way into Roksana's heart, a small poison that weakened her resolve more and more each day.

"I have been thinking of what to get you for the holidays." Precession giggled as a brown hen pecked at her boot, begging for more feed. A heavy wind whipped around her curly, vibrant red hair, the long jean skirt paired with heavy work boots so different from her fashion-forward counterpart.

Roksana frowned at the rooster who came into their circle, pushing the other hens out of the way. There was nothing she disliked more than a male who falsely thought he had more value than those around him.

These feelings were not exclusive to animals.

"You know, I've named them. That white one is Lacey because she's got the bits that stick up; they're very posh, her frills," Precession said, gazing too adoringly at the chickens.

"I like that little brown one over there. It's calm and doesn't peck at my feet," Roksana said.

"Oh, that's Romona. She doesn't seem to like the other hens too much, but does seem to enjoy some light opera."

"We are singing to the chickens now?"

"Whenever you go wandering into town. Who else do I have to keep me company?" Precession smiled genuinely. She didn't mind at all. She quite liked spending time with the animals. "Back to the subject of this gift. I'd like to make sure you approve of it first."

"Is it to expel those damn Vrae from our town?" Roksana's eyes were bitter. Precession knew that look, knew the longing in her sister's eyes.

"No," Precession's light, sing-songy voice erupted with joy and laughter. She loved Roksana so much, even when she was a grump. "I was going to invite Amis back for a holiday dinner."

Roksana's face went through several shades of scarlet. She looked down at her fitted soft leather gloves, heightening Precession's joy even more while her own shame and giddiness lined the air.

She got her. She had found a gift that made her sister speechless.

Precession pushed off the embarrassment that hung in the air. Her sister amplified these feelings of insecurity, feelings that were only there in case she was wrong about her sister's crush.

It was an obscure magic, if anything, an unfortunate one. To always be surrounded by those who were experiencing the same heightened emotions, never able to worry or focus on herself. She could have no friends because of it, other than Precession, of course.

On the other hand, Amis seemed to be that spark of light, a flicker of hope in the darkness of Roksana's loneliness. Precession wanted that for her sister, wanted her to be happy.

"I was hoping you would say something that might be more productive," Roksana retorted after several minutes of silence.

"What did you have in mind?" Precession mused, the world spinning around her as if she lived in a vacuum. She stood tall regardless, with Roksana's arm there to steady her.

"I think our groundskeeper is a problem. He seems to believe our guests are a tribulation for this town."

"He would be correct, would he not?" Precession smiled. "I do not feel responsible for this town nor the Vrae, as you do, but I suppose a gift is selfless."

"I think it's a bit silly, celebrating the human holidays," Roksana brushed it off. "Anything to blend in, I suppose."

"You love this beautiful town decorated and lit up. I can see the spirit that grows in your eyes during this season. You, my dear sister, are secretly sentimental, despite your efforts to appear otherwise."

Roksana scoffed like nothing could be more preposterous, not even singing opera to chickens.

Despite being outdoors, mental walls suddenly began to close in on Precession, her mind feeling trapped and forced to focus on something new. It had been too long. Too long since she could have a normal, teasing conversation with her sister. Too long since her magic, her own power, wasn't too consuming to speak of anything else.

She could manage the spinning, the tether, but this was something else.

Precession closed her eyes, absorbing the soundless instruction coming into her body and letting it flourish. She wanted to see, wanted to learn. Something was growing, something was coming. A tickle in her throat and a twinge of her stomach told her to be ready. Ready for what, however, was not clear.

Her hints at the future never quite were.

"When faced with eternity, it's best not to be buried in sadness, dear sister." Roksana said before noticing the shift in Precession. She stepped close, pressing their foreheads together.

"What is it?" Roksana whispered. "Something is wrong."

Precession's eyes opened, her eyelashes darker, clumped, and wet.

"There's so much," Precession began, staring out into the property, gaze not settling anywhere, "beauty."

Precession's premonitions did not come in the form of visions. The outcomes were not changeable, unlike Reign's time jumping. They presented more similarly to a thought, something that she couldn't quite hold on to as it slipped away like water through a strainer.

As she rotated the Earth and kept the moon tethered, the future, the past, and the present all spun around her. Every so often, it would get caught within her mind.

When she'd been a child, she'd assumed she was daydreaming, but then it would transpire within the real world. She knew it was special, that it was real, then. She hadn't been making it up.

"There's a sky, pink and blue with a golden light shining down on a body of water that is so clear it reflects the sky. It's a world where there is no horizon. Under those waters, a reef, vibrant and filled with marine life from both worlds, coming together as one realm."

Roksana frowned and rolled her eyes as she watched her sister's face, bright and filled with wonder. A childlike awe had been painted from Precession's forehead to her cheek. Roksana half expected her to reveal that she was looking at the heavens, a world that wasn't theirs.

"The place you describe does not exist. Most reefs are dying out," Roksana stated and turned to look over her shoulder towards their home. Voices were shouting, and Precession fell out of her thoughts. Her gaze turned towards the group of Vrae bodies running out of the house while waving their arms and pointing upward.

"What are they doing?" Roksana asked, eyebrows raised.

"I think," Precession said, her words barely audible, "that they are trying to protect us."

"Protect us from what?" Roksana asked before she was struck by fire and thrown thirty feet away from her sister.

"Mother," Precession heard Jenny scream, "stop."

Another burst of fire shot out of nowhere. Precession couldn't see the source but fell to her knees just in time to feel the tinge of flames passing over her. The fire hit the earth as chickens fled, some not so lucky as they looked for the last remaining feed on the ground.

"Perry!" Precession let out a sob as her younger rooster was now gone. She quite liked that one. He seemed like a gentleman.

"Looks like you get a new chicken for your present," Roksana said gruffly as she limped towards her sister, her clothes shredded to ribbons.

"Watch out," yelled Saul as another ball of fire flew toward them.

Roksana jolted and tackled Precession down flat, both girls panting face to face in the grass and loose dirt as they both narrowly avoided the next blast of fire.

More yelling came from the Vrae, sharp and distraught, but Precession tuned it out. The soreness from the fall to the ground crept through her back, shoulders and skull.

"I did not," Roksana started as she pushed herself up, "move to France with the intention of living an action-packed life."

Her sister grabbed her hand and began to yank Precession up to her feet. She kept her eyes closed, focusing on the tether, not allowing this all to be a distraction.

"Of course, it's you," she heard Roksana say under her breath. Precession let her eyes open, curious to see who the firebringer was. She scanned the estate, the beautiful green grass with lush trees in front of her singed. It was such a pity to have to regrow all of that.

Precession's gaze fell on a figure in the distance, hovering in the air outside the gate that separated her property from the road. It was nearly translucent, closer to water that held its form in the shape of a woman, blue flames sparking from the ends of her hair.

"Can you leave?" Roksana demanded, unimpressed by the

goddess that seemed hellbent on destroying their property. "Absolutely no one invited you here."

"How in the world are you so cavalier about all of this?" Killian huffed, running up to the two Kinnari women and the rest of the Vrae. Though still in human form, their eyes were red. They were all ready to hunt.

"Did this catch you at a bad time? Were you all ready to go out and murder the rest of the town?" Roksana sniped and rolled her eyes.

"My goodness, you're such a bitch." Jenny burst out laughing before diving, avoiding another ball of fire.

"Mother," she yelled back toward Ayurveda. "It almost seems like you are ready to kill us as well."

"Thank the goddess," Roksana mumbled. Jenny huffed as she picked herself up from her dive.

"I think that last one took out the goats." Saul turned behind him and frowned.

If there was a heartache to be had, it was the loss of her beloved small farm. Those animals did not deserve to be roasted alive. With no fear in her heart, Precession trotted towards the edge of the property, her steps carrying her in a zigzag as she felt the heat of another ball of fire go past her.

"Should we have a conversation, then?" Precession asked in her ethereal feminine voice. The goddess, angry and filled with little more than malice, hesitated as she watched Precession continue to approach.

"Please do not kill anymore of my chickens," Precession said, raising her head up to meet Ayurveda's stare.

"I am here to collect the girl," the goddess said, her voice sounding so close it was as if she was whispering into their ears.

"What girl?" Roksana hissed.

"The girl that I implanted into a Kinnari womb. The girl that I am truly a mother to. The girl with wings made of glass."

Silence lingered after she finished speaking. Precession and Roksana took in the implications of her words. As the creator and bearer of life, Ayurveda took responsibility for the creation of Hadley.

"That girl is not with us," Roksana answered, standing forty feet behind her sister. She moved, working to close the gap. To offer protection that maybe her sister didn't need. Precession felt sure. She did not fear. This was something that she could handle alone. After all, was her own magic not as powerful as those of the gods? Sometimes, it appeared so. She could feel it as it was drained out of her as she continued the rotation.

"Hadley has never stepped foot on this property," Precession told Ayurveda, who gathered more flames in her hands. "We also do not know her current whereabouts. You may be on your way before I call out to my own creator."

Ayurveda seemed to consider this for a moment. Her lips were a thin line that moved downward into a visible frown before she slowly shook her head, first left, and then right.

"Karmakara has no stomach for battle," Ayurveda said in her eerie whisper.

"No, but kill another one of my sister's pets and see what type of stomach I have," Roksana said, the heightened state of her anger reaching Precession, who did her best to wave it off.

"More bees with honey, dear sister," Precession said, trying to calm Roksana so that this did not escalate more than it needed to, before turning back to the impatient goddess.

"That's not the saying," Roksana grumbled, but went ignored.

"Why is it that you think that she is here?" Precession continued.

"My other children are here, working to betray me." The air stilled, and Precession's cheeks dropped for just a moment. The Vrae, she was talking about the Vrae.

"We are not here to betray you," Jenny said.

"Do not lie when no one needs you to," Ayurveda said, responding by letting the fire in her hands go, hitting the spot where Jenny stood. Sounds of rocks hitting earth exploded, and the woman stood no more. There was no body to be found.

With a deep howl that sprinkled pain and broken hearts onto

anyone who could hear it, the Vrae fell to their knees, shifting in their grief. Their human skin turned to polished rubber, shiny and a true black, like that of a void, like staring into the color of nothingness.

White, long, dagger-like teeth erupted from their mouths, fangs from a deeper side of hell that could bite through bone as if it were lettuce. Claws, long and sharp, cracked from now disfigured fingers as their eyes turned a more piercing red, the red of fear and defeat. It was the shade of red that conveyed that all was lost.

Precession could feel Roksana's edge turn slightly towards fear, confronted with the fully turned Vrae alongside her. A soft hand slid into hers as Roksana caught up to Precession. The twins were fully engaged, ready to fight alongside each other.

"Are you fighting for the Vrae?" Precession teased.

"As if," Roksana scoffed before shaking her head. "The things we do for Arryn, I suppose."

"I think they have a way of growing on you," Precession added, thinking fondly of the full dining room table and the camaraderie. It wasn't something that she'd realized was missing from her life. She had that once when they all lived together at the temple.

"You may leave, or I will let go of it all and destroy this planet that you no doubt need for whatever you are trying to do here." Precession's lovely voice carried an undertone that relayed her seriousness.

She was tired, tired of being the frail Kinnari, tired of constantly needing aid to even move about the day. It sounded like a relief, letting go.

She watched in her mind as it played out, her tether released and pure gravity flowing back into her. Precession's magic sitting in her body, ready for her to use as she willed, could be a terrifying yet wondrous thing. The life she could live as she watched the planet likely die would be a similar feeling to watching a pedestrian cross the street, wondering what it would be like to hit them with a car.

No, no, she would not go there, but she could. When faced with Ayurveda, that could be enough.

"Please, do it," Ayurveda dared her. "It would only help me. The work and effort it would save would be tremendous. I've considered burning it all down, every morsel of land, anyway. The girl, however, stops that need. Her ability to control makes it so I can be merciful as I take control of both realms. The Kinnari have done a terrible job at ruling. It's my turn."

"But we do not rule," Precession whispered, though Ayurveda had no trouble hearing her.

"That's exactly the problem, isn't it? You, Precession, could be dazzling and mortifying, yet you live under someone's thumb. You allow your natural enemies, my children, to live among you. You are a disappointment. You are feeble."

Precession was sure Karmakara would disagree, and that was the only one who had any right to be disappointed. Precession did the only thing she could think of, the politest way to say fuck you. She curtsied deep, bending to the ground, her eyes never averting Ayurveda's gaze as her lips curled into a large smile.

"Get up, sister," Roksana urged.

Fear, that was fear from her twin, circling around her. Precession pushed it off, not letting Roksana's magic get the better of her. The silver-voiced female didn't normally hold grudges, but she was really unhappy about Percy. She had raised that rooster since he had hatched. He didn't deserve that.

"Take us with you," Francis yelled, running up towards the gate.

"We can help you," his sister, Priscilla, echoed, following his steps.

"You certainly switch sides fast," Roksana grumbled.

"Indeed," Ayurveda said, her voice engulfing them all, pressing in like night taking over the sky. A darkness fell, and the tone shifted as heat visibly radiated off the goddess hidden in the sky.

"Morning, miss, et lady," the twin's groundskeeper waddled onto their property, waving a newspaper in the air, oblivious to the heat waves hovering closely overhead.

"Have you seen this? All of the North Island of New Zealand has burned down. The world is going crazy. There are rumors of a dragon, but I didn't catch where. Can you believe that?"

"That all sounds entirely improbable," Marcus said, emerging from the rest of the group of Vrae with his hands in his pockets, utterly laughing.

"What is so funny," Michel asked, his French accent thick.

"Your timing," Marcus answered.

With that, flames crashed through the air, and Michel yipped, diving behind a hen house. Precession turned her head over her shoulder and saw scorched, blackened bones where Marcus once stood.

"What in the hell was that for?" Ramsey yelled at Ayurveda before diving out of the way of another thrown flame. The Vrae that had stood beside him, Dravus, Bruce, and Leonardo, were not so lucky.

Ayurveda placed her palm by her mouth and blew a kiss of fire, the kiss of death. It was subtle, no instant destruction or obvious flames, but inch by inch, a breeze of embers so small they were nearly invisible approached. Their size didn't matter, though. It was no normal fire, not of this earth. This was the sun.

A river of fire caught ablaze before Precession's eyes, diverting around her as if she were an island. Every blade of grass, every tree, every man made possession disappeared under a wisp of smoke within seconds. Every remaining Vrae burned before her eyes as well. Priscilla, Saul, Jenny, Francis, Ramsey, and Killian were all gone, leaving only silent screams behind.

"I can count that as my holiday gift," Roksana yelled to her from on her own patch of grass, surrounded by fire.

A pit settled in Precession's stomach—her home, her land, her guests, all of it gone. Ayurveda smirked and evaporated into herself, taking the heat with her as the winter air settled back down around the estate.

Disheveled and seemingly emerging out of nowhere, Michel appeared, rising from the ashy dirt.

"Just like a cockroach," Roksana grumbled.

"I think I will find a new place to work now," the Frenchman said, raising a finger up in the air. His eyes were wide, like he'd seen a ghost, and he trotted off the property, ranting to himself before disappearing beyond the gate.

24

Arryn | Glacier, Myrilosis

Arryn was groggy the next day, awakening in the shabby room in which he had drunkenly fallen asleep. He wasn't quite sure how he had made it there. He remembered Reign going to bed after volunteering him to do . . . something.

Good lord, what is it that I agreed to do?

His head ached, proof that the barmaid had continued to refill his cup repeatedly. If he hadn't healed yet, he must have been on the brink of alcohol poisoning.

She was a beauty, that barmaid. If he had any decent skills at flirting, he might have been able to wake up with her next to him.

No, no. Stop.

He shook the thought off while reminding himself of his current task. He needed to know how Allienna got pregnant. He would avenge her death, and whoever had a hand in the creation of that girl, Hadley, was going to be held accountable. Daughter seemed like the wrong word, just like she seemed wrong.

He wasn't quite sure what he would do to them. He was not an action star. His style had always been to throw anything that seemed hard to deal with into the realm they stood in and hope nature would kill it. After seeing that there was a whole town in front of him and that civilizations in this world existed just as in the Earth realm, Arryn learned that there was a plethora of evidence that this plan had worked against him.

The large Kinnari male rolled off the single bed, and the metal frame squeaked in protest. A dresser with a mirror was positioned on the opposite side of the wall. His blond hair was disheveled, and his dark blue eyes were decorated with bright red veins pointing to his irises.

I look like shit, he thought.

Arryn took a moment to shape his hair, his magic grabbing hold of the atoms and giving it a bit more length so he could tuck it behind his ears. He refreshed his clothes, now wearing a long black wool jacket and hearty boots. His wings were tucked in, and he would keep them that way. His popularity in this realm was a joke at best, so keeping his true nature hidden was best.

Arryn left his room, grabbed the skeleton key off the dresser, and walked into the hallway before heading downstairs. Balizar was sitting at the desk, looking as unpleasant as ever. His eyes shifted away from the newspaper he had his nose in to glance at Arryn before he rolled his eyes and returned to his reading.

"Do you not ever go home?" Arryn asked as if he were talking to an old friend.

"Why would I ever want that? When I get to stay here all night and clean up after the original creator, the Kinnari, who gets blasted drunk and creates anything anyone at the bar can think of? A river of beer through the middle of the floor? I suppose you've got to keep your popularity up somehow."

Arryn grinned. That explained why he felt so loose.

The fire under his skin was almost non-existent. Despite his beautiful ability to heal quickly, the hangover seemed to stick around as it did for anyone else, but he could still quickly swoop up the grumpy creature and give him a big hug.

"I made some friends then, did I?" Arryn asked.

"Oh, no, no. Don't get things twisted. Everyone still hates you. No one here knows what to do about it now that your presence is public. Not a very violent group here in this town. I wonder, though, if your companions know the real reason why Kinnari hate has spread in this town. I wonder, do you even know?"

Because before humans were created, I made more Kinnari and left them in this realm with the rest of you.

"They know what they know," Arryn said, suddenly on edge, his eyes darkening. Balizar looked incredibly unimpressed and pulled his newspaper up, covering his face.

"A lot of suffering, a lot of blood has come from your actions alone. Your friend, the little girl, is she under control?"

"It's hard to keep her from stealing my ale, but otherwise, she's a peach."

"Hmph."

Arryn sucked on his bottom lip, his two front teeth showing. "Well then, speaking of Reign, have you seen her today?"

"I suspect she is getting ready for your journey south," Balizar scoffed.

"Good morning," the lovely voice of the barmaid rang through the lobby. "I suspect you'll want some breakfast for that headache."

"Now, why would you think I've got a headache?" Arryn asked, leaning against the front desk as Balizar pushed his chair back, looking offended.

"Oh, well, you musta had at least thirty pints last night."

Is she blushing? She is blushing.

"Is that a new record or something?" Arryn batted his long eyelashes.

"Words cannot express how weird it is to see you flirting." Reign walked in, impressively commanding the room despite her petite body. "Cool new hairstyle. I like it. You look like someone who lives in Portland."

"Portland?" the barmaid asked.

"It's an Earth realm thing," Reign responded, putting her hands on her hips and tapping her left foot impatiently. "Well, are we going or what?"

"The Earth realm? Is that where you live?" the barmaid asked but was ignored.

"You are a simple girl, Celestine, and we love that about you," Balizar grunted.

"Where are we going?" Arryn asked Reign, confused.

"You promised to heal some land after a fire last night. Don't you remember?"

I remember you making that promise for me.

"Do we have to do that today? I had plans." Arryn shook his head.

"You don't have plans." Reign laughed out loud. "How can you have plans when you don't even have a phone?"

"How are those two things related? I show up. It's worked for me for the past ten million years."

"Oh, wow, you're quite older than me," Celestine awkwardly piped up. "I'm going to go grab you both some plates."

Arryn watched the barmaid walk away. It was better not to know her name and not to get attached. He hated hearing it and couldn't pretend to forget it. His gaze lingered on her hips before Reign walked up to him and punched him in the stomach.

Allienna. Allienna. Allienna.

He felt too good. It was a new kind of danger—a lazy sort of recklessness. He needed to halt the use of his magic. He needed the burning to return so he wouldn't lose focus.

"How long is this journey?" Arryn rolled his eyes.

"If you walk and swim, maybe a ten-day journey," Balizar said, returning to his newspaper. "If you have money, boats and vessels keep you dry."

"Swim?" Arryn scoffed.

"What, you can't turn yourself into a fish?"

Arryn cocked his head. He had never considered that. If he could manipulate atoms to make his hair grow, there was no reason why he wouldn't be able to transform and shapeshift fully.

"We will be flying, obviously," Reign said. "Can we go now?"

With that, Arryn watched, amused, as Reign grabbed him by the arm and used all of her body weight to push him towards the door unsuccessfully.

"It's going to take more than seventy pounds to move me," he chuckled.

"You will move, you will fly. You will fulfill your obligation."

Arryn straightened, Reign's magic every bit as powerful, even in child form.

"Are you not havin' your meal now?" Celestine came back, holding two plates. "It's my favorite outta wha' that kitchen puts out. Biscuits and jam with henthrop eggs scrambled on top."

"Ah, leave them alone, woman," Balizar said as the barmaid stuck out her lip and let her shoulders sink forward. "That must have been the tenth meal you've brought him since they arrived last night."

Arryn, despite dying to know what henthrop was, couldn't engage. He waited for Reign, his hand landing on the handle, bound by her command.

"We will return soon. Thank you for your kindness," Reign said to Celestine as she bounced right up to Arryn, who held the door open for her. The bitter cold stung his hands as the low temperatures bit into his exposed skin.

"Warm one today, lucky us," Balizar grumbled as Arryn let the door shut behind them, leaving the inn behind.

ARRYN HAD no idea where he was going as he flew behind Reign, his long black jacket in his hand as his wings, cyan blue with streaks of gold, splayed out fully. It was hard not to like it too much, this newest self and the freedom he felt with it. It was only going to get worse, more addicting, as he used his magic continuously.

It would get harder to accept the burning that lingered under his skin. He would get used to the euphoria, maybe even crave it.

Reign turned mid-air to face him, her shiny black hair blowing around her face. She smiled and waved her hand towards her before pointing down at the mass of land that would be New Zealand in the Earth realm.

It looked nothing like the land he had seen when he last visited Waihema. There was no lush greenery to greet them,

No, as they descended, Arryn could easily see the destruction that would have made Reign so eager to volunteer him for the job. It didn't look like there had been a fire; it looked like a nuclear bomb had been dropped.

Arryn's boots touched the earth, pieces of rock, shards of glass, and other debris crunching under his weight as he stepped forward. Seeing the aftermath of a war was sobering. This had to have been a calculated crime. Nature didn't behave like this.

"It's—" Reign started to say but seemed to have lost her words as she stared, wide-eyed, at the foundations of buildings that once held life. Stone and cement had been cracked open and splayed across the scene as if the material was pliable.

"It's all ash," she exhaled, bending down to pick up black soot and studying it as she sifted it through her pinched fingers.

"There must be survivors. Where are they?" Arryn asked, jumping up on a pile of crumbled stone to look around, though it fell apart underneath him.

"Easy there, big guy," Reign said. "If there are survivors, let's give them a reason to return. Let's nurture this realm the way you have given to Earth. Everything you've done has been done with only one realm in mind. Let's heal all of this. Hell, both realms will benefit."

She was right. Allienna would have wanted the same thing. He could remake this land—a final gift to Allienna, a final way to grieve. He could say goodbye, for real, this time. He could heal this land and his heart.

Arryn crouched down, putting his hands to the ground, shards cutting into his skin. He let the destruction, the pain, be a part of him as he was a part of it, tiny droplets of his blue blood squeezing out of his palm.

He closed his eyes and let his head fall as he huffed, holding back a sob that had his body trembling. He missed her.

He missed her so damn much.

He missed the way her cheeks turned pink when he made her laugh. He missed the way his heartbeat quickened when she whispered in his ear. He forgot how they fought, passive aggression consistently winning out, always returning to normal as if nothing had happened.

He missed that the most, feeling a sense of routine.

Arryn let himself flop back, his legs out before him, and sat like a child playing in sand on the beach. He rooted his hands into the ground.

"Are you ready?" He looked at Reign. He hadn't used his magic like this since he was a child. The next closest time was when he had remade their temple, their home. He might get completely lost in it, in creating. He might be unable to return to the person she knew now.

Reign only nodded, her fingers twitching by her sides. Her brown wings, limp behind her, scraped the rubble around her feet.

Arryn took a breath and let it all out. He let the power within his chest, legs, and fingertips move away from him, grabbing onto every atom around him. Millions upon millions of pieces, just making up the few square inches around him, began to melt, form, and change colors entirely.

A vibrant green, the color of health and life, spread around him like sand in the breeze. Grass, thick and dense, grew underneath him. He looked up to see Reign beaming, watching the growth. It felt so good to release it all. So damn good.

Patches of new grass flourished closer to the shore as his magic spread, the golds and oranges dancing in the settling sunset. Arryn stood, his eyes set on the east side of the land, where life thrived.

He stopped the growth, pulled it back, and shifted the atoms in new ways as fields took shape before his eyes, growing potatoes and cabbage. Orchards filled with rows upon rows of trees sprouted, the sweet smell of fruit wafting down to him as apples and kiwis bloomed from the branches.

"What else do you have up your sleeve?" Reign challenged him, not hiding her glee, her childish giggle that seemed to call the stars out from their slumber as the sky darkened.

Arryn only cocked his head, feeling light, feeling free.

He placed his hand on the ground again, looked up at her, and raised a single eyebrow as the land split in multiple directions. Reign looked at him, confused, as the beauty he had already created was being destroyed.

No, not destroyed. The landscape was only being added to.

He could not destroy, not in the true sense of the word. The openings began to fill with water, eventually leading out into the ocean, and Reign finally saw what had been done.

Canals, so many canals holding crystal blue clear water sparkled, even under the night sky. Reign gasped and did a double take once she saw the smallest blue creatures, shaped like sprites, jumping in and out of the waters.

Some landed on the surrounding grass and blew air on the spots as sturdy trees emerged with silver among their yellow leaves.

"Who are they?" Reign asked, her voice emulating wonder.

"I thought they could help me finish the job."

Indeed, the thumb-sized creatures seemed to spread life and greenery every time they touched land. There was an extra beauty, something so out of the ordinary in the fauna they created. Flowers that glowed, changing colors as the wind whispered through them, sprung up in small groves. Large natural stones were spread across the landscape with a luminescent enchantment.

Arryn had begun to feel light-headed, but the energy that ran through him shone through. He was soaking in adrenaline, in power.

He welcomed it. He wanted more.

"We are not done," he shouted into the sky as a waltz of vibrant teal and green hues floated against the black of night.

"Arryn," Reign gasped, "it's ... it's otherworldly."

Arryn let his head roll from his left shoulder to his right, and he hazily tripped over his coat, which had now been forgotten on the ground. This brought him back to attention, his eyes moving from sharp to unfocused. He wasn't going to stop.

Bridges of stone and steel were constructed out of thin air over the canals, providing easy and safe walking access. Pathways continued to grow from there as homes made of enchanted wood blended into the environments with moss and vines wrapped all along the structures. It was quaint yet ethereal. A product of imagination, of a world Arryn would have wanted to live in. A world that he knew Allienna would also love to be.

"Seventy-six, seventy-seven," Reign counted the houses, the communities on each side of the canals that developed within minutes.

"Arryn, we don't know if anyone is here. It might be too much."

He shook his head and continued, making more homes, a market on the west side, a school on the north. Eventually, he propped his body up by placing his hands on the tops of his thighs while his head bobbed.

His chest thudded. Never all at once had he created like this.

"I can keep going," Arryn grunted as he tried to lift his head to meet Reign's eyes. She was noticing how he was deteriorating. She noticed that his smile was toxic, nearly frightening. There was a manic gleam in his eyes; he knew because he could feel it, a drunkenness overtaking him.

"Are you okay? We should stop. This is plenty."

"It's for her. It's for Allienna. I have to finish." Arryn panted.

Reign walked towards him, placing her hand underneath his chin, and lifted so their gazes met.

"I think that this is enough, Arryn," she said, her words soft, understanding. "It's so beautiful. I've never seen a place like this. It's perfect for her."

"I don't think I can stop," Arryn said, his head hanging low. He didn't know how to stop needing her, thinking of her, hoping he could still find her.

If she was gone, could he find a way to bring her back? The magic that got her pregnant was what he needed to see. That magic could be what he needed to show her this land. This land now entirely and wholly belonged to Allienna.

"Arryn," Reign whispered, "no one is here now. This place you built will be swallowed by nature as it grows. You're hurting yourself somehow, I can tell. Will you please stop?"

He lifted his head, ready to say no. So much was still missing: a medic, a theater, and a library. Allienna loved to read. He could build the grandest of libraries for her and whoever she shared it with. She wouldn't be alone with only him again; she would have this whole town. He needed her to thrive.

Arryn raised his hands towards an undeveloped area alongside the beach, with views of the volcano sitting off the bay. His head throbbed as he found his magic, and its overuse made him woozy.

Ignoring the feeling, he constructed red bricks, one wall, two, then three. Then, Arryn's vision went black, and he could not push anymore. He fell, hearing Reign curse. He chuckled at that, her sweet voice and those vulgar words. She was angry, and she should have been.

"Arryn, Arryn." She shook him as his chest and face were imprinting on the grass. "What the fuck is going on with you?"

"I'm sorry," he said, falling into a state of blackness. His consciousness slipped despite his magic reaching, searching, and wafting from his fingertips.

25

Reifoel | Wyvern Back

Reifoel's teeth were chattering. This type of cold was odd. His waters were unbearably cold, down so deep that light didn't touch, but this was different. This was dry wind, frigid air hitting his skin like needles, cracking the surface as if his body were no different than the red-brown cracked earth of a desert, a barren landscape.

The wyvern he sat upon couldn't have been flying more erratically, its wings casually turning from right to left as if it were swaying to a song. He was going to be sick as he held onto the large black curled spike in its back, the object separating him from Sheng.

Hadley was sitting with him. Sheng held onto her, her backside pressing into him.

When they had first started flying, Reifoel could see how stiff and uncomfortable she seemed. Hours had passed since then and Hadley had sunk into him, her head resting against his chest with her wings covering Sheng's face. It didn't seem to matter; his hands were resting in all the right spots.

Well, the wrong spots.

Yes, he was going to be sick.

Reifoel couldn't quite process what had happened on the ground just before Sheng had shown up. A man collapsed, irrefutably dead. He had noticed the look in Hadley's eyes, the fear, and the . . . guilt. Yes, that was guilt that sat in those dark blue irises.

He could plunge into her eyes; they reminded him of the ocean and home. He had been watching, studying how expressive they were, and when that happened, she thought she was responsible for it. He just had no idea, no sign that he could see, of what she had done.

When that man had turned into glass, resembling her wings before he shattered, Reifoel realized that he couldn't handle it.

He couldn't handle her.

He knew he would need to put some distance between them, though seeing how comfortable she was in front of him stirred up a new emotion. He was jealous.

She should be sitting on my lap.

The set of arms that were wrapped tightly around Reifoel were not as charming, as Isadore clung on for dear life. He had learned so much about the cousin that he could not stand since they had left, one of those facts being that he did not deal well with being suspended in the air. Reifoel could see that Isadore's hands were as cracked as his were, though the crevices were possibly even deeper. They needed to get into the water soon.

After several more moments of staring daggers into the back of Sheng's head and watching his hands and where they lingered, the wyvern bobbed to the left again but began a spiral descent. They were in thick white clouds, the moisture slightly relieving his broken, splintering skin. It was short-lived, as the wyvern continued to circle down, forcing him to deal with the g-forces.

Reifoel closed his eyes, the bile in his stomach threatening to come up and out of his mouth. He rested his head against the spike, praying that this would be over fast.

This is awful. I'm ready to go back home.

His stomach growled.

And sit with a nice cold plate of Mom's cooking.

His body jolted, his teeth clamping down too hard as the wyvern's feet hit solid earth. He didn't move at first, didn't open his eyes. Reifoel only listened to the wind and felt it harshly whip against him. The moisture in that wind took away that slap, turning the harshness into something pleasant, something to savor.

Isadore let his arms drop, leaving Reifoel feeling suddenly exposed. Reifoel heard his feet plop and jumped off the creature, though the sound of a crunchy yet wet landing made him curious. He opened his eyes, his stomach still swirling, to see a world that looked no different than flying through the clouds. White surrounded them, untouched with slightly gray and blue tones as the sunlight faded.

"Have you been here before?" Reifoel heard Sheng say to Hadley. He couldn't see her face; he couldn't see what her eyes expressed, and it killed him, gnawing at his chest like a rat was trapped inside, desperate for escape.

"Have I been to this mountain covered in snow and frostbite? No, this is probably the first time."

Reifoel watched as she pushed his hands off of her. She moved slowly, and her skin was several shades too red, too purple. She hurt, just like he did, just like Isadore.

Sheng, on the other hand, looked untouched, unbothered. As if he had taken a comfortable cruise down a beachfront highway in the middle of summer. Sheng's hair was disheveled, but it did not look bad; no, he could see it being interpreted as dreamy.

Reifoel frowned.

"Jump down, cousin," Isadore yelled up to him. Reifoel looked back down and noticed Isadore lying down fully, partially rolling his body in the crunchy white substance. "It feels like water. It helps so much."

That was enough. That was all he needed. If Sheng could look like that after the awful ride, he could level the playing field a little more. Reifoel let himself fall down the ten feet that separated him from his cousin and nearly yelped from joy as he plopped into several feet of snow.

"Does it work? The same way water does?" Hadley asked, hovering down to them with much more grace, her wings fluttering as fast as a young hummingbird's.

"Snow is made from water, Hadley." Sheng let out a booming laugh, nodding his head.

Hadley gave Sheng a look that lifted Reifoel's spirits, a look of absolute and utter disdain. He shouldn't care, but he did. He should have found relief from the sound, a mixture of hissing and slurping, that his skin made when he touched the snow. It was a sound he was confident only he could hear, but one that was overshadowed by his focus on Hadley.

"Where are we?" Isadore demanded.

Sheng patted the wyvern, the only one who remained on top of the beast. It let out a dramatic puff from its nostrils and closed its eyes, curling up its body.

"Hold on, girl, you're not done." Sheng looked down. "We need your fire."

Hadley looked up to him and then marched over to where the Serelune princes stood.

"This really is your first time here, then. You were not just being difficult?" Sheng asked Hadley, too much eagerness in his voice. "It took me a long time to find this place. I've searched for this Earth realm entrance for most of my life. I've only been inside once before, from where it connects into Myrilosis.

There were a few times where I was suspicious that the temple moved mountains, always to one I wasn't searching. I would just use my own personal portal, the one I built my home around. You've seen it, that pentagram in the ceiling."

Hadley blinked at Sheng, giving no reaction, no expression.

"Luckily though," Sheng continued, "the wyvern seemed to know the way; we just had to figure out how to align our goals and communicate. You were a big part of that; she wanted to get back to you."

Sheng jumped down and marched through the snow, putting his arm over Hadley's shoulder. Reifoel noticed how she stiffened. Anger snuck in on him, and he had to look down at his feet, worried that his temperature change might melt the snow. He hadn't had much experience yet with snow.

How dare he put his hands on her.

"I don't speak magic, so your words mean so little to me," Hadley said as she rolled her shoulders back so Sheng's arms rolled off of her.

Sheng tilted his head towards her, and Reifoel tried to hide his visible frown. There was something genuine in the way Sheng looked at her. He was an asshole, but Reifoel knew that there was still a threat somewhere there. It couldn't just all be for show, Sheng's affection. There would be quicker, more efficient ways for him to get what he wanted from her. A soft spot existed.

"No, I suppose you wouldn't." Sheng gave her a sincere smile. "I can't promise that I can keep you safe, Hadley, but I want to take you somewhere where we might have a better chance. Ayurveda is hunting for you. Hell, she nearly killed me when I sent you away."

"She's searching for me?" Hadley asked, her voice quiet but impatient. "Why would I hide? I've been trying to get back to her."

Sheng's smile dropped.

"This, this is me, trying to do what's best for you. What's best for the world," he said. "Tell that wyvern to blow fire right over there, could you? That moonstone is helping, too. She seems a lot more settled, more at peace."

Reifoel blinked, the necklace feeling heavy as Hadley pursed her lips and looked at the creature, who seemed to be snoring.

"Only because I'm cold," she decided and walked up to it, reluctant in her movements. She was still scared, still wary of it.

Hadley put her hands on the wyvern's belly and rested her cheek against it, moving up and down with its breath. Her eyes flickered to the distance, focused as if something was there, something she communicated with silently.

Sheng stood there with his arms crossed, smirking.

What an ass.

Isadore flopped back down into the snow, soaking in as much moisture as possible, bliss creeping into his normally stoic face.

As if pulled by a thread, the wyvern began to move its head in the direction Sheng had indicated, lazily glancing at a mountainous pile of snow that stood before them. It opened its jaws, revealing teeth just shorter than Hadley, and erupted.

Deep from its gut, a rumble thundered as a fire jet hit the snow. The wyvern turned back with the intention of returning to its nap. Reifoel noticed Isadore, his eyes wide, staring at where the fire had hit.

There, where snow once stood, was a partially revealed temple. Gold reflected onto the snow from the ancient stone. Reifoel could make out carvings and history depicted on its outer surface.

"A door," Isadore said, pointing, "there."

"I seriously love you," Sheng declared, putting both hands on Hadley's shoulders before turning away with his arms outstretched for the entrance.

Reifoel froze momentarily at those words. What words they were.

Isadore pushed Reifoel from his backside, guiding him to follow Sheng as his curiosity was building, his excitement almost showing. Reifoel forced himself to walk. Hadley did not approach as they did.

Sheng used his bare hands to brush snow off the thick door, looking for a handle.

"This is it," Isadore whispered.

Reifoel wasn't focused. He couldn't see Hadley when she was directly behind him. He didn't like it.

"What?"

"Get your head out of the clouds," Isadore hissed. "A temple, on top of a mountain of snow. We did it, cousin. We found the temple hidden in the snow. The man, Kinnari, must be here."

Reifoel blinked as the door groan echoed all around them. More snow fell from the temple exterior as Sheng jolted it open. They all stared down the hallway.

"It's pitch black," Reifoel said.

There was an eeriness there. Something powerful, something ancient, was once inside, maybe even still there. If they had found the Kinnari, the one from his mother's stories, Reifoel now wasn't sure that it was wise to meet them. Nature had a way of working itself out. Maybe he didn't have to intervene.

"I definitely thought you would die before we got here," Isadore scoffed, boldly walking up to the hallway and taking a step inside.

Sheng smiled wide. "Indeed, I didn't expect it either. Good on you, little man," Sheng clapped his hand on Reifoel's back before turning to take Hadley. He held out his arm, offering it to her.

"My lovely wife, will you please accompany me? There is a whole new world that you deserve to see."

Hadley stood there in silence, her eyes flickering a few feet to the left of Sheng.

He knew it. He knew she was looking at something.

Hadley let her head fall before she shook it, left to right. She walked toward them, her hand slipping off the wyvern's belly. Skin purple and red, she looked up at Sheng's face, the two no more than six inches apart. The heat from their breaths was visible, building a micro-cloud between them. She took his arm, her eyes then immediately went towards Reifoel.

His stomach lurched. She looked at him first.

"I'm not going because I like you," she said, turning back towards Sheng.

"No, of course not," he replied, his chest puffing out slightly. "You're going because you need me. You're a creature of perseverance."

Reifoel watched as she opened her mouth to protest, but before she could, Sheng scooped her into his arms and carried her into the darkness. Reifoel, with Isadore at his side, begrudgingly followed.

26

Hadley | Kinnari Temple

Hadley pushed against Sheng's chest, kicking her legs like a child.

She forgot how hard he was, how solid. It felt like pushing against a brick wall, a marble statue. How cliche, really, a demon with a rock-hard body. A devil with abs sculpted like a Spartan warrior that could lift her, shield her, throw her out of harm's way, and hover over her to protect her from a blast with his breath hot, panting against that sensitive spot on her neck.

"Put me down," she demanded.

With a laugh, Sheng set her down. Her feet touched the stone as they continued down the temple hallway. The freezing temperature outside still crept in, but the temple was overall insulated from the brittleness that welcomed them on the mountain peak.

"I will repeat it." She turned, unable to see him in the darkness. "You are not to touch me. Why do you continue to show up even when I try to get away from you?"

"Do you think we can have this conversation when we are not all standing in a black abyss?" Isadore asked. "My eyes were made to acclimate to this, and I still cannot see through this. Ooph, watch your step."

"Sorry, sorry," Reifoel panted. "I wonder if it's because of our human-like bodies; our skill set doesn't apply outside the water. I bet if there was a way to get in the water without changing, we'd be worthless swimmers like them, too."

"Hmph." Hadley let a smile escape since no one could see her. Isadore's constant hums of displeasure were a silly little highlight for her.

"Are we going to encounter anything terrifying here?" Reifoel asked.

"You arrived here on a wyvern. You are the terrifying thing," Sheng said.

Hadley reached out her hands, trying to feel around. She touched stone walls, feeling the rivets in the otherwise cool and smooth material. She could feel hot breath on the back of her neck, likely from Sheng. She pulled her arms back in as she continued to walk forward, waiting to run into something or fall down a hole that she would never come back out of.

Why the hell am I the one in the front?

"To answer your question," Sheng continued, "I made a wrong assumption. I had thought that you would be the womb, the creator of a creature, to truly match the power of the gods. To be a true protector from their wrath."

This is all bullshit.

"I realized my mistake, though; that power is you."

He said it so simply, so matter-of-fact. The man, the street vendor, flashed through her mind: the death, the shattering of glass. She could control the masses of people to follow her without demands without fear. She could do that, too. Use fear if she wanted.

It was time to accept that she was no longer the sad, orphaned teenager that she once was with regular human problems. No, she was so much more than even the Vrae, the demon who locked her up, stood behind her, trying to weasel his way back into her heart.

I'm not scared anymore. I can decide that. I can choose to not be frightened.

A noise, a clatter, echoed from ahead, and Hadley shrieked and jumped back, Sheng's arm wrapping around her protectively.

Damn it, I'm still fucking scared.

"What was that?" Hadley whispered, slightly out of breath. "All this magic between us, and no one can conjure a light?"

"We are not witches." Sheng chuckled. "I suppose your father could."

Her damn father. He apparently could do anything. She hated hearing about him.

Hadley could feel Sheng trying to press forward. Her lower body now hung slightly underneath him, his foot stepping in front of her.

"Can we not inch closer to the monster that is obviously up there?"

At her words, another scuttle was heard, but this time, she was paying attention and could hear more clearly.

Wings. That's the sound of wings.

Hadley let Sheng walk her forward, and now her curiosity was slightly piqued. Was there another one of her kind in there, trapped in the darkness, unable to find their way out—just like she was once, trapped in a closet with a chain around her ankle?

I'm coming, she thought. *I'm coming to help.*

She would not let it happen to someone else. She would not let them be abandoned and alone. She could stop it, be a change, and be better.

Hector flashed through her mind, his face dedicated and loyal beyond all measure as he died, as Hadley sentenced him to death. She had told herself he deserved it. She had told herself he had abandoned her. Maybe he did do those things, but was her choice, her pain, justified?

"Hello," she said, her footsteps quicker. She nearly stumbled on an uneven stone, but an arm reached out and steadied her.

"Woah there," Sheng said.

"No touching," she reminded him, yanking her arm away.

She took one more step, then something felt different. The walls were further away. They were in a large open room now, and she heard wings fluttering again.

The footsteps behind her stopped. Reifoel and Isadore caught up to them. She wasn't sure if she was hallucinating already, not able to see even her own hands in front of her face, but there was now a tiny ember in the corner of the room. A warm light, small and inviting, drew her closer like the gates of heaven, pulling someone out of death, out of unconsciousness.

With that last step, the change was sudden. Blinding light forced Hadley to bring her arms over her face and crouch down. It was Reifoel's hand on her shoulder, his skin still a bit rough, that convinced her to raise her head and look.

She was staring at a large bird.

It wasn't just a bird, though; it was something more spectacular. It made her feel every emotion all at once: happiness, sadness, hope, and loss. Its body, glorious as it sat, appeared on a long communal table, shimmering in gold and red with feathers that looked painted on. It was perfection, too impossible for nature.

"It's a phoenix," Isadore said, unimpressed.

Hadley grabbed her cheek with her hand and pulled down, snapping out of her wonder at the bird with Isadore's nonchalance.

"I have to say that it's an obnoxious pet for Arryn to have, though also not surprising. I can't decide if I'm impressed or not," Sheng said.

"You two might get along quite well," Reifoel said, laughing at the both of them.

"What, why would you say that?" Isadore demanded.

"Can we just not appreciate this damn magical bird?" Hadley rolled her eyes. "Did you say Arryn? As in . . ."

Hadley shifted uncomfortably, putting the pieces together.

"Yes, Arryn, your father. This is the Kinnari temple. I once murdered one of them in here. It feels like just yesterday."

Hadley turned to stare at him, shock in her face. She had known he was a monster, having firsthand been under his thumb, but she hadn't actually seen him do anything to someone else.

Her mind flashed to something he once said to her: that if a devil existed, he would be worse. She should have shivered and been worried, but oddly, she felt only relief. Here was someone worse than her, a more definitive evil. She was a victim of circumstance. She was learning how to survive and how to act now that she was living with any sort of ability.

He's worse than you.

Hadley took in the rest of the temple. The table on which the phoenix sat was huge, not just in length but also in thickness. It looked as if all twenty regular-sized people it could seat could also drunkenly dance on top of it.

She imagined sitting at it and blowing out birthday candles on a cake.

A home.

This could have been her home with her parents if they had stayed together. It was another world that could never exist, playing out in her head.

The air inside was cool and crisp, tinged with the faint scent of ancient stone and a hint of ozone reminiscent of the sky after a snow-storm. Enormous stone perches jutted out from the walls at varying heights, each wide and sturdy enough to support the weight of the enormous winged creatures. These perches were adorned with soft, glowing moss, providing a comfortable resting place.

Sheng moved over toward a natural wood counter with an immense sink basin. It was a kitchen, the shelves almost hidden but popped open at a touch, filled with stone and marble tableware and supplies. As he stepped forward, he paused and looked down before a large grin moved across his face. His hand felt around the stone floor beneath him before finding a handle. A large hatch on the floor that would accommodate wings opened up into a cool natural fridge section with no food, only wine. Lots and lots of wine.

"We could have a lot of fun here," Sheng smirked, looking at Hadley. His gaze devoured her, eyes scanning up and down. She tried to look away, but his eyes were so demanding that it was hard not to indulge him.

He was dressed simply in an oversized sweatshirt and slim-fit hiking pants, which reminded her of the sweatpants he wore when she met him at the gazebo. She had liked those sweatpants, the lines in his abs making an arrow point down.

Yes, he was worse than her, but maybe she was a monster, too. Perhaps the devil could fear her, too, one day.

The blush that warmed her cheeks faded as his grin grew, and her shadow self appeared.

Don't be a fool, she reminded herself; *it's him you need protection from.*

"Where is he?" Isadore commanded the room, his fists down at his sides.

"Where is who?" Sheng answered.

"The Kinnari. The creator. He is who we search for. We find him to tell him that the earth's rotation is slowing and may be causing fire waves, and then we can go back home. We both have a throne to prepare to take over one day."

"Just me," Reifoel scoffed at him. "I'm the only heir. I've missed your obnoxiousness, cousin. I thought you were getting mushy on me."

"Hmph," Isadore grunted in response, his eyes fixed on Sheng.

"Well, if you look around, he is not here. Also, you were there when the ship was destroyed. It was the wyvern. That has nothing to do with the moon. Do not worry, though; this is not our final stop. I'm shocked my mother dearest hasn't already destroyed this place. It's in perfect condition. It looks brand new as if it belongs in a theme park. Don't you think?" Sheng winked at Hadley.

"We cannot travel with you if your intent is not to find him," Isadore said.

Hadley noticed Reifoel had fallen quiet, his shoulders buckling forward and drawing into himself. He stared at the floor with the occasional glance up at her.

He wants to stay. He wants to stay with me.

Hadley wanted him to stay, too.

If Sheng had something sinister planned for her, if she was being an idiot by not protesting louder, letting her shadow self plunge into him and take control of his very body, then Reifoel would be there. He would do something. He wouldn't leave her in the dark.

Hadley smiled at Reifoel.

The next moment, his eyes fluttered back to her, and she saw him relax slightly, nearly smiling back. He was so kind and so loving, but there was hesitance, as if loving was new to him, like contemplating taking a drug for the first time.

I could be his drug if I wanted it. Do I want it? Does he even want me?

Yes, yes, he did.

Between Sheng and Reifoel's stares, both so different but communicating the same thing, Hadley could search for the confidence she once had in her former job. Men, sex, those were basic. She could navigate it. She could find a way to get what she wanted with it, find a way back to Ayurveda and live among the mountains, away from every damn person and being that would undoubtedly hurt her in some way.

"It's true. My intent is not to find him. My intent is to hide and protect her. I highly suspect that it will involve running into him." Sheng began pacing towards the opposite side of the temple. Another hallway parallel to where they entered was now pulling at her attention.

Something began to pull at her, an ancient whisper running through her heart and body. That hallway was where Sheng was leading her, and unlike in his East Sacramento mansion, her instincts were not to run away. No, quite the opposite.

Don't be afraid.

Her shadow self, in its usual dark form, danced playfully around Sheng, urging her forward. Sheng held his hand to her but then quickly pulled it back.

"I'm sorry, I forgot. No touching." He raised his eyebrows as he looked her up and down. "Will you please come with me? I am trying to find a way so no one can ever touch you again. To hide you from the goddess that wants to use you like a tool."

She saved me. Don't let him get it twisted. When I had no one, she came.

"Will you trust me?" Sheng gestured his hands to the side, stepping back so she could walk through.

"What about this bird?" Isadore huffed, walking towards Sheng and nodding towards Reifoel, who was side-eying whatever was happening between her and Sheng.

"Let's go, Your Royal Highness."

Hadley's shadow self skipped out of the way, Isadore nearly marching right through her, and made a vulgar gesture at him. Hadley smiled at her lovingly, adoringly. Her smile seemed to lighten up the room, and Sheng bellowed.

"I knew you would come around. If it makes it easier, wife, I can give you a bite. Just a small one." He raised his eyebrows at her and cocked his head, both shoulders shrugging as if it were a viable option.

"I guess we'll just leave it. Someone's probably coming back for it." Reifoel pursed his lips as he replied to Isadore.

"Why in the world would you think I'd want that?" She shook her head, the smile immediately fading from her face, and she followed Reifoel into the hall, passing by Sheng.

His frame hung over hers as she passed.

He hissed, "There was a time when it seemed that you craved it."

She paused, just for a second. The unmistakable scent of a tea tree clinging to his sweatshirt brought her back to his bed with his arms wrapped around her, his teeth piercing her neck as his fingers found their way between her thighs. That drunk, hazy feeling washed over her, that obsession that was so scary when she broke out of it but so safe, so complete when it overtook her.

"I would get out of bed each morning, soaked in blood. Another night slip ruined, another mattress to be replaced." She moved her chin up, her breath on his. "How you would think that I liked that, that I like being feed for a monster, is fucking psychotic."

Her breath was heavy. She was angry, reminded that she was a pet, a prize, kept imprisoned in her own body. She pleaded, begged this being, still and beautiful as marble, to stay with her. How weak that little girl was. How naïve.

No, she would not let him lure her.

"Excuse me," Isadore cleared his throat from the end of the hall. "There is a big door here. Are we opening it?"

Sheng slowly turned his head, not changing his posture or moving any further away from her. Hadley's shadow self emerged from the dark hallway, waving her finger at Hadley like she was a naughty girl. Hadley's eyes rolled, and they stalked right through her to catch up to Isadore and Reifoel.

"You can open it," Sheng yelled. Hadley wasn't sure, but she thought she heard defeat in his voice.

No, you are not allowed to feel bad for him. You were his victim.

Isadore pulled on the thick stone door as it creaked open, a natural gray light and chilling wind pouring in. Wings flapped behind her as she turned to see the phoenix flying straight for them. She ducked, letting it pass and fly outside into the open sky. She looked down, looking out at the land now there, the snow and the white and the vast nothingness.

The landscape was identical to what she had seen when the wyvern had landed.

"Did we go through the same door we entered from?" she asked, brows furrowed.

"This is the land where I was created," Sheng said, walking up behind them.

"Our home exists here, too, Serelune. There are some wonderful cities between here and there, such as New Eldhem and Crystalfen. I have so many memories in Whispering Bay," Reifoel told her.

"Myrilosis, the realm of magic to some, the realm of the discarded to the rest," Sheng added as the group moved forward, their shoes crunching through the snow.

27

Amis | New Zealand

One thousand sixty-eight miles, Amis had to walk. He could not fly with the five children on his back, in his arms. Three had wings, but they were new and untested.

He couldn't expect them to make such a long journey in the air, let alone keep up with his own pace. No, he had to settle for this, settle for a week-long journey as he switched off carrying Salome, Noah, Luca, and the other two nonwinged children, who he had come to learn were Rangi and Ahora.

"My feet hurt," Noah whined.

"I'm hungry," Rangi moaned.

The land was still barren and covered in ash. The damage was extensive, and as they continued south, Amis was continuously surprised to see that Ayurveda had managed to destroy the entire northern island.

"Up, I want up," Noah demanded, raising his chubby hands as his wings dragged behind him.

My merry bandits, full of mischief, Amis mused to himself before letting Salome down and letting Noah jump up. All of the children's paces had slowed. Their temperaments got worse as they marched further south.

"We haven't eaten in nearly two days," Salome said as she watched Amis wrestle Noah onto his shoulders. Noah protested, wanting to be held against Amis' chest, to be cuddled.

Amis had definitely spent most of the journey carrying Noah.

He looked around, the toddler's hand slapping him in the face.

He felt hopeless. He saw nothing, no food. There was nothing that he could feed them.

If they moved to the shore, Amis could learn to fish. He could leave the kids on the shore while he used his bare hands and deplorable swimming skills to somehow nourish them.

Amis would have to build a fire after that. None of these were skills that he had. Even his stint as Sheng's bodyguard did not allow him to learn any valuable skills that applied to this situation. When he lived in Waihema, the women had done everything regarding food and prepared it all.

Noah hit him in the face again, snapping his attention down to the grumpy, rounded face with pressed lips.

No, he couldn't leave them on the shore.

This one here would surely figure out a way to drown, he thought.

"We have to get going. Once we reach our destination, I will find you a feast you couldn't even dream about."

Gods, I hope I can find that.

They continued like that for another hour, hobbling and dragging their feet as the children sighed and groaned. Noah would cry on and off, screaming in Amis' ear. Amis wondered if his arms were going to fall off, slightly intrigued by how heavy the thirty pounds climbing all over his torso felt and how the small amount of weight pulled and dragged him down.

"I don't feel good," Salome said, her voice tight. Amis looked over right when her eyes rolled to the back of her head, and she collapsed right on her wings.

Fuck.

"Sa-wome-ey," Noah wailed, crying again.

Amis set the toddler down and sat beside Salome, his head between his legs, as he tried to process the situation and come up with a real solution.

He couldn't keep these children on their feet after everything that happened. They were literally starting to drop. He would have to carry them one by one in the air and cross his fingers that no one died in the process. Maybe it wouldn't be such a big loss if the non-marked children died, a small weight off his shoulders.

No.

That was the ruthlessness his balance allotted him; that didn't have to be who he was.

No more dead children. That could be the new standard.

Amis smiled at the thought, ignoring that his magic would react and eliminate them, if balance required.

"The ground is being painted green," Noah tugged on Amis's untamed, tangled long hair, bringing more than a couple stranded with him after pulling away.

Amis looked up, wincing from the forced hair loss, and pulled his chin back. His brow scrunched as he looked to see what the hell the toddler was talking about.

"You are oddly correct," Amis said back, a big grin crossing his face as the burnt wasteland rapidly changed in front of his eyes. Someone in Myrilosis, a beautiful, powerful magic, was healing the land. Whether they knew it or not, they were saving the last of the Waihema children at the same time.

Now, they might get to that damn portal.

Noah, Luca, Ahora, and Rangi stared, their eyes lighting up in that way of a child seeing magic for the first time. Trees exploded into the sky all around them as if it were untouched, undeveloped virgin land. It probably was on that side of the realm. Amis doubted that the cities and settlements had ever gotten so big as to fill an entire country.

Thin, green leaves hung off those trees, followed by small

bounces of green, partially opened shells. Rangi and Ahora immediately ran towards them at a speed Amis wished they could have brought with them on their journey together.

"Pecans, Noah," Ahora yelled back at them. "Just like from home."

Amis studied the land again, realizing that it did look familiar. They were close, so much closer than he had thought to Waihema, to where their village had once stood, filled with homes and parents who hugged them every night.

He would have to bring them there and hope that they didn't recognize it, recognize the undeveloped land, and fall into grief.

Hungry, tired, unconscious, and hurt were hard enough to deal with. He didn't know how he could get them to safety if they all broke down, remembering what had just happened to them.

Amis looked over at Salome, sleeping deeply. He frowned, her breaths more rapid than he would like to see. He ran his hand across her brow.

No fever, good.

He just needed to let her sleep and get some nourishment.

Amis stood up, pausing to investigate if his knees were cracking like the middle-aged man he felt like. That soreness, those aches, should be healing faster. He wasn't even two billion years old; he was too much of a spring chicken to have these issues. Granted, he didn't have a reference for what constituted as old and withering for a Kinnari. He was immortal. He should be perfect forever.

Gods damn it, Ayurveda.

It was her fault that his knees were cracking.

"Up, I want up." Noah's arms reached for him.

Okay, maybe it's your fault a little bit, too.

Amis swooped Noah up, the ground underneath his feet now lush with grass, and threw him up into the air. The toddler's face was filled with both shock and an irresistible smile. A sound of thrill, a squeal, and a giggle erupted from his lips as his wings slowed him down, and he descended right back into Amis's arms.

"Again!" he yelled, buck teeth showing from his giant smile.

"Come on, Luca," Amis said over his shoulder to the teenager, who began walking towards the pecan trees. Rangi and Ahora were already seven or eight feet up in the trees, sitting on branches and shelling nuts, stuffing them into their mouths and grinning.

Amis walked under the tree next to them, the breeze blowing the branches gently over his head. It was amazing; the difference it all made, some greenery, some life, could affect all of their moods and outlooks.

After picking pecans with Luca and Noah hanging off his arms as they tried their best to climb the trees, Amis brought handfuls back to Salome's seat. He gently pushed her dark hair off her brow and lifted the back of her head with his hand.

"Hey there. Here, let's sit you up," he said gently, supporting her back with his opposite hand. Her wings were draped over his forearm.

Salome's eyes opened slowly, wincing from the movement.

"I've got some food," he continued while she turned to look at him, confused though sitting fully upright.

Amis held out the shelled nuts towards her.

"For you."

Salome picked up her hand and took a single pecan, smelling it before warily placing it on her tongue. She began to chew and then closed her eyes in bliss.

"More, have more," Amis offered.

The seven-year-old girl grabbed a large handful, stuffing them all in her mouth and puffing her cheeks out like a chipmunk.

"Is this the place? The place where we are safe?" she asked after swallowing.

Amis shook his head no, smiling softly, a sadness washing over him as he realized that he really had no way of protecting them forever. The worst thing that had ever happened to this little girl, to this child, happened when he was right there with her. And they may not be any safer now.

"We have to get you to a place of magic, a place where someone can raise you, a place where we can figure out why you children have sprouted wings so young."

"But I like it here," she whimpered. "It reminds me of home. It has similar trees and skies."

A silence fell between the two of them as Salome picked more pecans out of Amis's palm.

"I know why," Salmone eventually said between chews. "I know why our wings came early. Our village, our stories say our wings come in for our protectors. When the fire came, when we all ran and were afraid and dying, there was no protector."

The words blindsided him.

Waihema had gone through periods with no protector, no winged Kinnari, before. When that happened, though, there were no Vrae raids, no real blue blood for them to hunt. This was no longer a question of biology but of how beliefs and stories shaped by centuries could coax and change the magic within them.

What it meant exactly, Amis didn't know, but he was grateful for it. It was a blessing. These children, so beautiful, filled with smiles and life even though their whole world was ripped apart, just over something so simple as tree nuts, were what made a world worth saving. It's what made a Vrae balance his sinister nature with protecting the world from his creator.

Amis looked over to the trees, chuckling as a happy toddler lay passed out in the grass. His belly, rising and falling with his breaths, was the only part of him that he could see besides his toes. The other three were sitting near him, lazily enjoying the shade from the branches overhead, giggling as a gentle breeze tickled the backs of their necks.

"Let's all get some rest," Amis said to Salome as he flopped back beside her, staring at the sky before closing his eyes. "We can continue after."

When he awoke, Amis blinked twice before taking in the night's atmosphere filled with blazing, bright stars. They danced, twinkling for him despite the vast distance between them. Other worlds, other realms potentially, ones he would never see or know anything about. All those stars were so beautiful, yet they were all her. All of the suns were Ayurveda.

He realized then just how pathetic they really were, how they were all ants, the only difference being that the Kinnari were ants that bit back before you squished them, before you burned them with a magnifying glass.

He waved to the sky, hoping that the balance he kept in the realms of this planet had a humble effect on anyone else who lived among Ayurveda suns, on their homes, too. The Life Gifter's other creations were possibly ruled by terror by Ayurveda already, perhaps shaped into worlds she wanted to replicate here. He hoped not.

It was still early in this war. They couldn't let it get any worse. They had to bite. Hopefully, there were enough of them, enough little ants, to cover her whole and bite hard.

Amis saw a dark figure crawling up to him from the corner of his gaze and quickly sat up, alert.

"I'm scared," Rangi's voice came from the shadow on all fours. "It's too dark."

Amis exhaled in relief, his sense of immediate danger fading, and patted the ground beside him. "I'll keep you safe. You can sleep."

The wingless Waihema child tossed and turned with some effort, eventually settling into a light sleep. Amis kept watching over him and the rest of them until the light began painting the horizon.

With the sky ablaze in the morning oranges and blues, all five children were on their feet, stomping behind Amis with the occasion humming and playful tag match. It seemed like very little time had passed before Salome stopped with her eyes wide on the familiar, darkened forest of trees that once separated Waihema from the volcanic ocean waters.

Home, she knew that they were home.

"We are not supposed to go into the forest." Salome gulped. "My mother forbade it."

Amis held out his hand to her and scooped Noah into his arms.

"You can trust me," Amis said to her.

Salome nodded and took his hand as the six of them ventured where the light could not touch, where the trees were so thick and old, even renewed, that they carried an ancientness, a secret.

The children's feet dragged with apprehension as they left the light, the beauty of the regrown world, behind in exchange for shadows and places that filled their nightmares.

Amis felt the energy and perfect balance between realms just three, four, maybe five steps ahead. They just needed to cross that threshold.

"It's time. We are here," Amis muttered as Salome, Rangi, Noah, and Ahora stepped forward, holding onto each other. With the flap of a hummingbird's wings, the smallest moment in time, they all disappeared into the air.

28

Reign | Kiwiva, Myrilosis

"Wake up, you son of a bitch," Reign yelled, kicking Arryn in his side.

Her small foot bounced off of him like a pebble tossed gently at a concrete wall. This small childish body was growing more and more inconvenient by the day. She understood why Tristan chose to hide in the subconscious of others, never participating in the real world, and how belittled he must have always felt. That and he didn't have to deal with Arryn.

Gods, you suck.

She kicked him again, wishing her commands worked on the unconscious.

Reign tried to understand what had happened. Arryn seemed drunk and manic about creation. She supposed he had never created that much at once before, not even at the Kinnari temple before they entered Myrilosis. He could have stopped, though, which made her frown. No one gets to that point, to the point of collapsing, without feeling weakened and altered, especially not in a Kinnari body that is used to healing rapidly.

How fragile they could truly be.

Reign huffed and puffed, letting out a few mumbled curses, and walked around Arryn, trying to pick up his feet and drag him.

"Of course, you would weigh the same as an elephant." She collapsed, breathless, after just a few seconds of effort. If she counted correctly, it had been four days since she had been stuck here with him. He was breathing. He wasn't dead, but he wasn't responding either.

"What did you do to yourself, friend?" she whispered to herself.

At least it was beautiful where she had been stuck, this little world that Arryn had tried to kill himself making. Still, she decided to leave him there, asleep in one of the houses on the other side of the canal instead of on the grass. She couldn't wait around forever; she had an online store to start and a mortgage to pay.

Reign sighed and flopped down beside Arryn, hating his stupid face. Maybe she should return to Earth and find a nice family to adopt her. She could go to school and let others take care of her. She didn't know what that felt like, to be taken care of. She's had to be strong, always. Her words and her commands demanded a confidence that showed others that she was to be depended on.

Let's be real; that would be a nightmare.

If she needed an adult, she supposed Grant would pretend to be her guardian. If he thought Reign's stepdaughter was in trouble, she knew he would help.

Reign jumped up as a pig-like snore erupted from the silence, Arryn's mouth opening as his head angled towards his shoulder.

He moved.

"Oh, finally," she spat out, jumping to her feet. It looked like the coma was over; he was healing. She planned on him being awake very soon, and they could fly back to Glacier. That town had grown on her, and the bitter cold kept her mostly inside that pub. She could live a few years stealing pints from Arryn, learning about the world he created when he was a child, learning what it had become.

Internet store, don't lose focus.

If it did well enough, she could replace the bamboo floors on the second floor. There was always that faint smell of urine that lingered there since her client ruined them. She could get cork flooring instead and try something new. It could be fun.

What an exciting future.

It was getting harder to think of home, her best friend hiding a hug's distance and raising her child without Reign knowing. The more and more Arryn grieved, the more she thought of the Kinnari that had abandoned them both, and the harder it was for her not to feel anger.

Where Arryn felt sadness and shame, she felt isolated and closed in, searching for someone she thought was in trouble.

There was that moment with her, the moment when they had been together, when Allienna asked her about her romantic feelings for Arryn. Reign often got hung up on that, thinking nothing of it then. Now, alone in her bed, the words haunted her. Were they all cast out because of jealousy and mistrust? She hoped not. It would have meant a lonely last few years for her best friend, raising Hadley alone.

Reign stood up and kicked Arryn in the shin, frowning while he had no visible reaction.

This is going to take forever.

The sound of thumping feet made Reign's heart stop. No one was here. There should be no life on this island. No one should have survived.

Someone was alive.

A scurry, the sound of bushes rustling not twenty feet from her, had her turning in the opposite direction as something dark jetted across the grass, heading away from the homes and from the town using a speed that was too fast for just two legs.

Reign reacted without thinking, sprinting after it, her brown wings opening behind her as she took to the air, following it. It ran under trees and foliage, giving her trouble tracking it with only the occasional tussle of the greenery it brushed against.

There was no stopping or resting. The speed of the dark creature's dash did not waver, despite the fact that Reign had been tracking it for twenty, then thirty, then forty minutes. She was even slightly out of breath from hovering above it in the air. After her dominatrix gig had ended, she really just did not get enough cardio.

A disruption into trees too thick to see through signaled that it had run into a forest ahead. Reign dove down, touching her feet to the ground right outside this darkness where light could not touch. A shiver ran up her spin as she stared inside, unable to see tree trunks even ten feet in front of her.

She blinked before jolting back.

Eyes.

Bright red eyes were in the distance, staring back at her.

Reign whirled around, looking back, searching for that glowing gaze that could only belong to one thing.

Vrae.

They were in a truce. They could not hurt her unless this Vrae existed only in Myrilosis. Unless this Vrae was not a part of Sheng's clan. Was there more than one clan?

The eyes had vanished so quickly that she questioned if they were ever really there. She didn't make them up. She chased that creature, the possible Vrae, into this forest.

Or did I?

She needed to get back to Arryn. If Vrae were running around, maybe she'd been led away from him on purpose, leaving him defenseless. Was coming to this land a set-up? Did the creatures in Myrilosis really want them eliminated to the point where they would go through such extremes?

Shit. Probably.

She turned, wings ready for takeoff to return to him, setting herself up to find the worst.

Maybe it won't be that bad, maybe he will die and turn back into a child. She wouldn't be alone in that way anymore.

Reign mentally swore at Tristan, realizing that he could just come around more, and they could complain about it all together. He sulked around, acting like a grumpy old man frowning as kids ran across his front lawn. She could do that. She probably already was doing that to a certain point.

Who was she kidding? She loved him for it. Reign had a soft spot for the assholes.

"I'm scared," a voice bounced off the forest trees, halting Reign in her tracks. "It's still so dark."

It was a child's voice, a boy's voice. She had never seen a child Vrae before, but at least it would be closer to her size if it came to a fight.

"I know you're in there," she yelled, heart racing. "Come out now with your hands clasped behind your back."

Leaves rustled, and multiple feet dragged along the dirt, and Reign was surprised.

Not a single being came out, but an entire group. Their postures were fully alert, and they obeyed her command with their hands mentally handcuffed behind them. She was impressed with herself, with the accidental blessing of unknowingly staring into their eyes through the darkness, her magic still working.

They were kids, and really, they all seemed familiar.

She studied them, all covered in dirt and blood. Her jaw dropped when she finally noticed the wings. Three of them were Kinnari.

"You look like us," the eldest girl's voice rang through the clearing. "Amis, she looks like us."

Without missing a beat, the silhouette of a grown man emerged behind them, his warm skin also covered in dried blood and soot, his hair wild down his back. Reign had never seen Amis look so wild. He usually was polished and poised, as if nothing could bother him. The most rattled he ever seemed was when they had been around Roksana.

"You are a sight for sore eyes, my friend," Amis's smooth voice pulled her anxiousness out of her chest. The source of balance was here. Everything would work out in the end.

Wouldn't it?

"Who are they?" Reign asked though didn't mean it. She felt like she knew, from a dream from such a long time ago, perhaps. She stepped towards the children standing with their arms behind their backs. "Oh. Resume as normal, as you are."

The five children relaxed, their hands coming forward. The toddler trotted right up to Reign, ducking under her wings as if he were playing a game.

"Get back here." Luca stomped after him, circling Reign with his eyes on his subject, intent on catching the giggling toddler. Reign smiled, unsure of how to move, her body becoming a small jungle gym until she was surrounded by all of them. The energy was infectious, and she couldn't hold back her grin.

"You're apparently the new Pied Piper of the last of Waihema," Amis chuckled. "This is why we are here, actually. I want them to be protected and loved. It seems like we are off to a good start."

Reign cocked her head at that, staring at that Kinnari male.

"The last of Waihema?" she replied softly. "The fire destroyed—"

Amis cleared his throat and looked down at his feet. "I don't want to talk about it too much in front of them. They've been through so much. Reign, please meet Salome; Luca here is the oldest male; Ahora and Rangi are our non-marked children, and of course, the baby Noah."

Reign's smile faltered, but the children playing didn't notice much.

"Can you fly?" Luca asked Reign, slightly panting from the fun. "I cannot fly. I can barely move these wings."

"I can do much more than fly with these wings." She smiled. "I can travel through time if I'm going fast enough."

She realized that she hadn't time jumped since she was mutilated, since teeth tore at her flesh, her wings. The insecurity of her lack of strength and possible inability to fly fast enough to do it crept in. She pushed the worry aside. It was such a nuisance, anyway; she shouldn't want that.

Reign watched as Noah and the other children jumped up and down excitedly.

"Do it,"

"Is it scary?"

"Can we see?"

"Woah,"

"Fwa-why, fwa-why!"

Amis clapped his hands twice to command their attention and calm them down.

"I think I have to discuss a few things with my dear friend, Reign," Amis announced.

"Are we there? At the safe place, though?" Salome asked.

"Amis." Reign shook her head. "I think I followed a Vrae here from the north. I just realized that I have left Arryn defenseless and alone."

Amis raised an eyebrow and smirked. "Defenseless? I could never imagine Arryn incapable."

Reign noticed what separated herself from the children was the stillness. They stood there, fidgeting with their hands. They swayed back and forth and twisted their upper bodies left and right. They were so filled with life, with hope. How different than what she would have expected.

Reign, on the other hand, was statuesque. She embodied wisdom and grace, the qualities of an adult woman. Her self-consciousness about her body eased a bit; she was still who she was. Her body did not change her strength or mental fortitude. Funnily enough, it took standing next to lives that were the actual age that she looked to realize that.

Amis waited impatiently, but was finally satisfied once Reign explained what had happened. She watched his lips grow tight and his fists close.

"It took me a long time to heal from Ayurveda's havoc. My knees pop even still. Are we weakening, or were these imperfections a part of us always but have never been noticed?"

Reign stood silent, letting him ponder his question.

"We should get to Arryn," he finally said. "How long of a journey is it on foot to him? I cannot carry them all in the air."

"No." She smiled. "But we can carry the two. Let's teach the children how to fly."

Cheers and joyful screams erupted as Luca and Salome's giant grins tackled her to the ground, knocking the wind out of her slightly.

"Looks like they've got a new leader." Amis chuckled.

Reign sat up on her elbows, smiling from ear to ear as joy was infectious.

"Let's get started, shall we?"

THE NEXT FEW hours that followed were grueling. If there were a unique torture that someone was looking for to get information out of hostages, Reign would recommend trying to teach a toddler something difficult.

Noah would get immediately discouraged in his flying lesson, throwing his fists down and crying as he'd jump three inches into the air and come immediately back down. Reign was realizing that there was never a sound that filled her body with more stress than the shrillness of a toddler upset.

Allienna was a saint for wanting this.

Reign slapped her cheeks with her hands and pulled down so the pink of her bottom eyelids was visible on his seventh or eighth attempt. The crying resumed, so high-pitched and filled with a special whiny tone that really nailed the physical feeling of nails on a chalkboard.

"I'll just carry him." She threw her hands up in the air. "I can't listen to it anymore."

"Seems like you have the patience for kids, there," Amis poked fun at her. He looked perfectly relaxed, as if there was no effect on him. She couldn't believe that. No, he had to be losing his temper under that facade he presented.

Despite the tumultuous montage regarding getting Noah in the skies, Salome and Luca caught on beautifully and without faltering.

Reign picked up the toddler, realizing that his 30 pounds was almost half of her own body weight. How was she supposed to fly with this thing in her arms?

"Let's try this one more time." She bent down to get on Noah's level, looking at him in the eyes as his chubby cheeks seemed to poof a little more as his bottom lip quivered.

"Up!" he demanded, his fingers crawling at her thighs.

"Noah," she said. "You will fly right now with the wings on your shoulders."

With determined eyes and a too-straight back, the power of Reign's command pulsed through the toddler. His chubby forearms raised parallel with his shoulders and his wings pushed out with them as he started to run. His breath was frantic, overdramatic, and comically audible, but after ten seconds or so, he was airborne. His toes lifted behind him as his wings pulsed down, pushing the ground further away.

Noah did a twirl and giggled, looking down at Reign.

"Up!" he repeated as everyone cheered.

Amis scooped the two wingless children into his arms, and everyone was airborne. Reign was the last to join them as they hovered, waiting for her as if wading casually in a pool. With a quick lift, she was with them, the wind blowing through her hair and the smell of the ocean pulsing through her lungs.

She had been away from Arryn for too long, and they were flying so slow. It was faster than walking, of course, but she thanked the gods that there were no ladybugs or flowers in the sky to distract the toddler even further as he moved towards clouds, brushing his hands through them.

Salome, the saint, would fly after him and grab his hand, course-correcting the ticking time bomb that was the three-year-old.

If Arryn had been eaten by a Vrae, it would be her fault.

Maybe.

Some time later, Reign began to see the buildings, structures, and canals that were built in the furthest north part of the land. She directed the others, waving her hands before she began her descent. Relief flooded her body as she circled down, locating a conscious

Arryn who was sitting up with a knee to his chest, watching them and waving.

"Well, look what the cat dragged in." Arryn laughed, slowly getting to his feet and clumsily walking towards Amis with his arms out wide, ready for an embrace. "Look, you've brought an entire family."

Noah tromped right along her side, taking her hand. She looked down at him and frowned as he sucked his left thumb, not a care in the world.

He was cute, even covered in blood, especially when he wasn't crying.

"I think it's time we dunk you in those canals." Reign laughed and picked him up. "What do you think, Arryn? Should they all just live here now?"

Arryn frowned slightly. "I want to get back into town. I need those answers, Reign. I cannot stay, but you can do whatever you wish."

Oh, I know I can do what I wish, you bastard, she thought *and rolled her eyes.*

"You're quite capable of ruining a good mood," she brooded as she guided the children towards the waters. "They will need fresh clothes," Reign yelled back to Arryn, who seemed to do his best not to hear her.

ARRYN AND AMIS walked up to them once they were all bathed and dressed, no more blood and ash covering the children's skin.

"There was something hovering over me when I woke up. It was silhouetted against the sun, so I couldn't tell what I was looking at. Then, it was gone, leaving right before you came," Arryn said to Reign, his voice hushed. Amis' eyebrows were raised as he waited for her to reply, bowing out and giving her the moment.

"I saw a Vrae, Arryn. I chased it, I followed it, and that's how I ran into Amis as it disappeared."

Arryn didn't react with more than a subtle frown and a nod. He turned to look at the children, who were taking turns rolling on the grass and tickling Noah. The giggling was a nice reprieve from the child's cries when he was learning to fly.

"Amis was telling me he wishes for these children to live in a world of magic, surrounded by those who can teach and care for them. I think it's time to go back to Glacier. It will be a rough journey for them, but between us all, we can carry who is least capable," Arryn said.

"You want to carry ordinary mortal children all the way to Glacier?" Reign scoffed.

"Excuse me, miss. Just because we don't have wings doesn't mean that the two of us are ordinary." Ahora's big brown eyes stared with sincerity as she twisted the water out of her hair. "We survived the culling; there is some Kinnari blood that runs through our veins."

Ah, yes, the cull, Reign thought. *I temporarily forgot how shitty Amis is.*

Reign sighed and put her hand on Ahora's cheek. "I hope you all like the cold."

Ahora seemed confused but nodded, putting on a brave face. Arryn easily picked up both of the two wingless children.

"You will sleep through this flight," Reign said as their eyes closed instantly. "I thought it would be better," she explained to Amis, who raised a single eyebrow.

"Can you do this one, too?" He laughed, picking up the toddler. "It's too far a journey. I planned on carrying him."

Reign commanded Noah to sleep. Then she took Salome and Luca each by the hand as they all took flight.

29

H adley | Glacier, Myrilosis

WIND WHIPPED through her hair and her skin, cracking her lips as she traveled down from the temple. She was missing the wyvern, the fire and the warmth. If all were quiet, if all were still, Hadley might be able to hear her own teeth chattering uncontrollably. She was not dressed for this; her attire was still more appropriate for the beaches of Bangladesh.

She had made it, made it to this place of magic. She hadn't seen any proof of it yet, and if it weren't for Reifoel, she would have absolutely not believed that they weren't just walking down the other side of the mountain.

Heat trickled down the back of her neck, and it was hard not to sink into that breath. Sheng's voice whispered along with the wind.

"Let me hold you."

Hadley shook her head, very aware of how close his teeth were to her exposed skin. No, she would not fall into his trap again. She would not let herself be used again.

"Don't touch me," she said, trying to distance them. She wasn't achieving that goal too well, her feet were frozen, likely unable to carry her much longer. She would need to fly. She should fly. She should fly away from them all.

Fingers intertwined with hers, and Hadley saw red, turning around to shout and let her shadow self jump straight into Sheng. Instead, she was met with Reifoel's gaze, his fingers laced with hers.

"Are you okay?" he asked.

Hadley felt the blood rise in her cheeks, and she turned away, watching as her shadow self danced around them, making kissing lips, giggling at her. Hadley rolled her eyes and marched right past her.

Keeping her gaze ahead of her, Hadley saw rooftops in the distance. There, a town existed, and she closed her eyes, bringing her chin up towards the sky in relief. She was so tired of almost dying.

She was sure that if she was mortal, she wouldn't have made it this far in the cold. Somewhere in that town was a bed with a hot bath, and behind her was a Vrae who was richer than anyone else she knew. Hopefully, his wealth could be applied to this world too and they could get proper lodgings.

She couldn't focus on the magic around her, the beauty of the multi-colored bugs lighting up around her as she walked, the different species moving about, staring at her skin, blue and red with wings of glass reflecting the sunset behind her.

She could only move absentmindedly.

Someone grabbed her hips and guided her until she was inside, in a bed, under covers. Her head sunk into a pillow, and her eyes fluttered closed, taking in Reifoel as he walked out and closed a door behind him.

∾

HADLEY'S SHADOW self snuggled up next to her, their backs touching. She couldn't physically feel the contact, but there was comfort in knowing she had herself and could protect herself. It was the greatest gift she could have asked for: not ever truly being alone.

After awakening, she felt sore throughout her body. An ache that pulsed even through her fingernails had her wincing as she swayed herself back and forth until she had the momentum to sit up and stand. The window reflected a night sky with more stars than she had ever seen before, giving it a dazzling hue that gave the illusion that the town before her was under a spotlight.

Hadley's eyes widened as she watched ghostly pale figures float in the air. Their faces looked incredibly busy and determined, but their bodies gracefully wafted as if they had nowhere to go.

What are you?

A knock came at her door, and she jumped, the repetition startling her. She stared, wondering if she should open it or pretend that she was still sleeping. She was leaning toward pretending.

The knock came again, more urgently than before.

"Hadley," Sheng's voice came from the other side of the door. Hadley searched for her shadow self, who was dancing in front of the vanity mirror, unbothered.

Of course, you wouldn't be scared.

Her shadow self looked over to her, sticking her tongue out at her own thought.

"What a wonderful world it must be to have a terrifyingly powerful magic at your fingertips," Hadley said out loud to the figure.

"What was that?" Sheng's voice returned through the other side of the door. "I didn't hear you there."

Shit.

She'd forgotten he was there.

"I'm just here to see if you're okay," Sheng said, his voice softening. Hadley stared at the door, at its plain wood texture. When she gazed at this door, she did not feel like magic was around her. It was so normal, so ordinary. It was surprising how good that felt.

Her mind flittered to Hector again, the weight of his memory.

Him spinning her around as he convinced her to take drugs and dance was once as normal as the door that she stared at.

"Hadley, we are all downstairs, eating. It's hot food. I think you should eat."

If she stayed quiet, he might leave.

"I'm not going to go away," he muttered, making her furious.

So he could read her thoughts now, could he?

You are not similar. You are not alike.

"Hadley," Sheng said, almost pleading.

Don't open that door. Don't be an idiot.

She watched as her shadow self twirled up to the door and walked right through it, smiling like a lunatic.

Maybe I'd be better off alone, after all.

Sheng knocked again.

"Fine," she shouted, strutting up to the door and flinging it open. She scowled at the man before her, hating that his arm rested on the doorframe above her. His strong jaw angled down towards her face. His lips curved into a smile that conveyed mischief, satisfaction. His eyes, smoldering, lit up when her gaze met his.

He is your enemy.

Hadley looked at his hand, inches from her, and scowled at him. He understood right away and lifted his hands up and away, taking a step back.

"I know, I know, no touching." He smirked as if he were a god, doing her a favor.

Asshole.

"There are Kinnari downstairs; we are all eating together. I think you should come down," Sheng said.

Kinnari. That word again.

"I don't want to see them," she said instantly.

"Then what are you doing here?" Sheng asked. "What is it that you are trying to find?"

She gulped, taking in the scent of his body as he stilled, hovering over her.

"I'm looking for peace," she practically spat before turning to slam the door in his face. Sheng stopped her, stopped the door from closing by pushing back. He grabbed her wrist with his other hand and pulled her into him, her right ear up against his chest.

Hadley was momentarily breathless but immediately looked for her shadow, ready to jump into the Vrae, color switching from black to translucent.

She couldn't make up her mind. Did she want him dead, or did she want control?

His chin brushed against the top of her head as he pushed her back and let go.

"Sorry, it was a physical response. I couldn't help it."

She tried not to look into his gorgeous eyes or ignore his sincerity. "You are the worst," was all she could say, her stomach fluttering, her breath catching.

"Oh, I can be bad, that's for sure," he chuckled, his gaze lingering on her collarbone. "How about I step in and help get you bathed so I can show you how bad I can be?"

He didn't look away, he just stared into her, pulling her apart without even knowing.

"If I come downstairs, will you leave my doorway?"

Sheng's smile faltered for a moment, long enough for her to notice. He straightened his posture and nodded his head.

"I'll wait for you at the top of the stairs," he said.

"Please don't."

Hadley shut the door, found a tub, and filled it with hot, steaming water.

ONCE SHE HAD FINISHED bathing and dressing, sporting a long-sleeved wool-like burgundy dress that was conveniently left hanging in the modest closet, Hadley took a breath and opened the door, stepping into the hallway.

The wooden rail let her see down to the first floor, revealing the lobby of a small inn. A grumpy creature sat at the front desk, nose buried in a newspaper.

Sheng stood at the top of the stairs, a knight protecting his princess.

"I told you not to wait," she said, walking right past him and down the carpeted steps, her blonde hair whipping against him as he shuffled, trying to give her space.

A bouncing, excited blur sprinted towards her, picking her up and spinning.

"I was a little worried about you," Reifoel said, placing her down. "I'm glad I intercepted you before you got into the dining hall."

Sheng reached the bottom of the stairs, clearing his throat. "I believe I was her escort."

"I can take it from here." Reifoel smirked, grabbing her hand, pulling her over to a sofa, and sitting her down. Sheng smiled, with all his teeth, and there was no doubt in that moment how dangerous he was. Reifoel looked nervous despite his best efforts to stay calm, to look strong.

Sheng bowed, not breaking eye contact, his terrifying smile not faltering.

"This is me, able to give you space. A perfectly healthy marriage we have."

"We found him. He's here," Reifoel said, watching wearily as Sheng slinked off. "The man from our mother's legend. Isadore has been buttering him up all night."

"Thank you," she said softly as she stood up.

"What for?" Reifoel asked, pulling her gently towards the opening that would bring them into the next room.

Hadley could hear the laughter, the joy that came from that corridor. She could smell meat and unfamiliar spices but delicious spices. She knew, though, who was there. She knew her father was who they had sought. She possibly would have rather been back in that closet, chains around her ankles, then to be rejected by him again.

She could feel in her bones his utter disdain for her. The one and only time they had met, when they stood face to face, he had acted as if she were irrelevant. This man who could have easily changed the course of her life, even potentially made it a happy one, had the world to give yet gave her nothing.

"You still haven't told me why you were thanking me," Reifoel reminded her as her gaze wandered back to him.

"For getting me away from him, from Sheng," she said. "I don't think I can go in there. They are all in there, aren't they?"

"I don't really know who you are talking about specifically, but yes, there is a large group table that takes up most of the dining area. They're drawing a lot of dirty looks from the locals. It's entertaining."

Reifoel held out his hand to her, a gentle smile gracing his face while he made his offering.

"Are they—are they waiting for me? Do they know I'm here?" Hadley swallowed, her mouth dry and stomach rumbling. When was the last time she had eaten? She was having trouble recalling.

"I won't leave your side unless you want me to," he promised her, his fingers spreading wider on his open palm.

"What if I never want that?" she asked sincerely.

She felt safer with him around, like a security blanket. He was warm, soft, and gentle, all things she had never had in her adult life. She took his hand, his skin smoother than she had ever felt it before. Her touch lingered, and she could feel his urge to pull away, his inexperience and insecurity.

"You feel nice," she said. Reifoel's eyes beamed at that, and she saw the tension he hid leave his neck as the muscles along his jawline and shoulders relaxed. His eyes widened as he drank her in, his gaze lingering on her exposed collarbone and the curve of her breast.

"I sat in the bathtub for a few hours while you were asleep. My body needed it. I will have to return to the ocean soon enough, especially now that we found the one we've been looking for."

The two walked a few feet, the doorway again looming before them. Hadley could see the brown tables, unfussy and perfect in a casual pub setting. She held back a laugh as she watched a creature that seemed covered in frostbite spill ale all over itself by tilting the cup back before its lips made contact.

Lively music played across invisible speakers, but it was not louder than the conversations. No one was there for dancing, but everyone in the dining hall sure was enjoying the company that they were keeping.

On the further side of the hall, parallel to a separate entrance that led to frost and winter outside, were six or seven full-length tables pushed side by side. Hadley spotted Isadore at the edge, his left leg kicked out, and he bounced as if planning to stand at any minute. He was sitting next to a large blond man with cerulean wings that took up the width of a single table, even folded in.

Hadley saw what Reifoel was talking about. Every creature that opened the exterior door and walked in spotted him immediately; he stood out incredibly. Their open hearts were tucked away, their brows furrowed as they took in the Kinnari, her father.

He is certainly not welcome here.

"What did he say?" Hadley's eyes bore into her father's back. "What did he say when you met him?"

"Well, he seemed a bit drunk." Reifoel chuckled, his dimples appearing. "Isadore took his task very seriously and explained who we were. The Kinnari man seemed a bit unimpressed."

This sounds typical, then.

"Then I told him my mother, the queen, had sent us to find him. To tell him that we are suspicious of the Earth's rotation slowing."

Hadley noticed Reifoel's pause, his eyes darting away from her as if he didn't know what to say.

"Well." She squeezed his hand, letting her thumb brush over his hand. "Then what did he do?"

"He was drunk. It doesn't matter," Reifoel mumbled, but quickly lifted his gaze and refocused it on her. "I wanted to apologize to you."

Hadley caught a glimmer, a speck of a ghost. Her chin didn't move, but her eyes followed it. Her shadow self was in this new form as it stalked over towards Arryn, her almighty and mythical father.

Did she want him dead? Could she even do that? A human was one thing, but something large and powerful like him seemed like it was untouchable.

Her shadow had jumped on the table. The warm light of the bulbs overhead added a haze over her as the illumination learned how to interact with this new and untested physical state.

She danced along that table unnoticed, passing the rest of the group, which was funnily enough, mostly children. Some had wings, while a few did not. All but one seemed bored, the others sleepy, laying their heads down on their arms or holding their chins up with their fists.

Sitting next to Amis was a bright-eyed girl who Hadley guessed was around ten years old, chugging ale from pint glasses and laughing too loudly every time the barmaid with breasts entirely too bouncy not to stare at walked away from their group. Hadley watched as that barmaid slid her hand over Arryn's shoulder, how he turned his head and let his eyes linger as she walked away.

The filthy pig.

"Reign, you are killing me." Amis snorted loudly.

Reign.

Hadley knew that name from another life. She knew that woman who seemed to want to be there for her. Her eyes scanned the table again and settled on where Amis's eyes were looking as the seemingly tipsy child became very familiar to her. Those dark eyes, hair, demeanor, and posture held an air of maturity and superiority.

"Let's join them. We can sit right next to Sheng." Reifoel caught the look on Hadley's face. He immediately corrected himself, "I will sit next to him, and you can sit next to me if you'd like, of course."

At least there was a buffer, and she could avoid more direct contact with her kidnapper. The glimmer of her shadow self made the air dance around her while she hovered right between Sheng and her father. Both males who had helped to destroy her life, her confidence, and her well-being were right across from one another, and she was expected to just sit there.

Would they expect her to smile? To be nice? She wouldn't do either of those things. Her thoughts were much more murderous than that.

Her shadow self was such a tease, such a test of her self-control.

She could jump, plunge into them both if only to see if they too could turn into glass, like her own wings. She could then shatter them like they'd shattered her own heart.

Reifoel tugged on her hand as she followed him, walking up to the table. Arryn's booming voice, tinged with a looseness that could be blamed on the ale, could be deciphered as they stepped closer.

"Why would I need such a thing, a child?" Arryn laughed, slamming his hands down on the table. "Look at them. They are no fun. They are asleep when there is only liveliness around them." Arryn motioned towards the children that littered the opposite ends of the table.

"I only meant that I hope to find someone to help raise and nurture them. Show them that these wings can be a blessing. They only know them to be a curse."

Arryn turned his nose up at that, taking another long drink from the glass in front of him, discomfort thick in the air around him.

"You took care of a boy in the gladiator training camps. You could be a father." Reign stood up, her eyes meeting Hadley's, her cheeks flushed with surprise. "You even have a flesh and blood daughter. You could easily help care for one of these children."

Arryn slammed his hand down on the table with his now empty glass.

"That girl is no child of mine. She is responsible for her mother's death. There is nothing that can convince me otherwise. That girl could die tonight, and I wouldn't mourn. The love of my life, my Allienna, would be avenged."

Reign's mouth hung open as she stared right at Hadley, her hand wobbling on the table. "Arryn, how could you say that?"

"You know how I feel," he grumbled, turning with his empty glass waving in the air, looking for a refill. Everyone else took notice of Hadley, took notice of Arryn's kin standing right behind him, a picture of distress, a pillar of anguish.

Hadley felt her world fall down around her, like large chunks of ice breaking off of a glacier, falling into sub-zero water. There were so many eyes on her, too many that all stared at her as if she were a dying puppy, as if she just needed a treat and a pet to feel better.

Reifoel pulled her back, closer to him, and whispered, "Let's go," but she didn't hear him. She didn't hear anything except for the man accusing her of killing the one person she had ever truly had in this world, her mom. He claimed her. He acted as if her mother belonged to him. No, no, she couldn't allow him to think that. She couldn't allow her to live in his wretched memories.

The glimmer was there, hovering over him, and Hadley nodded, giving her shadow self permission.

Dead, he could be dead.

That would solve her problem. He could break, like a pathetic crystal vase, knocked to the ground by a careless elbow passing by, not giving it any thought. She smiled, and Arryn turned to see what everyone else was looking at.

"Ah, of course," he said, her shadow self picking up a leg to jump into him. "Of course, it's you. I suppose you heard all that? Quite the mood you've killed here."

Speechless. Hadley was speechless, and her shadow self cocked its head towards her, confused, asking what to do.

Reifoel tugged on her arm again, and this time, she stepped with him, walking backward until the table, the dining hall, was out of sight. She clutched her free arm to her shoulder, wrapped around herself like saran wrap, holding in whatever was about to burst out from her heart. Her breaths were short, gasping in through her lips while forgetting to exhale, giving way to the anxiety that trickled down her throat and into the pit of her stomach.

It could be her fault. She didn't actually know. She was sick, so sick, her mother. Her father was an asshole, absolutely, but he rejected her entirely, without remorse. There had to be truth in there, then, for such an absolute belief. She was learning more and more every day about how deadly she could be and how manipulative she was.

It was possible her father wasn't the asshole. He might have been the good guy. She was the evil that plagued this group, murdered loved ones, even potentially unknowingly.

Sheng is worse than you. Sheng is worse than you.

Hadley looked back towards the entryway that led back into the dining hall. She was looking for Sheng, the monster that plagued her nightmares but would not leave her side. He was there with her forever. She could feel that, whether she wanted him or not. He would not reject her; he never had.

Hands wrapped around her navel, and Hadley felt herself being pulled into the body behind her. She let it happen, utterly numb to the outside world, trapped within the grief that caused the tears welling into her eyes. She pushed those tears back and turned to look up at Reifoel, the worry on his face evident.

"Are you okay?" he asked. "Let's get you out of here."

"Take me back upstairs, please," she begged, her words so soft, so damaged. "I don't want anyone to look at me."

Reifoel nodded and tried to guide her towards the stairs on the opposite side of the inn, but she didn't budge, move, or breathe. She just stared up at him, feeling so tired and sad. There was a hole inside her, and she just needed to feel like a real person, someone who wasn't broken. She needed to fix those broken parts of her, fill up that emptiness like she was clinging onto an oxygen tube right before getting pushed out into space.

"What is it?" he asked, her breath hot against his neck as he stared into her eyes, pleading, longing, filled with pain and ruin and desperation.

Hadley grabbed the collar of his black crewneck sweater and pulled his lips down to hers. There was a fullness there, as she sunk into the kiss and let her mouth part. His tongue slipped into that opening, and she sucked lightly before he pulled back and kissed her again, then again.

She was voracious, hungry, and he seemed to be the same, responding to her body by pressing more into hers until she felt a wall behind her.

A loud, obvious grunt sounded, and Reifoel pulled off of her. He looked over at the creature that tended the front desk, his nose buried in the newspaper.

"There are private rooms upstairs; I suggest you explore those," his gruff, disapproving voice said.

Hadley beamed at Reifoel, whose brow was heavy. He shook his head and grabbed her hand. This time, she followed as they passed a few pieces of furniture, a coffee table, and couches and walked up the very stairs that Sheng had brought her down from not twenty minutes ago.

They walked down the hallway and stopped in front of the door to his room. Reifoel looked at her, and instead of going inside, kept walking until they reached her door. She didn't care where they went or where they were. She just needed the touch, the comfort. She needed that acceptance, someone wanting her for her, not because they paid for her, not because she had magic in her blood.

Reifoel and Hadley crashed through the door to her room as it slammed dramatically against the wall on the other side. Hadley's hands were on his chest, and he moved down to his pants, looking for the clasp that kept his body hidden from her.

Feverish kisses pressed along her neck, descending to her collarbone while his hands explored her. He was cautious, gentle in his touch, as his palms pressed into her breast, massaging down until he reached her hips, fingers hungrily tugging up on her skirt, trying to find their way underneath.

They stood in the middle of the room, twisted around each other, audible breaths providing the soundtrack to their passion. Hadley moaned against another kiss, Reifoel's lips caressing hers as he triumphantly found the end of her dress.

She let her head fall back, feeling his hands move up the sides of her thighs; the contact with her bare skin had her breath out loudly, almost a shudder, while everything continued to hit her: the rejections, the lack of control, the constant pain of not knowing who she was supposed to be. A small tear escaped the corner of her eye while Reifoel's lips moved along her skin, her chest.

He paused, raising his chin to study her. She quickly wiped away the evidence, the sadness from her eyes.

"Please," she gasped, "please don't stop." Her chest heaved, her dress pulled halfway up over her body while she leaned back, fully supported in his arms.

But he didn't continue. He just stared at her, and his face, which had been so filled with passion and heat, was now concerned, even scared. It reminded her of how he looked at her in Bangladesh when he had stepped a little further away.

"What's wrong?" She breathed in his scent, salt, like the ocean, like his home.

"I can't," was all he said. "Look at you. It's not right. Not like this."

He let her go, his arms coming back into his sides as her heart shot up to her throat. Empty, she was empty again. He was leaving. He didn't want her. No one wanted her.

She looked up at him, hurt evident in her face.

"You're upset," he said. "I can't take advantage of you like this."

"You can stay, you can hold me," Hadley said, holding back a sob as more tears began to freely flow.

"It's just not right. I'm sorry. I really am."

Reifoel walked through the door, still open, without another look, without another word, and shut it behind him.

Hadley stood there, staring at the back of that door, exactly where she was earlier, as she contemplated pretending to still be asleep and took short, quick breaths through her mouth. She walked toward it, turned, and let her back slide down as she sat. With her knees pulled into her chest, she let it all go, the sound of her cries loud enough to be heard by the innkeeper down the stairs.

Alone, she would always be alone. She hated Reifoel for leaving her and her father for rejecting her. It was a mistake to have followed any of them, to play around, pretending that she was a part of some little family.

A glimmer moved towards her, her shadow self in its deadliest form.

"Find her," she instructed through sobs. "Find Ayurveda, bring her to me."

30

Reifoel | Glacier, Myrilosis

He'd had her in his arms, her scent lingering on his skin. She had tasted like nothing he could have imagined, so sweet, yet there was a tang that he couldn't let go of that made his blood boil. This kind of heat was so new, so raw, and he could see why, for the first time, a male would give his life to protect it, to preserve it, to savor it. He needed to get into the water and get rid of the skin that was so hard between his two legs before he considered strangling the creator, Sheng, or anyone who had hurt her.

The more time Reifoel spent near Hadley, the harder it was to hide this pull towards her, this passion that built like a current underneath calm and cool water. He was no longer denying it. He was no longer hiding it. He was infatuated with the Kinnari girl. She haunted the corners of his mind constantly, and she certainly scared the shit out of him.

He would do this correctly; she deserved the world, and the least he could do was properly court her. To make love with his human body for the first time was a thought that put a slight savagery into his decisions. He wanted to push her into the wall, throw her onto the bed, and make love for hours. He had a feeling that she had never had that before, someone to focus entirely on her, someone who would very well come undone simply by watching her do so.

His eyes gleamed at the thought as he sucked on his lip, walking into his room at the inn, which he was sharing with Isadore. It was identical to hers, except there were two smaller beds, making the space feel crowded even if there was no one else.

That tear that fell when they were in the middle of something new, something exciting, had stopped him in his tracks. The Kinnari male that they had sought was an ass, unfortunately, but facing that kind of rejection had to have affected her. She needed time, and he would be there, even if it was from afar, to give it to her until she was ready for him. Ready to not be able to leave their bed because she couldn't properly stand.

Reifoel cracked a fiendish grin, looking down at his feet as he walked straight toward the bathroom. He would soak in that tub all night and check in on her once she had some sleep, maybe even bring her down to breakfast. He could follow her forever to wherever. Whatever she needed to accomplish, whatever it was she needed to do, he would be there every step of the way. His home, his family, his ocean, behind him. Another life he would gladly give up for her, to kiss her so tenderly, to marvel at the power that he didn't understand, couldn't understand. He could embrace it, though. He just needed the pep talk, the one from himself that reminded him what he wanted, where his heart pointed to.

The door opened and closed behind him as Isadore stomped into the room and flopped down on his own bed, his long blond hair floating down behind him while his long limbs hung over the side, foot slumped on the wooden floor.

"This is much better than that cave, I have to say." He snorted, throwing off his shirt and tucking under a taupe blanket. "Bath time again? You're certainly missing home, aren't you now?"

"I just need to think," Reifoel said, turning away.

"Yes, well, now we can think about returning to Serelune. We have done our task. It is not our fault the oaf will not take our words seriously. This journey has all been one massive waste of time, and I could have very well been spending it figuring out how to become the true heir. Let's be honest, I know you don't want to be king."

Reifoel massaged the spot between his temples. "Cousin, I thought we had . . . what's the saying, turned over a new leaf?"

"I have no idea what that means." Isadore laughed and flopped back on a pillow, his arms behind his head, "I just know that to be king means to marry and rule at home, and we all saw how Hadley did under the water. I don't think that's going to work out very well for her."

His cousin wasn't wrong. She had drowned under that water, she could not live a full happy life there. It was better, perhaps, that he had walked away from her. He would hurt and suffer and pray to any deity that she would not end up with Sheng, but he couldn't negate his born duty, no matter how much he dreamed of doing just that. He couldn't give up his title and live on land, in the Earth realm of all places. That would rip out his mother's own heart.

You could. You would. You want to.

Though he would love it, he would love spending the rest of his life in a cottage or a lighthouse and having a human job in the Earth realm. He could give his mother grandchildren and convince her to see the surface, a place that he wasn't convinced she had ever actually seen. That could be his life together with Hadley.

If Hadley still wanted him.

But there was a special hell inside him that imagined his cousin winning, wearing a crown of bone on his head.

"I will marry whoever I am betrothed to once that time comes," Reifoel said, trying to seem bored, waving the conversation off as if the entire accusation was a fallacy.

"If you say so, then. We shall start our way back after some sleep. Hopefully that water will be warmer than the air in this town."

Reifoel took two more steps toward the bathroom before the wall in front of him dislodged, blasting fire and brick onto him as he fell down to the first story. The floor underneath him was gone, and walls were falling apart around him. Anything flammable had disintegrated from heat alone. Reifoel's skin was cracked, devoid of all moisture. He couldn't move from the pain, the crackling, he was about to fall apart. It happened so fast that at first, he didn't understand, didn't comprehend what was happening.

Frigid wind whipped through him, a sharp smack against him like a scourge coming down angrily and making contact with his back, cheeks, and knees as the realization dawned on him. They had been attacked.

Water. I need water.

"Isadore," Reifoel yelled. Snow fell from the night sky, and the small town that was visible was perfectly intact. There was no answer from his cousin, his enemy of circumstance, his companion who he had indeed learned to love. There was no bed where Reifoel last saw him, no floor, just a gaping hole.

"Isadore," he repeated in a whisper this time. It was a prayer, an understanding that he would not get a reply. He was surprised that he himself could even move his lips, use his throat, or make a noise. A snowflake hit his arm and it hissed, harmonizing with the ever-relenting gusts.

White creatures floated down, lining up around the town square, and began to freeze, perfect cubes forming around them.

Sunrise, it was almost sunrise.

"You can't go," a voice, nearly lost in the wind, floated up to Reifoel. His eyes glanced down. The most movement he could manage through the sharp pain that followed was possibly not worth the sleuthing.

"She doesn't want you," that same voice shouted again.

He knew that voice. It was Sheng's voice. He was angry, upset, running into the middle of the square, presumably talking to no one. It looked like he had lost it, had gone insane, but did Sheng have the power to blow up a building? Reifoel wasn't convinced of it.

"I'm going. You cannot stop me." Hadley stepped out, her hips swaying back and forth. There was so much magic and power around her that she almost glowed, a glimmer in the air circling her as she moved. Her wings were out, large, sharp, and translucent, giving the snow behind her a tint of blue from the moon and night sky.

Her blonde hair blew violently in the wind, and something in the way she moved told him that she was tired—tired of being cornered and mistreated. She was leaving them and didn't plan on returning, even if the world burned behind her.

"I have found you, my daughter," words that echoed through the sky caressed Reifoel like the lull of a warm, relaxing tide, allowing him to ride until he was ready to wake, unaware of where he might be.

"She is not your daughter." Arryn ran out, speaking to someone Reifoel still couldn't see. Arryn shook his hands up towards the sky at its darkest peak. The sun would rise at any moment.

"Who do you think that Kinnari came to," the mature, worldly voice filled the air around them again. "When she begged to be able to carry a child? She gave her life for the ability, and I helped execute it."

Reifoel watched the creator, the Kinnari, Arryn's back straighten. The words sobered him up, and moments later, he fell to his knees and sobbed in the snow, his shoulders convulsed with his alcohol-infused sobbing.

"It was you," Reifoel deciphered through Arryn's cries as he repeated himself. "You killed her."

Light, vibrant orange with peaks of angry red hit the horizon, and as Reifoel watched the sun rise, fear finally sunk into him as a figure emerged. It radiated heat, and haze outlined a woman's body, emerging from the sunrise rapidly approaching. A blast of fire erupted from her chest, hitting the building next door to the inn. Reifoel heard screams and saw creatures flee, those who could travel by air the only ones fast enough to avoid the next blast of fire, making Reifoel's skin hissed as it hit another building nearby.

"This world is mine," the figure hissed, her mouth opening into a smile that would terrify the most brutal of creatures. "I am your Goddess; I am the sun."

Ayurveda.

Reifoel hadn't known that the Gods were real, they were a part of myths and stories, but he did know that not one of them would mean anything good for the living. Gods were not symbols of bounty and harmony, they were symbols of retribution, of penance, of brutality. There was a special kind of sinister motivation, to create life and then torture it throughout its existance.

If he could have moved, Reifoel would have cursed Arryn. He was just as bad, crying in the snow as if he were the victim.

"You found me," Hadley's voice was filled with relief and joy, and she tiptoed into the sky, her wings bringing her towards the Goddess, the one being that seemed to have earned her trust. That talented, powerful woman was so hurt, so rejected, that she'd become the villain. She had been torn away from her, convinced of the pain the two of them would cause together, and yet, here she was looking at Ayurveda as if she were her savior, her family.

Hadley yelped as Sheng jumped unnaturally high, his mortal body changing to that of smooth, oil-black skin. His head was perfectly round, and his mouth looked cut from ear to ear. With eyes a murderous red and an opened, dagger-toothed mouth, Sheng bit into Hadley's shin as she screamed. Sheng looked like he had hit a wall, unconscious, and fell to the ground while Hadley floated down to nurse her leg.

"I'm so sorry," the words unexpectedly fell out of her mouth as she limped towards Sheng. She doesn't know that I love you. I forget sometimes, too, about my love for you."

Love? She hated him.

Jealousy hit Reiofel instantly, and he found the strength to take a step. It was agony. His skin was nearly powder, falling around him while he was safe on an undestroyed beam that creaked and rumbled with even the thought of moving too quickly.

Water. I need water.

"It looks like we are just in time," a lovely high pitched voice sang out. Two redheaded Kinnari appeared, seemingly out of nowhere. They moved to Arryn's side, helping him stand.

"We will need you to leave this world to us," said the deeper-voiced redhead. Reifoel noticed how similar they appeared, realizing that they were twins.

He turned his head to the right, where the bathroom should have been, to see water bursting through broken pipes.

"Oh, thank Gods," he whispered. His eyes flickered to Ayurveda, hovering in the sky, an ominous presence over the beautiful town. "Well, I'm not thanking that one," he added.

Reifoel let the heat, the scathing dryness of his skin, sink into him. He embraced the searing, the stinging, the pain and let it become a part of him. It was the only way he could face the agony of getting to that water. If he didn't, he would surely die, like his cousin. He couldn't let that happen. He couldn't imagine his mother's grief. The guilt she would face for the rest of her life for sending him on this journey. That was not something anyone deserved.

No, he had to survive, for his mother. For his father.

They needed an heir, his home, his people, needed him.

He kept moving, unaware if he was screaming or sobbing or holding his breath. The water was there. It was so close. If he could just take a few more steps, he could reach his hand out. That would be enough.

The edges of Reifoel's vision fogged, a darkness creeping in until he couldn't see. There was only blackness, but the swift movement of air pushed against him.

I'm falling. I'm falling, and there might not be a floor to catch me.

Something did indeed catch him, and it was unclear if he had been unconscious for just a few seconds or much longer since he thankfully did not feel the impact. The skin that peeled off of him would have surely caused a level of agony when he hit the ground.

Reifoel opened his eyes, grateful that he had landed perfectly in line with the support beam he was inching his way along. Small flicks of heaven, of perfectly wonderful relief trickled through him. It was stardust, magic, giving him a new thread of life to hold on to, to pull himself away from death.

The water, he fell close enough to the spouting waterline. Reifoel pulled his arm out from underneath his body, wincing from the rough contact as he freed it. He moaned and then gathered his breath, reaching all the way down to his fingertips for the smallest puddle, the smallest splash of water that rested on the beam's edge. Those mere ounces could be the mercy and salvation that he couldn't dream to ask for. Not here, not with this heat and death unfolding beneath him.

He understood it, the hate for the Kinnari. They were so careless, throwing all caution to the wind. Everyone and everything, including members of their species, seemed disposable, like they were just playing gods in a simulator.

Reifoel's fingers connected with the ounces of water that sat, dripping down the beam's edges as it collected more sprinkles from the spouting pipe. His breath evened out, and his heartbeat grew stronger. No more water dripped; instead, he soaked in it, the moisture traveling through him, healing him.

He wanted to weep. He knew he was on the brink of death. A Serelune devoid of any moisture would be the same as a shark that couldn't swim in its sleep.

More shouts and sounds of fire hitting buildings nearby shook the beam. Reifoel held on with his right hand, not letting his fingertips break contact with that water. Minutes passed, and skin that had been just falling off of his bones looked nearly healthy once more. His legs weaved together as the tough exterior of a finned, shiny black scaled tail formed.

Reifoel planned to stay there, clinging to that water and beam, hoping that what was happening on the ground and in the sky would be over quickly.

A blast of fire shot over his head, hitting a tower behind the inn. Reifoel closed his eyes and wondered what Isadore would do.

31

Precession | Glacier, Myrilosis

"So much death, so much destruction," Precession sang, the normal meekness in her voice absent. She pulled her arm away from Roksana, not needing the support. She was barely tethered, letting gravity and the moon fall further away from her as she confronted the Goddess who had destroyed her beloved home and scared away her gatekeeper.

It was so hard to find good help these days, even if Michel could be a nuisance. He was still family. Those Vrae had become a sort of family, too, though Roksana surely would never agree. How empty the silence had seemed since her home was destroyed. Since her farm animals and little pet demons had all met their demise. Precession wasn't one to talk ill of someone, but she did not like that, she did not like that at all.

Precession turned around, her eyes leaving the Goddess hovering in the air as she noticed a young girl dragging the bodies of what appeared to be children out from the mostly depleted building. That building was hanging on by a thread, and that girl was Reign.

Well, it was good that they were all together again, then.

"Amis," Roksana gasped. The Kinnari who fed her sister's passions and fire emerged behind Reign. He was carrying out children, too, children with wings.

A creature that Precession didn't recognize, pale and white with glasses that desperately hung onto his nose, was working with the two Kinnari, trying to provide aid. He was limping. The creature was hurt while the children seemed passed out cold. Precession hoped that their chests rose and fell and that she was just too far away to notice.

"Would you believe that this is the second time they've been in this situation?" Precession heard Amis say to Roksana by way of greeting him as she ran over to him, trying to help. "I promised. I promised I would keep them safe."

"They're alive," Roksana shouted over the chaos as more buildings broke apart around them. "It's okay; they are alive."

A woman hobbled out behind them, wearing a barkeep dress. There was something about her, so calm and collected, a healing energy surrounded her. Precession wondered if anyone else saw it.

The woman seemed content to be ignored while she made her way to Arryn, holding her hands out like they were wet, like she was planning to do something with them. Instead, the barkeep put her hands on Arryn's back. The massive blond Kinnari male seemed frozen, not moving. with his body plopped in the snow. He stayed down, not responsive to the barkeep's touch, his head in his hands. That woman placed her hands on his shoulders, then lay her chest over his back in comfort.

"Please don't ya cry, now, big guy," she said, her hushed voice in a tone carried by the wind, letting Precession into the private moment.

"You cannot help her," a dominant male voice made Precession turn back around, noticing Hadley laying full length in the snow on her stomach, blue blood gently pulsing from her leg while a Vrae in his full form held onto her.

Hadley whipped her body around slowly to look at him, her eyes filled with what looked like love.

"You will follow me," he said to her.

"I will follow you." She nodded her head.

"I love you," the Vrae said back to her. "One day, you'll say it back to me without a bite. I'm sorry for breaking your rule."

Hadley just stared back at him, saying nothing. Her head bobbed slightly, as if she were drunk, as if she were not herself.

If there was one thing that Precession understood so deeply, so fully, was the responsibility of the power she held. She had been trapped by it, like a lion in a cage, obedient and thankful for the scraps of meaningful life she got to experience. This girl, there was no difference there. She was so young. She was still growing into her powers. She would be chained to Ayurveda for her entire life, just like Precession was tied to the moon.

Precession couldn't let that happen.

She looked up to the Goddess, who wore an expression of amusement as embers rained down from her hands. The Vrae twisted his body in an effort to avoid them but failed, instead flailing his body over Hadley, protecting her as his skin smoked and burned.

"You do actually know that Vrae," a young boy's voice said as a new figure appeared next to her, brown curls in his hair and a scowl that reflected how much more he knew about this situation than them all.

"Hello, Tristan." Precession's voice was like wedding bells amongst the dismay. "I wouldn't have expected you to make an appearance."

Tristan tsked, then ran his fingers through his hair. They watched together as the Vrae screamed, a flame now ignited on his lower back. Hadley seemed suffocated, lost underneath him, staring at his face with the awe of a girlish crush.

"I need the girl. The alternative is to destroy this world you love so childishly. I am trying to save you from yourselves." Ayurveda's voice was weary, a promise of affection—an affection that they all surely didn't want.

"I've been waiting for this day since I was killed." Tristan laughed with his entire body, pointing his thumb casually at the Goddess in the sky. "She's a riot, isn't she?"

"Is this it, then?" Precession asked, "when I scream?"

The merriment on Tristan's face disappeared, his hands settling into the pockets of his trousers.

"That Vrae, there, he was the one that let Amis live. Once the others had their fill with me, he pulled the rest of them back. Is he on our side? Probably not, but he sure as hell is not aligned with the Goddess who made him."

Something large, something heavy, whizzed by them right at the Goddess. A giant ball of ice and snow, in a futile hope to defend the town, had been cast.

"You are not welcome here," a voice of wisdom and beauty said. It was a giantess, a woman so lovely and tall that she seemed to float on a skirt of white roses curved from snow. She was accompanied by a choir of her peers, seven or eight of them together, taking up most of the town square.

Together, they were forming another ball of snow, ready to defend their home and all that they loved.

Ayurveda instantly flamed, an inferno in the sky blazing orange and red. Everything around them began to melt as the sun blazed too close, too hot, not pulling back. The giantesses wailed, their bodies melting, eyes and noses dripping down into puddles. They were made of snow, not flesh, and yet, they were alive.

These beautiful creatures, these creatures that Arryn had made, gone so quickly.

Precession glanced at Arryn, still lost in his moment of grief, in the unsatisfying closure he'd received. It was such a pity, such an anecdote of abuse and mental harm, their love story. Yet he couldn't let go because he couldn't see it.

He never would.

That was not his story. His story was of pure hearts, sacrifice, and dedication to one another. It was amazing how he never could see, but Precession supposed that they all had been blind to what had been happening under their noses. None of them had known what Allienna's loneliness would lead to.

"You cannot hurt him," Hadley screamed, pushing the burning motionless Vrae off of the top of her body. The flames hissed against the wetness, the melted snow that surrounded them.

Hadley stood, her eyes filled with malice and despair. Her chin was up as she made direct eye contact with the Goddess, her wings humming, moving so fast that her feet lifted so lightly, so delicately off the ground.

"You need me, child," Ayurveda's voice echoed, her hand raising, an offering to the young Kinnari girl.

"She needs us," Precession sang, quickly stepping up into the air to join Hadley. "There is a reason you destroyed my home. Unlike you, I am not afraid. You cannot take what you want here; destroy what you will without consequences."

"You have no power to use either, sweet girl, without risking all the same things. We are equals in that way," Ayurveda said, still ablaze.

"It's time to let go," Tristan shouted from the ground. Precession understood. She knew that her purpose was deeper, fuller than how it appeared. Deep down, there was a sacrifice, a life that never belonged to her. It had been such a curse, this power, this tether that she was solely responsible for. The fear of all that death, all that life that Arryn created, that the others nurtured, would suffer for this choice.

It wasn't a choice, though. She had every intent of keeping life going as much as possible. Ayurveda, pulsing through the world and realms, meant only more heat and death. A sacrifice to avoid being ruled by a Goddess who looked down at them all as if they were trinkets, pebbles, useless things, was worth it.

Precession opened her arms, taking in the heat and radiation that burned her skin. It felt chemical-like, the searing from this distance.

Tears pooled in Precession's eyes as she looked up to the sky, shuddering out a breath. She raised her chin and closed her eyes and the tether that had a hold on her since she was created, that had been slowly slipping away these last hundred years or so due to her exhaustion, her loosening empathy, and her strengthening desire to be something more than a shell, an empty cosmic power.

Nothing. For the first time, do nothing, she thought to herself.

If she once held onto her tether with ten fingers, then she had recently held on with nine. She let a strand go, now eight fingers, and another strand, seven fingers.

The land shivered, and snow on distant peaks shifted at the obvious slowing in rotation.

"If you intend to scare me, to threaten me, then it's not working," Ayurveda said, burning ever brighter. Precession could feel her hair singe. The heat on her face was violent, a gentle kiss compared to what the Goddess could actually do.

That was okay. Precession could do worse.

Another strand lifted six fingers.

Five.

Then Four.

Three.

Two.

"No," Arryn yelled out, crawling in her direction and holding out his arm. "You will kill us all."

She noticed it then, the smallest piece of what she held onto, there with her, near her. Her grip on her tether was so loose that, for the first time, she could feel a moonstone hidden in plain sight. She turned her head slightly, trying to locate it, finding that it was hanging off of a neck, off of a creature with a tail stuck on a metal beam, hanging on for its life.

That was what she needed. All fear and worry faded away; the reassurance was somehow there. Ignoring Arryn's cries of warning, of despair, Precession let go of that last and final thread.

The redheaded Kinnari woman gasped. For a moment, she felt so normal. No pain, no pull, no lightheadedness. She was complete in a way that she had never felt before, in a way she didn't even know was possible to experience.

I feel good.

"Precession?" She heard Roksana's voice scream, but then she heard nothing. She had no senses, no sight, no smell, no touch. She wasn't anything or anyone. It was peaceful and quiet, floating in both light and darkness. It was a place that she was content to never leave, to never want, to never think. Precession welcomed the complete opposite of everything she had experienced in her life so far with open arms. If she even had arms. She wasn't sure.

The moment didn't last.

Precession was hit with a beam of power, an insurgence of all magic and nature around her. It felt like vengeance for letting go, for breaking order. It felt like hell raging through her. She was finding death and being reborn at the same time.

She let it flow through her, not knowing what to do with the energy but absorbing the pain. She couldn't scream out. She wasn't sure if she even had a mouth. She just felt the beam holding her up emptying into her.

When it stopped, the ache reached a new threshold, and she was convinced she was being pulled apart. She had lips again, a mouth, and she used it to scream. She screamed so loud, with her entire body, that surely anything nearby would know her dread, her plight.

This was what she had seen: her death. She might have died a hundred times, based on how her heart felt in her chest.

My heart, I have a heart, too.

Precession pulled back, her screams now closer to moans, as she mentally scanned her body. Wings—she still had wings—were holding her up off the ground as her legs were dangling underneath her.

Eyes, she still had eyes. It felt as if her head were buried in mud, but she attempted to crack her eyes open nevertheless and once she did, she was hit with an immeasurable amount of light. She blocked her face with her hands; she had glorious hands, but there was no relief. Her lids shut tight and that was when she realized that the light was her, inside her. She would get no relief.

Precession gazed ahead fully, her pupils not visible, only pure gold, an energy that harnessed the gravity of the earth, the core of the world.

Power. She had endless power. She felt dangerous.

Precession's vision had adjusted, and she took in a laughing Ayurveda before her. She cocked her head, not understanding the humor. Why couldn't she see, couldn't feel what was right in front of her? She was careless and arrogant.

That's when she started to notice the sounds around her again, the panic and dread in shocked voices on the ground.

"Can you not see what you just did?" Ayurveda smirked.

Precession's heart dropped as she looked at a world untethered, just now being able to see and pay attention to the consequences of her choice.

The rhythm of days and nights had already been disrupted, and she watched the moon inch across the sky. Tides in the far distance swirled, angry while the earth shook underneath her, natural disasters beginning to form, to run rampant. There was no going back. It was done.

Ayurveda launched her fire toward Precession, unphased by the destruction around her.

"I tried to be merciful," the Goddess's voice echoed. "I tried to create one of you, an equal, that could painlessly aid me in my goal. Instead, you all stole her from me, the only fragile thing that I cared about."

Precession lunged into the sky, her wings feeling slow with the weight of the power inside her.

Close, she was too close.

Precession pooled all that was inside her and threw her hands down. Her power, bursts of gold matching her eyes, hit the ground with the crack of hundreds of lightning strikes. She could feel it. The rhythm of the earth, the core underneath large fissures in the land, called to her, sang to her. It felt so familiar, the gravity of that song. It was her, everything she was created to be and to tame.

Precession smiled. It was a victorious smile, a smile that would make any opponent second guess themselves. Then she used that song, that golden energy within her, and directed it into the earth below her. There were more screams, but she couldn't look, she couldn't worry. She had one task only, and that was the goddess before her. She would eliminate the threat somehow.

"Even stars as bright as you," she sang, "can be eclipsed."

The earth below split, massive cracks forming while hissing geysers and enraged molten lava bubbled and sprayed several feet above the surface. Precession guided them both into a spiral with her left hand, directing it toward Ayurveda like a cannon. When she was hit, there was no reaction, no signs of weakness. Once the elemental cannon fire was gone, Ayurveda turned her head left and right. Then her body beamed.

Radiation, she was beaming radiation.

Precession covered her face, her entire body burning, and she looked for that tether that she had let go of, the moon that had already floated so far away. She grabbed it and harnessed its light, weaving it into silver threads and directing the moonlight back at the Goddess. It was working. Ayurveda was cooling off.

There was a small moment of relief, but then she realized, she could not win. She had given everything, letting go of her tether and the force of the Earth's core, and Ayurveda had not flinched. She had put the Earth in peril. The destruction that inhabitants would be experiencing right at that moment in the furthest lands away from them would be catastrophic.

Precession looked down for the first time, seeing mountains in the distance depleted of snow from massive avalanches. The climate was usually cold, but she saw bodies frozen, not moving with the long night they were likely in. Furious storm clouds brewed not too far from them, lightning visible between hail and tornadoes. No one could live here anymore—not without some special help.

She felt herself float down, wanting to fall into those cracks, to be enveloped by the elements that held her. Her prison, her cage, might have been an illusion. She could not defeat a Goddess. It was a laughable thought.

Teetering on the edge of a fissure in the earth, Precession wiggled her toes, ignoring Ayurveda floating right above her, closing their distance. The radiation had returned once hopelessness had set in. It seemed the Goddess was right. She had been trying to be merciful. She was willing to let most of life here continue. Now, that was no longer a possibility. They would all die soon.

A real death. The connection to a destroyed Earth would undoubtedly release their magic back to their creators. There would be no purpose. There would be nothing.

Tears welled up in her eyes, and she looked up, the gold beams that filled her still present. She exhaled and nodded as Ayurveda looked down at her with the wrath and brutality of the sun, the relentless exhaustion that could only come from a star.

The heat intensified for just a moment, making Precession wish she were dead, but it quickly faded back to normalcy. She looked up and realized why. Glass wings were flying back up to the Goddess, the light shining through them creating more heat and power.

32

Hadley | Glacier, Myrilosis

The ground was splitting right underneath Hadley, rumbling so loud that she thought her eardrums might burst.

Move, we need to move.

Sheng was partially lying on her, unconscious. The smell of his cooked flesh weaving into her hair and his slumped, dead body weight had woken something inside her. He had bitten her, that bastard had bitten her.

I had one fucking rule.

He was in his Vrae form, and it was much easier for her consciousness to break through the chemicals that flowed through her blood. It's not like she could love a monster.

He's not completely unattractive when he looks like this though, her body, the venom, coaxed her on. To have a monster in your bed, under your own control, could be a fun thing indeed.

Look at him frail, helpless, as you pull him into your lap.

Hadley shoved the thought away, staring at his open mouth, at his extraordinarily long, sharp teeth. Those teeth had pierced her leg. She hadn't even stopped bleeding.

Another rumble hit them, snapping her attention back to their surroundings. It didn't matter if she hated him or loved him; if she didn't get them both to a safer place, neither of them would have any life left to contemplate it.

Hadley screamed as lightning hit close by; it was far too close. She jumped up, Sheng rolling over on his side since his head was in her lap. She shoved her hands underneath his arms, ignoring the new sensation of his Vrae skin against hers. It was so supple, so firm. If leather and rubber had formed to create something new, it could maybe feel something like this.

You can have that skin all over you. He would stay in this form if you asked him to.

Hadley shook away her body's response, thankful that her head was fighting the bite so well this time, and pulled. Sheng was too heavy. She barely moved a few inches. Looking around desperately, she cursed and wondered why she couldn't have been gifted with supernatural strength.

You know, it's something that might actually be useful, she thought, grimacing as she pulled again and again. The ground continued to quake. She looked over to the distance and saw the actual split inching closer and closer towards them. A thick beam of golden light, of energy, was pulsing down into that crack from the floating Kinnari in the air.

"Mind if I assist?" A young boy crept up behind her, making her jump and letting Sheng fall to the ground with a thud. She was at a loss as she took in his brown curls and casual manner while everyone else was running for their lives.

Reifoel, where is Reifoel?

She pushed the thought away and nodded, the two of them teaming up to pull Sheng's body back far enough. A few quaint buildings remained standing, trembling under the endless threats that hovered above. The three of them posted up under the thinner structure as Hadley eyed the shaking ceiling, mentally threatening the universe if it fell down on them.

The crack had moved fully, enveloping the land where they had been standing. Steam, water, and hissing black and red lava erupted from the cracks at the Kinnari's hand.

She was going to save them all; that redhead was a hero.

No, Hadley argued with herself. *You must go to Ayurveda. She came here to find you. This is all over if you simply go to her.*

A glimmer caught her eye, relief flooding her, knowing her shadow self was staying close.

You should kill him. You should kill Sheng and run into Ayurveda's open, fiery arms.

Hadley knew that, and she knew how easy it would be with that glimmer nearby, waiting for instructions, waiting to help her. The venom in her blood would not allow it. The attraction to him made her consider stripping all her clothes off and bringing him to consciousness in the most filthy of ways.

She was his, and he was hers, even if she hated him. Even if she didn't trust him. That venom in her blood told her something she knew, something she had accepted, that he was in her life forever. His words rang true through her, that she would fall in love with him. It felt like he could be right about that.

No. It's not you. Leave him to die.

Everything was wet, hot, and cold all at the same time. She felt sticky and frozen and wasn't sure if the burning in her skin came from the wickedly cold wind, the Goddess burning in the sky thirty feet above her, or the lava that had just shot up from the opening in the earth.

The powerful redheaded Kinnari woman had begun to descend from the sky, her head hanging low in defeat. She did not look harmed, so Hadley was confused by her actions.

Stay and fight. Fight for us.

The heat burning off of Ayurveda seemed to intensify. Hadley looked down at her arms to see raw skin, her flesh peeling back as she watched, somehow not feeling the pain. She tsked and shook her head.

Only you can stop this.

Hadley stood and pumped her wings as she slowly floated into the air, wincing as she got closer to the Goddess.

You cannot leave Sheng, you love him.

She pushed the thought away, telling her body that this was the only way to save him, that she could come back. She fought that battle inside herself ruthlessly, wondering if she was even moving.

But she was, she was moving vertically, and once she was fifteen feet in the air, her hair and eyebrows felt like they were on fire. She looked down at Sheng, still blissfully unconscious.

Good, he won't have to see this.

While she moved her head up to turn towards Ayurveda, she stopped. Her eyes lingered on what had been the inn—what was left of it anyway. There was a beam, a post barely standing, and on top of that post was a frozen mermaid.

Reifoel.

Hadley's heart sank to her stomach. She could save him, too. If he were still alive.

No.

She stopped ascending as Ayurveda looked down at her and smiled, reaching a hand out for her and pulling back her heat, her blaze.

"I've been waiting for you," the Goddess echoed through the town.

Hadley smiled back and nodded, raising her hand back and flying upward despite the pull from her body. The urge to stay with Sheng and protect and to fight was too strong, but that was now exactly what she was counting on.

Hadley looked for the glimmer of her shadow self and gave it the permission it had been craving. Not breaking her eye contact, Hadley watched as Ayurveda's eyes widened as her shadow self jumped through the Goddess. It was likely stupid and ineffective, but she had to try something.

You're not as bad as him.

Hadley closed their gap and touched Ayurveda's extended hand.

She could not kill a Goddess; Hadley wasn't naïve. She didn't expect Ayurveda to fall over and die, and as Hadley's fingertips touched hers, she went right through; no solid mass was there, only gasses and heat. Like her shadow self, she went right through Ayurveda. Her heart stopped, and she turned to see the sun that hung too low, too close, had begun to crystalize like that man in Bangladesh had.

Ayurveda's face was one of betrayal and wrath, and within seconds, she was a solid piece of dragon glass suspended in the air.

What did I do?

At first, the start of Ayurveda's scream sounded like the whistle of the wind. It grew louder and louder until it turned guttural, deep, like a wounded animal who would not yield. Hadley waited and watched as the dragon glass started to crack. She hoped and prayed that the pieces would fall apart, and that would be it.

But that would be naïve.

The glass did shatter, but as those pieces fell, Ayurveda was there, like a snake breaking out of its skin, ready to strike.

Ayurveda did not look at Hadley or move towards her. She simply pushed her arms up, opened her mouth, and let out that belly-heavy groan, a groan that made Hadley realize that they had lost.

Run. Grab Sheng and run.

She began to descend, slowly, hoping the Goddess would not notice her while singing her war song, while distracted by whatever Hadely's magic had done to her.

Sheng is a monster. Leave him.

Hadley glanced at Reifoel, his eyes closed and visible heat leaving his lips and nose. He was alive. She let out a sigh, choking slightly when she inhaled too quickly, but the relief and joy she felt when seeing his chest move felt the same as breathing air after swimming out of the cave.

Ayurveda screamed.

Hadley looked up at her, seeing the fire and energy emanating from her, but it was nothing like before. There was so much less power and so little threat.

"It seems, lovely girl," Ayurveda's voice echoed around them all, cackling triumphantly. "That there is no reason to rule over or even save this planet."

That laugh wiped the smile right off of Hadley's face as she watched, confused. What wasn't she seeing?

Ayurveda was changing forms, circling into herself to form a sphere resembling golden sand. Small pulses of energy and light spilled out from it as she raised into the sky and enlarged, taking her place as the sun. The energy pulses enlarged as well.

"Solar flares," the redheaded Kinnari said, her voice sweet and lovely.

"What do they do?" Hadley asked, her feet touching the ground alongside the Kinnari.

"Nothing good, I would expect. I'm Precession, by the way, your soulkin."

Hadley turned to face her, raising her eyebrows and stepping towards the still intact building.

Stop wasting time, get back to Sheng. He is your life, Your focus.

"Soulkin, family not related by blood." Precession giggled as if it were a common phrase. "It's mostly used among gods and goddesses, those with world-creating magic like us. You should meet my sister; she'd hate you."

Hadley couldn't help but smile and try to stifle back a laugh, her eyes moving back up towards the sky, toward the very visible beams of light, the solar flares being emitted by the sun.

"Should we help the wounded?" Precession asked, "Starting with you, your leg hasn't healed from that bite. That's odd."

Hadley looked down at the small puddle of dark blue blood underneath her and was just as surprised. She touched her fingers to the bite and winced, bringing it up to her face to study it. It smelled of Sheng, and suddenly, Hadley's blood boiled. That smell, that scent, was something that she had to have. She stood up and began pulling her top down over her shoulders, her eyes roaming towards where Sheng's Vrae body still lay unconscious.

"I think that you should—" Precession began as Hadley started to march off. Her words were interrupted with a faint thud. The two Kinnari looked up, watching as those solar flares made contact with the moon, so distant, still floating free.

The sky was filled with light, an orange haze that glistened and looked beautiful and enchanting. Precession slid her fingers into Hadley's and squeezed, a look of worry across her face.

"She wouldn't," Precession muttered, "she couldn't."

Footsteps approached behind her, sloshing through the melted snow. Hadley turned to see the same Kinnari holding her hand, except her eyes held a different kind of intensity, one of judgment and annoyance.

Hadley felt annoyed all at once, too. She was annoyed by the chemicals in her body pulling her toward Sheng, annoyed that her leg wouldn't stop bleeding, annoyed that she wasn't in bed with her own mother on a weekend, watching silly dramatic movies and making fun of them together. Hadley gulped, the hollowness she felt inside painful.

"You're the sister, I suppose," Hadley said to the twin.

"I don't like her." Roksana crossed her arms, looking at her sister.

"I told you she wouldn't." Precession smiled. "This is Roksana. She will heighten your emotions and if hers are particularly strong, they will rub off on you."

That explained the sudden annoyance.

"You're just in time to see the explosion," Precession said, offering her sister her other hand. "Ayurveda is doing her worst, and I am a bit in awe. It's impressive."

Roksana accepted her sister's hand and the three of them stared in silence, watching the sky. The cold, freezing wind whistled around them, but they did not move. Hadley let herself drift off into the orange haze and the beauty she took in. There was a moment of peace as the venom wore off in her body, and she was there with someone who called her family. Precession had called her soulkin, and it felt good.

That moment of peace, of acceptance amidst the eerily calm, didn't last much longer. The thudding had stopped, and without another sound, trapped in the vortex of space, Hadley watched as the moon split apart.

33

Arryn | Glacier, Myrilosis

He squeezed Celestine in his arms as her body shook from the cold and the fear. Arryn had picked her up and swept her away as soon as the ground started to quake, feeling no obligation to get involved in the conflict. He had lost his love, his passion, and it was Ayurveda that had taken her away from him. There was no anger, though there was plenty of agony and defeat. That was it, though; it was time to admit it, give up, move on.

Move on.

No, clearly, he couldn't do that, but he could hold it in—the pain. He could walk, talk, and hold on to the burning underneath his skin, not creating and living like he did when she was here. That was the only way to pretend things were normal and that he was okay.

The woman in his arms could fill some void. She was beautiful enough, as long as he could keep her alive.

They had taken shelter, if you could call it that, behind the rubble of a fallen building on the opposite side of the town square. Arryn watched Ayurveda's attacks aimed toward the inn, toward whoever opposed her in the sky, the two of them were tucked slightly behind her.

He didn't know if he could stop this other than handing over the girl to the Goddess. That was all she wanted, one single being, and yet, he seemed to be the only one who thought they should just do it, accept it, and lose the Kinnari, his daughter.

Arryn watched Hadley in that sky, watching her do nothing other than look around frantically, and yet there was something he could not see. It piqued his interest for a moment when Ayurveda turned into glass, but that moment was quickly replaced with horror as he looked up into the sky. Precession, Hadley, and Roksana stood near the large fissure in the ground, watching the moon break apart as it was beaten down with hundreds of solar flares. Without the tether, the moon had drifted too close, and now Ayurveda would show her wrath by destroying the planet that she could not rule over.

The moon was crumbling like a dry cookie, the broken pieces of lunar rock getting caught in the atmosphere and falling toward them. The sky began to darken as volcanic activity heightened around them, the ground shaking again.

"What do we do?" Arryn's new companion asked, her teeth chattering. "Can't you, can't you save us? Can't you repair it?"

Arryn didn't answer, but his throat bobbed. He didn't know how to save them, and he couldn't save them. He'd passed out creating an entire town, an eco structure. It would take him years to restore something like the moon. Especially since he hadn't created it in the first place. Putting it back together would be guesswork.

"We should go," he said, taking the woman's hand and tugging. He didn't know this place, this world, very well. If the world was ending, he would face it in the comfort of the temple, at home.

His wings ripped out of his back, destroying the shirt and jacket he wore to fly them over the fissure. Precession turned her head toward them and waved, her smile solemn, a goodbye.

"Where do you think you're going?" a demanding young voice splashed up to Arryn out of nowhere.

"You know, I think I find you more annoying as a child," Arryn grumbled as Reign pouted at him.

"I have quite a few unconscious bodies over there under that building. Amis and I could use your help."

"Where do you want me to put them?" he asked, rolling his eyes.

"Wherever you two are headed would be fine," she responded and turned, walking towards the building she had pointed at just a moment ago.

"We have to help," Celestine said. "I want to help."

The world is ending, and I can't have even one moment of peace.

"Fine." Arryn gritted his teeth and dragged the barmaid behind him. He noticed the three Kinnari women, still holding hands, turn to watch them. Hadley frowned at him like he was the problem. She looked so much like Allienna right there with her brow furrowed at him. He hated it. He hated her.

Once Reign had stopped moving in front of him, arriving at where they had taken shelter, she immediately began to hoist a winged toddler up. His eyes were closed, his mouth open. The amount of heat and breath that came out of him was barely there. Too little, he didn't have long.

"Arryn, how many can you carry?" Amis asked, with two children in his arms.

"If we are in the air, I have to carry Celestine, too. I'm unsure if I am that extra set of arms you need."

"I think I can help," a voice unfamiliar to Arryn said. He turned his head casually to see his daughter and the twins with her.

"Be my guest," Arryn said, holding back a sadistic laugh. She was barely bigger than Reign, and there were too many bodies in the area.

"We can probably leave the Vrae," Reign said. "He's likely already dead at the next building over."

"It looks like you've finally stopped bleeding," Precession said in her sing-song voice to Hadley, who smiled and nodded.

"Can someone get me back to the temple as fast as possible?" Hadley asked.

"I believe Arryn is the strongest in the air," Amis said.

"I cannot help; I have others to carry." He couldn't believe that they all had expected him to help her.

"You don't need to carry me," Hadley responded. "I just don't know the way. Please, I have an idea."

"What do you have to lose?" Amis asked, curling his body over the children he held, trying to keep their heat in.

Arryn closed his eyes and lowered his head, taking a deep breath. He felt the barmaid shivering so hard that he imagined she was about to face hypothermia. At least he could get inside the temple; what the girl did wouldn't be on him.

"Fine." He snapped his head up and scooped Celestine back into his arms. "Let's go." Without another word, without any warning, he was airborne and flew north from Glacier, leaving everyone behind. He didn't bother to look if Hadley was following him or keeping up. He couldn't care about someone else, someone new. There was no room for her.

She looks so much like Allienna.

Arryn weaved through hail and snow that seemed more violent and less forgiving than the storms he was used to. It made sense that the weather would change and that the landscape would become unlivable. It would take days, maybe weeks, but he expected to hide away in the temple as the rest of the world died. He couldn't have helped; it was too much. They couldn't ask that of him.

Low clouds hid the top of the temple's mountaintop, soaking through his clothes as he flew through them. The barmaid's skin was red, purple, and blue. She didn't move. She didn't blink after he landed. He looked down at those wide-open eyes.

"I have to set you down," he explained to her. Celestine was holding on for dear life, and he had no time left. Arryn pounded on the block of snow covering the temple, looking for the door. Once he got the handle uncovered, Hadley landed behind him.

"She's not well," his daughter yelled at him over the wind. Celestine collapsed as Hadley caught her. Arryn rolled his eyes and pulled the temple door open before turning to pick up the barmaid and get her inside.

Obviously.

It was quiet inside, the wind not audible through the stone. Arryn quickly walked into the large room, pulling atoms together to ignite a fire in the wood-burning stove. He brought a plush, velvet lounge chaise into existence and gently placed the barmaid on top of it, keeping his arms there for his body heat to help warm her.

"I'll be right back," Hadley said.

Arryn didn't respond, letting his daughter walk through the opposite hallway before disappearing. He looked over his shoulder and frowned once she was out of view, but quickly brought his attention back to Celestine, trying to scoot the chaise a little further away from the fire in case he was warming her too quickly.

He was nervous about nerve damage, and as far as he could tell, she was entirely human, fragile. What was such a breakable thing in such a harsh place?

The ice that clung to her ashy dark brown hair had melted, and Arryn watched as the rise and fall of her chest began to move into a steady rhythm. She had such long, dark eyelashes. Arryn stared at those eyelashes, stuck together from moisture into near-perfect triangles, listening to her breath for what seemed like a day, a week, a month.

It was foreign to be needed like this without being asked. He was helping her because he wanted to. Such a surprising soft spot he had. It was something that even he didn't understand.

Arryn sat in his moment of calm, listening to the fire crackle, letting its heat warm him. He hadn't had this peace without the guilt or sadness in so long. He touched the back of his hand to the barmaid's cheek, making sure she was heating up. A beautiful quilt woven with a serene green thread appeared in his hands, and he covered her, letting her rest.

Once his nerves calmed and let himself fall victim to relaxation, he was quickly thrown back into the reality of their situation, hearing a bang at the end of the hallway that destroyed that moment of calm. No, the two of them were still not alone. He had his daughter to deal with.

More bangs came until Arryn heard a thundering crack, reminding him of the moon's collapse and the natural disasters accumulating right outside. Stone fell and was thrown by a force as Arryn listened to the outside of the temple fall apart while he waited patiently, hovering over Celestine and staring at her lovely eyelashes.

The front of the temple had collapsed. He could hear the wind again, feel the cold inching in from the open air. However, there was one thing he wasn't expecting, and that was a feral shriek of something significant that was not produced by a storm.

A familiar rumbling shook the walls around him. It had been so long since he felt something like that, and once realization dawned on him, Arryn swept up the barmaid, her head against his chest, and pressed up against the temple wall with his body protecting her.

Dragon fire shot through the hallway and into the great room. Furniture was thrown to the side, aflame as it was hit with embers. The chaise flipped, hitting in the back of the legs.

Dramatic exhales from the dragon sounded down the hallway as more stone toppled, the size of the creature destroying more and more, and it came in closer.

"What's happening?" Celestine whispered, still pressed against him.

"You're awake," Arryn said, relief evident in his tone.

"Maybe not for long," she said, peering around him as a dragon's head emerged into the room, followed by its neck and its back. It was a deep burgundy color.

"Kismet," Arryn choked, not believing it. "Kismet, you came back."

"Who is Kismet?" Hadley's voice yelled out, and as the dragon came into the room, he realized she was sitting atop it, the two looking perfectly comfortable with each other.

"How did you find her?" Arryn asked, stepping towards Kismet, unsure if the beast would remember what he had done, that he had left her.

"She came to me when I was lonely in the mountains trying to heal. And supposedly, she isn't a dragon. Not anymore."

Arryn noted her two legs and grimaced, not wanting to know what had happened.

"Do you know this creature?" Hadley asked.

"I created her when I was lonely, when I, too, was trying to heal."

He hated it, admitting the similarity. The two of them didn't have to be anything like each other. He would prefer it that way, to keep a distance, to not learn about her.

"That's beautiful," the barmaid whispered behind him.

"I have been calling her Aqurya, but I, too, once went by two names." Hadley leaned her body forward, sweeping her arm back and forth, giving the creature compassion and appreciation.

"I'm going to take her into town. We can carry most of the survivors on her back. Can they take refuge here? It seems spacious enough."

There had been a point when filling this temple with a family was the only thing he'd wanted. It had been a different kind of family Allienna had craved, not one of biology, but of all those souls that had grown up together in this very place. They had all left, and he hoped that they would come home. He saw it then that this was the closest that he would ever get, the wounded, the damned, and even fucking biology. If Djoser was here, he imagined that he would never hear the end of it.

"If you could go anywhere," Arryn asked, ignoring her question, "anywhere, right now, where would it be?"

Hadley sat atop Kismet and blinked, looking confused.

"I'm sorry. Are you trying to have a conversation with me?"

Arryn shook his head and huffed. "You get that sarcasm from your mother. She was so gentle, so simple, but when she got heated, that brilliant mind would present itself, reminding me how lucky I was to have her with me."

His chest eased, his body settled a little bit more into their conversation. Here was someone willing to talk about Allienna, willing to keep her alive, even in memory. Everyone else seemed to avoid the subject, too intent on moving on.

Hadley looked down at Kismet's scales, petting the creature, her hand so small against its back. Arryn doubted that it could even feel the affection.

"That's where I would go," she said. "I grew up in a little house that neighbors a city. It was always so warm; the sun would shine, and I would spend afternoons laying in the grass after some poor guy mowed it for my mom. They would disappear after that. She would never give them the time of day. It was only the two of us against the world. She never wanted anything more. I would go back to that house, and maybe I would never leave. I would be happy basking in those memories forever."

"You should. You should go there now, honey," Celestine said, breaking the silence that followed. Arryn could see Hadley wipe away tears and he realized that she was maybe just as sad as him.

"I can't. I have to go back. I said I would go back. I am not a monster," she said, urging Kismet to move through, smashing stone and causing chaos as it tried to get to the portal, into Myrilosis. "Tomorrow is a day."

"Now what is that supposed to mean?" Arryn asked.

She's crazy.

"Nothing, it's just something an old friend used to say," Hadley yelled behind her as they faded into the land, into Myrilosis.

"You can bring them back here," Arryn ran after them, yelling. "Did you hear me? It's okay!"

34

Hadley | Glacier, Myrilosis

ismet.

The name rang through her, pulsed as if it were her name, too. Their bond felt more natural, more solidified now that she knew who she was sitting atop.

"Kismet," she rang out like a bell, a hysterical giggle choked out of her throat.

The wyvern purred in response, bobbing down and up as if nodding with its entire body. Hadley smiled at the simplicity that the name, the knowledge, brought to their relationship. She knew now who this creature was, where it came from. Hadley wished for everyone to have that, to know who they were so they could yell it loud to the world.

Dark clouds presented vortexes and tornadoes, even at such high altitudes as this. Gusts of wind nearly knocked Hadley off of Kismet as she tucked her head against the warmth of the wyvern scale and held on, tucking her wings in with her.

She thought of her home again, in a pocket away from things like mountains, the nearest ocean a hundred miles away. But it was right on one of the biggest fault lines. She had heard it all her life growing up, to prepare for that type of disaster. She wasn't even in the same realm, but she prayed it was safe there. She hoped all those people that lived in her hometown, people she didn't know but still were somehow her community, were not dead.

The moon crumbling in front of her, now completely gone from the night's sky, was eerily beautiful. Like watching a flower get plucked, each rose petal melting away into darkness. She knew it would be bad. She knew it meant the end for most anything living on the planet, she just didn't know if there was anything to be done about it.

She could at least do this. She could try.

She had been so angry, so hurt, that she couldn't see straight. She couldn't think.

Hail fell down upon them, Hadley's fingers bleeding as she was hit with a piece the size of a basketball. Blue blood pooled up around three of her fingernails, but within minutes, she was healed, though she continued to get hit in her back, in her thighs, in her wings. She couldn't let go of Kismet to protect her head; her thighs were not strong enough to keep her seated. The poor wyvern was being pelted far worse than her. She worried for Kismet, helpless.

Hadley opened her eyes to see a familiar glimmer, a friend.

I need you, she thought to her shadow self, *I need you to gather them all.*

Loyalty, she needed their loyalty.

The last time she had done so, had her shadow self jump into a mass group of the living, had been to orchestrate death. It had been to bring them to Ayurveda, to help her grow her power so that she could rule over this planet with Hadley being the liaison. Together, they were a fearsome team, she knew. Hector's face flashed again in her head and she deserved it; she deserved to miss him. She deserved that pain, that regret. She would not let it go in vain.

Her shadow self darkened, becoming the more familiar form she had met. The silhouette nodded at her and did a backward dive off the wyvern, shooting past Kismet at an even faster speed.

Find all the injured, Hadley communicated to her shadow self, *Anyone alive. Save them all.*

They approached the village, barely visible in the darkness. Only stars existed now in the night sky, but they were all completely covered by storm clouds. Kismet landed, her two legs sinking deep into the new powdered snow. Once Hadley's eyes adjusted, she saw the faces that surrounded them, haunted, gaunt, as if everyone had aged a hundred years in the short amount of time she had been gone.

She counted nineteen. Only nineteen survivors were there with an undying loyalty, a loyalty instilled in them that would make them crawl to her if they had no legs. That's exactly what Reifoel would have had to do, she realized, as she stared into his eyes nearly devoid of life and personality, with a tail stretched out behind him.

Alive. He is alive.

She saw Sheng, still in his Vrae form, staring at her with that familiar snack time expression. Hadley tried to not to smile back at him, tried not to show that she was happy that he hadn't burned to death. All the Kinnari that were present stared back at her, looking mostly unscathed. The children that were once unconscious had their eyes open, which she took as a good sign, though their expressions were blank.

A few other bodies, other creatures of the town, were there, too, and she was thankful. Hadley was thankful that an entire town, an entire culture, was not decimated from this realm. Her heart couldn't have handled that. She couldn't take anymore guilt, not after she had forgiven herself.

"Get on," was all she said, her voice nearly carried away in the wind. Those on the ground didn't need a moment, they didn't need to think about what she said. They just simply obeyed. Some climbed onto Kismet's wings, while most climbed onto the wyvern's back. Hadley helped each one, reaching her arm out to pull them up.

Roksana was hit in the head with a large, heavy piece of hail, though seemed to barely notice, blood running down her face. It didn't seem to matter to her, didn't seem to slow her down.

Kismet stretched out her wings, long and powerful, and then launched into the sky while carrying the extra weight without a struggle. The wyvern circled around, gently diving down to pick up Reifoel with its clawed foot before flying back to the temple.

They landed on the top of the mountain, snow already covering the stone that had been flayed to the side as Kismet emerged through it, breaking down the walls. The creature shuffled through the hallway and Hadley could already feel the air become warmer, smell the savory spices of a feast. There was comfort waiting for them all just ahead.

Once in the great room, Hadely was relieved to see a banquet sized table spread out with mass amounts of food accumulated on top of it. There were twenty or so single beds laid out on the opposite side of the temple. Arryn and the woman that he was with had gotten it ready for them all and Hadley felt only grateful.

She didn't yet know how the magic of her shadow self worked, if the emotion that was inserted into people had to wear off or if she could control that better.

Hadley yawned, the comfort of the temple letting her adrenaline burn off. Her magic was something she could figure out later.

"Eat, sleep, heal," she said and watched as the survivors dispersed. No conversation was had, no hope sounded, just the whistling of the wind and the brutal clash of thunder could be heard from the broken temple walls on both sides.

"I should fix that," Arryn said, walking up to her. "The walls, I mean."

"Can you fix the world? How does it all work?" she asked, skeptical of the man who was treating her like an actual living being for the first time in his life. The woman that stood behind him gave him a nudge after he looked down at his hands, not answering.

"I have limits, too, how much I can do. It's something I've just recently learned," Arryn said. "Maybe, over time, if we can survive the initial storms, we can figure something out."

Hadley slid off of Kismet, patting her head and letting the wyvern close her eyes. She looked out through the room, seeing Reifoel in a bed. Sheng, too, was just a few beds over from him.

Reign and the other children were sitting at the banquet table, eating and warming themselves with a handful of the other survivors. When she spotted Amis, she frowned, remembering how much distrust she had for him.

He walked up to her and Arryn, free of whatever magic her shadow self had cast upon him.

"How did you do that?" she asked. "How did you get free?"

"Are you talking about that cute little trick you can do? I am balance and you, my dear, do not clash well with balance." He snickered.

Hadley didn't have the energy, the patience, to show her annoyance at the Kinnari.

"Arryn." Amis turned to him. "I heard you propose to heal and repair. I might explode, destroy things accidentally, nonsensically, if that were to go on for too long. Might I propose . . ."

"Yes. Please," Arryn answered right away, without pause. "I can try it, but I have never created like that, someone who once existed. Can you help somehow?"

"Let us try together," Amis said, nudging Hadley out of the way. She watched her father bring his hands together and then apart, staring intently at a spot hovering above the flooring. Amis, too, seemed overly focused on that same spot.

"Ah, a famously weird family reunion," Reign's voice chirped, the loyalty fading, her personality coming back. "What in the world are those two doing?"

Hadley just shrugged.

"Those kids are doing alright," Reign said to Hadley. "Honestly, I think they'd follow me to the end of the earth if I led them. They're all tough."

She shrugged, bringing her focus back to Arryn and within a blink, was surprised to see a body, a person where there wasn't one before.

"You're doing it," Amis shouted in encouragement.

Hadley watched as a broad, tall man with olive skin came into consciousness and took a step. His dark eyes with flecks of green were alive with curiosity.

Arryn, Amis and Reign didn't hold back their excitement as they surrounded the newcomer, shouting words about him coming back from the dead. The man smiled, his teeth beautiful, white and gleaming, but then quickly shook the others off. Djoser raised his head and looked right at Hadley, taking steps to close the gap between them.

END.

SERIES ORDER

∾

For updates, join the mailing list at

www.ellekaelee.com

GLOSSARY

This glossary is inclusive for book two, Burning Glass. It will be updated as the books progress so that accidental spoilers do not occur.

Ahora

One of the last five Waihema children.

Allienna

Hadley's mother, a full Kinnari, is the one who dies, catalyzing the story. Ethereal and regal.

Amis

A complex Kinnari and caretaker of the Waihema children. Known for internal conflict, magical balance, and reluctant protection. Helps resurrect Djoser.

Aqurya

Hadley's original name for Kismet, a wyvern created by Arryn from sorrow and snow. Breathes fire and shares a deep, magical bond with Hadley. Kismet and Aquarya are the same creature.

Arryn

Hadley's father is a powerful, emotionally volatile Kinnari and the creator of Kismet. Capable of atomic-level creation magic. Grieves Allienna.

Articiren

Towering, dainty giantesses standing fifteen feet tall, with an otherworldly elegance. They resemble women with Victorian-style hair piled high, wearing wide floral skirts that make them appear to glide across snow. Their skin tones vary like the Kinnari, but are marked with imperfect rectangular patterns—similar to a giraffe's coloring—across their faces and limbs.

Atheri

Angelic beings in Ebonspire with radiant, genderless forms and ambiguous motives. Made by Arryn to destroy Vrae with their heaven-esque light.

Balizar

Cynical innkeeper in Myrilosis. Provides commentary on the Kinnari legacy and magical restoration.

Celestine

A kind, awkward barmaid in Myrilosis. Helps Arryn and Reign and shows affection for Arryn.

Djoser

A destructive but loyal Kinnari. Represents death and resurrection.

Glaciels

Species adapted to life in the town, Glaciel, is often emotionally reserved. Physically resistant to cold and attuned to Myrilosis's mountain realm.

Glaciel

A temple town in Myrilosis, carved into a mountainside. Closest in proximity to the Kinnari Temple.

Glass Wings

Translucent, painful wings, Hadley grows as a Kinnari. Beautiful but burdensome.

Hadley

The protagonist, a powerful Kinnari with a hidden past and

evolving magic. Endures captivity, betrayal, and transformation. Also known as Hailey in her sex work scenes.

Hector

Hadley's close friend from her mortal life. His memory haunts her decisions.

Isadore

Aquatic noble from Serelune, cousin to Reifoel. Cynical, protective, and a skilled fighter. Distrusts Hadley and her magic.

Jenny

A cloaked follower of Sheng. A Vrae who serves him loyally.

Karmakara

Cosmic balancing force. One of the gods. Appears to Luca and offers glimpses of future paths.

Kinnari

Winged magical beings created to protect life and Earth. Their glass-like wings and powerful blood make them targets of the Vrae.

Kismet

Hadley's bonded wyvern, created by Arryn. Formerly known as Aqurya. Formed from snow and sorrow.

Kiwiva

The Northern New Zealand area of Myrilosis, destroyed by fire.

Life Gifter

The supreme creator god who governs cosmic laws, immortality, and the ability to create life.

Luca

A Waihema child marked by the Kinnari.

Lumes

Light-based ethereal bugs.

Marthrend

Crustacean-like beings who offer shelter in Emerald's Peak. Live in an icy region near Myrilosis.

Myrilosis

A mirrored magical realm of Earth. Connected by portals. Houses temples, sacred sites, and magical storms.

Noah

One of the five Waihema children. Survives storms and temple collapse.

Precession

Frail, prophetic twin sister to Roksana. Dreams of future events, receives visions.

Rangi

One of the Waihema children. Present during the exodus to Myrilosis.

Reifoel

An aquatic prince from Serelune. Has a growing romantic bond with Hadley. Calms the wyvern, possesses water healing.

Reign

Hadley's fierce, sarcastic godmother. A Kinnari who can regenerate into a child. Protective of the children.

Roksana

Blunt and protective twin to Precession. Amplifies emotions around her.

Salome

A Waihema child marked by the Kinnari. Protected by Amis. Loyal to Reign.

Saul

A Vrae cultist under Sheng.

Serelune

An underwater kingdom ruled by Reifoel's family. Suffers partial destruction, later begins reconstruction.

Shadow Self

Autonomous magical reflection of Hadley. Capable of moving independently, resurrecting, and manipulating life or death.

Sheng

The first Vrae, created by Ayurveda. Hadley's former captor and complex romantic antagonist.

Soulkin

A term Kinnari uses for non-blood-related family.

Temple

Original Kinnari temple located in the Himalayas. Contains ancient magic and serves as both a battleground and a sanctuary.

Tristan

A Kinnari boy, presumed dead, returned via prophetic dreams. Informs and guides others like Amis.

Vrae

Demonic beings created by Ayurveda to consume Kinnari. Can walk as humans or transform into monstrous forms with gaping jaws and red eyes.

Waihema

A remote village was created by the Amis to protect half-Kinnari children. Initially a breeding ground, later a sanctuary.

ACKNOWLEDGMENTS

Editor: Taylor Robinson

Cover Artist: Gretchen Cobaugh

Map Artist: @veronikawunder

List of commissioned artists for the series art so far:
    @foxlore_art
    @hexbayne
    @eburnsillustrations